D0763585

# ROCK WEDDING

## BY NALINI SINGH

NEW YORK TIMES BESTSELLING AUTHOR

eISBN: 978-1-942356-37-0
ISBN: 978-1-942356-38-7

Cover image by: Jenn LeBlanc/Illustrated Romance
Cover design by: Croco Designs

# ROCK WEDDING

# PART ONE

# CHAPTER 1

SARAH KNEW TODAY WAS A bad day for Abe. The anniversary of Tessie's death always was… and it didn't matter that today was also the anniversary of the day Sarah and Abe had first met. Any happiness he felt at being with her was crushed under a black cloud of grief that descended the instant the clock ticked past midnight.

Sarah understood that Tessie came first, always had. She wasn't jealous. How could anyone be jealous of a sweet girl who'd only lived for eight years before her life was cut cruelly short? It seemed deeply unfair that someone so innocent was gone when such ugliness continued to exist in the world.

No, Sarah would never be jealous of Abe's beloved baby sister.

All Sarah wanted was to be there for Abe. He'd refused to share his grief with her on their first anniversary, but they'd been married nearly two years now. It was time she took the bull by the horns and made him understand that she'd always be there for him—in the darkness and in the light. Through the good and through the awful.

Why he didn't already understand that, she didn't know. Sarah had stood by her husband through the drugs and the stints in rehab and the backsliding. She'd been there every step of the way, had never, not once, given up on Abe—but he didn't seem to realize she'd bleed for him, die for him.

Sarah loved Abe with a devotion that terrified her.

She knew he didn't love her back. That was okay. She could accept that—she'd never expected someone so magnificent to love her. But he wanted her and he needed her and he was *wonderful* to her when he wasn't poisoning his body with drugs and alcohol. Only last month, he'd surprised her by taking her to see the live taping of her favorite television show. And the way he touched her... she felt precious.

It was more than she'd ever thought she'd find, more value than she'd ever believed anyone would see in her. If only she could help him with his grief in return.

Four years after Abe and his family buried Tessie, following the rapid onset of a disease against which Abe's sister stood no chance, and the loss remained an open wound inside him.

The outside world might look at him and think he'd given in to despair, but Sarah knew the truth. Her husband was full of *rage*. He held it within, his screaming at fate silent, but his anger, it never died. And sometimes, when there was too much inside him and he couldn't hold it within any longer, he took drugs and turned into a man she didn't know—and then he raged in truth.

Broken furniture, holes in the walls, Sarah was used to all of it. But no matter how awful his mood, how much poison ran through his veins, Abe had never, not once, turned that rage on her. He took it out on stone and concrete, leaving himself with bloodied knuckles he refused to allow her to bandage.

The last time, she'd called David in desperation. The drummer had come, gone toe to toe with him, made him calm down.

She hoped tonight wouldn't be a painful echo. *Please let Abe be all right tonight.*

Heart aching in the post-midnight quiet, she padded barefoot down the hallway of the airy and light-filled house and pushed open the door to the music room where a black baby grand piano sat in solitary splendor. The cover had been pulled off, dropped to the side; the stunning instrument gleamed in the moonlight that speared through the gauzy curtains hanging over the folding glass doors to its right.

Those doors were open, the curtains waving in a gentle breeze.

"Abe?" she said after running her eyes around the room and finding no sign of him.

She stepped through the curtains and out onto the patio beyond, the stone surface slightly gritty under the soles of her feet. The pool sparkled in the moonlight, the lawn pristine green velvet thanks to the gardeners who came in weekly.

Sarah would've liked to have set up a garden of her own, plant some happy, pretty flowers, but what did she know about gardening? She'd probably make an embarrassing hodgepodge that'd mess up the immaculate beds created by the gardening team, beds full of roses far more elegant and genteel than Sarah would ever be.

Tugging down the high hem of the sparkly gold dress she'd worn for dinner tonight, a dinner where Abe had sat darkly silent until he got up to stalk off into the night, she looked away from the ice-white roses that climbed up one side of the house and scanned the lawn, the trees at the edge of the property.

Abe sometimes walked there at night, but she couldn't spot him today despite the light of the moon.

Her heart began to thump. "Abe?"

He'd been clean for a month this time, but if anything was going to send him into a downward spiral, it'd be the anniversary of Tessie's death. "Abe!"

Her voice echoed in the silvered darkness.

Wondering if he'd left the house, gone drinking on the town or out with one of his bandmates, she padded back into the house. She flushed when she realized she'd tracked a little dust inside, quickly went back outside and brushed off her feet on the mat by the door. Sometimes she thought she'd never figure out how to be refined and ladylike and look as if she belonged in Abe's world.

Not the glittering, hard-edged world of a rock star. That, she could fake.

No, it was the world of the Bellamy family that left her feeling lost. The world of Ivy League educations and old money and people who used words she'd only ever read in the novels that had been her friends throughout life. At least, because she read so much, she understood the words even if she couldn't pronounce them. That was good.

Once, when she'd dared mention to Abe how out of her depth she felt, he'd given a bemused shake of his head. "You're perfect, Sarah. Smart and beautiful." An arm around her neck, tugging her to the muscled warmth of him. "I don't have a snooty degree either, remember? Stop worrying."

That had made her feel better. But still, she couldn't do as he'd said, couldn't stop worrying. Because while Abe had forgone a degree to pursue a career in rock music, he was an accomplished classical pianist, had been playing since he was a child. And unlike her, he *could* go to an Ivy League university if he wanted to. His mother, Diane, was proud of his stellar school record, had told Sarah of it.

Of all the people in Abe's world, it was Diane Bellamy whom Sarah most admired. Abe's mother never had to raise her voice to get attention; she did it by dint of her presence and her quiet grace. Sarah wanted so *much* to be like her, to have that elegant confidence and certainty about her place in the world.

After using a tissue she had in her pocket to brush away the dust she'd tracked onto the gleaming wooden floors, she scrunched up the tissue and put it back in the pocket meant for a phone and ID when going clubbing. There wasn't much else to this strapless sequined dress—she'd worn it tonight because it made her feel pretty, but mostly because the last time she'd worn it, Abe had hauled her close and kissed her stupid.

"Abe?" she said again, her hopeful tone starting to tremble.

A knot grew in her throat.

He'd left her alone again, gone off to deal with his demons on his own—or in the company of the people he did love. Fox, Noah, and David, his bandmates and best friends.

Sarah knew she should be grateful, and she was. Anything that helped Abe, Sarah would accept. She just… She just wished he wouldn't shut her out. His reserve was like a stone wall she couldn't penetrate no matter how hard she tried.

Despite all the good times in their marriage, all the times they'd laughed together, all the nights they'd spent tangled in one another, the closest they'd ever been was on the night they'd first met.

He'd been alone that night and so raw in his pain that she'd wanted only to comfort him. She'd held him, then later given him her body. She hadn't known it was the anniversary of Tessie's death then, but she'd known he needed her and she'd wanted only to give to this man who made her soul come alive. Even the knowledge that he was out of her league hadn't stopped her, Sarah the moth to Abe's flame.

*There you are,* a hidden part of her had whispered the first time he spoke to her. *I've been waiting so long for you.*

But last year on this date, he'd spent the night away from her. The four members of Schoolboy Choir had recorded all night, gotten Abe through the anniversary while Sarah walked alone in the house.

She'd never known it was possible to be lonely in a marriage until she'd married Abe, married the man she loved beyond life.

Eyes burning, she touched careful fingers to the piano, not wanting to leave fingerprints on the glossy finish but unable to resist its beauty. It was such a lovely instrument, but she'd never heard its song. Abe had never, not once, played it in the time since she moved into his home.

It seemed wrong to her that the instrument had been silenced.

Taking a seat on the piano stool, she looked at the pristine black and white of the keys. She hadn't had the chance to learn music as a child, but she'd made a real effort at learning the piano since marrying Abe so that she could talk to him about his passion. Her teacher had declared that she was "pedestrian but stubborn."

That was fine with Sarah—she had no dreams of being a great musician.

*Her* passion was Abe; music was just a way to get closer to him.

But even a pedestrian musician could learn fairly complex pieces over a year and a half of intensive study comprised of ten or more hours of lessons a week. It helped fill in the time when she was alone in the house except for the housekeeper and the chef who came in for a short period each day. During the weeks while Abe was on tour, she asked the piano teacher to come every day. And then there were all the days when Abe was recording or planning songs with the band.

Sarah had a lot of time on her hands.

Staring at the keys, she lifted her hands, put them immediately back down.

This was Tessie's piano. She knew that without ever having been told. It was obvious from the way it stayed draped in covers all year except on the anniversary of her death. Though Abe never talked about Tessie with Sarah, she'd seen the photos he kept around the house, seen the joyous smile and dancing eyes of Abe's much younger sister, her tightly curled black hair in adorable little pigtails.

Tessie had been a midlife surprise for her parents, born when Abe was thirteen. Rather than being resentful of the tiny interloper, Abe had adored her.

"He was such a good big brother," Diane had told Sarah one day while they shared a coffee before a family dinner. "He used to call her from boarding school and tell her bedtime stories, always took her on 'dates' during his vacations home. And whenever she asked him to play the piano, he'd play, and Tessie would put on her little tutu and dance and dance."

Sarah didn't think a girl with such joy in music would've wanted this piano to sit forever silent.

"For you," Sarah whispered and put her fingers to the keys. The piano was in perfect tune.

As she played a haunting nocturne, she realized Abe must keep it that way even though he refused to play the instrument. Her entire chest hurt for him, for her beautiful man with his broken heart and scarred soul. If only he—

"What the fuck do you think you're doing?"

# CHAPTER 2

JERKING TO A STOP WITH a jangling of the keys, Sarah stood up so fast she knocked over the piano stool. "Abe!" Her pulse a racehorse, she stared at the man looming at her from only two feet away. "Where were you? Didn't you hear me calling?"

"Get the fuck away from the piano."

Even during the worst of the drugs, he'd never spoken to her with such dark anger. His eyes glittered in the moonlight, his black shirt and black jeans only increasing the sense of danger that clung to him, her husband with his skin the shade of rich mahogany and his wide shoulders.

"I'm sorry," she whispered, stepping away, then bending down to right the stool.

He didn't help her, didn't move, just stood there staring at her with those cold, hard eyes in a face that was all harsh good looks.

Her stomach twisted. "I just thought—"

"I didn't marry you for your brains."

His vicious words tore open her deepest vulnerability, stabbing right into her secret knowledge that she was a high school dropout from the wrong side of the tracks playing at being a sophisticated woman who belonged in this big north Santa Monica home with its shining floors and glittering chandeliers.

Sarah blinked past the stinging pain; she knew Abe was hurting. She wouldn't take what he'd said to heart. After all, he didn't know about her past. As far as he was aware, she had the same level of education as him and she'd been born in a normal, boring suburb, her equally normal parents killed in a car crash at the end of her high school years.

He couldn't know how much the words he'd spoken in anger hurt her.

Holding on tight to that thought, she said, "You shouldn't be alone tonight." She moved to him, reaching out to lay a hand on the muscled heat of his forearm, his skin appearing exquisitely darker in this light. "Why don't we talk about Tessie?" she said gently. "Think of all the good memories, the fun times you had with her. I'd like to know her too."

Shrugging off her hand, Abe strode to stand just outside the open doors, his eyes on the landscape beyond. "Get out."

"Abe—"

He turned, shoulders bunched and hands fisted. "You don't get it, do you, Sarah?" Shoving aside the curtains so there was no barrier between them, he said, "You're a hot piece of ass who managed to get into my head and into my pants while I was out of it. I married you because you told me you were pregnant—"

The sneer in his voice broke something inside her. "I *was* pregnant!" The miscarriage had devastated her. Abe had been so tender then, had held her as she cried. He'd even stayed home for an entire week, and she'd fallen asleep in his arms.

She'd almost felt loved.

Tonight he shrugged in a way that made it clear he saw her as a scheming liar. "The point is I don't love you. I don't want to share things with you." Hard, staccato words. "Your job is to keep looking like a hot piece of ass and to hang on my arm when I need you to. Otherwise, stay the fuck out of my life."

Fighting tears, Sarah tried to remember this was grief and rage talking. "You don't mean that."

"Jesus, Sarah." He stalked toward her, grabbed her upper arms, almost lifted her off the floor. "How much clearer can I make it? You're a groupie like countless others I've fucked. You just lucked out that I was stupid enough to fuck you without a condom."

She'd felt so needed that night when Abe had first taken her to his bed, so *wanted*. Afterward, as he'd slept in her arms, the lines of pain erased from his face, she'd felt useful for the first time in her life. "It was more than that." She refused to let him destroy her memories. "We stayed together all night." Limbs entwined, hearts beating in time. "We began a relationship."

Abe put his face an inch from hers. "I was high and you were available."

Sarah flinched, feeling cheap and trashy and... like nothing.

Abe continued before she could respond. "So if you want to keep this nice life you've managed to con out of me, stay the fuck out of my sight unless I want you there." He released her. "You just have to spread your legs when I ask and smile for the cameras when necessary. That's our *relationship*."

Sarah shattered inside, spiderweb cracks spreading out from her heart to create jagged shards in every corner of her. Trembling and with her tears starting to fall despite her attempts to hold them back, she looked into Abe's eyes and couldn't tell if he was sober or not. "You've been drinking." The words came out shaky, a plea.

"Do I sound drunk?"

No, he didn't. But his body was so used to the alcohol and the drugs that it was often hard to judge his sobriety. He could well be under the influence. Sarah tried to hold onto that… and couldn't. Not in the face of the ugly things he'd said to her.

Never had he spoken to her that way.

And she knew.

Abe didn't just not love her. He didn't even *like* her.

He definitely didn't need her.

She was worthless.

Again.

Turning on her heel, she ran from the music room. Her tears threatened to blind her, but she managed to make it up to their bedroom and pull out a small suitcase. It was a fancy Louis Vuitton one. She didn't really like the colors or the design. Left to her own tastes, she would've bought the much cheaper one that looked as if it had travel stickers all over it. But this was the kind Abe's mother used, and Sarah had copied her because then she could be sure of not making a mistake and embarrassing Abe.

Wiping the backs of her hands over her cheeks as her tears continued to fall hot and wet, she threw clothes into the bag. She wasn't quite sure what she was packing, but it didn't matter. Shoes, she needed shoes. Going to the large walk-in closet she'd spent hours organizing and reorganizing because she couldn't believe it was hers, she found her cheapest, oldest pair of tennis shoes and thrust her feet into them.

She wiped her forearm across her face as she went to the cubby that held folded sweaters for when Abe wanted her to go somewhere cold. Mostly he never took her with him on tour, but a couple of times she'd attended music events in colder places; events where he'd needed his wife to "hang on his arm."

Almost bending over from the pain, she gritted her teeth. Once it had passed and though her tears refused to stop, she took out the sweaters and put them neatly in another cubby. Even now, she couldn't bring herself to treat the beautiful cashmeres and silks with anything but care. Right at the back, hidden in a small box, was her stash of emergency money.

Abe had given her credit cards that had no limit, didn't care what she bought, but Sarah had never been able to fully trust the cards. So she'd withdrawn money on them. If Abe or his accountants noticed, they didn't say anything. She'd never withdrawn much. A hundred here, a couple of hundred there. Enough that she had a fund just in case.

She didn't know what she'd been preparing for. Maybe this.

A woman who knew she wasn't loved could never quite settle in.

Taking out the two thousand dollars she'd accumulated in the time since their marriage, she put some in her bra, some in her shoe, some in the suitcase, and just a little in her purse. If she got mugged, they wouldn't get all of it. She took the cards too. A woman who had no family, no one to whom to turn, couldn't afford pride.

And if the husband she adored thought she was nothing but a gold digger, useful only for spreading her legs and being an ornament, then she might as well live up to that expectation.

15

Swallowing down the new wave of raw tears that threatened, she carried the suitcase down the stairs and threw it into the dark green Jaguar parked outside. It wasn't her car, but she could use it whenever she wanted. Trying not to think about how Abe had taught her to drive, how he'd just shaken his head and laughed when she accidentally reversed the Jaguar into his SUV, she checked that she had her purse, then put the Jag into gear and peeled away. She'd leave it somewhere safe after she found a place to stay, call the housekeeper and tell her where it was so one of Abe's drivers could come pick it up.

Sarah might be trailer trash, but she was no thief.

Her mouth twisted as she thought of the credit cards.

Abe had given those to her, she reminded herself. *I have every right to use them and not feel guilty about it.* And she would. If she couldn't reach his heart, she'd hurt his wallet.

Sobs wracked her. "Stop it," she ordered herself. "No one cares if you cry."

No one ever had.

Sarah didn't know where she was going, but when she found herself in front of a good but not A-list hotel, she stopped, parked, and stalked up to the counter. They stared at her when she asked them to pre-charge the room for a week, but since her card was black and clearly had her name on it and she had her ID, they did it. Now, even if Abe canceled the cards, she'd have a place to stay for a week.

She was rolling her own bag to the elevator when the doors to that elevator opened and a well-dressed man in what she recognized as an expensive suit walked out. Patrician-faced and golden skinned with blue eyes and dark hair threaded with fine

16

glints of silver, he immediately made her feel grubby and small. He had wealthy and cultured written all over him.

Then his features creased with concern. "My dear, you look distressed. What's the matter?"

Sarah just shook her head, unable to speak in the face of his unexpected kindness.

"Shh, it's all right. Let's get this bag and you up to your room." He carried her bag up for her, and when she fumbled the key card, he took it and opened her door.

That was when she belatedly realized she'd been stupid to so easily trust a stranger. But before she could panic, he put her case inside, placed her key card on the nearest flat surface, then stepped back out into the hallway.

"This hotel has apartment levels," he told her. "I live in the penthouse." Reaching into his pocket, he took out a business card. "Here. Take this. Call me if you need anything."

Sarah's fingers closed over the black gloss of the card. "Why are you being so kind?" Her voice was hoarse.

"Because you're a beautiful woman in distress, and I want to play knight in shining armor." His smile was disarming, his teeth Hollywood perfect against tanned skin that didn't look fake but as if he'd caught exactly the right amount of sun. "And because I hope someone would help my sister if she was ever in the same position."

Tears threatened again, this time in relief. He was just a nice man, not someone who wanted her to "spread her legs." Abe's ugly words, they still hurt so bad, still made her feel so dirty and used. "Thank you."

"It's my pleasure." His smile faded. "Now go have a bath, order room service, and remember, you can call me anytime."

Nodding, Sarah shut the door.

Then, though she didn't consciously realize it, she waited. Because if Abe *had* been drunk or high when he said what he had, Sarah would give him the chance to make things right. And, even as she made it clear that he had to get sober, this time for good, she'd try to forgive him for the wounds he'd placed on her heart. Maybe it wasn't the most sensible choice, but Sarah loved Abe too much to simply walk away without a backward look.

So she made sure her phone was charged, that it was always with her, that she was never in an area without a signal. And she waited.

For hours. Then days, then two long weeks.

The cards still worked, but instead of staying on at the hotel, she moved to a much more ordinary apartment where the rent was such that her neighbors were all hardworking, blue-collar people who smiled at her and made her feel normal for the first time in two years. She couldn't embarrass herself here, could be just Sarah who had only a partial high school education but who could work hard too, who'd done blue-collar work herself before she met Abe.

And she continued to wait.

It was on the thirtieth day after she'd walked out of the house that she accepted Abe wasn't going to call her, wasn't going to apologize for the horrible, hurtful things he'd said. The man she loved with every beat of her heart didn't care that she was all alone in this huge city, didn't care about her tears or her broken heart or the fact that she missed him so much she couldn't breathe, couldn't sleep.

*I don't love you.*

*Your job is to keep looking like a hot piece of ass and to hang on my arm when I need you to. Otherwise, stay the fuck out of my life.*

Flinching at the memory, she got out the credit cards she'd only used for food and shelter at that point and went to methodically cut them to pieces, then thought *fuck him*. If he could shit on her dreams, if he could treat her like she was worthless trash, then he deserved all the pain she could dish out.

Sarah stood, washed her face, put on her best day dress, and slipped her feet into flats. Ready, she went on the shopping spree to end all shopping sprees. She wasn't stupid; she'd been poor too long to be stupid. She bought the kind of clothes a woman would need if she was looking for work. Not skimpy dresses suitable for a rock star's wife and formal gowns appropriate for music awards.

Simple skirts and pants, clean-cut but quality shirts that'd last, neat work dresses. She bought shoes to go with them.

She bought a fucking car because she needed a vehicle to navigate this sprawling city. It was a candy-apple-red MINI Cooper with a white top, cute and fast and so much more Sarah than the Jaguar that had always made her feel like an imposter. She bought jewelry, not because she wanted the jewelry, but because it was an asset she could put in a safe-deposit box and sell off if necessary.

She bought groceries, focusing on supplies that wouldn't go bad for months or even years.

She bought meals for every homeless person she saw, bought double meals for the homeless teens.

And she withdrew cash as many times as possible.

The cards finally stopped working on the third day of her determined spree.

NALINI SINGH

By that time she'd spent more than enough money to hope-fully hurt Abe a little, but she knew it was nowhere near as badly as he'd hurt her. Again and again, she heard the words he'd thrown at her, felt the bruising pain of taking hit after hit, and she wanted him to shatter as he'd shattered her, but she didn't know how to find the kind of pit bull she needed to make Abe feel as she was feeling.

It was then that her eye fell on the glossy black of the busi-ness card she'd kept, of the man who'd been so kind to her that horrible night. He'd been kind afterward too. The two weeks she'd been at the hotel, he'd ordered her room service, including a bowl of strawberries and cream that came with a handwritten note that said he hoped the strawberries made her day sweeter.

He'd rung once every day to check on her, and when she'd told him she was moving into the apartment, he'd insisted on driving her over himself. Since then, he'd stayed in touch with a call once a week. And though his eyes were admiring when they looked at her, he was always a perfect gentleman.

He made her feel like a woman worth respect. Not a cheap, gold-digging whore.

Picking up the phone, she dialed his number. "Jeremy," she said. "Do you know the name of a good divorce attorney? A really mean one?"

A pause before Jeremy Vance said, "I know a man affection-ately spoken of as the Rottweiler. Will that do?"

Sarah clenched her stomach, hardened her heart. "Yes."

"I'll call him for you if you like, set up an appointment. We're friends, so you're more likely to get in to see him that way than if you call yourself."

"Thank you. I'd appreciate that." Sarah made herself breathe.

Abe was getting *no more* of her tears.

"Anything for you, Sarah." Jeremy's tone was warm. "Would you like me to accompany you to the first meeting? I know you're still fragile."

Sarah went to say yes, shut her mouth. She was so scared, so alone, but she'd been that before, and she'd survived. Jeremy was nice, but Abe had been nice once too. The only person she could rely on was herself.

Same as always.

Her every breath hurt.

"No," she said to Jeremy. "Thank you, but I'll go alone." And she'd make Abraham Bellamy rue the day he'd taken on a girl named Sarah Smith.

A girl who would've once carved out her own heart and laid it at his feet should he have asked it of her.

# PART TWO

# CHAPTER 3

SARAH SAT IN THE SOLARIUM of the lovely dual-level house she'd bought using part of the proceeds of her divorce settlement. Her knees were tucked up to her chest, her legs covered by a heavy knitted throw she'd found in a thrift shop; she cradled a mug of coffee in her hands while, beyond the window of the solarium, she could see the daisies she'd planted cheerfully bobbing their heads.

It had made her so happy to buy this house with its stylish appearance and neat gardens and delicate metal fencing. In a solid family neighborhood, nothing about it said that the woman who owned it had a de facto stepfather in prison for the murder of her mother.

No, the woman who lived here had *value.*

Today Sarah smiled tightly at the memory of her defiant thoughts the day she'd moved into this house less than two years earlier, a month after her divorce from Abe became final. She hadn't had value. Not then. Not in the way she wanted. She'd bought this house with Abe's money, furnished it with Abe's money. Her Rottweiler of a lawyer had more than earned his fee, but in the end, Sarah had been left feeling sick inside.

Because she'd never wanted the divorce. She'd wanted Abe to fight for her.

He'd fought her demands, but never had he fought for *her*.

Now she had this house and this garden and this broken heart that had never quite healed right. And once again, she was alone. Her fingers brushed her cheek, still able to feel the bruise that had blackened it two weeks earlier. "I never thought Jeremy would treat me that way," she said to Flossie. "He was so kind, so supportive once. He never ignited my heart, but he was a good man at the start."

Sarah's mutt of a dog, chocolate colored and with those incongruously silky ears Sarah loved to stroke, looked at her with mournful eyes darker than her furry coat.

"No," she said in disagreement. "I wasn't so careful about keeping my assets out of his reach because I didn't trust him. That lesson came courtesy of the divorce." After the Rottweiler, she'd hired another lawyer who'd tied up her divorce settlement in ways no one else could touch. No one had had to tell her to do that—she might not have a high school diploma, but she'd grown up in a home where what little her mother made, her mother's boyfriend claimed as his own.

And though Jeremy had been wealthy from the start, she'd still never considered accepting his help to manage her finances. He'd offered after the divorce, but had taken her demur with good humor. No pressure, no snide remarks. "He *was* a good man," she reiterated. "But he changed as I changed." Sorrow made her blood heavy. "I think if I'd stayed the same, we might've made it."

Jeremy Vance had rescued a broken bird, expecting her to stay broken.

26

But of course Sarah hadn't been willing to be frozen in time.

Sarah had grown stronger day by day, become independent, a business owner. At first, Jeremy had celebrated her successes. Only later had she realized that Jeremy didn't want an independent lover. He wanted Sarah as she'd once been: the lost girl searching for help.

She should've walked away the instant she realized that.

Part of the reason she'd stayed had been the baby.

Her hands clenched hard on the coffee mug.

Memories cascaded through her mind of going out to get groceries the week after she first filed for divorce and seeing Abe's face splashed on the front pages of a major tabloid. He'd been out partying the previous night, half-naked groupies hanging all over him, their hands possessive on his chest and their eyes smug.

Sarah's splintered heart had broken all over again. Because even then, while they were in the first bitter stages of their divorce—at a time when Abe was refusing to even sign the papers—she'd hoped. She had loved him *so much*, but the photographs made it clear he'd thrown her away like yesterday's trash, that he'd already moved on. The only reason he was refusing to sign the papers was because he was pissed off at the settlement her lawyer was demanding.

Jeremy had been there to catch her broken self as it fell.

He'd come to see her that night, brought her flowers to cheer her up. A chance visit he'd said. Then, it hadn't occurred to her to question him, to wonder why he'd turned up the very day the photographs of Abe partying hard hit the tabloids. But again, he'd been nothing but kind to her at that point—he could've honestly believed he was coming over to help her deal with the ugly situation.

She'd been so out of it, so emotionally numb that, for the first time, she hadn't resisted when he tried for a kiss as he so often did. When he began to push for more, she knew she should stop him, but she'd felt so distant that it was easier to just let it happen, get it over with so she could curl up and rock away her pain.

She'd been a fractured ragdoll whose heart no longer beat.

Only Jeremy hadn't disappeared afterward. No, he'd stuck around and openly said he wanted a relationship; everything he'd done had made her feel important and wanted and even a little loved. When he'd asked her if she'd have a child with him within a relatively short period of time, she'd been shocked. Then he'd told her that he adored her and explained he was getting on in years, didn't want to be too old to play with his child… and Sarah had thought of how much she'd loved the baby she'd miscarried.

The baby Abe had accused her of faking.

Looking back, she knew she'd still been in a terrible emotional place, in no state to make such life-altering decisions. Jeremy had to have known that, had taken advantage of her pain to tie her to him. So clear to see now, but then, she could think only that any child they created together would be wanted by its father. So she'd said yes. And in that, Jeremy hadn't let her down: he'd stood by her, even put their future child or children into his will right after she told him she was pregnant—so that if anything happened to him, their child would still have his or her father's support.

Sarah hadn't loved Jeremy, but at that instant, she'd known she'd do *anything* to make the relationship work. This man, she'd thought, was a good human being. Her child would have a father and a mother, would have a proud history. Her child wouldn't be a forgotten piece of flotsam other people could crush and hit and abandon.

Pain splintered through her.

Because her precious baby was gone, buried in a peaceful plot underneath the wings of a guardian angel. He'd been so beautiful, so perfect with his tiny toes and his tiny fingers, and so very, very still. No cries, no breaths, his light brown skin stark and bloodless. Her womb hadn't been able to sustain him as it hadn't been able to hold on to her and Abe's child.

Putting down her coffee mug when her hand began to shake, she clenched her fingers in Flossie's coat when her dog whined and nudged at her. "I know, Flossie," she said on a wave of heart-deep pain. "I should call Lola." Her best friend wouldn't thank her for trying to handle this day of all days on her own—but Sarah was well aware Lola had stresses of her own right now.

The woman who'd once been a teen single mom and was today a successful entrepreneur—though still very much a mom to her now college-aged son—was normally resident in Los Angeles. Six weeks earlier, however, after her father suffered a severe fall, Lola had flown to Houston to help her mother cope. She and Sarah spoke on the phone at least twice a week and aside from those who'd been there that night, Lola was the only one who knew about Jeremy hitting Sarah.

She'd recommended they "fry the bastard's balls" and "feed them to him."

Lola could be a little scary when the people she loved were hurt.

29

Wanting to smile through the pain lodged inside her, Sarah made the call. Not just to lean on Lola's shoulder, but to ask after her. It turned out her friend had needed a chat, too. "I love my folks," she said toward the end of the call, "but I'm hanging out to see you. Hopefully it won't be too much longer. Dad's improving rapidly."

"If you do need to spend more time in Houston, I'll fly to see you."

"Sarah, you have no idea how much that means to me," Lola said before she had to hang up to take her father to a medical appointment. "And hon, be kind to yourself today, okay?"

Choked up by the love inherent in that gentle order, Sarah couldn't reply with anything but a wordless sound.

The ring of the doorbell a second after she and Lola ended their conversation had her jumping. No one should've been able to get past the gate. She must've forgotten to lock it. That should've worried her. The fact that it didn't worried her.

Flossie woofed as the doorbell rang again.

Ignoring it because she didn't want to deal with anyone, and if it was Jeremy, she might just be tempted to walk out and knee him in the gonads, she picked up her mug, took a drink, then put it back down. She had to get up and out of this chair, start doing all the things that needed to be done. She couldn't do this every single month, couldn't X out the fourteenth in her diary because she knew she'd be a wreck unfit for company.

Her business hadn't yet felt the impact, but it would if she didn't find a way to deal.

Because Sarah was no longer a nobody. She had a small but thriving business, had employees who relied on her and clients who did the same.

A flash in her peripheral vision.

Giving a short yelp, she scrambled out of the armchair... to stare frozen at the big, muscular man on the other side of the glass of the solarium. Abe raised a hand, said something that didn't penetrate the glass; his eyebrow piercing glinted in the noon sunlight, the metal cool against the warm, dark brown of his skin. That piercing and his unexpectedly clean-shaven head put all the attention on the harsh but gorgeous lines of his face. Sarah felt her own skin flush, her heart thunder. She hadn't seen him since that terrible night at the Zenith Music Festival fourteen days ago—the night Jeremy hit her.

The blow had come after she told Jeremy their relationship was over. She'd known it for a while, had stayed only because of residual loyalty from when they'd first met and he'd been so kind to her. In truth, it had been months since they'd even really touched. And nothing, *nothing* in Jeremy's behavior to that point had suggested he'd ever get physically violent with her; she'd never have broken up with him alone in the dark otherwise.

On the other side of the glass, Abe pointed toward the back door.

Sarah shook her head, her heart thumping.

Abe was the one who'd hauled Jeremy off her. She hadn't even known he was nearby until he grabbed Jeremy with an enraged roar and slammed the other man up against the side of one of the heavy-duty buses the band had been using as their living quarters while at the outdoor festival. She and Abe had spoken earlier in the night, too, after Abe came up to her during the party to celebrate that day's performances.

She hadn't expected him to track her down, had expected what he'd said to her even less: *I'm sorry, Sarah. I should've said that a long time ago—no excuse as to why I didn't except that I'm an asshole.*

That, she could've borne. As he'd admitted, the apology had come far too late. It had no power to worm its way under her defenses. Then he'd said: *You're still the most beautiful woman I've ever seen.*

Given that Abe had just seen Sarah talking to Oscar-nominated Kathleen Devigny, a woman who was heartbreakingly beautiful even when she was dressed down, the words had hit her hard. The cynical part of her might've accused him of laying on the charm, but Abe wasn't charming. He'd never been charming. He was just Abe. Blunt and honest and violently talented.

And a man, she'd realized that night, who still held the power to hurt her.

Today, on the other side of the glass, Abe folded his arms and spread his feet on the soft grass she babied all year around and mourned when water restrictions kicked in. Jaw set, he locked the deep brown of his eyes with her own.

He wasn't going to leave.

Eyebrows drawing together as years of withheld fury roared past her grief, Sarah gave him the finger and mouthed, "Fuck you," before turning on her heel to leave the solarium.

She roared out of her internally accessible garage ten minutes later, leaving Abe waiting on the lawn.

# CHAPTER 4

SARAH HAD GIVEN HIM THE finger.

Abe shook his head, still not quite able to believe it, even though the incident had occurred several hours earlier. His wife... ex-wife, he reminded himself, didn't indulge in public displays of affection, didn't swear, and she *definitely* didn't make vulgar gestures. The entire time he'd known Sarah, she'd been elegant and ladylike and contained.

Even when she was trying to convince him to kick the drugs, even when she was frustrated to tears by his behavior, she'd never *once* used a four-letter word. In his worst moments, he'd tried to push her to it, but Sarah hadn't ever snapped and told him to fuck off or called him a son of a bitch.

And in bed, when he'd lost himself in her, he'd had a tendency to get very dirty with his mouth. Sarah had never told him to stop, had, in fact, reacted with molten heat, but she'd blush and go quiet if he asked her to say dirty things in return.

He'd always found that cute—and it had given him a challenge. One day, he'd thought, he'd get his wife to whisper naughty, naughty words to him in bed.

His smile faded.

Running his fingers over the piano keys, he picked out a melody that had been humming in the back of his mind for hours. He didn't know where he'd heard it but it would bug him until he played it out. So he played, and he thought again about the night he'd fucked up his life with Sarah. She'd done nothing but try to love him, and he'd done his best to wound her beyond repair.

"You were a goddamn asshole, Abe," he gritted out, the melody turning hard and angry under his fingers.

That he'd been on a cocktail of drugs, his body so used to them that he'd showed little outward effect, didn't matter. He'd made a mess of things, kept doing it in the days, then weeks that followed after she left him. For some fucked-up, drugged-up reason, he'd been angry at *her* for leaving him when he'd done his best to push her away. He'd woken up each day expecting to see Sarah back beside him in bed, and when she wasn't there, he'd gotten angry all over again, hit the booze and the drugs.

David, Fox, Noah, they'd have slapped him to his senses if they'd known he'd fallen into the abyss, but all three had been out of town for reasons he couldn't now remember. As a result, Abe had been free to attempt to drug and drink away his demons. In the fleeting moments of coherence, he'd been glad Sarah wasn't there to see what he'd become. He never wanted her to see him like that.

Noah was the one who'd finally caught on to what was happening. He'd walked into their favorite bar a couple of days after all three men returned home, to find Abe partying with a dozen groupies, white powder scattered openly on a glass table in front of the sofa where Abe was seated. Noah had known he couldn't make Abe move, not in the belligerent mood Abe had been in at the time.

So the guitarist had gritted his teeth and just kept an eye on him.

Later, Noah told him he'd kept shouting, "She sent me fucking divorce papers!" As if *he* was the injured party. Eventually, sometime during the night, the drugs and the alcohol had done their work. He'd passed out... to wake the next day and discover his three closest friends had hauled him physically into rehab.

Eight weeks later, he'd come out sober and angry. Always so angry. At fate. At God. At Sarah. She'd *left* him, wanted to *divorce* him. Even then, he hadn't realized he should be begging and crawling on his knees to make up for what he'd done, how he'd abandoned her.

No, he'd fallen back on anger, the emotion that made it easier not to feel pain, not to feel panic, not to feel the staggering sense of loss that would've rocked him had he stopped for a second and thought about what those divorce papers actually meant. Anger was a great insulator. Furious, he'd gone to get his wife, to remind her she'd taken vows with him that he wasn't about to allow her to forget, but he'd been months too late.

His demons had awakened with a vengeance when he pulled up and saw Jeremy Vance kissing her on the doorstep to her apartment.

He hadn't been sober for most of their divorce battle.

He was stone-cold sober now. But while he'd gone through rehab and stuck to it this time, stuck *hard*, there was one thing he'd never done until Zenith: apologized to Sarah. Not because he didn't think she deserved it. No, it was because he hadn't been able to face her. Sarah's opinion of him meant everything—and he'd screwed that up beyond redemption.

He'd known seeing disgust or hate in her eyes would kill him.

Even more, he'd thought she was happy with Vance, was painfully aware he didn't have the right to push himself into that happiness. He'd given up all such rights. The fact he missed her each and every day didn't change that.

But the moment at the music festival when he'd realized Sarah was bare feet away, he couldn't have kept his distance if his life depended on it. He'd barely breathed until she met his gaze... and he saw no hate in her, only a guarded wariness that was a thousand times worse.

The apology he'd given her that night was nowhere near enough to make up even a tiny bit for the monumental bastard he'd been to her. Part of him said it was selfish to push himself back into her life, even if it was to say sorry a thousand times over.

Another part of him said she deserved a pound of his flesh.

Pushing back the piano stool, he stood, grabbed his keys. Sarah wouldn't expect him to show his face again so quickly after she'd flipped him off—and he knew where he was most likely to find her if she wasn't at home.

He swung by her neat little house first; the gate was locked, the windows all closed, and no one human responded to his long press of the gate buzzer—but he did hear a canine woof or two from the fenced-off backyard. He'd jumped the gate earlier today, but given that he was much bigger and stronger than the asshole who'd hit Sarah during Zenith, he wasn't worried that Jeremy Vance would do the same. Still, he'd make it a point to tell her about the possible security vulnerability.

If she didn't punch him in the face the first second she saw him.

Getting back into the rugged black SUV that was the only vehicle in which he felt truly comfortable, he drove out to the Los Angeles County Arboretum. He wouldn't even know the place existed but for Sarah—and he'd lived in LA far longer than her. One day soon after their wedding, she'd disappeared without warning; when he'd called to check that she was okay, she'd told him she'd discovered "the most amazing garden" within easy travel distance of the city.

Abe had gone with her during the good times, enjoyed the peace of the serene landscapes. Enjoyed even more how bright and bubbly and happy his wife was as she told him about the flowers, his sexy nerd who fooled people into thinking she was a party girl without a brain. Abe had always known different, always known Sarah had one hell of a mind to go along with that knockout body.

He'd figured she'd study further once they settled in, get herself a bunch of letters after her name. It had given him a proud kick that his wife was so intelligent. The only thing he hadn't factored in was his own assholishness. How the fuck was Sarah supposed to study when he was off his head half the time?

"Kick yourself later, Abe," he said. "Today, you get on your knees and apologize to her."

Arriving at the arboretum about an hour later courtesy of LA traffic, he discovered the parking lot comparatively empty thanks to the fact it was only about a half hour from closing time as well as being a weekday. He pulled into a spot next to a little red MINI Cooper, then paid for admission and walked straight to Sarah's favorite spot in the arboretum: a wooden bench that overlooked Baldwin Lake, with the graceful presence of the Queen Anne Cottage on the other side.

And then there she was, standing on the edge of the lake, looking at the mirror-still water, a faraway expression on her face. Beautiful didn't describe her, wasn't good enough a word for her. She was *Sarah.*

Unique and stunning.

Her African-American, Puerto Rican, and Japanese ancestors had left their mark on her in different ways—that glorious, deep brown skin that glowed under the kiss of the late-afternoon sun, the thickly lashed brown eyes that had a feline edge to them, the sharp cheekbones and masses of curling black hair.

He'd always loved her hair, but Sarah insisted on straightening it more often than not.

Today, however, it ran wild around her head and over her shoulders, the sunlight picking up reddish glints in the glory of it.

His fingers curled into his palms, skin tingling with the urge to touch.

It was then that she saw him. It was as if a steel rebar had replaced her spine, shutters slamming down hard to wipe the expression off her face.

# CHAPTER 5

A S HE CLOSED THE DISTANCE between them, she tugged the dark gray of her shawl tighter around her body before turning to face him.

Her legs were exposed by the knee-length sundress of cool blue with white flowers that covered her body, and those legs were as phenomenal as always. Sarah loved to dance, and it showed in the fluid muscles of her body. But she wasn't all muscle over bone like some dancers became. No, Sarah had serious, dangerous curves along with all that tone. And when she stood straight up as she was doing now, she came to just below his chin.

It made her very tall for a woman.

It made her the perfect height for Abe.

Coming to a halt a couple of feet from her, he looked at her face, specifically the spot where that bastard had punched her. "The bruise is gone." Fury rumbled in his gut regardless. If he ever saw Vance again, the man would lose that smug face of his, become unrecognizable even to his own fucking mother.

Sarah tugged the shawl even tighter around herself. "What do you want, Abe?" The words were harsh, holding none of the innate gentleness that had first drawn him to his wife... but her body, it trembled.

As if she'd shatter if she didn't physically hold herself together.

"To apologize properly." He barely restrained the urge to take her into his arms. He wasn't used to Sarah looking fragile. Gentle or not, Sarah never looked fragile. Sarah was tough enough to kick his ass and tear him a new one.

It was exactly what she'd done the times she'd found him with drugs.

"For the things I said the night you left me"—God, what the fuck had been *wrong* with him—"and for the bastard I was during our marriage."

Sarah stared at him before turning to face the lake once more. "Fine." The word was flat. "Good-bye."

Abe flinched. He'd known this wouldn't be easy. He didn't *want* it to be easy. He wanted her to be angry with him, wanted her to be full of fire... wanted to know he hadn't doused that wild, rare fire with his ugliness. "I don't expect forgiveness," he began, "but—"

"But what?" Sarah turned on her heel. "This is part of some twelve-step program you have to complete to lay your demons to rest?" She shoved at his chest with her hands, the shawl dropping unnoticed to the soft green grass. "How damn noble of you!"

Her touch rocked him to the core. It always had. "Sarah—"

"I don't want your apologies! In fact, I don't want to see your face ever again!" Each word was punctuated by fists pounding against his chest. "Go. *Away!*"

Abe was a big man. He could take Sarah's fury. What he couldn't take was the shimmer of tears he glimpsed the moment before she spun away. "Sarah." He pulled her into his arms without thinking about it.

"Go away." A whisper this time, her voice wet and her body no longer of the valkyrie who'd launched into him. "Please go away and let me grieve in peace."

It hit him then. Today's date. Eighteen months to the day since Sarah's baby had been born, a painful fact Abe knew because he'd never been able to stop himself from listening for anything to do with her. The little guy had never taken a breath outside the womb, never known his mother's smile or her love. Because Sarah would've loved her child with a fierce will. It was what she did: love so deeply that she didn't hold anything back, didn't protect herself.

Sarah had no walls or shields when she loved.

And that was when Abe knew he was wrong. The baby *had* known Sarah's love—she would've loved him from the day she first learned of his existence.

"Ah, sweetheart." He didn't release her, couldn't release her when she was so very hurt. He just held her as the sun inched lower in the sky, and at some point, she began to talk about her baby, about her boy.

"I named him Aaron," she said in a voice husky with withheld tears. "I always liked that name, but originally I planned to call him Luther, one of my other favorite names." She stared out at the water, her cheek against his chest and her arms folded up between them. "But he looked like an Aaron when he came out."

She swallowed. "When I talked to him, I called him Baby Boots because of how he'd kick inside me... But it was important he have a proper grown-up name too, so officially I named him Aaron."

41

Speaking through her sobs, she described her baby boy with his perfect little nose and his tiny hands and his round belly. "Why didn't he breathe, Abe?" It was difficult to understand her now, she was crying so much. "Why couldn't I keep him alive? I tried so hard. I did everything the doctors said. I ate the right foods—"

And then there were no more words, only Sarah breaking in his arms.

Lost, helpless, Abe just held her and he wished to God that he could take her pain. He knew what it was to lose a young life, what it was to watch small hands go still and a small face stop smiling. But unlike Abe with his sister, Sarah didn't have any living memories of her baby, no echoes of joy to balance out the agony of loss.

"I'm so sorry, sweetheart. I'm so goddamned sorry." He rocked her in his arms, and when he saw a security guard heading toward them as if to say it was closing time, he gave the man a look that said his life was forfeit if he came any closer.

The guard went in another direction.

And Sarah, she just cried until he didn't think he could bear it... but he did, because no way in hell was he leaving her alone. Not this time. Not even if her tears tore him in two.

SARAH FELT WRUNG OUT, WORN away. She didn't know how this had happened, how she came to be sitting in Abe's car, driving to the cemetery where she'd laid her baby to rest. "I hate seeing him there," she whispered, arms wrapped around her middle over the shawl Abe had picked up and put back around her shoulders. "I made sure he had the most beautiful white casket all lined in blue, but he shouldn't be there. My baby shouldn't be in the ground."

Abe said nothing, but he was listening. She could tell. When he was sober, Abe had always been good at listening, and today she couldn't stop the words from tumbling out. She needed to speak about Aaron; Jeremy, when they'd been together, hadn't had the patience to understand her grief.

No, that wasn't totally fair. He'd been excited to greet his son, in that she wasn't mistaken—he'd been determined to name their child Jeremy Vance Junior for one, a fact on which they'd still been in discussion—and he'd grieved when that son was born without life. But he'd also shut that part of their life away behind an iron door, refusing to talk about Aaron when Sarah wanted so much to talk about their little boy.

Maybe it had been his way of dealing with the loss, but later, when her own grief continued to haunt her, he'd told her they could always have another one. As if Aaron was replaceable, like a broken washer or car.

Aaron was *Aaron*. Her firstborn. Sarah would always remember the tiny, perfect body the nurse had put into her arms. She'd been a kind woman, that nurse, had treated Sarah's baby with respect, touching him as gently as if he were a living, breathing child. "I sat with Aaron in my arms for hours, memorized every inch of him."

And Jeremy, for all his faults, had made sure no one interrupted her precious time with her son.

"He was so beautiful, Abe." The grief that never seemed to grow any softer thickened her voice again. "I wish you could've seen him." What a foolish thing to say to the man who'd once been her husband but who had never voluntarily wanted to give her a child. She'd asked so many times after the miscarriage, but Abe had always said no.

"Did you take any photos?"

Surprised by the question, she nonetheless scrambled for her purse, wiping away her tears at the same time. No one aside from Lola ever asked to see pictures of her baby—as if he hadn't existed. But he *had*. He'd been a gorgeous, perfect little boy with honey-brown skin and long, long lashes. "Yes, there was a volunteer photographer," she said, pulling out the photos she kept always in her wallet.

"The nurse called him after asking me." The elderly man was retired, but he came in whenever a parent or parents lost a baby to stillbirth or neonatal complications and wanted a tangible memory of their child; in his faded blue eyes, Sarah had seen a father who'd once held his own silent baby. "Here."

Abe brought the car to a stop near a grassy shoulder, and it was only then that she realized they'd entered the peaceful green of the cemetery. "Let me see," he said, holding out his hand before she could become angry again at the fact her baby was here, under the cold earth.

She passed over the photos of her baby, her own gaze greedy on the images that were all she had of the son for whom she'd decorated a nursery, a son she'd dreamed of taking to school and playing with in the park. "He looks like he's sleeping, doesn't he?" Such a sweet, peaceful face.

"Yes." Abe touched his finger to the image as if stroking her baby's cheek. "How did you even carry him? He looks like a linebacker."

Sarah laughed through her tears. "God, he used to kick so hard." It was why she still found it so difficult to understand why he hadn't made it. "They said he had defects in his organs, that he never formed right... but he looks perfect to me." Would always be her strong Baby Boots.

"Definitely an Aaron," Abe said, his hands careful with the prints and his eyes taking in the details she pointed out. "Playing football and getting all the girls. And maybe even being a little preppy. Just enough to have that bad-boy-pretending-to-be-good vibe that girls love."

Sarah laughed again, so happy to hear her son's name on someone else's lips, hear an acknowledgement that Aaron had been born even if he'd never lived. Putting the photos away with care when Abe returned them, she took a deep breath, then directed him to the place where the babies lay, sleeping under the sheltering wings of a guardian angel.

She'd come here first thing this morning. Of course she had. She might not like seeing her child here, but she would *never* leave him alone. "Hey, baby boy," she said, kneeling down to the lush green grass and straightening the furry blue-and-yellow dinosaur she'd gotten to keep him company. She didn't leave flowers. Babies didn't care about flowers. They liked toys and colorful balloons.

Sarah had brought him bright orange ones this morning, gently anchored the strings in the ground beside the small headstone. They bobbed in the breeze as Sarah sat and talked to her baby as she did at least once every week. Abe sat beside her, a big, quiet, patient presence. It was getting dark by the time she rose to her feet.

"Good night, Baby Boots," she whispered before bending to press a kiss to Aaron's headstone. "I hope you're making mischief up in heaven." That was the only way she could bear this—if she believed that her baby's spirit had flown away and this gravestone was only a place for the living to grieve. He wasn't here any longer.

"Good night, Aaron."

Abe's words made her lower lip quiver. "Thank you," she said through the rawness inside her. "For treating him as if he existed."

Abe put his arm around her shoulders. "He did."

She didn't shrug off his hold, instead soaking in his warmth, his strength. "Were you okay last year? On the anniversary of Tessie's passing?" It had always been the worst time for him, and when the date had rolled around, she'd worried, watched the tabloids, only breathing a sigh of relief when she saw no mention of Abe indulging in self-destructive behavior.

"I hung out with the guys," he told her now, "stayed the night at David's place." He stroked his thumb over her bare upper arm as he said, "I take her balloons too. She always loved chasing them."

It was the first time he'd ever shared anything about how he mourned for his sister. "You visit her often?" Sarah knew Tessie had been laid to rest in Abe's hometown of Chicago.

Less than a year later, Diane and Abe had buried Abe's father beside her, the physically fit man dying of a sudden heart attack. "A broken heart," Diane had said to Sarah one day. "These Bellamy men, when they love, they go all in. And my poor Gregory, he couldn't survive losing his baby girl. It was the helplessness that got to him—not being able to fight her dragons for her, slay them."

Like father, like son, Sarah had thought at the time, already starting to understand that Abe, too, was haunted by how

46

helpless he'd been made by the disease that had taken his sister's life.

"Whenever I'm in the city," Abe said now. "Mostly I only go to support my mom. I carry Dad and Tessie here." He touched his heart, right on the spot where he bore a tattoo of a tiny wood sprite peeking out through long reeds. Such a delicate tattoo for this big, tough man, but Sarah knew it was his favorite.

"The wood sprite tattoo," she said, "it's in memory of your sister, isn't it?"

To her surprise, Abe shook his head. "No, it's not in memory. It *is* a memory—Tessie's the one who chose the design," he told her. "While she was in hospital that last month, I used to read to her and I asked her what my next tattoo should be." A smile in his voice. "She never blabbed about my tats to our folks. They didn't know back then, thought I was the most clean-cut rocker on the planet."

Sarah held her breath, not wanting to break the moment, not wanting to lose this instant when Abe was trusting her with a piece of himself. It was far too late for them… but it still mattered that he would.

"So Tessie picks up the fairy book I'd been reading to her and says, 'This one.'" He laughed. "I got it that week—she saw it before…" His smile faded, his hands fisting at his sides. "It fucking sucks that assholes get to live and Tessie and Aaron didn't. That my dad didn't."

The blunt words were so what Sarah felt that hearing them unexpectedly eased her grief. "Yes, it does."

Beside her, Abe closed his eyes, took several deep breaths, and seemed to consciously force himself to unclench his hands.

Sarah felt her eyes widen.

He'd never focused on control that way when they'd been together; he'd worn his fury at the world on his skin. She'd been able to feel it shoving to escape at every moment, had worried constantly what would trigger it. It had never been directed at her, not until that last night, so she hadn't worried for herself but for him, what it was doing to him.

This man… he released another breath before opening his eyes. And when he turned to her, despite the grief and anger that still lived in him, he was the Abe she'd seen only rarely during their marriage: the gifted musician who felt deeply but who was at peace with himself.

"I'll drive you home."

She started a little at the deep sound of his voice; she'd become so lost in trying to come to grips with the change in him. "My car's still at the arboretum."

"I'll have a driver pick it up," Abe said as they walked back to his SUV, "drive it back for you." He helped her into the vehicle.

Sarah went to argue, realized she really shouldn't be driving. She was too exhausted from the emotional storm that had just passed. "All right. Thank you."

Not saying anything in return, Abe drove them to her house in a silence that slowly became filled with a thousand whispers of memory. Sarah had always loved being in the passenger seat of Abe's car, had been so proud to be his wife, to have the right to sit beside him.

Not because he was a rock star. Because he was Abe, talented and incredible.

He still drove as easily and as confidently as he'd always done, as if LA traffic wasn't a serious nightmare—and he got her home in far better time than she would've made herself.

"I should've stopped, picked up takeout," he said as she pushed the button on her key-fob remote to open the gate, then the garage. "You must be starving."

Sarah shook her head. "I'm fine."

"Sarah." Parking in the empty garage, Abe turned to her, tipped up her chin. "I know what grief can do to a person, and you've clearly already lost weight. You gotta eat, sweetheart. Come on, I'll make you my famous omelet."

She laughed, and it was a startling thing to have her lips curve up instead of down, to feel the knot in her chest begin to loosen. "You make terrible omelets." The last time he'd made her one during a silly, fun weekend when he'd stayed home the entire time, it was only half-cooked and she'd had to pick out pieces of shell.

It was one of her happiest memories of their marriage—seeing Abe grin as he banged pots and pans and declared himself her personal chef for the weekend.

"It's the thought that counts." His grin hit her hard as they got out of the SUV, reality colliding with memory.

She lowered the garage door, and then for the first time since she'd run out of the music room on the anniversary of Tessie's death, she invited Abe into her home.

# Chapter 6

Tension simmered in the air between them, but it wasn't like it had been at the music festival. Then it had felt as if she stood precariously balanced on a razor-thin tightrope, her heart braced for further hurt from this man who'd always meant too much to her. But Abe hadn't hurt her. He'd apologized... and the look in his eyes, it had shaken her.

*You're still the most beautiful woman I've ever seen.*

Today... today he was *her* Abe. The big-hearted man who'd envelop her in his arms and make her feel tiny and petite and protected. All things she'd never been. That Abe had drowned himself in drugs and alcohol and rage until she'd thought him forever lost. But here he was in her kitchen, making her a terrible omelet while she let Flossie in and gave her a treat to chew on. Afterward, she put on some toast, then dug out a package of ham Molly had bought for her.

The fiancée of Schoolboy Choir's lead singer had insisted on restocking Sarah's pantry before allowing her to move back home, Sarah having stayed with Fox and Molly until her bruise faded and the locks were changed at her place so Jeremy couldn't corner her after she returned.

All of Abe's bandmates, as well as the women who loved them, had done so much for her after the shock of Jeremy's punch left her a trembling wreck, but none more so than Molly. Sarah was still a little bewildered by the other woman's kindness, but she couldn't argue it hadn't been genuine.

"Molly's not going to survive in Hollywood if she keeps being so nice," she said to Abe as she put the ham on a chopping board.

Abe went with her abrupt and—to him—probably inexplicable choice of topic. "Don't worry—Moll's got an excellent bullshit detector," he told her. "Developed it with all the crap she went through as a teenager."

"What?" Sarah asked before shaking her head. "Sorry, I shouldn't have asked. She deserves her privacy." Especially after her compassionate gentleness toward Sarah, the sheer friendly warmth with which she'd welcomed Sarah into her home.

Abe's eyebrows drew together, that silver piercing of his making her want to tug at it, play with it. He hadn't had any piercings while they'd been together, just those tattoos she'd loved exploring with her fingertips and her lips while he lay lazily relaxed in bed.

Heat kissing her cheeks at the vivid memory that suddenly flashed into her mind, of his big body sprawled naked on white sheets, she glanced away just as he said, "Molly's history was splashed all over the tabloids after that bottom-feeding creep taped her and Fox in their hotel bedroom. You didn't see?"

Chopping up the ham, Sarah pressed her lips into a tight line at the idea of the awful violation. At least she hadn't helped fuel the media frenzy. After the divorce, she'd given up even glancing at the tabloids in an effort to avoid any and all mentions of Schoolboy Choir. The only time she'd broken the self-protective rule was on the anniversary of Tessie's death last year.

"I heard bits and pieces, but that was all." It had been difficult to totally avoid the news since radio, TV, everyone had covered it. Though Sarah hadn't known Molly then, she'd felt sick for the other woman and Fox, so much so that she'd shut down anyone who'd tried to talk to her about the video. As far as she was concerned, the screaming interest and attention only encouraged other disturbed individuals to emulate that kind of behavior.

Fame was fame to some, regardless if it equaled jail time.

"Yeah, well, the media dug up her past, so it's not a secret," Abe said. "I don't think Molly would mind if I told you— especially since I think she's a badass for being who she is despite it all." He gave her a quick précis of the other woman's past.

"She's tougher than she looks," Sarah said afterward, deeply impressed by what Molly had survived as a teenager, *and* by how she'd held on to her core of kindness rather than giving in to bitterness and anger.

Flipping out the first omelet, Abe poured in the second one. Sarah dropped the chopped up ham into it before it could set. "You need more than eggs," she said when he raised an eyebrow. "There's lots of ham, and I'll cut some cheese, too, for sandwiches." Abe was a big guy and it was all muscle.

When they'd made love, she'd felt deliciously overwhelmed.

Face flushing at her second inappropriate thought of the evening, she moved away from the stove and prepared the sandwich fixings. She had everything on the table by the time Abe flipped out the second omelet. She hadn't thought she'd be hungry today, the grief having hit her brutally hard this month for no reason but that some months—some *days*—were just tougher than others. However, one bite of the omelet and her stomach made itself felt. "No shell," she said to him with a smile.

His grin devastated her all over again, reminding her of who they'd once been together, those precious times untouched by drugs or alcohol or Abe's inner rage. It still hurt inside to know it had all been a mirage, a romantic fantasy she'd spun in her mind in her desperate hunger to be loved, to be wanted.

"Here." She put together a sandwich for him after finishing her omelet. He'd already demolished his own as well as another sandwich. "Wait, I have that mustard you always liked." Getting up, she dug around in the pantry until she found it. "That should keep you going for a couple of hours at least."

"You think you're joking, but I'll probably be hungry again by ten." He shrugged. "I get one of those services to bring me meals that I can stick in the fridge and raid at night. Lean meat, vegetables, that kind of stuff."

Sarah stared at him. "Hollow leg?" He'd been haphazard about food when she'd known him.

"I've been working out more." He bit into the sandwich, chewed and swallowed before adding, "Helps keep me focused and away from all the bullshit."

*All the bullshit*, Sarah thought, was code for alcohol and drugs. "Good." She'd hated what he was doing to himself. "Not that you need to be any more ripped." Abe had always been fit, despite his addictions, but from what she could tell, he was now carved out of granite.

A smile that held more than a hint of male satisfaction, white teeth flashing across the handsome face she'd fallen for at first glance. But his face alone would've never captured her interest and held it. It had been the electricity between them, the vivid, visceral connection that made it feel as if he'd been made for her, she for him.

Looking back, she could see that their raw compulsion toward one another hadn't been the firmest foundation for a relationship. But she'd had so much love to give, had thought she could make it enough. And Abe... he was so solid, so big and strong and confident that he'd seemed able to handle her need, to be the rock on which she could stand.

"Hey." He reached out, tapped her cheek. "Where'd you go?"

She gave him a rueful smile. "It's been a day." The anniversary rolled around every month like clockwork, and every month she ended up curled in a corner, sobbing out her heart. Perhaps because she had to keep her grief contained the rest of the time—people didn't think she had a right to mourn. After all, her baby had never lived.

No, that was unfair. It hadn't been "people," but Jeremy. He simply couldn't understand why she didn't just get over it.

That bastard was now out of her life... and she wasn't rocking in a corner tonight. "Thank you," she said to Abe as they stood to clean up the table.

His expression was suddenly difficult to read. "You—" Running a hand over his head, he held her gaze. "Anything you need, Sarah."

The potency of the connection was too much, a taut string vibrating in the air between them.

Breaking it, she said, "Even your keyboards?"

He groaned. "Why the fuck did you want those keyboards anyway?" he asked as he filled the dishwasher while she started the coffee. "It was the weirdest thing you asked for in the divorce."

Sarah shrugged. "I was mad because your lawyers said I cheated while we were married." That had hurt, really hurt, because if there was one thing Sarah knew how to be, it was faithful. "You were the one who went out with groupies while we were still only separated." Those pictures had broken her heart.

"I was high as a fucking kite," Abe said bluntly, no excuses in his tone. "After you left, I lost any solid footing I had, went totally off the rails."

Sarah's heart ached, wanting to see in his confession a sign that perhaps she'd been at least a little important to him. "How long have you been clean?"

"Since partway through our last major tour."

Sarah did the math, felt her eyes widen. Abe was closing in on a year in just a couple more months' time, give or take. "That's wonderful, Abe." It made her want to hug him, tell him he could keep going, that a year could become two, could become ten. "Was there a catalyst?"

"You could say that." His lips twisted. "I almost killed myself."

Sarah sucked in a breath, the idea of a world without Abe in it incomprehensible to her. "Cocaine?"

"No, I did manage to give that up after our divorce. Decided to focus on hard liquor instead." He rubbed his hands over his face. "Nearly drank myself into a coma, had one hell of a fight with the guys afterward when they pointed out I was useless to them as a keyboardist if I couldn't keep my shit together."

And the shocks kept coming. Sarah could barely take it in—the four men had been friends since they were thirteen years old. She'd thought nothing could ever tear them apart. "That's what finally got through to you?" Sarah asked, grateful to Fox, David, and Noah. "That you might lose your place in the band?"

"It was one hell of a hard push, got me thinking. Then…" Jaw grinding, he twisted the dishtowel in his hands before putting it on the counter. "I kept the incident from my mother… but she knew. I could see it in her face when we next spoke, could see her breaking as she prepared to bury another child."

"Oh, Abe." Sarah's eyes burned; she understood Diane Bellamy's pain far better now than she had before she lost Aaron. "That had to be awful for your mom, but I'm so glad it made you realize what you were doing to yourself and to her."

"Yeah." Leaning back against the counter with his hands gripping the edges, he held her gaze. "I've been totally clean since. Not even a Sunday beer or a pill to take the edge off."

The intensity of his focus made the tiny hairs on her arms rise. "You look better than I've ever seen you look," she said, taking in his healthy, glowing skin, his gorgeously defined biceps, the clean line of his jaw.

A flame flickered in his eyes. "So do you." His eyes skimmed over her body as if she were dressed in skintight leather rather than a simple sundress.

Flushing, she went to pick up a mug for the coffee, but Abe was suddenly right next to her, his heat blazing against her skin. He cupped her cheek with one hand, just held it there in silent invitation until she turned her head to look into his eyes.

She shivered at the molten heat that awaited her.

Electricity arced between them, formed in the raw passion that had never died even when everything else collapsed into ruins. Sarah knew she shouldn't, that this was a bad, bad idea, but she'd hurt so much today, and it had been so long since she'd been held. So long since she'd felt like a woman and not just a shattered thing that had once been Sarah.

When Abe bent toward her, she tilted back her head, parted her lips. His heat branding her, his scent sinking into her, his lips touching hers… and *ignition*. Her entire body went up in flame, her pulse rocketing. Moaning in the back of her throat, she gripped at his T-shirt and rose on her tiptoes to deepen the kiss, the craving inside her a feral thing.

A rumbling sound in Abe's chest that vibrated against her hands, and then he was spinning her around and picking her up to put her on the counter. All without breaking the kiss. Pushing her thighs wide apart without apology, he settled in between and, stroking one hand up her back to grip her nape, used the other to shove up her dress so that his palm was on the bare skin of her thigh.

He'd always been demanding, always *handled* her during sex.

Sarah liked it, liked how it made her feel small and feminine when she'd grown up being the big girl in every one of her classes, instinctively hunching in a futile effort to make herself smaller. She never felt too big or too tall with Abe. She felt exactly the right size. God, he was so strong, so hot.

Since Abe had shaved off his hair, she gripped at his neck, his shoulder, all the while sinking deeper and deeper into his kiss.

He moved his hand higher up her leg, onto the hypersensitive skin of her inner thigh, bare inches from her panties.

Sarah whimpered.

Chest heaving, Abe broke the kiss, said, "You want to do this?"

Sarah's nod was firm even if her breath was ragged. She wanted this more than anything. For the first time in eighteen months, she didn't feel numb inside. She felt alive and real and full of something other than sorrow.

"You sure?" He ran his thumb over the skin of her inner thigh and the slight roughness of his touch rasped sparks straight to her nipples. They tightened almost too much, until the sensation straddled a fine line between pleasure and pain. He stroked again, a man with a pianist's gifted hands but who played guitar enough that his fingertips weren't smooth.

She'd always loved his touch.

"You've had a tough day." Abe's deep voice, his hand going still on her aching flesh.

Sarah found her voice in the need that clawed at her. "I know you're trying to be a good guy, Abe, but don't." She kissed him again. Hard. "I want this and I'm an adult. I don't need babying."

A smile curved his lips, the kind of smile that would've made her clench her thighs if he hadn't been between them. "Oh, I know you're an adult, Sarah." Lifting his hand from her thigh, he closed it over her breast, big and bold and unapologetic.

Sarah shuddered, deeply conscious that she'd set herself up for a night of heaven and hell. Because this man, he knew her body in a way no one else ever had. As he tore down the strap of her dress and bra to expose the breast he'd so bluntly fondled, she tightened her abdomen, but nothing could prepare her for the feel of his thumb and forefinger capturing her nipple, rolling it.

She cried out.

Abe kissed her cry into his mouth, all the while continuing to torment her sensitive flesh with a touch *just* this side of painful. When he closed his entire hand over her bare breast even as he licked his tongue against her own, she shuddered and wrapped her legs around his hips in an effort to tug him impossibly closer.

She wanted his body crushing hers, wanted to feel him thrusting hard and demanding into the molten heat between her thighs, his breath harsh in her ear and his rhythm a thudding drumbeat that slammed through her.

Shoving up her dress even farther, Abe pushed his thumb under the side of her panties and ran it along the seam of her thigh. Her legs quivered, her panties so damp that she wanted them off, wanted his hands on her. She pushed at his shoulders.

Breaking the kiss, Abe shook his head as if to clear the fog of lust, stepped back. "No?" he asked, his pupils dilated and his dark skin flushed with heat.

"Yes." Hooking her hands into the sides of her panties, she tugged them down her thighs, and then Abe was there, pulling them all the way off and throwing them on the kitchen floor. He pushed apart her thighs once more, but instead of coming between, he bent and took one long, luscious lick that had her screaming as her back arched.

"Now!" Almost sobbing with need, she grabbed at his shoulders.

He came up in a powerful rush, slamming his mouth against hers. He tasted of her and oh God, why was that so erotic? She could feel his hand moving between them, feel him undoing his jeans, freeing his cock. And then he was slotting the thick, rigid length of it against her and she was so frantic with want that she pushed forward as he thrust in and oh, he was big. Her body ached, adapted, their mouths colliding again as they became locked together in a hot, sweaty, primal dance that tore her apart in a matter of seconds.

She felt his cock pulse as he came inside her, the wetness an intimate heat.

# CHAPTER 7

"I'M ON THE PILL," SHE said ten minutes later while she lay curled up in Abe's lap in the armchair in her solarium. He'd carried her there, her legs too weak to support her body in the aftermath of the earthquake of that orgasm. Her panties were still on the kitchen floor, but she'd righted her bra and dress while he'd fixed his jeans but removed his sweaty T-shirt.

"You're safe from a paternity suit." It was a lame attempt at a joke, the idea of having another child in her womb an agonizing one. Sarah didn't know if she could ever again take that risk. What if her baby died again?

"You wouldn't have to sue me, Sarah," Abe said, one big hand still on her back, the other warm and almost proprietary on her thigh. "If I made a kid with you, I'd step up."

He took a deep breath, released it. "I don't remember all of what I said that night, but I remember accusing you of pretending to be pregnant to trap me—I'm more ashamed of that than anything else I've ever done. I saw your pain after the miscarriage. I know damn well it was real. I know sorry isn't ever going to be enough, but I'm so sorry, sweetheart."

Sarah's eyes burned, because this Abe? He was the one she'd fallen for until she had not a hope in hell of protecting her heart against any blows he chose to deliver. The good, strong man who believed in family and loyalty and taking care of those who were his.

"And you don't have to worry about anything else either," Abe added, running his hand up and down her back. "I'm clean."

She felt the sharp bite of jealous teeth inside her, aware the reason he knew that was because he'd no doubt been for a checkup after his alcohol- and drug-fueled hookups. But all she said was, "Me too." She couldn't believe she'd been so careless today—but Abe had once been her husband, and in the midst of the painful need that held her captive, she'd forgotten he wasn't any longer.

Her body had known only that when she and Abe were naked, it was bare, his cock sliding against her desire-slick flesh.

"You should go," she whispered, knowing she couldn't let this advance any further. She hadn't lied when she'd told Abe she wanted to be with him, had spoken the pure truth when she told him she wanted him, but she also knew she *was* still emotionally fragile.

If Abe kept being so nice to her, she'd start to imagine things that didn't exist, had never existed. Sober, Abe was an amazing man, but that man had never loved Sarah. She couldn't afford to forget that—he'd almost broken her the last time they'd danced. Now, with her heart already in pieces after losing Aaron, she didn't think she could survive another round with this man who was her Achilles' heel.

Abe stirred. "I can stay on the couch." His voice rumbled against her, his frown apparent in his tone. "You shouldn't be alone."

Swallowing past the tears thick in her throat, Sarah shook her head, then forced herself to push away. He released her with obvious reluctance, watched her rise to her feet in silence. Those dark eyes, so beautiful and evocative, she'd dreamed of them so many times since the day their marriage shattered. "I'll be all right." She touched her fingers to his jaw in a quiet good-bye before dropping her hand. "Thank you for staying with me today, but I need to be alone now."

It was such a horrible lie. Sarah *hated* being alone, had had too much of it in her life. But she'd learned to bear aloneness even when it hurt... and she had to protect herself from Abe. High, he'd brutally hurt her. Sober, he could destroy her.

Because love? The kind of love she'd had for Abe? It never really died.

Getting up, Abe tucked a curl of her hair behind her ear. "You call me if you need anything."

Sarah nodded, knowing she wouldn't call. This was it. The farewell they'd never really had. "Good-bye, Abe."


ABE COULDN'T STOP THINKING ABOUT Sarah. A week after they'd come together in that primal and passionate coupling that had left him happily wrecked and truly satisfied for the first time since she'd left him, and he couldn't get her out of his head. He hadn't so much as looked at another woman in the interim. And despite the fact Sarah had made it clear he'd receive no return invitation, Abe hadn't stayed totally away.

He'd sent her flowers the next day.

He knew how much his wife—*ex*-wife—loved flowers, and he couldn't simply have sex with her, hold her, then let it go without acknowledgment. He hadn't known what to put on the card, what words she'd accept from him, so he'd just written: *For you – Abe*

She'd replied by text message: *Thank you.*

That was it. Not even the most hopeful man could read any kind of an invitation in those stark words. Abe wanted to anyway. He'd been *so* fucking stupid to let her go; she was the best thing that had ever happened to him. She'd loved *him*. Not Abe the rocker who was one quarter of a multiplatinum band, or Abe Bellamy the heir to a large family fortune. Just Abe. He'd been too drugged up, too obsessed with drowning his grief to see the value of what he was destroying.

"Yo, Abe, you with us?"

Abe looked up from his keyboard at Fox's gritty voice. The lead singer's dark green eyes were intent, as if he'd see right through Abe's skin. Breaking the eye contact, Abe played his fingers across the keys. "Just thinking about that last line." He, Fox, Noah, and David were jamming together in the music room at his place, playing with ideas for their new album.

He hadn't thought about the ramification of having the session here, but now he realized he'd been an idiot. Because every time he looked around, he saw Sarah running from him that night, saw the tears streaking down her face, relived the hurt he'd inflicted. Fuck, fuck, fuck.

His fingers wanted to pound down on the keys.

"Uh-huh."

Abe glared at Noah. "You have something to say?"

"Nope." The blond guitarist—so handsome as to come perilously close to pretty—strummed a few chords.

"How's Kit?" Abe asked, not trusting the glint in Noah's eye.

The glint became emotion of an intensity so deep Abe could almost touch it. "Good, she's really good." A grim smile. "Now that her fucking stalker's locked up, she's starting to breathe easy." He moved his fingers on the guitar strings.

Abe joined in, as did David on the drums and Fox on another guitar, and they played for a while. The glint was back in Noah's eyes when they paused. "You heard from Sarah recently?" he asked Abe.

Abe forced himself to shrug. "Why would she contact me?" He didn't intend for even his closest friends to know he and Sarah had fallen back into bed—or rather, onto a kitchen counter. The moments had been secret, a private gift. "Fox, you and Molly heard from her?" Sarah had stayed with the couple after that bastard Vance assaulted her. It had kept her safe and protected and out of the media spotlight while the band's publicist—and David's fiancée—Thea, took care of organizing a locksmith to go in and change the locks at Sarah's place.

It was a smart precaution, but Abe didn't think Vance would be back. The man was a coward, and since Sarah had physical proof of his violence toward her, he wouldn't take the risk of aggravating her and her calling the cops.

Abe's hands fisted against the urge to crush that scrawny fucker's throat.

"Yeah," Fox said as he jotted notes on a music sheet, his guitar held on his lap with one arm hooked around the neck. "Molly and Sarah met up for coffee a couple of days back."

Abe blinked. He hadn't really expected to hear that Sarah had stayed in touch with Molly—she'd always been a little distant with his bandmates. Maybe because, a harshly unforgiving part of his brain pointed out, her husband was a dick who left her alone a lot while he jammed with the guys or toured with them.

No wonder she hadn't wanted to hang out with Fox, Noah, and David.

"Molly said she's looking much better," the lead singer added. "Healthier, stronger." He passed the music sheet to David, the two of them so used to writing together that they could overwrite or overhaul each other's suggestions without risking bruised egos or anger. "Sarah's business is going really well—she's considering a small expansion since she's having to turn down potential clients at this point."

Abe felt a surge of warmth in his chest; it took a second for him to realize it was a lash of fierce pride. He hadn't been able to keep himself from reading about her when she'd been profiled in the business pages of the newspaper. So he knew Sarah had built that business on her own, had been her own first employee.

Soon after leaving him, she'd gotten a job as a cleaner who worked for a company that contracted people to work at various businesses. It messed with Abe's head to know his wife had taken a minimum-wage job rather than rely on the money at her disposal through the credit cards he'd had issued in her name—at least until something set her off on that crazy shopping spree to end all shopping sprees—but he was simultaneously proud of her for rebuilding her life on her own terms.

According to the article he'd read, one day the owner of a restaurant, impressed with her quiet work ethic and scrupulous honesty after she repeatedly turned in small change she'd found on the floor, had asked her if she'd also be able to clean his family home. He and his wife had been so pleased with her work and, more importantly, her discretion, that they'd recommended her to other friends.

"Everyone knows my wife and I went through a messy patch in our marriage," the restaurant owner had said in the piece. "Sarah had a front-row seat to some very private fights, but she never, not once, said a word to anyone. She even protected us from ourselves by making sure our trash was clear of anything the tabloids could dig through."

Sarah had soon identified a small niche market—wealthy and famous people who were understandably paranoid about privacy—and set up her own cleaning business after doing a night school course to learn business basics. Her firm promised total discretion and had quickly built up a reputation among the glitterati. No one minded paying more than they would for a regular service—Sarah's motto was if she paid her employees well, they had no reason to sell exclusives to the tabloids.

She'd also done something else extremely smart.

"We're tight-knit," she'd said in the interview. "I'm the majority owner, but each of my employees has a stake in the business, depending on seniority. We all rise or fail together."

The fact she'd held on to the company despite her relationship with that prick, Vance, and that the company had gone from strength-to-strength in a relatively short period of time, was a testament to Sarah's drive and will. A man like Vance would not want "his" woman to have any independent passions, things he couldn't control.

NALINI SINGH

"She's changed, hasn't she?" David looked up from where he sat in the armchair next to Fox's, his hand stilling on the music sheet.

"Yeah, Sarah never struck me as entrepreneurial." Noah's voice was thoughtful rather than judgmental. "But man, she was really young when you two first hooked up." A nod at Abe. "Twenty-one right? I guess she's just growing up and into herself."

Abe nodded, unable to speak past the sudden knot in his stomach.

He couldn't understand the reason for that knot until Molly dropped by an hour later. She was on her way home after running an errand in the city, but she'd picked up a box of fresh-baked muffins for them. "Wouldn't want my favorite men to starve," she said with that warm, wide smile that marked her as far too nice for Hollywood.

As Fox demanded a kiss, then asked her about a project she was working on for her one-woman research and editorial business, Abe realized Fox and Molly were growing together. Being each other's support and strength.

Sarah was alone. Had always been alone in many ways. Even when she'd been married to Abe.

The realization was a gut punch that crushed all the air out of him.

"How're the wedding preparations going?" David said to Molly.

Molly beamed. "I'm so glad you asked!" Running back into the hallway, she returned with a giant bakery box. Inside were at least ten tiny boxes. "Cake."

"I love cake," Abe put in, trying to get into the mood of things—he wasn't about to ruin Molly and Fox's excitement because he was sick to his stomach over his fuckups.

"Charlotte's going to make the cake," Molly told them after pressing another kiss to Fox's dimple, pure delight in her expression as she spoke of her best friend. "She arrived in the country two days ago without telling me, and today she gave me the surprise of my life by turning up at the house with two sets of handmade cake samples."

A pointed glance at Fox. "Funny how she had the code to open the gate when I hadn't yet given it to her since she was meant to arrive tomorrow."

Fox just whistled.

Laughing, Molly kissed him again, then pointed to the box. "This is the second set. I'm taste-testing the first set with the women tonight. I need you all to tell me your favorites since Fox is being no help at all. When I ask him what flavors he prefers, he shrugs and says, 'Cake is cake.'"

"Swap out cake with pancakes," Fox drawled, "and I'd be your man."

She put a little notepad on the coffee table on which she'd left the muffins and cakes. "I'm going to let you taste the samples in peace," she said. "But if you don't give me some real feedback, I'll stop bringing you muffins."

As a threat, it was effective.

After she left, they decided to get some coffee and try the cakes before working on another piece.

Fox made notes for Molly. "See?" the lead singer said. "I'm being helpful."

The four of them were proud at being able to narrow things down to a rich vanilla cake with chocolate-buttercream frosting; a cake that was labeled as "champagne," with a frosting they couldn't figure out but that tasted hella-good; and a passion fruit cake with cream cheese frosting.

Happy for his friend but still pissed off at himself, Abe was glad to get back to the music. It had always given him firm ground on which to stand. A little while later, after they paused so David could fix something that was out of alignment on his drum kit, Noah said, "Um, so…"

Schoolboy Choir's guitarist never sounded like that. He usually projected an image of not giving a shit about anything—the rest of the world might be happy to go along with that, but his close friends all knew it was a front, Noah a man you could count on to be there when you needed him.

"Are you going red, man?" a wide-eyed David asked as all three of them focused on Noah.

"Shut up," was Noah's pithy response, and yeah, there was a hint of red on his cheekbones.

Not a blush though, Abe thought with a frown. This color seemed to have more to do with a surge of emotion. Whatever he wanted to talk about, it was important to Noah. Staying quiet, Abe let Fox handle this—the other man knew all Noah's secrets, though David and Abe had witnessed his demons, could guess terrible things underlay them.

"Hey," Fox said, staying relaxed in his chair. "This is us. Blood brothers forever." A reminder of the promise they'd made on a boarding school playground after getting involved in a fight against a group of bullies that had left them bloody but victorious. "What's up?"

# CHAPTER 8

"I HAVE THIS THING," NOAH SAID at last.

Blowing out a breath, he shoved a hand through the golden blond of his hair. "A song. It's not Schoolboy Choir material."

"If it's yours," David said, "it's Schoolboy Choir material. We're not a threesome—" He groaned as the rest of them, even Noah, cracked up.

Fox was the one to say it. "Sorry, David, you're a nice guy, but ain't no ménage à trois happening here."

Rolling his brown eyes, David said, "You idiots know what I mean. Schoolboy Choir has four members. It is whatever we bring to it."

Abe nodded, his grin fading as Noah's expression turned nervously hopeful. Even with friends, the guitarist didn't often show emotion so openly. "Play it for us," Abe said. "If we don't like it, you know we'll tell you."

Others might not have understood why that made Noah's shoulders relax. Those people hadn't made music together for over ten years, from the time they first started the band way back in boarding school. They didn't understand what it was to put your soul out there and hope people didn't kick it. Having friends who had your back? It was everything.

*Sarah had always had his back.*

The thought was a hard one to bear—because Abe knew he hadn't had hers. Not the way she deserved. Not the way she needed. If he could go back in time, he'd pound himself bloody, but he couldn't. He had to live with the consequences of his actions, live with the fact that he was the one who'd made Sarah leave. It was all on him. No one else.

Music in the air, faint and quiet, a melancholy backdrop to the words Noah began to sing. The guitarist had a good voice, and this song, it needed that smooth, powerful voice, not Fox's gritty edginess.

The song he sang was about a sparrow with a broken wing, and it fucking tore Abe's heart right out of his chest, left it bleeding on the floor.

A stunned silence was Noah's applause after the final word faded from the air.

Then Abe and David blew out their breath almost at once while Fox just looked at Noah in a way that made it clear exactly how deeply the song had impacted the lead singer.

"Goddamn. That's powerful, man," Abe said, his voice thick with a bucket load of emotions. "It made me think of Tessie, like she's flying free same as that bird in the song."

Noah's dark gray eyes held Abe's, his throat moving as he said, "Yeah."

Nothing more needed to be said. Abe didn't talk about Tessie, not even to his closest friends, men who'd all known and played with his baby sister and who'd stood beside him at her funeral. Sarah had pushed open that door with the raw honesty of her own grief and now "Sparrow" had shoved it open wide.

A deep but gentle rhythm, David beating it out on the drums.

Nodding, Fox picked up the guitar he'd set aside and began to weave his music with David's.

Abe wasn't even aware of moving from his keyboards to Tessie's piano.

It just felt right to pull off the dustcovers, to take a seat on the piano stool and add the beauty of the keys to the music his blood brothers were creating. "Sparrow" wasn't a song for keyboards or fancy arrangements. It was pure and beautiful, and it needed the same accompaniment.

When Noah began to sing again, Abe knew they'd gotten it right.

And as he played, he knew Sarah's heart would break when she heard this song… but that she'd love it too. Because heartbreaking as it was, "Sparrow" also held a deep vein of hope of which Abe wasn't sure Noah was aware.

Abe wanted to grab on to that hope, use it to feed his hunger to fix the worst mistake of his life, but he knew the hope didn't belong to him. Sarah had told him to go. He had no right to challenge her decision, to fight to be allowed back in. He'd given up that right the day he'd lied to protect himself.

The day he'd told her he didn't love her.

PART
THREE

# CHAPTER 9

ALMOST EXACTLY THREE WEEKS AFTER the hot, sweet, passionate hour that had haunted her thoughts no matter how many times she told herself to forget it and move on, Sarah braced herself to see Abe again. There was no way to avoid it, not when, in approximately twenty hours' time, she'd be attending the wedding of Schoolboy Choir's lead singer.

She still couldn't believe she was about to spend the night at Molly and Fox's house prior to the other woman's wedding. After her and Abe's drawn out and bitter divorce battle, a battle fueled by pain and hurt and a love that refused to die, she'd never expected to be invited back into the band's world.

Then the men had sent her flowers after Aaron was stillborn.

And Sarah had realized for the first time that maybe Fox, Noah, and David *did* see her as a person, not just as the woman who'd been Abe's arm candy for a few years. The fact that Abe had sent her flowers too? Sarah still wasn't sure she'd truly processed that. Her ex-husband would've never done such a thing... but *her* Abe would have.

But this, tonight, it wasn't about her and Abe. It wasn't about the boys at all.

It was Molly who'd invited Sarah to a coffee date not long after Sarah left the sanctuary Molly and Fox had provided after Jeremy hit her. Sarah had offered to go to a hotel, or to Lola's empty apartment, but Molly wouldn't hear of it given Sarah's shocked and shaken state and her need for protection from the paparazzi. Sarah had expected it to be a one-off kindness, their paths never crossing again; with Molly engaged to one of Abe's closest friends, she'd figured the other woman's loyalties wouldn't permit her to be friends with Abe's ex.

Then Molly had reached out.

That first coffee meeting had been followed by others where Sarah got to know Kit and Thea better too. They—as well as Molly's best friend, Charlotte—had all had the best time at Molly's "Cake-Testing Fiesta" a couple of weeks earlier.

Of course, both Thea and Kit had been around while Sarah was married to Abe, but back then, jealous and feeling like a fraud, Sarah had rebuffed what, in hindsight, she could see had been attempts to foster a friendship. Thankfully, neither woman was holding the past against her. And tonight all of them would help celebrate Molly's impending wedding.

Smiling at the idea of the "girls' night in" that Molly had chosen in lieu of a bachelorette party, she checked she'd gathered everything she needed to take to Molly's. That didn't include a wedding gift—as per Fox and Molly's request, she'd made a donation to a small charitable foundation that helped children deal with the loss of one or both parents. Knowing what she did about Molly's past, Sarah understood the charity must speak deeply to her, but what the other woman couldn't know was how deeply it spoke to Sarah as well.

Perhaps if their friendship endured—and she so hoped it would, would work hard for it—she'd talk to Molly about it one day.

As it was, she'd made a far more substantial donation than could be expected of a wedding guest, and she intended to add them to the list of charities to which she donated regularly. All had to do with helping lost children. The safe arms of this charity would've been out of her reach even had they been around in her part of the country, but as long as it helped *one* child, it was worth it.

Shaking aside the memories of the ruins of her childhood, she took another look at the dress she intended to wear for the wedding. Knee length, with the fabric a deep shade of turquoise, it bared her arms but had a high neck. The interest came from the origami-style folding on the upper left, from her shoulder to the curve of her breast.

Elegant and pretty at the same time, the dress spoke to both parts of Sarah—the girl who loved sparkle and shine and prettiness, and the woman who knew the world treated you better if you appeared confident and wealthy, with no hint that you'd ever once worried about looking trashy.

On her head, she'd wear a fascinator that matched the dress except for some subtle accents in a vibrant citrine.

Sarah touched her fingers to the pretty confection of it before closing the hatbox in which it sat.

She adored it as much now as she had in the shop where Molly had taken her girlfriends so they could all get hats or other headgear for the wedding. Sarah would've never picked something like this on her own, would've thought it made her look foolish. It didn't. As Kit had said, it made her look like one of those upper-class English people who went to "posh" country weddings.

Grinning, she checked a box that held a pair of simple black spike heels and an equally unadorned clutch. The heels, they were a gift from Abe. Not the shoes themselves but Sarah's comfort in wearing them. Before Abe, she'd always worried about her height, aware she topped most men. Put her in heels and she topped the *vast* majority of men.

But with Abe...

*"You're perfect sized." A sudden grin, his hand cupping her face. "I get to kiss you as much as I like without getting a crick in my neck." He claimed her lips in a molten kiss to underscore his comment. "And in bed, we line up exactly right."*

Toes curling at the memory, Sarah realized her cheeks were flushed to the burning point. It didn't help when she had to walk into the kitchen to retrieve her keys; her eyes went immediately to *that* counter, the one on which Abe had taken her so hard and deep, where he'd made her come until her thighs quivered.

"*Breathe*, Sarah," she ordered herself even as her fingers trembled on the keys. She couldn't go back down that road. She'd admitted long ago that Abe had the ability to hurt her more than any other man on the planet.

*That* was what she had to remember, not how good he made her feel when he put his hands on her.

Because he'd be there tomorrow afternoon at Molly and Fox's "backyard wedding," as Molly was calling it. She and Fox were determined to slide under the paparazzi's noses and have a celebration unmarred by flyovers as the media fought to take photographs. As part of that, the guest list was strictly limited and everyone knew not to say a word to anyone who might purposefully—or accidentally—spill the beans.

All staff hired for the event had the same reputation as that which was the foundation of Sarah's business: flawless discretion about clients.

Getting into her car after loading everything she'd need tonight and tomorrow, Sarah turned the vehicle's air-conditioning to high, then drove out. Despite how friendly Molly had been, Sarah might have felt awkward about tonight, as if she were barging in, except that Molly had made it a special point to ask Sarah to come.

"We can hang out and talk," Molly had said with that huge smile of hers that made it impossible not to smile in return. "And as a bonus, we'll all be here for the morning pampering and makeup session."

"Are you sure?" Sarah had asked, undone by Molly's generosity. "I don't want to intrude."

"You're my friend, Sarah." The other woman had squeezed her hands, her brown eyes luminous. "We might just be starting out in that friendship, but I know it's one that'll last."

Keeping Molly's words in mind, Sarah drove through the gate after someone opened it for her without her having to push the buzzer, bringing her happy little red car to a halt in front of the house. Three other vehicles were already there: a black sports car, a midnight-blue BMW, and a large, dark gray SUV with rental plates. She'd just opened the back passenger-side door to start gathering up her things when the front door of the house was thrown open.

Molly ran out, dressed in a fabulous halter-neck swimsuit in black, a white sarong tied at her waist. "Sarah!" Her eyes sparkled, every inch of her bubbling with joy. "You're here!"

Laughing, Sarah met Molly's hug halfway. "So," she said, "you're just slightly happy to be getting married?"

"Hah!" The other woman pushed playfully at Sarah's shoulders. "I can't wait to be Molly Webster-Fox!" She looked about an inch away from floating off the ground. "I've decided I'm going to be that newlywed—you know, the one who gets monogrammed towels and shows off her wedding photos at every opportunity."

Infected with Molly's happiness, Sarah grinned and said, "Why not?" She pulled out the garment bag in which she'd zipped up her turquoise dress.

"Let me take that." Molly folded the bag carefully over her arm, then took the hatbox so Sarah could grab her overnight bag and the shoebox. "I'm so glad you could come. We are going to have way too much fun. There will be giggling and cocktails and dessert."

Sarah'd had girlfriends when she was growing up, but her home life hadn't allowed her to spend time over at their homes or ask them to visit hers. And after she'd run... Well, she'd never actually hung out with a bunch of women and giggled. It sounded oddly appealing.

Having grabbed everything, Sarah shut the car door, then followed Molly into the house. The curvy woman with creamy skin and soft, ink-black hair that curled wildly when not tied back, led her to a large downstairs room. "This is our dressing room," she said, hanging Sarah's dress on a clothing stand.

There were already three other dresses on there, as well as Molly's wedding gown.

Molly brushed her fingers over the antique lace on it before putting the hatbox on a table and indicating Sarah could place the shoebox beneath it. "Come on, I'll show you where you can leave your overnight bag."

That proved to be another downstairs room, this one set up as a guest room. "I thought you'd like the view into the garden," Molly said. "It'll be private even during the wedding since the garden's hedged off to be a secret nook."

"It's wonderful, Molly." Sarah put down her things. "Thank you."

The other woman beamed. "You want to change into your suit? We're going to hang by the pool."

Sarah felt a stab of that old lack of confidence, a sudden awareness of her height and size. "Can I spy on what the others are wearing first?" she asked in a whisper.

Molly winked. "Sure. Let's go up."

Having kicked off their shoes, they padded up the stairs toward the sound of other female voices. "We'll be doing makeup and hair upstairs tomorrow morning," Molly told her on the way. "It's sunnier and we'll have a view of the water."

An instant later they reached the sprawling open-plan kitchen/living area.

"Sarah!" Closest to the stairs, Kit came over and kissed Sarah on the cheek.

The actress wore a two-piece in checked red and white, the bottoms little shorts and the bikini top simple but supportive with two thin straps. It gave off a slightly old-fashioned vibe that Sarah liked. Given Kit's profession, her body was flawless, toned and without an ounce of fat.

"Hey there, my fellow CEO. You want a glass?" Thea held up a bottle of champagne, her golden skin glowing in the early-evening sunshine that flooded the area.

The leggy publicist, whom Sarah had always secretly admired for her innate sense of style, wore a sleek red one-piece over which she'd thrown a floaty garment that covered her arms and came to her thighs. The slick-straight strands of her hair were pinned carelessly in a knot at the back of her head, but somehow Thea still managed to look cool and sophisticated.

Thea had intimidated Sarah during her marriage to Abe. That was before she'd learned how ferociously the other woman protected those who were her own—and also how kind Thea could be. It was Thea who'd taken charge of ensuring Sarah's security was up-to-date and who'd brought over her things while Sarah was staying with Molly and Fox.

"I'd kill for a latte actually," Sarah admitted. "I know it's weird, but I've been jonesing for one all afternoon and wasn't able to get to my favorite coffee place."

Thea turned to Kit just as Thea's phone began to ring. "You're faster at the machine." She was on her phone seconds later, no doubt ensuring the media hadn't discovered Molly and Fox's wedding plans.

As Kit cheerfully used the gleaming coffee machine to make Sarah her latte, Sarah smiled at the last woman in the room aside from Molly—a petite blonde whose silky hair came to an inch or two below her shoulders. Seated at the break-fast counter, she was dressed in a cobalt-blue bikini top and a pair of short black board shorts. Her hazel eyes sparkled in welcome at Sarah behind the clear glass of her wire-rimmed spectacles.

"Hi, Charlie," Sarah said. "I meant to tell you—I think I put on five pounds after sampling all those cakes." It had been impossible to resist the deliciousness; Charlotte was one mean baker.

"That was probably her cunning plan all along." Molly jumped onto a breakfast stool beside her best friend. "To make us all burst the seams of our dresses while she remains tiny and adorable."

Charlotte elbowed Molly. "I would kill for your curves," she said before returning her gaze to Sarah. "And yours are seriously dangerous."

Confidence boosted by the friendly atmosphere and the fact all the other women were different sizes and shapes, Sarah smiled. "Thanks. Let me go get into my suit so we can head out to the pool."

It only took her a few minutes to change into the bronze two-piece that was her favorite. The top cupped her generous breasts firmly, then hugged her body to the waist. It also had small ties that caused pretty ruching along the curve of her waist on either side. The bottoms were simple and not too high cut.

Pulling on a floaty beach top similar to Thea's over the outfit, she walked back upstairs just in time to hear one of the women say, "…worried about fitting into the dress?"

Molly's laughter was open warmth. "My dress isn't form-fitting, but even if it was, I could still gorge on dessert to my heart's content." She glanced over at Sarah, filled her in. "They're teasing me about the dessert bar I had the caterers come in and set up by the pool."

Taking a sip of the divine latte Kit had made for her, Sarah smiled her thanks at the amber-eyed woman whose skin held a natural bronze glow thanks to her Venezuelan ancestry on her mother's side. "I guess we're all used to brides freaking out about their weight." Sarah certainly had prior to her own wedding—and all it had gotten her was the urge to binge-eat chocolate. "It's nice that you're not." Not that Molly needed to worry—she had a beautiful body, all soft curves and lush sexiness.

"I actually lost a few pounds without trying," Molly admitted. "When Fox and I went on that hiking trip."

"Yes." Charlotte grinned, her gaze wicked. "I'm sure it was the *hiking* that made you sweat, *Miss Molly.*"

Pretending to strangle her best friend, Molly blushed. Which only made everyone laugh and fueled further teasing until Molly ordered them all out to the pool.

# CHAPTER 10

FORTY MINUTES LATER, AFTER A swim in the clear blue waters of the infinity pool lit from below, Sarah took a seat on a lounger under the night sky that had eclipsed the last of the sunlight and tried one of the triple chocolate fudge brownies Charlotte had whipped up and added to the catered items. She groaned. "These are the devil's work."

Charlotte looked over from the neighboring lounger where she was sipping a cocktail. Her face dead serious, she said, "Thank you." Then she set aside her cocktail and used her fingers to make tiny horns on top of her head.

Sarah burst out laughing. And that set the tone for the rest of the evening. She'd never had a night like this, with women who were all close friends with each other... and who'd pulled her firmly into that circle.

Not once did she feel like an outsider.

The conversation flowed freely, as did the desserts and cocktails and food, though Sarah stuck to nonalcoholic drinks. Her stomach was a touch unsettled. Not enough to really bother her, but enough that she didn't want to aggravate it with alcohol.

"The men probably think we have a stripper here," Thea said at one point while she was treading water in the pool, the pool lighting making the water and her suit glow like jewels. "We could torment them by sending updates about our imaginary stripper," she suggested to a round of grins. "He could be wearing a fireman costume."

"Will he bring his own pole?" Charlotte asked with a sparkle in her eye.

Kit nodded. "An important consideration. What is a fireman without his pole?"

"That's like poetry," Thea said. "Where dost thou placeth thy pole?"

Slapping a hand over her mouth when a snort of laughter escaped her, Sarah met Molly's eyes. The other woman began to giggle too, and then it was all over.

In the end, they decided not to mess with the men's heads. Right now, the five males were having their own get-together at Thea and David's place.

"What about you, Sarah?" Charlotte asked innocently ten minutes later, the two of them alone on the loungers while the other women swam. "Are you seeing someone?"

Sarah felt her stomach drop in a steep dive. The correct answer was no, but her brain kept flashing back to how it had felt to be in Abe's arms again, to hear his deep voice in her ear, to see his smile. So right. It had felt so right. Not just the sex. Everything. Speaking to him about Aaron when she barely spoke on that painful subject even to Lola, listening to him speak about Tessie. All of it had felt right.

For the first time in forever, she hadn't felt as if she stood on shaky ground.

She was still fumbling for an answer when Charlotte reached over to touch her hand with her delicate one. "It's okay." Gentle words. "I know sometimes things are complicated."

Grateful for the quiet kindness, Sarah released a breath she hadn't been aware of holding. "How about you tell me about this T-Rex Molly mentioned."

Charlotte's cheeks filled with color, but her grin was wicked and sweet both. "That's what I secretly called Gabriel when we first met. He was my boss." Then, as Sarah listened, Charlotte told her about a relationship that had begun with a stapler thrown at the boss's head.

"He used to bring you cupcakes to say sorry?" Sarah sighed. "That is seriously romantic."

"First he'd drive me insane with his demands—Miss Baird, I need this. Miss Baird, why haven't I got this already?—and right when I was about to scream, he'd bring me cake." Charlotte's cheeks creased. "I adore him beyond life."

Sarah couldn't help but smile even as her own heart clenched; once, she'd worn her love for Abe as openly on her sleeve. "You two getting married as well?" She nodded at the stunning diamond on Charlotte's finger.

"In just under two months," Charlotte confirmed. "Molly and Fox are going to fly out to New Zealand for it. It's going to be a traditional church wedding." She found her phone, brought up a photo of four gorgeous and *built* men with their arms around each other's shoulders. "This is my Gabriel." She touched her finger to the image of the biggest man in the group, his shoulders and height reminding Sarah of Abe.

Both could've been linebackers.

Charlotte's Gabriel had black hair and steel-gray eyes, his skin sun-golden. One of the men in the photo looked very much like him except that his eyes were a startling blue. The other two were younger and had a warm brown skin tone, different features, but there was something about them… "Brothers?"

Charlotte nodded. "Sailor, Danny, and Jake." She scrolled through her photos to show Sarah several more not only of the four brothers but of a number of other good-looking men. Most were in sports uniforms that exposed strong thighs and biceps. Whoever else was in the shot, however, it also always featured either Charlotte's fiancé or one—or more—of his brothers.

"Gabriel used to play rugby professionally, and his two youngest brothers still do," Charlotte explained. "Sailor does it for fun." The petite blonde shook her head. "Most of Gabriel's former teammates are coming to the wedding, and at least half are currently single. I'm running out of single female friends to invite!"

Shoulders shaking, Sarah took a strawberry from the bowl Kit passed over before the other woman took a seat on the lounger next to Charlotte's. She bit into the juicy red flesh as Charlotte showed off her man and his brothers to Kit. As she'd already guessed, Charlie was head over heels for her "T-Rex," and if the look in Gabriel's eyes in those photos was any indication, he had a serious thing for the woman who'd taken the photographs.

Sarah swallowed and glanced away into the distance for an instant. She'd never had anyone look at her that way—as if she were his heart and his soul and his reason for waking up in the morning. Once, she'd hoped Abe would someday look at her with that depth of love.

That dream had died a hard death, but as the interlude in her kitchen showed, she was still dangerously susceptible to the man who'd been her husband. She'd have to be careful the romance of the wedding didn't seduce her into making a mistake that led her right back into his bed.

*Why?*

The question came from a sinful, hungry part of her that wasn't the least bit sorry she'd gotten down and dirty with Abe. Her face flushed even now at the memory; she was grateful the other women were too busy nibbling at dessert and chatting about the wedding to notice.

Not wanting to miss out, Sarah wrenched her attention back to the matter at hand and joined in. As for Abe and her response to him, she'd deal with that tomorrow.

THE NEXT MORNING—AFTER A WONDERFUL late night where they'd ended up talking for hours—Sarah showered, then put her pajamas back on and joined her friends in the kitchen. Kit had just come in from using another shower in the house and went straight to the coffee machine.

"Need caffeine," she said, her arms held out like a zombie's.

"You want me to do that?" Sarah asked Kit. "I think I've figured out the machine."

"No, let me." Kit yawned. "It'll wake me up a bit more. What does everyone want?"

Two minutes later, while Sarah was quietly and happily listening to Charlotte and Molly discuss the flower arrangements, Kit slid across Sarah's latte.

The aroma was heavenly. "Thanks, Kit." God, it was nice sitting here with women she liked, doing nothing in particular. She did miss Flossie though, but Sarah's pet enjoyed the rare times she got to go to a special "pet hotel" where she hung out with other dogs and had doggie sleepovers.

"What do you want for breakfast, Sarah?" Molly swung off the stool even as she spoke. "I can whip you up some—"

"Sit down!" Charlie's voice was unexpectedly fierce. "This is your wedding day. Act like a bridezilla."

Scrunching up her face, Molly stuck out her tongue at her best friend but retook her seat. "T-Rex is a bad influence on you, Miss Baird."

Sarah laughed at the darkly uttered words before getting up herself.

"Cereal's my usual—"

"No, no, I have something better." Charlie waved Sarah back down and, jumping off her own stool, went around the counter.

Lifting a cover, Molly's best friend said, "Ta-da!"

"Wow, those muffins look delicious." Sarah's stomach rumbled, though she wasn't usually a big breakfast eater. "Apple and walnut?"

"Pear and walnut." Placing one on a plate, Charlotte passed it over.

Sarah went to break it in half using her fingers, felt her eyes widen. "It's still warm!"

"I made them just before." Picking up another muffin, Charlotte put it in front of Kit, the actress having grabbed the stool next to Sarah. "Forget about being a superstar today," she ordered. "You'll still fit your clothes."

Kit drew in a deep breath, the scent of the fresh muffins filling the air. "I surrender." Putting down her coffee cup, she went to take a bite. "You're bossier than you look."

"T-Rex has a lot to answer for."

"Hush up, half of Foxy."

Laughter filled the air as Molly threw a crumpled up napkin at a grinning Charlotte. Once again, Sarah didn't feel the least bit out of place. Not with Molly, Charlotte, and Kit also in their pajamas and Kit stealing a sip of Sarah's latte while the actress waited for her second cup of the morning to brew. Then Thea joined them after her shower and began taking photos with her phone, promising solemnly that the images would never go online anywhere.

"This is for us," the publicist said as she made Molly and Charlotte pose together in their pj's. Both women were wearing boxers-and-camisole combos, their smiles so huge they outshone the sun. "Though"—she tapped a finger on her lower lip, eyes narrowed—"this will also make excellent blackmail material—except shit, Kit, you look far too good even without makeup and Sarah, you're glowing."

"Hey, what about us?" Molly and Charlie said in insulted concern.

A second later and everyone was talking over everyone else, and it was chaotic and fun. When the makeup artist and hairdresser arrived, they all watched Molly get done up—at least until the makeup artist banished them outside for making Molly collapse into giggles.

Sarah's turn came after Kit. She'd brought her own makeup just in case, but the artist had come fully prepared. "Molly told me the skin tones of everyone who was going to be here this morning. Wish all my clients were as organized." The small and no-nonsense Hispanic woman began to open a different set of compacts. "We can still use your stuff if you'd feel more comfortable that way, but I have a product I think you'll love."

"Let's go for it," Sarah said with a grin, the joy around her having infected her own spirit.

The makeup artist did a stellar job.

Then it was time to have her hair straightened as she'd requested, the hairdresser combing the long strands into a sleek updo.

FOUR HOURS—AND A CAREFULLY EATEN lunch—later, all five of them were ready to head downstairs to dress. After tidying up, the makeup artist and hairdresser left—but not before the makeup artist gave each of them a personalized touchup kit. If Sarah ever ended up invited to a big public event again, she knew exactly who she was going to call to do her face.

She caught Kit's eye once they were in the dressing room. The actress nodded before shooting Thea and Charlotte a meaningful glance. Thea gave a small thumbs-up behind Molly's back while Charlotte winked, then turned to her best friend.

"You need to get into your dress."

Molly shivered. "I love it so much." The other woman did a little dance and went to where the vintage gown was hanging. A creation of delicate lace with cap sleeves and a V-neck, it would—paired with her sultry eyes and deep red lipstick—turn Molly into the embodiment of old Hollywood glamour.

"Did you get the right underwear?" Kit asked, taking a seat in the beautiful armchair in the corner, the seat cushion a dark blue velvet.

"Yes, I found this really pretty set." Molly showed them the white lace bra. "The panties match."

Charlotte shook her head. "No, that's not going to work."

Molly's face fell. "No? But it's so elegant, and it doesn't show through the dress."

"You can keep it for another day." Thea spoke from her spot leaning in the doorway, her long hair having been fashioned into a romantic knot at her nape. "Today I think you should be demure on the outside and a vixen underneath—give Fox a sexy surprise."

Molly blushed. "I can go through my lingerie—"

"Or…" Charlotte picked up a small box sitting under the garment rail, hidden from view behind the dresses. "You could wear this."

"And this." Thea added her box to the pile, followed by Sarah and Kit, all of them having snuck in the extra boxes in their overnight bags.

"You guys!" Molly's eyes shimmered wetly.

"Don't ruin your makeup," Thea ordered her half sister, but her voice was affectionate, a softness to her features that Sarah had never before seen.

"It's waterproof," Molly protested thickly.

Hugging the other woman, Charlotte said, "Open the boxes."

Molly went from near tears to a hot-pink blush at first sight of the lace lingerie in rich cream: a *tiny* G-string, a lace bustier with fine boning, delicate silk stockings, a garter belt that would frame her body just right, and last but not least, exquisite lace gloves that set off Molly's gown and would only add to her lushly sensual look when she took off the dress.

Bright red at this point, Molly pointed a finger at them. "I am not putting this on with you as an audience!" But her lips curved and her eyes sparkled. "But thank you so much. I love it."

"Everyone out," Thea ordered. "Only Fox gets to see this masterpiece."

Shouting out fake boos, the four of them stepped outside and teased Molly through the door while she dressed. When she opened it, she'd put on her lovely gown of creamy lace but needed one of them to button it up in the back. Charlotte took up the task of slotting in the tiny fabric-covered buttons, her eyes luminous and totally unshielded—not simply because she was wearing contacts instead of her spectacles, but because her love for Molly was a visible light within her.

*We chose to be sisters,* she'd said to Sarah last night.

As Sarah watched, Charlotte hugged her best friend from behind, careful to keep her face turned so her makeup wouldn't get on the dress. "You look so beautiful, Molly."

"I'm just… happy. Really happy, all the way to my toes." Molly looked around as she squeezed Charlotte's hands. "Having you all here…" Her breath hitched.

"Hey, don't you get me going." Thea's voice rasped with emotion, the hug she shared with Molly a tight squeeze. No one who didn't know them would've guessed at their familial relationship; they were two such physically different women. But Thea and Molly, too, had chosen to be sisters after finding each other as adults.

It wasn't the last hug of the afternoon. One by one, Kit and Sarah wrapped their arms around the woman who'd brought them all together.

"Okay," Molly said afterward, the lace of her dress exquisite against her skin and her face aglow. "It's time for you to put on your dresses."

# CHAPTER 11

SARAH, THEA, CHARLIE, AND KIT dressed in a chaos of laughter and conversation.

Sarah's turquoise-colored dress fit as perfectly as she remembered. Kit, meanwhile, had chosen a dress of deep amber, while Thea was in rich violet. All three of their dresses came to just above the knee. Charlotte, however, was in a flowing, ankle-length dress of bright raspberry, as befit her position as Molly's maid of honor. The rest of them would walk out ahead of her as part of Molly's bridal party—it was Molly who'd asked them to choose jewel tones for their dresses.

"We look like a group of flowers," Sarah said when she glimpsed the entire group in the large standing mirrors placed against one wall.

Molly clasped her hands together, her smile huge. "It's exactly how I imagined."

Thea's camera clicked, capturing another image for Molly's wedding album.

"I don't want a stranger capturing these moments," Molly had said the previous night when it came out that Thea would be taking the majority of the photographs, backed up by one of

David's brothers who was an excellent amateur photographer. "I want it to be about friends and family and joy."

Thea had brought along a tripod, making it easy to set up the camera and use the timer to take group shots. Once everyone was dressed and they had arranged things for the next part of their outfits, she set it up to take a series of shots, then joined the rest of them.

The five of them stood side by side in front of the mirrors, Molly in the middle.

"Everyone ready?" Molly asked.

Nodding, they reached as one down to the hatboxes placed beside them, picked up their fascinators, and rose to their full height. Each headpiece was different, and each one suited the woman who'd chosen it. Sarah had never worn anything like this in her life, but she loved the pretty, frothy thing.

"That's so lovely," she said to Charlotte after spying her jaunty little choice with its curling feather of peacock blue. "Here, let me put in the bobby pin you need at the back."

"Thanks." Charlotte stood still as Sarah got the bobby pin in place without messing up Charlotte's updo. "I love yours. That black netting over your eye—you look like a femme fatale."

"She's right," Kit said, angling her fascinator a little more to the right. Her piece had a dramatic, curved shape that curled over the side of her head, the color a vivid blood orange that somehow went perfectly with the amber of her dress.

As striking was Thea's of deep pink, but the most beautiful was the bride's, as was only right. It was as if three-quarters of the front of Molly's hair was covered by tiny blooms. Anchoring the piece in her hair were feathers of purest cream, while the cream netting that came over her eyes was of a finer weave than Sarah's and went to her lips, a veil Fox would lift up during the ceremony.

"Something old," Molly whispered, touching her fingers to her dress. "Something to build a history on."

Thea placed her hand on one of the boxes that had held the lingerie. "Something new, to take into your new life."

"Something borrowed." Charlotte fixed a necklace around Molly's neck; it came to the top of her breastbone in twin strands of white gold, then became a knotted waterfall that ended just above the V-neck of her dress. "Mom would've been so happy you were wearing her wedding necklace on your own wedding day. And I'll love wearing it on mine, knowing you both wore it before me."

Wetness shone in both women's eyes.

"Something blue," Kit said, passing over a bouquet of riotous color that included several glorious shades of blue.

"And," Sarah added, "a silver sixpence in your shoe."

"What?" That question came from four female voices at once.

Sarah laughed. "It's the complete rhyme. I looked it up once." When she'd been about to be a bride herself. But today wasn't about her. It was about the generous woman who'd reached out to her in friendship. "I couldn't find a sixpence," she said, "but since it's meant to represent good luck and prosperity, I got you this little horseshoe charm I thought you could tuck in somewhere."

"Oh, I love it." Molly took the tiny charm and, with a sinful smile, tucked it inside the top of her corset, to all their approving laughter.

And then the other woman was ready, a bride who couldn't wait to meet her groom.

ABE SMOOTHED HIS HANDS DOWN the front of his charcoal-gray suit jacket.

Fox had chosen the same suit for himself and his grooms-men, all of them wearing white shirts with darker gray ties under their jackets. The only difference with Fox's suit was the flower thing in his pocket, which matched the bouquet Molly would be carrying. It had some fancy name that Abe couldn't remember at the moment.

"We're looking damn good," he pronounced after turning from the mirror.

The other men, including Gabriel Bishop, agreed with loud "Hell, yeahs."

The ex-professional rugby player and current hard-nosed CEO had fit seamlessly into their group in the time he and Charlotte had been in the city. Abe liked the other man a heck of a lot, even after Gabriel taught them how to play rugby and showed that, retired from the sports field or not, he could still kick their asses.

Gabe hadn't expected to be a groomsman, but with Molly's bridal party including four women, it would've left one woman without an escort had Fox only had his bandmates as grooms-men. However, what had started out as an offer made and accepted because of Molly and Charlotte's lifelong friendship had grown into a real friendship between all five of them.

This afternoon, they were all at David and Thea's home. Fox had been banished from his place the previous night,

Molly adamant he not see her before she walked down the aisle toward him. So, of course the five of them had to party—but they'd done it here rather than going out to a club or bar. Abe knew it was partly because of him; his friends didn't want to put him in a situation that might push him off the wagon and back into the hellhole of drugs and alcohol.

The fact that Fox was effectively skipping his bachelor party because of Abe would've made Abe feel like shit if his friend hadn't made it a point to talk to him beforehand.

"We've all partied before," the lead singer had said. "And we'll all party again, but I don't want to do some public deal the night before my wedding. I want to hang with my friends, play a little music, and stay close to Molly in case she forgets about her 'no seeing me before the wedding' rule and calls to arrange a hookup."

Abe chuckled at the memory as he snapped a photo using his phone. Fox was doing up the final button on his suit jacket while David had just flipped up his shirt collar to slide on his tie—he and Gabriel were the only ones who could knot the things flawlessly, so they'd been press-ganged into helping everyone else.

Noah stood not far from David. He was looking into a mirror while combing his hair, his scowl a thundercloud. "Now you know how much I love you, man," the guitarist muttered to Fox. "I only ever put on a suit and use a comb when it's a big premier or gala deal for Kit."

"I hear the suit works well for you," Gabriel said from where he was perched on the edge of a table, long legs lazily stretched out and crossed at the ankles.

Noah gave the other man the finger. It made Gabriel's shoulders shake. Yeah, the other man had fit right in, even to the point of ragging Noah about how designers had begged him—were still begging him—to do campaigns after he wore a tux to a black-tie charity gala he'd attended with Kit.

Bumping fists with Gabriel, Abe said, "What do you think the women got up to last night?" He couldn't stop thinking about the fact he'd be seeing Sarah again, and soon. Fuck, he couldn't wait. He'd missed her.

*No more lies of omission, remember, Abe?*

His jaw tightened. Because the truth was that he'd missed Sarah since the day she walked out. However, that dull ache had become a raw need after the hours he'd spent with her three weeks earlier, the Band-Aid firmly ripped off the wound he'd told himself was healed over, forever scarred.

"You think they got a stripper?"

Gabriel's growl of a question had them all freezing before Fox grinned and shook his head. "Nah. Molly wanted to do a girly thing. No men invited."

Five pairs of lungs expanded.

Then David chuckled. "We are so nuts for our women," he said, clearly at peace with his adoration of Thea.

And why not? Thea adored him right back, as Molly did Fox, Charlotte did Gabriel, and Kit did Noah. The latter two were still figuring out some stuff, but one thing was certain: they were a unit. *#NoKat* was not only a full-blown media phenomenon that showed no signs of fading, it was very real.

In this room, only Abe didn't have any claim on or right to the woman he'd be escorting at the wedding. His stomach clenched, but he refused to believe he'd lost her forever. As long as Sarah still wanted him, he had a shot. If he could get her in bed, addict her to him, he'd have the time he needed to prove to her that he was no longer the man who'd hurt her so badly.

There were no drugs in his system, no alcohol. Only healthy food and a boatload of determination. He'd also stopped picking up women. The guys didn't know, but until the explosive encounter in Sarah's kitchen, he hadn't been with a woman for months. Specifically since that night during their last tour when he'd shoved so much alcohol into his body that he'd almost ended up in a coma.

After sobering up—and quietly getting help to *stay* sober—he'd consciously confronted an ugly truth: that he found no pleasure in the meaningless hookups that had filled his nights since his and Sarah's divorce. The sex had simply been another way to drown out the things he didn't want to think about, the things that haunted him: Tessie's death and Sarah's absence from his life.

Hell, he was such a world-class bullshitter when it came to the most painful events in his life that he'd even managed to convince himself that he didn't love Sarah, had never loved her; he'd carried that belief like a talisman against the pain of losing the right to call her his wife... until the moment he laid eyes on her at Zenith.

The second he'd heard her voice, met those dark eyes that had once looked at him with unhidden love, he'd been slapped in the face with harsh reality: that he'd tried to bury what he felt for her, bury who she was to him, because he couldn't deal with the unforgiving fact that he and he alone was responsible for the destruction of his marriage.

Because Abe had only ever loved one woman: Sarah.

He'd fought it, lied to himself, told his friends he was over her, but his love for Sarah was woven into every part of his fucking heart.

"Hey." David nudged his shoulder, his eyes incisive. "You good?"

David and Abe had been best friends since they were thirteen. The other man had always had Abe's back—even when Abe was an asshole. He'd earned the right to ask Abe that question, as had Noah and Fox. "Yeah, I'm good."

"You sure?" David kept his voice low, their conversation sliding under the other men's discussion about a controversial call in a recent basketball game.

Abe ran a hand over his shaved-smooth head. "Sarah," he admitted. "She'll be there."

No surprise in David's expression. "I figured. You're still hung up on her."

Abe didn't bother to deny it.

"Look, Abe, I know all about being hung up on a woman." A deep grin. "But you and Sarah... Something toxic happened when you were together."

"No." Abe sliced out a hand. "I've forced myself to be brutally honest this time around—only way my sobriety is going to stick." His sponsor was a hard-nosed vet who'd understood that just in time to save his own marriage *and* who'd held on to his sobriety for twenty-five years and counting. "It was me, David."

No excuses, no bullshit.

"I was fucked up and I took that out on everyone, Sarah most of all." His friends thought they knew what he'd been like during his worst days, but they had no idea how many times he'd hurt his tough, sweet wife with his words and his lack of care, until even her generous heart couldn't love him. "All Sarah did was try to love me."

David nodded, his golden-brown eyes dark with the awareness that no one outside a marriage or relationship ever truly knew what went on inside it. "Whatever happens," he said, "I know you're going to stay sober this time around." No hesitation in his tone, nothing but absolute confidence. "You're different."

"Yeah, I am." It was as if a switch had been thrown in his brain. He finally got it: *he* was in charge of whether or not he lived a life that made him happy. And he understood that any self-destructive choices he made had a profound impact on others: David and his other bandmates, his dad when Gregory Bellamy had been alive, his mom... Sarah.

"Isn't it time to head over?" David's voice drew him back to the here and now. He glanced over to see that Noah had picked up an acoustic guitar.

"No, we still have a half hour." Noah strummed aimlessly, still managing to create music. "Small session to settle Fox's nerves."

"Fuck you." Fox's grin made it clear he wasn't nervous but impatient. "But why not? It'll be the last time I sing as a single man."

The other man belted out three of their hits over the next twenty minutes, with Noah on guitar, David tapping out a rhythm using a pair of sticks he'd left nearby, and Abe on the keyboard he kept at David's place for the times they jammed here.

Gabriel took over photographing duties for the duration, though when Fox called for him to join in on the chorus, he proved to have a voice that wasn't totally untrained. "Church choir," he admitted with a wince between songs. "My mum made all four of us join. At least until we turned thirteen."

Abe, Fox, Noah, and David grinned before launching into another song—because the event that had sealed the friendship between the four of them had involved a choir tryout.

As the session wound down, Fox looked even more pumped if that was possible. "I'm going to get married!" he yelled in his gritty voice.

They all roared their approval before setting down their instruments to check one another's clothes. Then, once ties had been straightened and cuffs nicely aligned, Fox's boutonniere—*that's* what it was called—neatly in place, they walked out to get into two separate cars.

Fox roared off first in his red Lamborghini, with Noah in the passenger seat. Abe followed in his grunty black SUV, David in back and Gabriel in the passenger seat. David would ride home with Thea after the wedding, Noah with Kit, while Gabriel's rental was already parked at Molly and Fox's.

"You staying at a hotel tonight?" Abe asked, aware the visiting couple had been staying with the lead singer and Molly since the day Charlotte pulled off her plan to surprise Molly.

Gabriel stretched out his legs in the passenger seat, at home in the big SUV that was the same size as his rental vehicle. Given that the ex-rugby player was Abe's size, a smaller car would've simply never worked.

"No," the other man said. "We're spending the night at the house."

Abe blinked while David was more vocal in his surprise. "I don't think Fox is into foursomes."

Chuckling, Gabriel looked over his shoulder at the drummer. "Molly doesn't know, but Charlotte and I arranged for the newlyweds to spend a few days at a romantic mountain cabin. I checked with Fox before we did it—he's all for kidnapping his Miss Molly right after the reception."

Abe's brain took note: there was a certain woman he'd love to kidnap for a sensual getaway.

"I've got romantic plans of my own," Gabriel added with a scowl, "so don't hang around too long post-wedding."

David snorted. "This is a rock wedding, Bishop. The party *might* end at dawn."

Abe's hands tightened on the steering wheel; he couldn't wait to party the night away with Sarah. No way in hell was he letting some other man try to pick her up. Abe would be the only one doing any seducing, putting in motion his plan to win back his wife.

He wasn't going to fuck up. Not this time.

# CHAPTER 12

SARAH STOOD WITH CHARLOTTE, KIT, and Thea behind Molly, bubbles of happiness popping effervescently in her bloodstream.

Facing Molly stood a handsome older man with light brown skin and salt-and-pepper hair: Vicente Rivera. David's father.

From what Abe had told Sarah that day in her kitchen, Molly's own father had been a useless excuse for a man before his death, but she'd become very close to the Riveras in the time she'd been with Fox. No surprise when her sister, Thea, was marrying their oldest son. The publicist, too, adored her future in-laws.

From the way Vicente pressed his lips to Molly's forehead, his big hands on her upper arms, the affection was deeply mutual. His golden-brown eyes glowed as he drew back. "With three strapping boys, I never thought I'd get to walk a daughter down the aisle." Wetness in those eyes, which he'd bequeathed to all his sons. "And what a beautiful daughter."

Molly threw her arms around him, squeezing him tight as his own arms came around her, the black fabric of his suit jacket dark against the lace of Molly's gown. "Thank you," she whispered, emotion thick in her voice.

"It is my honor." Vicente kissed her forehead again, then lowered her netting veil and held out his arm.

Taking a shaky breath, Molly curved her fingers gently around his forearm. Vicente put his other hand over hers, squeezed.

The wedding march began to play, picked out on the piano by David's youngest brother.

Molly turned to glance back at Charlotte and the bridal party, Vicente a solid presence by her side. No words needed to be spoken, her joy written in her smile. Charlotte came forward, touched her hand to Molly's, then walked out the sliding doors on the lower floor of the house. Thea followed, then Kit and Sarah, all of them preceding the bride down the rose-petal-strewn pathway bordered by potted plants bursting with blooms.

They all got smiles, but an audible "oooh" filled the air at the guests' first sight of Molly. Heart thumping for her friend, Sarah, too, was focused only on Molly as she, Charlotte, Thea, and Kit stepped aside to wait for her at the altar. Vicente walked with open pride by Molly's side, the bride glowing with so much happiness that she was radiant.

Sighing a little at the beauty of the occasion, Sarah watched misty-eyed as Vicente and Molly reached the top of the aisle. David's father left Molly with a kiss on the temple and a quiet word to Fox that had the lead singer giving a firm nod. Then the older man took a seat beside his wife—who was dabbing at her eyes with a handkerchief. Sarah's own steadfastly—foolishly—romantic heart was making her eyes burn. She'd just swallowed back the tears that wanted to escape when she really looked at the groomsmen.

All four were dressed in classic charcoal-gray.

Sarah knew she should be looking only at the bride and groom, but she couldn't keep her eyes off Abe. The last time she'd seen her ex-husband this dressed up had been on their wedding day. He looked even better now, the bluntly handsome lines of his face holding a new purpose and strength, and his body…

A heat wave crawled over her own flesh as, all gorgeous strength and intense eyes, Abe caught her gaze, held it. It was the wedding officiant's voice that snapped Sarah into the moment. And though her heart skittered inside her chest, she turned her attention firmly back to the two people whose love they were here to celebrate.

It was a beautiful, sunlit wedding.

The vows the couple spoke to each other made a lump form in Sarah's throat; they were so honest and passionate and loving. Molly smiled with her whole body throughout. And Fox's eyes saw only Molly as she stood in front of him with her gown whispering lightly in the breeze. The lead singer looked astonished, awed, delighted—as if he couldn't believe Molly was his.

But when he kissed her after the white-haired officiant pronounced them man and wife, there was no tentativeness. He claimed Molly's mouth with such heat and possessiveness that people whooped and Noah put two fingers into his mouth and let out a wolf whistle.

Ending the kiss with a grin on his face, a blushing Molly laughing beside him, Fox lifted their linked hands into the air. "We are fucking married, people!"

A cheer reverberated through the crowd.

Color and scent filled the air as Molly and Fox walked back down the aisle, the guests showering them in the flower petals that had been left in small baskets placed below each seat.

Then it was time for Sarah to step up and walk out behind Kit and Noah.

The guests would wait for the wedding party to leave, then head to the big pavilion that had been set up at the last minute to ensure it attracted no unwanted attention. Up ahead, Charlotte had been joined by a gray-eyed man who was as big and as muscled as Abe. *Gabriel.* He was glancing down at Charlotte with a possessive smile; the other woman looked tiny next to his linebacker physique—and yet somehow they fit. There was simply a resonance there, a deep vein of trust.

As there was between Molly and Fox, Thea and David, Kit and Noah.

Abe offered her his arm.

Pulse beating like a rabbit's, Sarah slid her arm through his and they walked behind the other couples. She tried not to inhale his scent, tried not to feel his muscles flexing under her touch, but it was impossible. The fresh, warm, and deeply masculine scent that was Abe's seeped into her every cell, his body brushing hers with every step they took.

It would've been logical for her mind to fill with images of their own wedding day, but her brain was more interested in replaying their far more recent encounter.

The kitchen counter under her.

Abe pushing apart her thighs.

Hot, tangled breaths, his body driving into hers, his fingers digging into the soft curves of her ass. Her scream as she came. His cock pulsing inside her.

*Oh, thank God.*

They were inside the house. Her knees quivered as she broke contact with Abe. The rest of the wedding party was already heading upstairs.

The whole time she was climbing up, she could feel Abe's eyes on her ass.

She told herself it was her imagination, but her tingling skin and flushed face didn't think so; then she reached the top of the stairs and turned... and caught him in the act. "Stop it," she hissed under her breath.

His response was a grin, his eyes traveling slowly up her body—and lingering on every curve along the way. Her thighs clenched, her body damp in that dark, secret place only Abe knew exactly how to touch.

"I'm a red-blooded man, Sarah," he said when he finally reached her eyes, "and, sweetheart, you have one hell of an ass."

She was both flattered and aggravated by him. Especially when he looked so damn good grinning up at her. And damn it, yes, it felt good to be told she had "one hell of an ass" by this man who had always pushed her buttons.

Glaring at him when his grin deepened—as if he could read her thoughts—Sarah stalked off to join the others.

Charlotte was laughingly picking flower petals out of Molly's hair. As Sarah watched, Fox shook his head, showering the floor with splashes of silky pink, cream, and deep yellow. Regardless of his action, his arm remained around Molly. The lead singer's smile was huge, the kisses Molly kept dropping on his cheek adorable; it was clear she was aiming for the lean dimple in his left cheek.

"Congratulations, man," Abe said, walking over to haul the lead singer into a hug that lifted him off his feet.

Grinning, Fox slapped Abe on the back before they broke apart to do that complicated handshake thing Sarah had never been able to master even after Abe tried to teach her one lazy Saturday morning, both of them laughing when she gave up and made up a random handshake of her own.

Pushing aside the melancholy that threatened to envelop her at the reminder of how young she'd been, how hopeful, Sarah bent to kiss Molly on the cheek, then gave her a heartfelt hug. "Congratulations. I am so happy for you."

"Thank you!" Molly's dark eyes were full of light.

Delighted for her, Sarah stepped back so Kit, too, could hug the bride. She ended up bumping straight into the hard wall of muscle that was her ex-husband. Who hooked an arm around her waist before she could move away. "You look edible," he murmured, his breath brushing her sensitive earlobe.

Which Abe knew all about.

Sarah's heart rate had never quite slowed down. Now it kicked again, the heat of his touch sinking through the fabric of her dress to soak into her skin. Turning on a wave of need, she said, "I like you in formal wear." She couldn't help herself; she reached over to fix his tie. It hadn't been out of place—she just wanted an excuse to touch him even knowing it was a bad, bad idea.

Allowing her hand to lie on his chest for a second, she drew in a breath… and glimpsed Noah watching them, interest alive in the gray of the guitarist's eyes. She flushed, dropped her hand, and turned to face the bride and groom once more.

"Let go of my waist," she muttered to Abe at the same time.

"Make me," said the man holding her prisoner.

Sarah knew she could move away, but she didn't want to draw attention to the two of them. And her traitorous body didn't want to break contact—having Abe messing with her was more fun than it should be.

Deciding to fight fire with fire, she shifted slightly, just enough to angle a look at him from under her lashes. It was a *very* specific look, one that had never failed to have a certain effect on Abe.

"Fuck." It was a hard, barely audible sound.

Despite that staccato word, he didn't release her. Instead, he stroked his hand down to her hip and began to move his thumb back and forth, back and forth over a particular spot. Their position at the end of the semicircle of friends meant no one could see what he was doing.

"*Abe.*" Her voice came out strangled.

Leaning close as if to ensure he heard what she was saying, Abe said, "You started it." His breath was hot, his chest hard where it touched her shoulder.

He moved his thumb again. "And it *is* a wedding," he murmured. "Aren't bridesmaids supposed to hook up with the groomsmen?"

"I'm not a bridesmaid," Sarah managed to get out, her self-control not totally in tatters.

"Close enough."

"A toast to Foxy!" Noah held up a glass of champagne.

Threatening to punch the guitarist, Fox grinned nonetheless and dipped his head to kiss Molly, soft and sweet and with so much love that Sarah's vision blurred.

"Hey." Abe's stroking turned into a comforting rub. "No crying."

115

"It's a wedding," she sniffed, using a finger to wipe away the tears that had escaped. The other women were doing the same.

Feeling a deluge coming, she was about to dig in her clutch for a tissue when Abe handed her a pristine white handkerchief. "It was part of the getup," he said, pointing at the pocket of his suit.

"Thanks." Sarah dabbed at her eyes.

The Riveras arrived then, David's two brothers included; more hugs and kisses were exchanged. Alicia and Vicente beamed as proudly as if it was their own child's wedding.

Vicente's hug of Fox was powerful, paternal. His words, however, were a growl. "You take care of my girl, Fox, or like a son or not, I'll be over here with a baseball bat."

"You'll never need to do that, sir," Fox promised.

The naked emotion in the lead singer's eyes when he looked at his bride had Sarah's eyes filling with tears once again.

"You always did cry at all the romantic parts in those movies you used to make me watch." Abe's rumbling voice against her ear, his body warm and supportive behind her... and the memories making her ache.

She loved romantic dramas and at the start of their marriage, Abe had watched with her, Sarah's body curled into his on the couch. She'd stopped asking him around the time she'd realized he was never going to take her on tour with him. Instead, she'd watched those movies alone in the big house in which she felt like a left-behind toy. And the tears she'd shed hadn't been because of the movies.

But back at the start, when she'd still been hopeful of winning a small piece of his heart... Abe had held her, teased her, made her believe she, too, could have her own happy ending.

That such endings weren't just for beautiful people with perfect lives, but for the broken and scarred too.

Today, as she leaned against Abe's strength, Sarah allowed herself to give in to the fantasy that they'd made it, that it hadn't all gone so awfully wrong. What harm could it do? The instant the reception was over, they'd head their separate ways.

# Chapter 13

A BE'S HAND WAS WARM AND possessive on her lower back when they followed the rest of the wedding party back downstairs and to the pavilion. Molly and Fox would enter last; the rest of them all wanted to be there to cheer on the newlyweds—and Sarah was dead certain Fox wanted Molly to himself for a couple of minutes so he could kiss her boneless.

She gasped at her first glimpse inside the pavilion: waterfalls of fine white fabric pinned to the walls like curtains in a luxurious outdoor tent, the floor lined with a luscious carpet of silver and cherry red, flowers everywhere. Meanwhile, the tables were set with white tablecloths, the centerpieces little tea candles floating in glass bowls surrounded by bunches of white flowers.

It was pretty and fresh and romantic, and Sarah adored it. "I can see Molly in all the tiny touches," she said to Abe as she took her seat at the head table, Abe holding out her chair. "No hard edges, just joy."

Abe undid the button on his suit jacket before sitting down beside her. "Like you," he said, his expression unexpectedly tender. "You've never had any hard edges."

Flustered, the fantasy suddenly too much, she glanced away and to her left.

David was just taking his seat beside her, Thea on his other side, his mother beside Thea. Then came the two empty seats for Molly and Fox, with Vicente, Kit and Noah, Charlotte and Gabriel on the other side.

"Hey. Stop ignoring your official wedding escort." Abe put his hand on her knee.

Sarah couldn't take his teasing anymore; she kicked him under the table.

He nudged his hand an inch higher in punishment. And Sarah saw red. Hoping nothing showed on her face, she used the fact that David was distracted by something Thea was saying to reach across and run her hand over Abe's cock.

Once, just once.

It was enough.

"Fuck." He ducked his head to hide the curse word... then finally removed his hand from her knee.

And she missed the warmth, the contact. *Him.*

"That was mean." He spoke against her ear. To anyone watching, it would appear as if he was just leaning in so they could speak without disturbing their neighbors.

"You started it," she said, turning his earlier words back on him while trying to convince herself she'd made the right call.

He stretched one arm out along the back of her seat. "You're having fun, admit it."

"No."

He tickled the back of her neck, well aware it was—weirdly— the most ticklish spot on her body.

119

"*Abe.*" Her voice came out strangled, and then she was laughing as she tried to tug away his hand without making a big deal of it.

Abe grinned, so gorgeous and sexy that she just wanted to kiss him.

"What's so funny?" David's question came right as Abe stopped teasing her in favor of simply bracing his arm on the back of her seat, his muscled strength brushing her back.

"Just checking if Sarah's still ticklish."

Sarah kicked him again as David's lips curved into a deep smile. "I'm going to kill you," she muttered to Abe.

His eyes glinted wicked promises at her.

Her breath caught, her face flushed. It was just as well that Charlotte said, "Time," from the other side of the table right then.

The wedding party stood as one. There was no need to make an announcement. The guests followed their lead, all eyes going to the entrance of the pavilion… just as the air filled with the gritty sound of the hard rock love song Fox had written for Molly. The lead singer and his bride didn't walk in. They danced in, Molly in Fox's arms as he spun her around, then caught her back against his chest before they laughingly danced the rest of the way in with their hands linked.

"Rock it!" Abe pumped his fist in the air as the other band members and guests hollered and clapped.

Sarah's palms stung, she was clapping so hard; her smile threatened to crack her face. This wedding was unlike any other she'd ever attended, and she loved it. When Fox's love song ended to be immediately followed by a classic rock song by a husky-voiced female singer, the couple waved the wedding party over.

Sarah wasn't usually comfortable under any kind of spotlight, but today she didn't hesitate; she went with Abe and they danced. She didn't even try to fight the sheer joy she got being in Abe's arms, his body moving against hers.

There'd be plenty of time for that later.

The speeches that followed the first round of dancing were short and funny and wicked.

Noah told a story about finding the newlyweds lip-locked in Fox's Lamborghini that had everyone laughing as Molly blushed and Fox kissed her cheek, his arm hooked around her neck. Then it was Charlotte's turn: the petite blonde's words were sweet and so emotional that they had everyone blinking back tears. Molly rose to hug her best friend, the love that existed between these two sisters of the heart out there for the world to see.

Vicente was the last to speak, his speech that of a proud father on his daughter's wedding day and his hand resting on Molly's shoulder. He also made it a point to say how proud he was of Fox too, how much it meant to him to be at the wedding of the "honorable, strong, and talented" man he'd watched grow to adulthood beside his own son.

Fox exchanged a powerful hug with the older man afterward, his eyes raw.

Then the music started up again and everyone was invited to party.

It was the least elegant and most fun wedding reception Sarah had ever attended, and that included her own. She ended up kicking off her heels partway through, dancing until her breath was ragged and her blood pumping. Those dances were almost always with Abe. The only other men to whom he'd relinquish her were Noah, David, Fox, or Vicente, and David's younger brothers.

It was scary how much she didn't mind his possessiveness. *Fantasy*, she reminded herself. *It's just a few hours of fantasy.*

When she ended up with Noah just as the pulsing beat segued into a slower song, she didn't know quite what to say or where to look, but the blond guitarist didn't push her on the topic of her and Abe.

He just said, "It's good to see you again, Sarah. Give Abe hell, eh?"

The comment startled her into a smile. "Will do," she said, and it wasn't until thirty seconds later that she realized the import of Noah's words and her response: he'd assumed she and Abe had a thing going, and caught in the fantasy, she hadn't exactly denied it.

*Careful, Sarah,* she warned herself, but when Abe came to reclaim her, she didn't resist. Nothing could happen here with so many people around them. His heart beat steady and deep beneath her ear, his body so warm and strong.

Always, she'd felt safe in Abe's arms.

She'd never slept well when he was on tour, had counted off the days and hours until he'd be home again... until he'd hold her again as he was doing tonight.

The party went from afternoon to night, as befit a hard rock wedding. Sometime after true dark, Abe bent his head to her ear and whispered, "Put your shoes back on," in a tone that made her skin go hot, her breasts seeming to swell beneath her dress. She knew she should end this here and now, but oh, how she'd missed him.

*Just one night.*

She found her shoes, slipped her feet into them, and didn't resist when Abe took her hand and led her out of the pavilion, his goal the black SUV parked a short distance away. "My car." She tugged at his hand to pull him back. "I don't want to leave it here." Where it'd be discovered the next morning, this fantasy night laid bare to the world.

Eyes hot, Abe kissed her wet and deep as his demanding cock pushed into her belly. "We'll come back for it," he promised. "*After.*"

Sarah's panties were so wet by then that she didn't argue or resist when he tugged her toward his SUV once again. They drove to his place in molten silence. In LA terms, it wasn't too far from Fox and Molly's home, but it was far enough that it felt as if her body would burn up if she didn't have Abe's naked flesh against hers, *in* her, then and there.

Whimpering when he screeched to a stop in his garage, she drank in his harshly spoken, "Sarah," and got her seat belt off just in time.

He came around to her side of the SUV as the garage door closed, hauled her out. Pressing her up against the side of the vehicle, he kissed her with such raw passion that she felt branded. *Owned.* She bit his lip, shoved at his suit jacket. Shrugging it off, he ripped off his tie while she frantically unbuttoned his shirt.

He literally tore the sleeves open, his cuff links making tinkling sounds as they hit the concrete of the garage floor. And then he was pulling off his shirt, sending the remaining buttons flying, and she couldn't stop from spreading her hands on the mahogany-hued beauty of his chest, leaning in to taste him kiss by openmouthed kiss.

He shuddered, thrust his hand into her hair.

Sarah's hand flew up. "My fascinator!"

Abe, his chest heaving, gave her a burning look... then smiled. "Come on." Gripping her hand again, he drew her into the house and up to what had once been their bedroom.

Memories crashed into her, painful and beautiful and heartbreaking.

"*Wait.*"

Abe didn't ask why she'd stopped in the doorway, digging her heels in. He knew. Eyes locking with hers, he said, "I've never brought any other woman here. Just you."

*God, this was so dangerous.*

But she let him pull her closer, shivered when he kissed the side of her neck; she'd barely begun to process those sensations when he spun her around to kiss her mouth.

Sarah didn't have the time—didn't want it—to think about the past. Not tonight.

"This first," he murmured after their lips parted in a whisper of damp heat.

Lifting his hands to her fascinator while she stroked the warm, smooth skin of his chest, he removed the bobby pins that held it in place, then put it carefully on the nearby dresser. Spinning her around so quickly afterward that she wobbled, might've lost her balance had she not left her heels in the SUV, he unzipped her dress. "Don't want this wrinkled."

A kiss to her shoulder.

Shivering again, Sarah let the dress fall off her body, stepped out. Behind her, Abe picked it up and threw it over the back of a chair. "There," he murmured, his hands hot and a little rough on her hips. "Now you don't have to worry."

124

A second tender kiss to the curve of her neck. She'd been hot, wet, ready for a wild session, but this was different, the night changing in front of her. Panicked, she shifted to face him, pressing her body against his in a silent invitation. His erection made it clear he was as ready as she was, but he didn't take her invitation, didn't push her down on the bed or against a wall and thrust inside her.

"Now, Abe," she demanded, dropping her hands to his belt buckle.

"What's the rush?" He lifted those hands back up to his chest, placed his own hands on her waist. "You are so fucking beautiful, Sarah." Kisses along her jaw, down the line of her neck. "Let me worship you."

Panic twined with need, with memory, and it was hard to think, hard to breathe. "Kiss me." She needed an anchor, needed him.

His kiss was deep and slow and as possessive as the hand he placed boldly over her breast. Shivering, she took and took, drinking him up. His breathing was harsh by the time they separated, his eyes glittering, but still he didn't strip her naked, finish it. Falling onto his knees in front of her instead, he leaned forward to press a kiss to the black lace of her panties.

"*Abe.*" Her hand on the back of his head, her knees shaky.

"Shh, I have you." Kissing a line along the waistband of her panties, he held her up with one arm around her upper thighs. A lick of his tongue over her hipbone that made her moan. Then, at last, he was shifting his arm and tugging down her panties and she was stepping out of them because she couldn't resist Abe when he was being so tender.

Throwing the crumpled lace aside, he clamped his arm around the back of her upper thighs once more and kissed her again. Only this time it was on her bare flesh. Sarah cried out as her knees threatened to crumple. Her hands fell forward onto Abe's shoulders, his body the only solid point in her universe.

"I have you," he said again, his breath hot against her flesh.

Then he did what he'd said: he worshipped her.

Rocked by pleasure over and over again, Sarah felt boneless, liquid, when he rose to scoop her up in his arms. Laying her down gently on the bed, he first got rid of her bra. Then, keeping his eyes on her the entire time, he stripped down to the skin. Taking the thick length of his rigid cock in one fist, he stroked once, twice, his jaw clenched.

Sarah's back arched, her lower body rising up toward him in a silent plea.

"I can see you," he ground out. "So fucking wet for me."

When he grabbed a condom from the bedside drawer, rolled it on, she wanted to protest. He was her husband— But no, he wasn't. Not anymore. He was her lover for this one fantasy night and tomorrow... Tomorrow she'd think about tomorrow.

She lifted her arms and he came over her, nudging her thighs apart to push into her in a deep thrust that made her want to cry out except that the pleasure was too much, robbed her of sound. Her sense of completion was absolute, her arms wrapping around Abe to hold him close. He didn't move hard or fast despite the fact he was viciously aroused. He took it slow, each stroke accompanied by a kiss, more than one, their bodies sliding skin to skin all over.

She kissed his shoulders, the curve of his neck, anything she could reach. She had missed him so much. Always she'd missed this man who'd once been her husband, but even more since the emotional, passionate hours they'd shared three weeks earlier.

Tears stung her eyes.

Abe spoke against her ear, the rumble of his voice cascading a thousand memories over her. "I haven't been with anyone else since that day in your kitchen." He drew back, thrust impossibly deeper. "You're in my blood, Sarah."

Nails digging into his back, she locked her mouth to his. She couldn't listen to his words, couldn't start rebuilding dreams that had splintered forever. This was a night out of time. After it ended, she had to put herself back together and figure out how to get over Abe Bellamy all over again.

# CHAPTER 14

SARAH FELT LIKE A FALLEN woman—a deliciously used fallen woman—when they drove through the gates of Fox and Molly's home around four thirty in the morning. They'd planned to come back much earlier but had fallen asleep in each other's arms in the aftermath of a pleasure that had melted her bones and twisted up her heart, would've probably slept through to dawn if Sarah's phone hadn't suddenly beeped with a low-battery warning that nudged them awake.

Thank goodness Abe had the code to let himself in, because aside from Sarah's car, Gabriel and Charlotte's rental was the only vehicle in the drive, the house quiet, lights all off.

The pavilion hadn't yet been taken down, but it was closed up tight for the night.

"We are so busted," she groaned. Someone would've noticed her car sitting out here pretty much all by its lonesome, would've looked for her, not found her. It wouldn't take a genius to put together one and one to add up to a sinfully sexy two.

"Everyone will have been too buzzed to care," Abe reassured her before coming around to help her down from her seat, his SUV high enough that it had a step built in. "They probably figured you crashed here."

He tapped her ass once she had both feet firmly on the ground. "Go get into your car, drive home. I'll follow."

She knew that by "home" he meant his place, but the cold night air finally succeeded in slapping some sense into her. "I think I better go to my place."

"Sarah," Abe began, his eyebrows drawing together.

"I have a meeting in the morning." She opened the driver's door, threw her clutch onto the seat on the other side. "I need to be up and ready for it." The meeting wasn't until eleven, but Abe didn't need to know that.

Her ex-husband slid his hand around the back of her neck, his hold warm and proprietary. "I'm not letting you go." It was a whispered promise. "Not this time."

Sarah shook her head, forced herself to speak. "I'm not yours to keep or let go." A piercing sense of loss tore through her as she broke away from him to get into her car. She and this talented man, they were so good together when they worked, but when they crashed and burned... "I barely survived our last round together, Abe."

Her door still open, she looked up from the driver's seat, met his gaze. "I don't know if I have the strength to go there again."

Abe braced one hand against the edge of the car's frame, bent down. "You're the strongest woman I know." His dark eyes held her captive, the look in them beyond passion.

Pure raw emotion.

"And," he said, "I'm not that asshole, the one who hurt you. I won't ever let myself become that man again."

Sarah wanted to believe him. She'd loved Abe so desperately and the place in her heart where he'd lived remained a jagged wound, but she'd been through too much to believe in rainbows and puppies and happily-ever-afters for herself. For the girl who'd gotten off a bus all alone in this huge city, then found herself alone again less than two years after she fell into the arms of this man to whom she'd given all of herself.

Blinking rapidly in an effort to stave off the torrent of sorrow that wanted to pour out of her, she swallowed, managed to form words. "I better go."

Abe let her shut her door and pull away, but when she looked in the rearview mirror, he was still there, watching as she drove off: a big, strong, and deeply talented man who still meant more to her than anyone else ever had... and who she couldn't let back in, not if she was to survive.

No matter if it felt like she was making a terrible mistake.

# CHAPTER 15

THREE DAYS AFTER A NIGHT that haunted her dreams, Sarah watched Flossie bound into the house. She'd just picked her pet up from a dog sitter—Flossie loved socializing with other dogs and Sarah didn't like to leave her alone when she was going to be gone all day.

She'd spent today with her accountant. They'd been working out if she could expand without it having an adverse impact on her compact but currently extremely high-performing business. It had been good to get out, to have business to focus on, think about. It kept her from going over and over what had happened at the wedding, how it had felt when Abe was so tender with her.

Her phone beeped an incoming message.

One glance at it and her lips curved. It was Lola, asking if Sarah wanted to go with her to a play. *It's months away, but I need to get tickets before they sell out, so yea or nay now or forever hold your peace,* the other woman had written. *Best news: Dad's well enough that I should be home in a week—though I have organized some home help for him and Mom. Over their objections, I might add. Two more stubborn people you'll never meet.*

Sarah's smile grew deeper—Lola had inherited that trait in spades.

*Kiddo blew off college to come hang with his grandpa and grandma for a few days,* her friend had added. *That really perked everyone up. Can't even read him the riot act now, though I am booting his ass back to college tomorrow. Anyway, I didn't want to interrupt your work day with a call, so ring me when you get home.*

Sarah made the call then and there.

"Hey, you!" Lola said into the receiver in her big, ebullient voice.

"Hey back," Sarah replied with a smile. She and Lola had met at an event designed to introduce small LA businesspeople to one another; Sarah had heard Lola laugh and turned with a smile to see who was making such a joyous sound. They'd hit it off right away regardless of the twelve-year age gap between them—and despite Jeremy's attempts to disparage Lola as "loud and cheap," Sarah had never stopped nurturing their friendship.

Never again would she focus only on a man. She'd made that mistake with Abe. Oh, he'd never once tried to get between her and any friends she wanted to make. No, it had been Sarah. She'd thought if she concentrated all her energy on Abe, if she gave him her everything, he'd love her.

As far as awful ideas went, it had been one of her worst.

Dropping her purse on the vanity after kicking off her shoes, she settled on the bed for a long talk with her best friend. Flossie padded in to curl up in the sunshine by the window, happy to nap while Sarah chatted with Lola. But though Sarah and Lola normally had no secrets from one another, Sarah couldn't tell her friend about Abe. Not yet. Not when she could still feel his touch on her skin, still hear the deep, rough murmur of his voice in her ear as he rocked into her body, his own body a wall of heat against her.

She felt too raw inside to expose her emotions to the light.

It was forty minutes later, Flossie still snoozing, that she and Lola finally hung up, having made plans to catch up once Lola was back home.

Sarah stood, was raising a hand to lower the zipper on her sleeveless and beautifully tailored red dress, when the gate buzzer went off, making Flossie bounce up from her position in the sunshine and bolt downstairs. Sarah walked out of her bedroom in a less frantic fashion and headed down the hall to look through the tall, narrow window at the top of the staircase. She could see the gate from this spot, and what she saw today was a familiar black SUV.

Blood rushed to heat her skin, her pulse a hard drumbeat.

Stepping back from the window, she just stood in place for half a minute, arguing with herself. As she did so, her eyes fell on the roses Abe had sent the morning after the wedding, roses she'd deliberately placed on a hallway table rather than inside her bedroom. The blooms were startlingly healthy and joyously red. When she'd first seen them, the bouquet had turned her mushy for a little bit—until she'd reminded herself that Abe was her ex for a reason.

The buzz came again. Flossie barked, as if wondering where she was.

"Don't be a coward, Sarah." Smoothing her hands down the front of her dress, she walked downstairs to the control panel in the hallway and pushed the button that would open the gate. She waited to make sure the gate closed automatically behind him.

Abe didn't appear to have a paparazzi tail, but you never knew with a rock star, especially one as successful and as loved by women as Abe. He was good for the paparazzi's bottom line even when he was sober. The only good thing about the current situation was that Sarah had never really registered on the paparazzi's radar even during their marriage—likely because Abe was so rarely photographed with her.

Her hand curled up against her heart.

It still hurt that he'd never been proud of her as Fox clearly was of Molly. The lead singer had been snapped hand-in-hand with his now-wife countless times while the two went about the daily business of living their lives. Picking up something at the grocery store, grabbing a burger, taking a simple walk.

Abe knocked, sending Flossie into paroxysms of exited barking. "Hush, Flossie," she said and pulled open the door. "Hello, Abe."

He smiled and bent down to pet Flossie as Sarah's traitorous dog sniffed at Abe's jean-clad legs and apparently decided he was okay from the way her tail began to wag. When he rose—after Flossie ran off to play in the enclosed yard—it was with a frown. "You got shorter."

"What?" She glanced down. "Oh. I'm not wearing my heels."

Abe's gaze lowered and Sarah couldn't keep her toes from curling into the carpet; she suddenly felt bare to the skin when she was perfectly well dressed.

"What're you doing here?" she asked in an effort to wrench back control of a meeting that shouldn't be happening in the first place.

"Using then discarding me, Sarah? Tut-tut."

"*Abe.*" This wasn't how it was supposed to go. He wasn't supposed to pursue her. Abe didn't pursue women. Not even his wife.

"Nice dress," he commented, hand braced on the doorjamb. "Sexy, but all business. You had a meeting about your company?"

Sarah didn't quite know how to respond. No man ever asked about her business—Jeremy hadn't cared, and all her employees were female. It had simply worked out that way, but she was glad for it. She wanted to give women like her a chance. Women who were alone and friendless and struggling in this big city.

"Yes," she responded when Abe just waited patiently for her answer. "With my accountant."

"Yeah? Business good?"

Again, Sarah hesitated. Why did he care? Abe had no interest in business, that she knew full well. "You want to go into partnership with me?" she joked in an effort to find her feet. "Doing your due diligence about the company's finances?"

His smile was sudden and gorgeous and it still made her chest squeeze so hard. No one had a smile like the keyboardist for Schoolboy Choir.

"I suck at business. That's why I have finance nerds to handle it."

Sarah rolled her eyes. "You do keep an eye on what they're doing though, right?" He hadn't when they'd been together. Back then, she hadn't been confident enough to offer to take on the task, hadn't known she had the potential for that kind of skill. The night classes she continued to take regularly had shown her different, shown her that she wasn't the "stupid, brainless brat" her mother's boyfriend had so often called her.

"Yeah, I check things now that I'm sober," Abe said, his deep voice slicing the dark memories in half.

He leaned in a little closer at the same time, his body blocking out the outside world. It should've made her want to step back; it didn't—it made her want to place her hands on his chest, raise her lips to his and taste him as if she had every right to kiss this man when he came to her door.

As if he were hers.

Abe's physicality had always spoken to her own. That was the one place where they'd never had any problems.

"You eaten?" he asked as she fought with herself to stay in place, to not give in to the tug between them.

"No," she answered. "I haven't been home that long."

"I know a place."

Sarah's toes curled deeper into the carpet, her battered heart skipping a beat. "I..." Shaking her head, she reminded herself how this had ended the last time around and knew what she had to say. "I think it's better if we aren't seen together."

That gorgeous smile faded as if a cloud had passed across the sun. "Right."

"I don't want to be sucked back into the media storm that surrounds you," Sarah found herself saying, hating that she'd stolen his smile, regardless of whether that was the only sensible decision she could've made. "They'll start saying we're getting back together and following me and..."

"Yeah." Abe pushed off from the doorjamb, dropping his hands to his sides. "You're right. I'll go before the bottom-feeders sniff me out here—just wanted to make sure you were okay."

Sarah fought the part of her that so badly wanted to ask him to stay, to say that they could just hang out at her place. Those words she could never say—because one thing had become clear to her: Abe was her deepest weakness.

He still held the power to hurt her more than any other man on this planet.

ABE MANAGED TO KEEP HIS distance from Sarah for the next seventy-two hours. That didn't mean he didn't think about her. He damn well did. He dreamed about the smooth beauty of her skin under his hands, the way her breath turned ragged when he stroked her just right, how her thighs tightened around his hips when he thrust into her.

He'd been waking hard as a rock and having to jerk off in the shower to take care of it. But their sexual chemistry wasn't what kept him awake at night. It was the memory of her laughter during the wedding and afterward. She'd glowed with happiness as she danced, her eyes sparkling.

Abe hadn't seen such joy in her smile since the first months of their marriage, and he knew *he* was responsible for snuffing out her light. No fucking wonder she didn't trust him anymore. A woman like Sarah rarely gave her trust, and he'd shit all over that precious gift.

Plowing his gloved fists into the punching bag in front of him on the morning of the fourth day, he blocked out the other sounds in the gym and attempted to lose himself in the rhythm of the mindless action. It worked for about a minute before his mind filled with Sarah again. Her shy smile when he gave her a compliment. The way she'd sit curled up under his arm and read to him on lazy summer days.

Hard on the heels of that memory came one of him throwing her books in the pool in a drug-fueled rage. She'd been sobbing as she tried to save them.

"Fucking bastard," Abe muttered, talking to his past self. He punched the bag so hard that it threatened to swing back right into his face. He didn't care. He deserved to have his face beaten in.

Ripping off his gloves afterward, he showered, then went straight to a bookshop.

It was too little too late, but now that he'd remembered his asshole behavior, he couldn't just leave it. Ball cap pulled low, he wandered the aisles… then realized most people here didn't care who he was; they were more interested in the volumes that lined the shelves. He spent an hour inside the murmuring quiet of the store, searching for the titles he remembered seeing on their bedside table. She'd definitely read him Jane Austen.

He couldn't remember which one though, so he bought the entire set.

And there was this one romance novel she loved and had read over and over again. He'd teased her it would fall apart in her hands one day. She'd just smiled and read him a paragraph that she'd told him was part of her favorite scene. What the hell had it been? *Yes, that was it.* In the end, it turned out the store didn't have that book in stock, so he bought her a bunch of new releases featuring people with dogs or puppies on the covers. He definitely remembered seeing covers like that in their home.

After spotting it in a display, he added in a nonfiction book about a woman who'd set up her own company while nearly flat broke and who was now a millionaire. At the counter, he paid extra to have the books wrapped up and packaged.

He'd called his car service earlier; the driver shot him a funny look when he put the package in the passenger seat and gave him Sarah's address. "I'm a courier now?" the stocky middle-aged man asked, having worked long enough for Schoolboy Choir that he was a friend. They'd all missed his calm demeanor and total trustworthiness when he broke his leg recently and had been out for a while.

"Best in the business," Abe responded.

The other man snorted. "I'll get it to her now."

Blowing out a breath after the gleaming black town car pulled away, Abe went to where he'd parked his SUV and got in. He didn't want to go home to his empty house, but he didn't want to barge in on his friends either. David and Thea, Noah and Kit, they needed time alone. As for Molly and Fox, while the newlyweds were back home after a short wedding trip, having postponed their honeymoon until later in the year, Abe wasn't about to bust up their love nest.

Gabriel and Charlotte probably wouldn't have minded the company since they'd been doing the sightseeing thing, but the other couple had flown back to New Zealand twenty-four hours earlier—after inviting all of them to their own wedding.

His phone buzzed right then.

Picking it up, he saw a message from Fox. *Molly and I are at that Thai place with the noodles you like. We saved you a seat if you want to join us for lunch.*

Fuck, he loved his bandmates. *On my way,* he messaged back.

Starting the engine, he tried not to obsess over if Sarah would call him after receiving his long overdue gift. Hell, he'd be content with her throwing the books at his head. All he wanted was for her to talk to him, to let him show her he wasn't that guy anymore, the one who'd destroyed them both.

# CHAPTER 16

SARAH SAT ON THE FLOOR of her living room, books spread out all around her.

Having worked nonstop for days, she'd given herself the afternoon off. First, she'd gone to see her son. The anniversary had rolled around again, and though she hurt, this month wasn't one of the bad ones. She'd talked to him, told him about her day, left him with a kiss.

Her plan for the rest of the day had been to get into her pj's and curl up on the couch with Flossie to binge-watch a favorite television series. Then had come the buzz at the gate that made her heart thunder and her skin flush... and the delivery of a most unexpected package.

*I hope you're doing okay today. Say hi to Aaron for me. I'm sorry I threw your books in the pool. I was a dick. – Abe*

Sarah stared at the note card again, still not certain she was reading it right. The first two lines, they turned her throat thick, but the rest... He'd been so high that day that she'd have bet her business he had no memory of the ugly incident. Sarah had never forgotten it: she could still feel the wrenching ache of the sobs that had overwhelmed her as she tried futilely to fish out books that had been well and truly drenched.

Abe, meanwhile, had moved on to throwing the pool furniture into the shimmering blue water.

Her fingers trembled as she picked up a leather-bound copy of Jane Austen's *Persuasion*. It matched the other Austen novels he'd sent her, the set a lovely reissue packaged for collectors. Beside the fancy collector's editions lay cheerful paperbacks with laughing couples and/or dogs on the covers.

She stifled a wet laugh. He'd clearly chosen those at random, but it was cute that he'd remembered she liked romances with animals in them. Half the time when she'd read to him or talked to him about her favorites, she'd thought he was mostly asleep. It hadn't mattered—she'd just liked being with him.

The most surprising book in the package was the one about the entrepreneur who'd gone from rags to riches on stubborn grit and sheer determination.

It gave her a funny, fluttery feeling in her tummy to realize Abe really did take her business endeavor seriously. It wasn't mockery, not when he'd gone to the effort of choosing these other books with her likes specifically in mind. He'd thought she'd like the book because she was an entrepreneur too.

Her eyes burned.

Putting down the book in her hand, she took another look at all of them, then got up and put the books neatly onto the "to be read" section of the bookshelf in her living room. Like so many booklovers these days, Sarah read a lot electronically— she loved being able to inhale a few pages on her phone while she was stuck in a queue or waiting room, loved even more that she could download a book any time of day or night—but she still also cherished printed books, always bought the print editions of her favorites, adored curling up with a paperback on a Sunday afternoon.

Maybe because to her books represented education and comfort. Security.

She loved walking into the room and seeing her favorites, complete with spines broken from how often she'd read them. Her books held so many memories—this one, she'd first read while her stomach was in knots the night before she went to sign the papers that would officially create her company. And that one she'd been given by Lola on her last birthday.

Today, as she arranged Abe's gift to her satisfaction, she patted the spines of the leather-bound editions, smiled at the paperback covers.

Picking up the torn wrapping paper and the note card afterward, she put the paper in her recycle bin before returning to the couch and to Flossie. One hand lying on the warm bulk of her dog, she turned the card over to look at the image on the front. She hadn't paid much attention to it earlier, more focused on Abe's strong black scrawl on the other side.

It was a drawing of a fairground.

Sarah's breath stuck in her chest for a long second. She'd asked Abe to go to a fair once. It had been toward the end of their marriage, when her husband was home so rarely it had felt as if he was actively avoiding her. That night, he'd turned her down to party with the guys instead. She'd gone to the fair alone, had ended up sitting in her car watching other couples walk by arm in arm, laughing and excited to be together

Had he remembered? Or was this just chance, the note card grabbed at random off a stand at the counter when he went to pay?

More importantly, what did she do about it?

Her hand went to her phone, but she hesitated, the memories of her awful loneliness while she'd been with Abe holding her in place. Curling her fingers into her palm, she picked up the television remote instead.

She *had* to keep her distance if she was to have any chance of protecting her battered heart. Because this Abe? The one who sent her flowers and books and who dropped by to make sure she was all right? He was more dangerous than the man who'd broken her to pieces.

ABE ATE, TALKED, MANAGED TO sound normal enough that neither Molly nor Fox saw anything amiss, but all the while he was waiting for his phone to buzz. Even after he returned home around ten that night, following a jam session that had ended up turning into an impromptu dinner at Noah and Kit's, he was poised to grab the phone.

An hour passed, two.

Sometime after midnight, he finally accepted that Sarah wasn't going to call him.

His jaw clenched as he sat on the edge of the bed, his muscles rigid and his emotions black and twisted. Before, he'd have gone for the drugs, tried to drown it all out. If he didn't feel, he couldn't hurt. Today he went to the baby grand piano that sat beside the glass doors that led out onto the patio. He stared at it, his soul aching.

Before Noah had shared "Sparrow" with them, he hadn't played it for years, not since the last day his baby sister spent in his home. She'd been healthy then, had come to stay with him while his parents went on a little vacation; he and Tessie had decided on their own vacation and gone to Disneyland three times in a week.

The rest of the time, they'd made music together, Tessie as drawn to song as Abe. After they buried her, his tiny sister who had never had a chance, he hadn't been able to bear the memories that came flooding back when his fingers touched the keys: of Tessie dancing while he played, saying, "More! More!" when he dared stop.

But those memories weren't the only ones that haunted him now when he looked at the piano.

*The anguish on Sarah's face, his wife's footsteps as she ran from him.*

Spinning away from the baby grand, he went to the other piano in the room, placed all the way on the other side. And he played. What came out wasn't hard and raw but soft, melancholy. A nocturne.

The one Sarah had been playing that night.

The birds outside were chirping in the predawn light and his hands ached by the time he stopped. And still there was no message on his phone.

He went to bed at last, only to be awakened four hours later by the buzzer that announced a visitor at the gate. Groaning, he put a pillow over his head and tried to ignore it. That was when his phone began ringing.

"What?" he growled into it without looking at the screen to see who it was.

"Abe?"

The husky feminine voice chased all sleep from his mind. "Sarah?" He sat up. "Is everything all right?"

"I'm here," Sarah responded instead of answering him. "Can I come in?"

Had Abe been on drugs, he'd have been sure he was hallucinating. As it was, he wondered if he was dreaming. "Yeah, sure. Give me a second." Getting out of bed wearing what he usually wore to sleep—nothing—he didn't even try to find the gate remote. He just made his way to the control panel and let her in.

He was still standing there butt naked when Sarah's car pulled up. "Shit."

Running to the nearest bathroom, he splashed water on his face, rinsed out his mouth, and grabbed a towel to hitch around his hips. He'd barely gotten it in place when the doorbell rang. Jogging over to open it, he said, "Good morning."

Sarah took a physical step back, her face blanching. "You look like you've been on a bender."

"What?" He shook his head, got his brain cells in order. "No, I was playing." He held out one hand.

Forehead wrinkling, she grabbed it. "Abe, your fingers are swollen! How long did you play?"

He shrugged, his eyes caressing the exposed curve of her nape as she bent over his hand. She'd swept her hair up into a neat little knot, was wearing a blue-green dress that had lots of panels that hugged her form. "A bit."

Sarah's lips parted as if she'd yell at him. But she snapped her mouth shut on the next breath, dropped his hand, swallowed. "We need to talk."

Abe frowned; her tone was so tight, her body held in such fierce check. But he wasn't going to interrogate her. Not when she was finally back where she belonged. In *their* home. "Yeah, sure. Come in."

PALMS DAMP AND SKIN FLUSHING hot then cold, Sarah walked into the house she'd fled two years earlier, hurt and lost. "Maybe you should..." She waved vaguely in the direction of Abe's body.

And God, what a body.

It was like he'd been carved out of rich, chocolate-colored marble. All ridges and valleys and glowing skin. Relief colored her blood: now that she was really looking, it was obvious he hadn't gone back to abusing drugs or alcohol. He'd never looked this healthy, this goddamn good during their marriage—and even then, he'd been difficult to resist. Now...

"Were you in the shower?" she asked when he just scratched at his stubbly jaw after shutting the door.

"No. In bed."

Her mind immediately supplied her with a hundred highly distracting images of Abe sprawled out, the sheets kicked off his bare body. Then her blood ran cold. "I'm sorry. I didn't mean to interrupt—"

"Alone," Abe said before she could finish, his voice firm. "Sleeping alone." He held up his abused hands. "Crashed after playing."

"Oh." She fiddled with the strap of her simple black purse. "Um, clothes?"

Her husband—ex-husband—looked down at himself as if he'd forgotten he was only covered by a teeny, tiny yellow towel that showed off far too much of his powerful thighs and seemed in danger of slipping off at any second. That buttery yellow shade should've made him look less masculine, but it did the opposite.

It threw his maleness into stark focus.

"Right." Abe's eyes lifted to connect with hers... and a slow smile crept over his face.

If he said anything teasing at that moment, she'd throw her purse at his head. Sarah swore it. Today was *not* the day for Abe to be all teasing and sexy and making her crazy. "Clothes," she repeated in a tone that brooked no argument, and pointed in the direction of his bedroom.

He chuckled and began to turn that way. "Back in a minute. You want to make yourself some coffee?" he asked over his shoulder. "I got a new machine Fox recommended."

Sarah went to say no, then decided she might as well find something to do with herself or she'd go mad while waiting for him. "I'll make you one too." She headed to the kitchen before she could give in to the urge to watch him walk way, his muscular buttocks moving against that flimsy excuse for a towel. "That's what got you into this mess," she muttered to herself as she reached the kitchen.

It was all black marble counters and white cabinetry, the appliances steel and the windows generous. A room full of light that she'd once made even more vibrant with fresh flowers, it had always been her favorite place in the house. She had so many great memories of this room—including a treasured one with Abe. He'd been mostly naked that time too, having just come out of the pool wearing only snug, dark blue shorts.

She'd been putting together a pasta salad for their lunch, and he'd wrapped his wet body around hers from behind, making her squeal. But she'd liked it, loved that he'd cuddled her, kissed her neck, maneuvered her unprotesting body to a wall before lifting her up so he could take her against that wall. She'd expected a hard, fast quickie, but he'd kissed her so much that day, his hands petting her body, and his cock in no rush inside her.

Her lower body clenched.

Slapping at her cheeks hard enough that it stung, Sarah told herself to snap out of it, to remember that, most of the time, she'd been alone and miserable in this room and in this house. She'd eaten more meals by herself at the freestanding counter than she ever had with Abe.

Turning to the coffeemaker on that sobering thought, she saw it was an easy one to operate, using the prepackaged little pods. She found those pods in the cabinet directly above the coffeemaker.

*Abe reaching over her head to grab something for her. "Here you go, Shortness."*

Fighting the assault of memory, of the only time in her life when she had actually felt short, she grabbed the pods and shut the cabinet door. Then she concentrated on choosing what kind of a coffee to make for herself, and, after that, on how to work the machine perfectly.

Having already brewed a half-strength cappuccino for herself, she'd just finished making an espresso for Abe when he walked in. From the fresh soap scent of him, he'd had a quick shower before he changed into crisp blue jeans and a black T-shirt with a V-neck. The tee pulled across his chest, hugged his biceps.

And her stomach, it wanted to flip again.

"Thanks." He picked up the espresso and threw it down his throat like the liquid wasn't even hot.

He'd always done that—and she'd always winced, just like now.

Looking away, she took more careful sips of her coffee while nerves began to twist and knot in her gut. "You want another one?" Abe had always loved espresso.

"I can do it." He moved to the machine, got it started before turning to her. "You look good in that dress."

Sarah could feel color rising to her cheeks, hoped her skin tone hid it. "Um, thanks." She'd learned how to dress herself as a businesswoman by looking up articles online. Before that, she'd been all short, ass-hugging skirts and glittery tops, the perfect rock-star groupie. Not that there was anything wrong with that look—Sarah still liked to pull out her glittery tops now and then—but it had never quite been her.

"I guess I finally found my style," she added when Abe didn't say anything further, his eyes lingering on her curves with open appreciation.

Her nipples ached.

Frustrated with herself and her susceptibility to this rock star who'd never loved her, she put her cup on the black marble of the freestanding counter in the center of the kitchen. "We might have a problem."

Abe raised an eyebrow in a silent question as he leaned back against the counter opposite where she stood, his hands braced behind him.

"I missed my period."

# CHAPTER 17

HER WORDS FELL LIKE A bomb into the silence of the kitchen. Suddenly the ticking clock on the wall was all she could hear, each movement of the second hand a jagged, bright sound that scraped across her already raw nerves.

"It's probably nothing. I'm probably just late... only, I'm never late," she said past the slightly sick feeling in her gut. Having this conversation with Abe, it was a nightmare repeating itself. "I wasn't lying about being on the pill. I did everything right this time!" She'd made sure to take the pill like clockwork, having no intention of ever again falling pregnant. Not after Aaron. "But I was on the final day of some antibiotics for—"

"Sarah." Abe strode forward to grip her gently on her upper arms. "I know you didn't lie about being on the pill."

"Right, okay." She nodded her head like a marionette. "I just didn't want you to think I'd been trying to trap you or anything." Her body began to shake. "I can't do it, Abe. I can't be pregnant again. I *can't*." She'd lost two babies already, her womb an apparently hostile place.

"Hey, hey." Abe drew her close, but she couldn't allow herself to rely on him. Not when he'd thrown her away so easily. Not when he'd forgotten her in a heartbeat.

Wrenching back, she touched a trembling hand to her face. "It might just be stress-related." Sarah hoped that was it. "But I can't face going to the doctor alone." Yet instead of calling one of her friends for the needed moral support, she'd come straight to Abe.

She couldn't explain why except that her head had started spinning when she'd realized she was late enough for it to matter, and the spinning hadn't stopped since. Her brain clearly wasn't firing on all cylinders. "What was I thinking? You can't come with me. If the media—"

"Fuck the media." Abe's harsh tone sliced through the air. "I want to be there for you."

Sarah took a trembling breath, glanced at that ticking clock. Abe's mother had given it to them as an anniversary present, and Sarah had always loved it. Simple wooden hands on a carved background of a darker wood polished to a shine, it had been handmade by an artist who worked with the natural grain and patterns of his chosen medium.

"Sarah, let me do this."

Regardless of her panic at the idea of being hounded by the paparazzi, Sarah knew Abe deserved to learn the truth alongside her. She cleared her throat, said, "The appointment's in thirty minutes."

ABE TURNED ON THE RADIO to cover the silence in the SUV as he drove Sarah to a doctor in the suburbs. Whatever her original reasoning for choosing that doc, a man she'd told Abe was her normal GP, the unintended result was that the media was unlikely to spring them. Good. Because he was not having anyone upset Sarah today.

His heart boomed like David's drums.

The idea of a kid...

Emotions crashed through him: joy, fear, grief, excitement, sheer terror... and shame.

He squeezed the steering wheel. "I'm sorry about our first time around." Sarah's miscarriage had been early on in the pregnancy, but she'd known, been devastated. It hadn't felt as real to him—maybe because he'd already been going down the rabbit hole, but still, he'd done okay then. He'd held her, listened to her talk out her grief, made sure she ate. But none of that mattered after the ugly words he'd flung at her the night he drove her away.

How the fuck did a man make up for that?

"It's fine." Sarah smoothed her hands over the skirt of her dress, her voice quiet. "Let's just get through this."

Abe wanted to reach out, touch her, convince her she never had to worry he'd repeat his drug-fueled behavior. "Whatever happens, I'll be there." Stopping at a light, he turned and spoke to her profile. "I won't cut and run. Not now, not ever."

Another jerky nod, her hands twisting on the strap of her handbag. "Light's green."

He drove on. The two of them didn't speak again until he'd brought the car to a halt in the small underground garage of the building where the doctor had his office. "Which floor?"

"Third."

He put his hand on her lower back as they got into the

elevator, kept it there as they stepped out. Their luck held. Miracle of miracles, there was no one else in the waiting room.

Smiling, the white-haired receptionist said, "You're in luck, Sarah. We've had two cancellations in a row, so you don't have to wait. The nurse will be right out to fetch you." A pause, her eyes on her computer screen. "Oh, wait, I see the doctor said for you to see him directly—he wanted to check up on that flu of yours. I'll have the nurse show you through."

"How did you end up with a country doctor in LA?" Abe murmured to Sarah as they waited for the nurse, his hope to make Sarah smile.

That smile was shaky. "Dr. Snyder *is* a country doctor—and the receptionist is his wife," Sarah whispered. "They only relocated to LA because their daughter and grandkids are here. I'm going to miss them both when he retires like he's threatening to do."

"Does she always call him 'the doctor'?"

Sarah nodded. "She's very proud of him."

Then the nurse, a short no-nonsense woman with a warm smile, was there.

Once inside the doctor's office, Sarah took a seat in the chair nearest a fifty-something male who sported a bushy black mustache and kind brown eyes above the white of his medical coat, his pale skin dotted with freckles.

Abe shut the door before taking a seat in the chair next to her.

"Sarah." The doctor's eyes scanned Sarah's record on the computer. "How's that flu you couldn't shake off? Any problems?" He put on his stethoscope and pressed one end to Sarah's chest.

"I'm—"

"Breathe deep," the doctor interrupted. "Now out." He made her do that several times before nodding. "Excellent. All clear."

Sarah's smile was tight. "The antibiotics took care of the chest infection in the first couple of days, but I finished the whole course like you said."

"Good, good." The doctor typed a note into her medical file using one finger on each hand, pecking at the keys as fast as a bird hunting for food. "So you just came in for the follow-up?"

Sarah swallowed, her hands gripping at her purse. Abe couldn't stand to see her so distressed. Putting one hand over hers, he met the doctor's eyes. "She thinks the antibiotics messed with the pill and she might be pregnant."

"The ones I gave you shouldn't have counteracted the pill unless... Did you throw up at any point? That could've had an impact on the effectiveness of the pill."

"Yes." Sarah swallowed, her fingers curling over the side of Abe's hand. "It was the night before the monthly anniversary of Aaron's death. I just couldn't keep anything down."

"Ah." The doctor looked gently at Sarah, and in his expression, Abe saw a deep understanding of Sarah's loss, compassion for the little baby boy who had never breathed. And he realized the kindhearted man had asked to speak to Sarah directly not simply because he'd wanted to check she was over the flu: Dr. Snyder was a rare being—a true healer, one who cared about his patients' mental as well as physical well-being.

"I'm guessing you want to confirm as soon as possible?" At Sarah's nod, Dr. Snyder said, "Home pregnancy tests are surprisingly sensitive, but if you want absolute certainty, I'd recommend a blood test."

Sarah nodded. "The blood test. I want to know beyond any doubt."

"Our blood test results usually come back overnight, but I can put a rush on it." The older man was already pulling up the form on his computer. "It probably won't be covered by your insurance."

"That's fine," Abe said.

Sarah was in no shape to handle any kind of a delay.

Squeezing her hand again when she parted her lips as if to disagree with his implicit offer to pay, he continued to speak. "Are we talking a couple of hours, half a day?" he asked Dr. Snyder.

"I'll draw the blood myself, send it by rush courier to the laboratory. You should have the results this afternoon."

SARAH WAS BACK IN ABE'S SUV within fifteen minutes of the start of the consultation, a tiny square bandage in the crook of her arm where Dr. Snyder had taken the blood sample. She felt as if she were living in a dream world, everything surreal. "I have a meeting scheduled for later today."

"Can you postpone?" Abe pulled out of the underground garage and into the searing sunshine of an LA day.

Sliding on her sunglasses, Sarah found her phone, made the call, still feeling oddly distant. "I should've kept it," she said after hanging up. "I don't know what I'm going to do while we wait to hear back from Dr. Snyder."

Abe placed one big hand on her leg, the touch one of comfort rather than sexual. She knew she should push him away, but she closed her hand over the warmth of his. She needed comfort today, needed to hang on to something or someone lest she shatter.

"We could watch a movie," Abe suggested.

"No, I need to *do* something or I'll lose my mind." She rubbed her face. "I'm going to clean my house from top to bottom." It would keep her hands and legs busy, hopefully distract her brain.

"I'll help."

"There's no need." She had to grit her teeth to make herself break the connection between them, gently nudging his hand back to his side of the vehicle. "I'll call soon as the doctor gets in touch."

"I'll go nuts waiting on my own." Abe shot her a look that hid none of his own tension, and she remembered there were two of them in this.

"And," he added, "I bet you never shift all the furniture to clean underneath because some of it's too heavy."

The chambers of her heart seemed to fill with nails, sharp and painful, at the same time that stubborn flickers of hope whispered awake inside her. She tried to shove them aside, the pain and the hope both. "I'll make you vacuum."

"I can take it."

Sarah wasn't sure she could.

Having Abe home, the two of them doing a domestic chore together, had been one of her stupid daydreams during their marriage. Instead of dreaming about going to big, glamorous events as his date or experiencing exotic vacations by his side, she'd dreamed small, domestic dreams.

And today, when she was at her most vulnerable, her most defenseless, one of those dreams was going to come true.

# CHAPTER 18

TWO HOURS LATER, ABE FELT like he'd moved every piece of furniture in Sarah's home. His arms ached, but the ache was a glorious one. In spite of her threat, she hadn't actually made him vacuum, but she *had* made him pick up and individually dust each of her books as well as her bookshelves. Sarah had a lot of bookshelves.

She, meanwhile, had changed into shorts and a tee and vacuumed with a vengeance.

When he saw her getting ready to spray some cleaning liquid on her already squeaky clean bathroom tiles, he grabbed the bottle. "Wait a minute. This type of stuff has all kinds of chemicals in it." He scowled at the laundry list of impossible-to-pronounce ingredients. "I don't think you should use this. Just in case."

Leaning slightly against him, Sarah looked down at the bottle with a worried eye. "Do you really think so?"

"Go. I'll do it."

When her face dropped, his wife obviously lost with nothing to occupy her, he said, "How about you make those egg-and-spinach things for lunch? I've got a craving for them."

Her eyes lit up. "I think I have everything I need to whip up a batch."

REFUSING TO NEUROTICALLY CHECK THE phone in her pocket for missed calls, Sarah concentrated on cooking the frittatas. They weren't difficult to make, but she took precise care with every one of the steps, from blanching the spinach, to setting the oven to exactly the right temperature.

When Abe came into the kitchen a half hour later, having stowed the cleaning supplies and washed up, she pointed to the table where she'd just put a jug of fresh lemonade and a glass. "Thanks for doing that."

Abe shrugged and poured himself a glass of the cold, refreshing drink. "It was pretty easy since you're so hyperclean anyway."

Sarah knew she was a bit OCD on the cleaning front, but when you'd spent time on the streets, cleanliness took on a whole new importance. At least she'd channeled her tendencies into a successful business. "What time is it?" It just slipped out.

"Just past noon." Putting down his glass after finishing his lemonade in one go, Abe hummed a tune. "Tell me what you think of this."

Butterflies erupted inside her at the slow, bluesy sound of his voice. Abe rarely sang on Schoolboy Choir albums, but she'd always loved listening to him when he mucked around at home. The sound sank into her bones, the lyrics wrapping around her, a man speaking of dreams that shatter under the weight of harsh reality.

"It's sad," she said after he finished. "But… it gets you right here." She touched her fingers to her heart. "Did you write it?"

Abe shook his head. "David—in his pre-Thea period, when he thought he'd never have a shot with her. He and the others want me to be lead vocals on it."

A smile took over Sarah's face, her obsession with the phone pushed aside for the moment. "That's wonderful."

"There's a reason Fox is lead singer," Abe pointed out. "The man has serious vocal range."

"Yes, but Fox's voice wouldn't work for this song." Sarah could see exactly why his bandmates wanted Abe to take lead vocals. "You should do it."

Abe tapped his finger on her kitchen table. "I'll think about it." A quick flash of white teeth. "I don't want to become a showboat like Fox and Noah."

Laughing at the old joke, she turned off the oven timer when it buzzed, then pulled out the tray with the frittatas. Abe helped her throw together a green salad, then the two of them sat down to lunch. Sarah tried to eat, she really did, but her stomach wasn't in the mood to cooperate.

Abe's dark eyes dropped to where she rubbed at her tummy. "You think it might be—"

Sarah interrupted before he could finish his question. "Just nerves." She picked up her phone, stared at its mockingly silent face. "I'm going to take a shower."

Abe didn't attempt to stop her, and she spent twenty minutes in the shower, another forty minutes drying her hair and putting on makeup, before pulling on tailored black shorts and a short-sleeved top in deep orange, a thin gold chain around her neck her only ornamentation. When she padded to the living room on bare feet, she found Abe sitting on the sofa with his feet up, Flossie beside him.

The two of them were engrossed in a documentary about penguins.

And her heart, it went all mushy at the cozy sight she would've given anything to witness during their marriage. Fighting the soft, squishy feeling, she left them to it and walked into the kitchen with the vague idea of baking something.

The phone rang.

Sarah had it in her hand with no knowledge of having pulled it out of her pocket, but she couldn't make herself answer it, though Dr. Snyder's name flashed on the home screen. Abe was suddenly beside her, his arm strong and warm around her waist.

He took the phone from her unresisting hand, put it on speaker, said, "Doc, we're both here."

"Sarah?" Dr. Snyder said in his slightly gravelly tone. "I need your permission to share your medical results with Abe."

"Yes," she whispered, then coughed and answered more clearly. "I'm here, Dr. Snyder. Please tell us both."

"There's no doubt—you're pregnant."

Sarah's knees buckled. Only Abe's quick response, the arm he had around her waist locking tight, stopped her from crumpling to the floor. She was barely aware of him thanking the doctor and promising to get back in touch; the noise inside her head was a swarm of angry bees.

Shivering, stunned, she only snapped back to herself when Abe swung her up into his arms. "Abe, I—"

"I've got you." His grip tightened.

Sarah hadn't been afraid he'd drop her. Abe carried her like she weighed nothing, and she wasn't a small woman. She'd

161

been about to say that she was better, could walk. But seeing the hard line of his jaw, feeling the rigid strain of his body as it moved against her, she kept her silence until they reached the sofa and he sat down with her in his lap.

Scrambling off to curl up at the other end, her arms around her knees, she forced herself to ask, "Are you angry?"

"What?" His eyebrows drew together over his eyes, his body angled toward her. "No, of course I'm not angry. I'm worried—about you."

"Oh." She swallowed, tried a wobbly smile. "Can't blame you when I nearly pulled a Scarlett O'Hara impression."

Abe stretched out one arm on the back of the sofa. "So." His tone said he wasn't about to be distracted. "We're having a kid together."

Sarah's hand crept over her abdomen, her terror as brilliant as the sudden burst of love in her heart. "I'm no good at keeping babies alive, Abe." Hot and wet, the tears locked up in her throat began to fall. "They die inside me."

"Sarah, sweetheart, don't cry." He hauled her back into his lap.

She didn't resist this time and he held her close, stroked her hair, her back, whispered things she didn't hear, his voice a deep rumble against her as she fell apart.


SARAH'S HEARTBROKEN SOBS DESTROYED ABE. He wanted so much to take away her pain, fix things, but he could do nothing except hold her safe while she splintered into a million pieces.

"I don't know if I can do this," she said after a long time, her voice a thin whisper.

A deep ache in his chest, he cupped the back of her head. "I'll back whatever you decide." That was all he could say, Sarah's pain too violent for any other response.

She didn't answer for a long time. When she did, it was another punch to the gut. "What if my body can't hold on to our baby?"

Abe didn't know how to ease Sarah's hurt, but he couldn't stay silent when the guilt in her voice was a heavy, suffocating blanket. "It wasn't your fault," he said. "You did everything right." He knew that without having been there for her second pregnancy, because during the first, she'd religiously followed all medical advice. "You hear me, Sarah? You did all you could. Some things in life we can't control."

Sarah didn't answer.

It wasn't until maybe an hour later that she stirred. Sliding out of his arms, she left without a word; he wanted to follow, see that she was all right, but he told himself to give her space. She knew he was here, his shoulders ready to help her bear this weight.

She returned after five minutes, having washed her face and redone the knot into which she'd twisted her curls. "We need to work out the logistics."

Abe wasn't surprised by her sudden calm. Sarah had always liked to organize things, had found serenity in ticking off items on a list. Back at the start of their marriage, she used to make lists for what he needed to pack when he went on tour. He'd find the list beside his phone, smile because she'd always add smiley faces next to stern warnings about essentials he couldn't afford to forget if he didn't want to be caught short. Those lists had been for fun anyway—Sarah had ended up packing for him more times than not.

He could still see her standing alone in the doorway, waving good-bye as he left her before that last tour. It would've been easy to convince himself that he didn't know why he'd left her behind rather than bringing her along, but Abe was through with self-deluding lies. He hadn't taken Sarah on tour because she'd meant too much to him. He'd been in no headspace to love anyone as much as he'd loved this sweet, smart, beautiful woman who'd tumbled unexpectedly into his life. So he'd tried to keep her at arm's length.

He'd been a coward and she'd paid the price for his spinelessness.

"I want to be there," he said today. "For the whole deal."

Sarah walked into the kitchen, busied herself chopping up ingredients for a salad. "We can work out visitation for after the baby is—"

"No, Sarah." Having followed her, he took a seat on the stool directly opposite her, only the speckled gray of her counter between them. "I want to be there for the pregnancy too." If she'd made a different decision, he'd have gone with her then too. "The scans and the vitamins and all that shit."

Sarah's knife stopped moving on the carrots she'd cut into teeny, tiny slivers. Huge, dark eyes lifted to his. "What?" Open disbelief.

He didn't look away, didn't flinch. It was time for him to man up and step up. No more hurting her because he was so fucking scared of how much she could hurt him if he let her in. No more being so terrified of losing her to death one day that he'd rather push her away. No more being an asshole who left her alone.

"I want to be there to drive you to the doctor's," he said, "and I want to be there when you find out if it's a boy or a girl."

He took a deep breath, his chest shuddering with the force of his emotions. "I might have been a failure as a husband, but please give me the chance to be a good dad."

Sarah blinked really fast, then returned her attention to the pale wood of her chopping board. Scraping the demolished carrot into a bowl, she picked up an orange bell pepper and, slicing it in half, began to clean out the seeds. "What about your music?"

The sharp words bit hard. But Sarah had more than earned the right to demand an answer, demand certain promises. "We're not planning to tour again for at least a year or two, and any other appearances that come up, I'll check first with you to make sure it doesn't clash with baby-related stuff."

Sarah began to cut the bell pepper into thin, rectangular pieces. "The others won't mind? Fox, Noah, David?"

"Hell no." He rubbed his face. "It was never about them, Sarah. You know my behavior was my responsibility."

The magnificent Amazon who was his ex-wife continued to slice the bell pepper, her expression difficult to read. "It's not a short-term commitment, Abe."

Putting down the knife at last, she placed her hands on the counter and took a deep breath. "If... if this baby makes it"—one hand going to her belly—"he or she is going to need you always. Do you understand that? It doesn't matter if life gets hard or if your addictions start howling, or if something horribly sad happens, you *still* have to be a dad."

She held up a hand when he would've spoken. "I know losing Tessie hurt you. *So* much." A thickness in her voice. "But what if your mom dies or one of the guys in the band? Would you still be able to maintain?"

Taking a quick breath, she continued. "Because if you can't, if you have even the slightest inkling that you might break, then you need to walk away." No anger in her tone, nothing but a passionate conviction. "I don't want my child exposed to a father who's here one minute, gone the next. I won't have a little boy or girl heartbroken because their daddy disappears for weeks or months at a time."

Abe took the quiet verbal blows without attempting to defend himself. Hell, those blows were far softer than he deserved. "I'll maintain," he vowed. "You can trust me."

No response.

Panic knotted his gut. "Give me the pregnancy to prove myself. That's nine months—"

"Four weeks less," Sarah corrected, a sudden heat in her face as she stole a glance at the counter where they'd come together in naked passion.

Abe's blood pounded. "Right, eight months, give or take." He coughed past the roughness in his throat, damn glad she couldn't see his lower half. Now was not the time to be sporting a rampant cock. "That's two-thirds of a year."

He waited until she met his gaze. "If I prove myself to you in that time, promise me you'll let me be a dad to our baby." He knew he could take her to court, get visitation, but Abe didn't want that. He wanted to be an everyday part of his kid's life, feed their baby a bottle, change a dirty diaper, sing him or her to sleep.

To do that, he'd have to become a part of Sarah's life.

Abe didn't think Sarah had realized that yet. She was thinking only of the baby. But Abe, he'd been thinking of Sarah for a long time. From the way she laughed, to the way she danced, to how she'd looked at him once, before he'd tried his fucking best to snuff out that rare, beautiful light inside her.

"All right," she said slowly. "Let's see how it goes."

It wasn't the most ringing endorsement, but Abe would take what he could get, work with it. This time around, he'd be the man Sarah deserved.

# CHAPTER 19

LYING ALONE IN BED THAT night, Sarah thought of the way Abe had pulled out his phone and made the call for her follow-up appointment with Dr. Snyder. Because of her history, the doctor would be monitoring her closely throughout her pregnancy. He'd also told her he'd be referring her for specialist scans at a far earlier point than he did with most women.

Sarah had no argument with any of it, just wanted her baby safe.

Appointment made, Abe had promised to return at ten the following day to take her to the first visit. Sarah knew that if he kept his word about wanting to be there for everything, the media would sniff them out sooner rather than later. However, the possibility that had horrified her only days ago was no longer her primary concern.

She stroked her belly.

If it meant her baby would have a father, a *real* father, then she'd suck it up and find a way to weather the harsh glare of fame. "Stay," she whispered to her belly. "Please stay. I promise you I won't ever hurt you. Please don't go."

Her eyes grew hot, her chest agonizingly tight.

Turning over onto her side, she stared out the window she'd left slightly ajar to let in the night breeze. Her bedroom was on the second floor and the window had a security latch, but she couldn't actually fall asleep until she'd closed and locked it. Even after all these years, she still didn't trust the night.

Bad things happened in the night.

Today she had no reason to get up and shut the window, her mind wide awake. Picking up her phone, she went to message Lola to see if her best friend was up, hesitated. She wasn't ready for anyone else to know about this pregnancy, which meant the only person she could talk to was Abe.

She scrolled to his name in her address book, hesitated with her finger hovering over it.

*I want to be there for the pregnancy... The scans and the vitamins and all that shit.*

Setting her jaw, she decided to take him at his word and made the call. To her surprise, he picked up almost at once. "Sarah? What's wrong?"

She bit down on her lower lip. "I can't sleep."

"Yeah, me either." Abe sounded like he was moving around. "You want to go get ice cream?"

"It's half past eleven at night."

"So?" A verbal shrug. "We live in LA. Someone's gotta be selling ice cream at this hour."

Sarah smiled, the tightness in her chest evaporating under the sudden bubbles of delight. "Why are you breathing so hard?"

"I was doing weights. It keeps the demons at bay."

That he'd said that without hesitation, trusting her with his continuing emotional struggle, threatened to crack the shield around her heart.

Telling herself to be careful, go slow, she said, "If I eat midnight ice cream every day of this pregnancy, I'll get fat."

Certain people might already consider her fat, but Sarah knew she wasn't. She was simply bigger than the current cultural norm—and in Hollywood, that norm was twisted to insane levels of thinness. She had the physique of a toned and healthy woman who could take care of herself—and of her baby. "I need to stay fit, keep my body strong throughout the pregnancy."

"Sarah, honey, you've got nothing to worry about, never have." Abe's response might as well have come with a visual of him rolling his eyes he was clearly doing it so hard. "But," he added as she glared at the phone, "if you want, I'll create an exercise program for you so you can eat midnight ice cream without guilt. Baby-belly friendly."

Sarah turned over onto her back, her stupid heart going all mushy at the affectionate tone of his voice. "Let's go get ice cream."


IT FELT LIKE SNEAKING OUT when she got into Abe's SUV, as if the two of them were doing something naughty. And then she caught a hint of his masculine scent, saw the bulge of his biceps as he put the car into gear, and it *definitely* felt like she was setting herself up for trouble. She should stop him right now, open her door, and go back inside the house.

She didn't.

Instead, she settled in and said, "I did a search, found an all-night grocer where we can grab ice cream."

"I got something better. Flossie going to be okay?"

And now he was asking about her dog. Next thing she knew, he was going to turn up with an armful of puppies and totally demolish her defenses.

"Happily asleep in her inside bed," Sarah told him even as she fought to keep her mushy heart from overflowing its bounds. "She won't need to go outside till morning now."

Waiting for her gate to close behind the SUV, Abe glanced at the skinny black jeans and red top she'd put on with black heels. "How did you manage to dress so nicely so quickly?"

Sarah's toes curled. "Practice." She'd also done her face in five minutes flat; it was part of her armor, how she survived this world where she was an imposter who didn't have the right background or connections. "You look good too."

Her rock-star ex was wearing blue jeans and boots, but instead of a T-shirt, he'd thrown on a collarless white shirt, the sleeves rolled up to his elbows. It was probably designer. When Abe was sober, he liked clothes... and he'd liked buying them for her too. Once, while he'd been on tour, she'd received the most enormous delivery from Chanel.

It had made her feel loved, made her almost forget that he'd left her behind.

"Thanks." His voice merged with the bittersweet memory of the phone call they'd shared that day, her in LA, Abe several states away. "I figured you'd look good so I better not turn up in sweats."

Sarah knew that even if he had, he'd have looked hot. Abe was just generally hot, so any effort at dressing up only took him into überhot territory. And she should *not* be noticing that. This new relationship of theirs was about the baby, nothing else. "Where are we going?" she asked, recognizing the street seconds later. "The restaurants along here will all be closed."

"You hear that Florentina Chastain is doing a limited run of midnight dessert sittings?"

Sarah's eyes widened. "*No?*" She was an acknowledged Scrooge with her money, but the one thing she bought without fail every month was a small box of Chastain's handmade chocolates. "She probably sold out weeks ago." The boutique chocolate and dessert shop had a five-star reputation among the chocoholics and the glitterati.

It was a pity many of the latter just came to see and be seen.

Such a waste of the most exquisite desserts known to mankind.

"This dessert-sitting deal is to support charity," Abe told her. "I rang and promised them twenty grand for a table."

"You just spent twenty grand on dessert?" It came out a squeak.

A shrug. "I have enough money for five lifetimes—and the charity's for feeding hungry kids, so I figure it's worth it."

Sarah went quiet.

"Hey." Abe glanced at her as he slid into a parking space not far from the boutique's storefront; the seating section was in the covered and air-conditioned courtyard in back. "I thought you'd like this, but if—"

Sarah made herself speak. "No, let's go. I'm excited." No lie—she wanted to do this, even if it reminded her too much of her past.

Because she had far more in common with those hungry kids than she did with the no doubt dressed-to-the-nines crowd inside. "How much were the actual tickets?" she asked after they'd exited onto the quiet and otherwise empty sidewalk.

"A grand each, I think."

It took them less than a minute to reach the boutique.

And then slender, striking Florentina Chastain with her dark Cleopatra eyes, pure cream skin, and hair as black as midnight was welcoming them. Dressed in a simple knee-length black skirt that hugged her form without being too tight, a white shirt, and black heels, her hair in a smooth roll at the back of her head, she epitomized effortless sophistication.

"You put me in a tough spot, Mr. Bellamy," she murmured in a soft voice that held the liquid accent of a faraway land. "I couldn't turn down the donation, but my courtyard won't fit another table."

Abe just held out the check he'd snagged from his pocket.

Sighing, the chocolatier took the check and shook her head, but it was with a smile. "Follow me—but first let me give this check to my assistant."

That done, she took them past the glass cases filled with chocolates and other sweet treats, through a door marked Staff Only, and up a flight of stairs so narrow that they had to go single file... only to emerge on a small, square rooftop that would be overshadowed by a nearby building during the day. At night, it had a glorious view of the sky and just enough room for a table for two. That table was draped with a pristine white tablecloth, atop which sat a grouping of white candles in crystal holders that refracted the light into a beautiful pattern of shards.

"*Oh.*" Sarah lifted her hands to her mouth, undone by the sheer romance of the setting.

Abe put his hand on her lower back, rubbed gently. "Better than the courtyard?"

She just nodded, though her already mushy heart was threatening to melt. She kept reminding herself that Abe was doing this to support her through the pregnancy, that it was really about the baby. Still, part of her wanted to believe that it wasn't, that it was just as much about her.

Florentina's expression made it clear she was pleased by Sarah's response. "I will return in a moment."

Smiling with the smug satisfaction of a man who knew he'd hit a home run, Abe pulled out her chair. She took it with the surreal sensation of being in a dream—as if one of her beloved romance novels had come to life. Abe had just taken his own seat when Florentina returned.

"We've paired a number of award-winning wines with tonight's dessert-tasting menu," the other woman began.

"No wine," Abe interrupted.

Sarah winced inwardly. She hadn't had the chance to tell Abe that she wanted the pregnancy to be their secret for a while. Until it advanced further, until she knew if their baby was going to stay. If she could, she'd have kept it secret until she held her living, breathing baby in her arms.

But Abe didn't give away her pregnant state. "Alcohol's permanently off the menu for me," he said in a voice that made it a simple fact of life. "Sarah's keeping me company in my sobriety."

Florentina smiled and didn't offer them the little menu in her hand. "In that case, I will accompany your desserts with our most decadent teas. Yes?"

Sarah was a coffee woman and so was Abe, but too much coffee wasn't good for the baby and this was an adventure. "Yes," she answered for them both. "We'd love to try the teas."

The first one that came up was, according to Florentina, "a light, aromatic herbal infusion with a hint of grapefruit and vanilla." Sarah liked it enough to reconsider her coffee-only habit.

Abe looked at it askance before making a face of total martyrdom that had her laughing. Then he threw back half the cup. "Fancy hot water," was his conclusion.

He was far more impressed with the poached pear in a light pomegranate cream that was their first course.

Sarah took a bite, groaned, eyes closing.

She opened them to find Abe staring at her in a way that sent the blood rushing to her cheeks. And not from embarrassment. A little breathless, she took a second bite, bit back the moan this time.

Of course, the pear dish was just the start. Next came a chocoholic's dream—a rich and sinfully dark chocolate mousse swirled to perfection inside a tiny bowl fashioned from the finest milk chocolate, then topped with curls of white chocolate sprinkled with sparkling gold dust. Florentina had paired it with a strong black tea that, to Sarah's tongue, held a faint undertone of raspberries, lush and juicy.

Sarah dipped her spoon into the mousse, took a taste.

There was no way she could hold back her moan this time.

"Jesus, Sarah." Abe's words were rough, ragged. "I won't be able to fucking walk if you keep that up."

She stared at him, swallowed the mousse... and realized she'd dropped a curl of chocolate right in the V of her red top. It was sitting on the plump curve of her breast. She didn't even have the chance to attempt to pick it up before Abe leaned over and wiped it off with the soft white of his cloth napkin.

"Behave," he ordered in a tone as stern as that of her junior high school principal. "I mean it."

Sarah took another bite of the mousse, slid the spoon out oh-so-slow from between her lips. She didn't know what had gotten into her except that Abe was looking at her like he wanted to eat her alive, and no one had looked at her with that much raw *want* for a long, long time—not even the man who'd once been her husband. He had back before everything went wrong, before the grief and the drugs and the anger turned him into someone she didn't know.

It was a heady feeling to see that look in his eyes again.

Swallowing the spoonful of mousse, she slid in another bite and closed her lips around it with lush deliberation. Abe's eyes were black flames across from her. When she let her eyes flutter shut and moaned in the back of her throat this time, she heard him push back his chair in a screech of sound against the concrete.

Lifting her lashes, she met his gaze, shook her head.

His jaw clenched as he pulled his chair back to the table, but that fire in his eyes, it didn't dim.

It seemed to flare ever brighter as she finished the mousse with exquisite patience before picking up the new cup of tea that had been delivered partway through by a slender man in black pants and a white shirt, their old cups whisked away. This tea was cold and cleansing, all peppermint and ice.

Shivering in sensory pleasure, she put the delicate cup of transparent glass on its matching saucer. And spoke for the first time since she'd begun her teasing. "You didn't eat your mousse."

Abe nudged his plate toward her.

Sinking her teeth into her lower lip, she shook her head. "There are multiple courses to come, and I've already inhaled a gazillion calories."

"Who cares?" He stretched his legs out on either side of hers, his big body in a sprawl that wasn't the least bit careless. "You always look hot."

The blunt comment got her right in the gut. Because he said it as if it was an unquestionable truth, as if the fact she'd been labeled "plus-size" by the media when they were being nice and "fat" when they weren't was a load of bullshit. As if she was gorgeous and sexy. She knew he meant it—because no matter how awful he'd become under the influence of drugs, he'd *never*, not once, made her feel bad about her body.

It was the one thing he'd always and enthusiastically loved about her.

"Thank you," she said, then smiled. "And you are seriously ripped. Like a model off the cover of that health magazine."

Eyes gleaming in masculine pleasure, he nodded at her chocolate bowl. "Not going to take a bite?" It was a dare.

# Chapter 20

NARROWING HER EYES, SHE PICKED up the empty bowl and flicked out her tongue to lick the edge. The rich, decadent taste of the mousse mingled with that of the creamy milk chocolate used to create the bowl. She couldn't control her shudder.

"Fuck!" Shoving back his chair, Abe rose and stalked to the edge of the tiny roof.

When she made a move to join him, her face flushed and in need of the wind she could see ruffling his shirt, he half turned and pointed a finger at her. "You. Stay. There." It was a growl.

Sarah stayed. Not because she was scared but because she wasn't sure she'd be able to keep hold of her senses or her clothes if she got near Abe when he was looking at her like *that*. Glaring at her until it was clear she'd obey, Abe turned back to stare out into the darkness. His wide shoulders rose and fell multiple times, as if he was taking deep breath after deep breath, but when he shifted on his heel to return to the table, she saw his body remained out of control.

"Quiet." He slammed back into his chair with that command, pulling it under the table enough that he could use the tablecloth to cover his lap.

Sarah felt a smile try to form, attempted to bite it back, but it just wouldn't die. The fight to withhold her mirth erupted into a small snort, and when Abe glared at her again, the snort turned into giggles. Giving in, she laughed harder than she'd laughed in an entire year, delighted with this night, with the rock star across from her, with the way the sensual memory of chocolate lingered on her tongue, with the entire world.

ABE HAD *NEVER* BEEN SO sexually frustrated. Sarah had always had a way of riling him up, but before, when they'd been together, he'd made her pay for her teasing—to both their pleasure. Often she'd teased him for exactly that reason. And he'd let her, having convinced himself their physical chemistry didn't mean anything, that it was just sex.

Yeah, which was why he'd never once cheated on her, no matter how many groupies threw themselves at him.

It had never been just sex, not with Sarah.

But watching her laugh, even if it was at his expense... it was better than sex. He hadn't seen his wife laugh for the longest time. Perhaps since halfway through their marriage. He'd forgotten how goddamn beautiful she was when she laughed, open and luminous and with zero fear of the world.

Sarah was magnificent always, but she was a goddess when she laughed.

Wiping her thumbs under her eyes to sweep away the tears that had fallen during the laughter, her cheeks still creased in a deep smile, she said, "Drink your tea."

He looked askance at the cup he'd ignored. Fine condensation had begun to bead on the sides, so it wasn't hot tea. "Why are there leaves floating in it?"

"Fresh mint. It's delicious."

Abe wasn't sold, but decided he might as well try to develop an enjoyment of other drinks since alcohol wasn't ever going to be on the menu and Florentina Chastain would probably be mortally offended if he asked for coffee. He drank. "It tastes like toothpaste."

"It does not!"

He drank some more, found the toothpaste-flavored ice water kind of grew on him. "Okay," he admitted. "I might drink that again." He almost told her to remember what it was called so he could order it again one day, as if she'd always be by his side.

Quick, confident steps sounded before the words could spill out, Florentina Chastain herself walking up to clear away their plates. She gave him a haughty look straight down the bridge of her aquiline nose. "You don't like mousse?"

Abe had a feeling that if he didn't answer right, he'd never again get a table here—and Sarah liked this place. "It's her fault." He pointed at the culprit. "She ate her mousse in front of me. Slowly. Very, very slowly."

Sarah's mouth fell open. "*Abe!*" Scrunching up her napkin, she threw it at his head.

Florentina's icy demeanor thawed as he caught the soft missile, an unexpected sparkle in her gaze. "Ah, then my chocolate has done its job, no?" Sweeping away the plates, she walked off, her heels making small tip-tap sounds on the roof.

"I can't believe you said that." Sarah pinned him with a scowl.

"At least she'll allow you to eat her desserts again."

Sarah went to speak, paused. "Hmm. Yes, you're right." She took a final sip from her cup before their usual server arrived to deliver their new tea and remove the old cups.

Florentina returned after the quiet, efficient male, this time with a pot of some creamy thing that she put in the center of the table. She then placed small platters of beautifully sliced and arranged fruit in front of them, including some exotic things Abe didn't immediately recognize. "Enjoy." A glance at Abe. "Perhaps you should eat slowly in front of her this time?"

With that wicked suggestion, she walked off to disappear down the stairs.

Abe looked at the tiny fork Florentina had left by his plate, then at his hand.

Yeah, no.

Using his fingers to pick up a slice of what might've been white peach, he dipped it in the sauce thing and threw the whole piece into his mouth, chewing and swallowing quickly. It was pretty good. The fruits weren't raw as he'd initially thought—they'd been cooked very slightly and coated with some spices that felt good on the tongue. He ate another piece, all the while deliberately *not* looking at Sarah. Until he realized she hadn't reached for a single piece of fruit.

Frowning, he threw the second half of an orange slice into his mouth. "You don't want to try?"

Cheeks flushed and eyes glittering, she ducked her head. But it was too late; he'd seen what she was trying to hide. His entire body heated up, his smile slow and dangerous. He hadn't been trying to tease her—he didn't know how, not unless he had his hands on her. Clearly, however, he'd managed to do so by accident.

Why not capitalize on his success?

Taking a piece of apple, he dipped it in the sauce, then lifted it to the lush curves of her lips. He fucking loved Sarah's lips. Back when she'd liked him, the things she'd done to him with that mouth... mercy. "Here."

Her gaze lifted to hold his as her lips parted. She bit down on the first third, chewed. He waited, fed her the second bite... then the last. When her lips brushed his fingers on that final bite, he had to force himself to drop his hand. His damn cock might burst otherwise. His balls were already beyond all hope.

Then Sarah smiled again and he realized it was worth it.

Why in hell had he let this woman go? Talk about a lesson on the evils of alcohol and drugs. But of course it hadn't only been the booze and the drugs. He'd been an asshole to her in his angry grief, but grief didn't excuse how he'd acted. Nothing excused it.

Sarah wasn't ugly in her own grief.

And that grief lived in her every second of every day, regardless of if she laughed; he understood that. He'd witnessed his mother's devastation at Tessie's death—he had some idea of what it did to a woman to lose her child. His father, too, had never recovered. Gregory Bellamy hadn't been like Jeremy Vance, hadn't just been able to forget his daughter and move on. He'd mourned her every day till he died.

Abe's heart ached at the memory of the man who'd been his example of manhood, who'd taught him about honor and keeping your word and how to treat a woman. He'd have been so disappointed at Abe's behavior toward Sarah—but Abe vowed to his father that he'd do better. This time around, he'd do it right.

He couldn't control fate, couldn't control what would happen during the pregnancy, but he could control his own actions: he'd make damn certain that Sarah was happy in every way he could make her. It wasn't atonement, wasn't redemption.

It was hope… and need… and love.

That last terrified him. Because there was a very big chance that he'd permanently snuffed out any possibility of getting Sarah to love him back. She'd *given* him that priceless gift once, and he'd thrown it back into her face. Abe wouldn't blame her if she never trusted him again.

SARAH SAT IN THE PASSENGER seat of Abe's SUV, replete and content and with her skin tingling in that anticipatory way that said bone-melting pleasure hovered on the horizon. Sarah looked out the window at the slumbering lights of Los Angeles, swallowed. She and Abe, the sex had always been good. Phenomenal. That had never been their problem. And now…

Her hand opened over her abdomen.

"You good?"

She started, not having realized he was paying attention to her actions, he'd been so focused on driving. "Yes. I just suddenly remembered I'm pregnant." Of course it was always there, the knowledge, but sometimes it faded into the background, and other times it burst right into the very front of her consciousness and took away her breath.

Abe nodded, his eyes on the road. "I wonder if it'll be a boy or a girl." A grin. "Can we fight over the names?"

*Who was this wonderful man so excited about the journey they were to share?*

She wanted him desperately.

Inhaling deep, then exhaling in a quiet release, she made herself look forward instead of at Abe. She had to be careful, so careful. Fear gripped her heart at the idea of falling for him again only to be rejected, to be left behind.

No, she couldn't permit that to happen. Their relationship had to remain stable and friendly for the baby's sake. Nothing more, nothing less. It didn't matter how fiercely she was attracted to the man Abe had become. "We'll definitely be fighting if you want a weird Hollywood-child name," she said, trying to keep her tone light.

"Nope. I like girly names for girls and manly names for boys. Traditional as they come."

She rolled her eyes, her lips twitching. "If we have a son, I'm buying him dolls as well as trucks, same for if we have a girl."

"Fine with me. As long as their names are girly for a girl or manly for a boy."

"We'll see." Sarah was just messing with him. The truth was that she liked the more traditional names too... and it was so strange to be having this discussion with Abe, with the man she'd never thought would come back into her life. Now, if nothing went wrong with the pregnancy, he'd be part of her life forever.

ABE BROUGHT THE SUV TO a stop in front of Sarah's gate, waited until she used the remote she had on her keychain to open it, then drove in. When she pressed the remote a second time to keep the gate from closing behind his SUV, disappointment was a cold, hard lump of stone in his stomach.

"Thank you for dessert." She unclipped her seat belt.

"Hold on." His seat belt already undone, he pushed open his door and jogged around to her side to grab her waist and help her down. His SUV had to be a bit of a monster to comfortably fit his big body; it had a step you had to stand on to climb up and down. Abe didn't need it, but Sarah did, and he didn't want her to trip.

*That's a load of bullshit, Abe.*

Sarah could handle his SUV. The truth was he hadn't wanted to let her exit the vehicle and leave him, the night over. And he'd wanted to put his hands on her, hold her close. "There," he managed to say, his hands lingering on her waist.

"Thanks." Sarah slipped the strap of her purse over her shoulder and made a small motion as if trying to step back.

Abe forced his fingers to open. "I'll wait until you're inside."

She gave him a faint smile, an unspoken tension between them that hadn't been present over the past couple of hours as they'd teased and played with one another. Something had happened on the drive home; he had no idea what. "You'll call me? If you need anything? Otherwise I'll be here to take you to the doctor at ten."

Sarah separated out her house key from the other things on the fuzzy yellow ball of her keychain. "You really want to come to all the appointments?"

"Yeah, unless it's something female where you don't want me there."

Laughing, the incredible woman who'd been his wife shook her head. "It's all female, Abe." She patted her belly. "I'll call you. If you can't come—"

"I'll be there." No matter what.

# CHAPTER 21

ABE MADE SURE HE WAS on time for Sarah's return appointment with Dr. Snyder. Mostly the doctor just took Sarah's vitals, ordered a few more blood tests to check she was healthy in terms of iron and other nutrients, then told her he'd call through a prescription for anything she needed once he had the results.

Abe had intended to pick her up, but she'd messaged for him to meet her at the doctor's office. Appointment over, they stood in the underground parking area under the building, protected from the scorching heat of the LA sun. "You working today?" he asked, taking in the tailored navy-blue dress that screamed professional to him.

A nod. "One of my employees is retiring, so I need to find a replacement. It's all interviews back-to-back." She glanced at her watch. "First one's in forty-five minutes."

There was so much of Sarah's life he'd missed out on, so much he didn't know about this woman she'd become. "I guess you'd better head out in case you get delayed in traffic," he said, even though he wanted to talk to her.

"Yes, it gets this hot and someone always loses it." Sarah gave him an awkward smile as she slid into the driver's seat, as if she couldn't believe they'd been reduced to talking about LA traffic. It was a favorite topic of locals, but they'd been too much to each other for it to come to this.

Abe gripped the door before she could close it. "You free this coming Saturday?" His heart pounded like that of a teenage boy asking a girl out for the first time.

When Sarah said, "Yes, I think so," he told himself not to celebrate prematurely.

Slipping on her sunglasses, she put her purse on the passenger seat. "Why?"

He curled his fingers over the red metal of her car door, the edge solid under his palm. "I have tickets to the symphony."

"The symphony?" A smile that felt far more real, far more his Sarah. "Let me guess. No one else will go with you?"

He scowled. "Philistines." In actuality, he hadn't ever asked anyone else. He usually liked to go alone, lose himself in the music so different from that which he made but that spoke to him on the same visceral level.

"In the interest of full disclosure," he said, "they're not the best seats and it's a matinee performance—I didn't want to be front and center at the fancy night session." True, except this time around, he'd bought *two* tickets, and when he'd chosen the seats, he'd placed Sarah's aversion to media interest over his own liking for the front seats where he could stretch out his legs.

Abe couldn't *not* be a big guy who attracted attention, but the symphony audience was different to Schoolboy Choir's audience. And even if there were rock fans in the crowd, most people didn't expect to see the keyboard player of a hard rock band at the symphony. Especially one wearing a button-down shirt and clean, dark blue jeans. And because they didn't expect it, they didn't make the connection.

Sarah placed her hands on the steering wheel, closed her fingers over it slowly as if she was thinking. His heart boomed a bass counterpoint to his breathing, his blood a roar in his ears.

"I'd like to go."

The words were an exhilarating punch to the gut. "Great. I'll pick you up around one thirty."

"See you then."

Abe shut her car door with a smile.

His wife was letting him take her out on a date. He could work with that.


THE REST OF THE WEEK dragged for Sarah until at last it was Saturday.

She didn't know why she'd said yes when she'd instructed herself to stay friendly but distant with Abe. Then he'd asked her and he'd looked so... wary, as if he expected her to turn him down flat, and her mouth had opened and she'd heard herself agreeing to go with him.

"Sure, Sarah." She glared at herself in the mirror as she put on her earrings. "You're doing this out of the kindness of your heart, not because you have a dangerous weakness for a certain rock star."

The glare didn't help; bubbles of excitement still popped in her blood at the thought of seeing Abe again.

She knew she was in trouble. Bad trouble.

Which probably explained why she still hadn't 'fessed up to Lola about the fact that Abe was once more in her life. "Soon," she promised Flossie. "I'll tell her soon."

Her dog didn't look like she believed Sarah.

Having Internet researched what people wore to early performances of the symphony, she'd chosen a simple black dress and paired it with a fine string of pearls. Those pearls were real, given to her as a wedding gift by Abe's mother. Diane Bellamy had placed them around her neck before the reception, kissed her on the cheek with what felt like real maternal warmth, and said, "Welcome to the family."

Sarah should've handed them back during the divorce, but she hadn't. It wasn't because of their value, but... "Because a mother gave them to me," she whispered to her reflection.

Sometimes, when things got really bad in their marriage and she was so lonely, she'd pretended Diane was her mom as well. In real life, however, she'd never dared make such a claim. It wasn't that Abe's mother hadn't been kind to her, but Sarah had always felt as if Diane didn't think Sarah was good enough for Abe.

*Or maybe those were your own insecurities messing you up, hmm?*

It was Lola's acerbic voice, a memory of one of the many conversations she and her best friend had had over the time they'd known one another. That particular conversation had happened while Sarah was cleaning a Bel Air mansion not long after she'd gone out as a one-woman-operator; alone in the house but for a slinky black cat with a diamond collar who'd purred up a storm when she petted it, she'd called her best friend, and they'd spoken while Sarah dusted and wiped.

Six months later, Sarah had walked into that same mansion on Jeremy's arm. No one but the cat had recognized her, though she'd cleaned that mansion for five months before she hired her first employee and handed off the house. People didn't ever really look at their cleaners for the most part, and dressed-to-the-nines and elegantly made-up Sarah, her hair slick straight, appeared a different woman from dressed-down Sarah with her curls pulled neatly back.

Lola had once asked her if she felt more herself without the trappings of sophistication.

Sarah's response had been immediate. "No. All those things—the nice clothes, the makeup, the ability to hold a cultured conversation—I learned them, *earned* them." Glossy Sarah wasn't a mask she put on; it was simply the look that helped her navigate certain situations in this life she'd clawed out for herself.

Could she have done it without Abe's money?

*No.*

Sarah had never lied to herself about that. The divorce settlement had been relatively conservative because of the short length of their marriage—and Abe's own Rottweiler of a lawyer—but it had been more than enough to give her what she needed to set up a new life.

Abe had also given her something even more dear to her: his name.

It had infuriated Jeremy that she hadn't reverted to her maiden name of Smith, but that name held only horrors for Sarah, far worse than the most painful memories from her marriage. She hadn't even cared when, right after the divorce, certain snarky columnists had called her a "first wife" who wanted to cling to the fame of her ex-husband.

Sarah paid her good fortune forward every single month, writing out checks to charities that supported and tried to offer help to teens on the streets. She'd been one of those lost children not that long ago, knew that sometimes a teenager had a home so unsafe the street was the better option.

*Flames. Fear. Grief.*

Those were her last memories of her childhood home.

"That's in the past," she whispered aloud. "No one will ever link Sarah Bellamy with the unwanted girl born in a one-bedroom shack in Miami, or with the teenager who became the star witness in a murder trial." She was gone forever, that fifteen-year-old girl with her skinny face and bruised arms and legs, her hair cut tight to her skull.

The people who'd known her then would never recognize her in Sarah.

And this strong, successful woman she'd become, she had a date to attend the symphony.

"I'VE NEVER BEEN TO THE symphony before," she confessed to Abe after they took their seats.

"Yeah?" A pleased smile as they waited for everyone to finish filing in. "It's fucking amazing."

Sarah bit back a smile as the blue-haired matron in front of them turned to give Abe an admonishing look. "Really, young man. Language."

"Sorry, ma'am," Abe said with a rueful smile. "Got a little too excited."

As Sarah had mentally predicted, the matron melted. Smiling her forgiveness, she returned her attention to her partner, an elderly man in a dapper brown suit and spotted bowtie.

"Charmer," she whispered under her breath to Abe.

"Nana Bellamy would call it good solid manners."

Cheeks creasing at his choirboy response, she said, "Do you ever think about giving up the band to join an orchestra?" He was a gifted classical pianist who'd been offered placements at prestigious music academies right out of high school.

"Nah." Abe played with the program for today's concert. "I love listening to it, but this isn't the kind of music I want to make—and those people would never be my family."

*Not like Fox, Noah, and David.*

Sarah glanced away, reacting as she'd always done to mentions of the band, her jealousy a bitter creature inside her. She turned back the instant she realized what she was doing.

She wouldn't make the same mistake twice, not after the way the band members, as well as Kit, Thea, and Molly, had closed ranks around her after the nightmare with Jeremy. Not after Molly had invited Sarah into her home and her wedding. Not after all three women had extended the hand of true friendship.

Abe was right—his bandmates had never been the problem.

"Noah and Kit," she said under the cover of rustling and mumbled conversation as people settled down. "I always knew they had chemistry, but I could've never predicted their relationship." It was obvious the couple was madly in love, however. Any idiot could see they were a unit, two halves of a whole.

Stretching out his arm behind her seat, Abe leaned down to speak against her ear. "Kit's good for Noah, really good. And he's nuts for her."

Sarah was having trouble thinking with Abe so close, his warmth enticing and his mouth almost touching her skin. "At Zenith, they did that thing with the eyes," she finally managed to say.

Abe's fingers brushed her shoulder. "What thing?"

Butterflies in her stomach, her skin hot, the bad, bad trouble becoming ever more dangerous. "You know, when couples don't speak but they're communicating with their eyes."

"Huh."

The lights dimmed on Abe's bemused response, the haunting song of a single violin filling the void until that void *was* music and there was no more darkness.

The concert was unlike anything Sarah had ever before experienced, the soaring highs making her feel as if she were flying while the somber notes brought tears to her eyes. She was on her feet with the rest of the audience come the end of the concert, clapping enthusiastically and calling for an encore.

They got one.

"That was so wonderful," she whispered in the aftermath.

Abe, his hand firmly clamped around hers as they stood to exit the concert hall, passed her his program to hold. "Not their best performance, but damn good."

"Not their best?" Sarah's mouth fell open. "How much better can they get?"

"You'll have to keep being my plus one if you want to find out." He maneuvered them through the crowd milling around in the large atrium outside the performance chamber.

Sarah didn't consciously realize he was still holding her hand until they were in the elevator to the parking garage, and then she didn't want him to let go. Just like she hadn't been able to stop herself from saying yes when he asked her out. Fear licked over her heart, quelling the breathless joy she'd found in the music.

Abe had hurt her *so much.*

"You want to stop for a snack?" Abe asked after they were in the SUV.

And the words just spilled out. "Let's go to bed." It was only chemistry, nothing more. She'd surrender to it, let it burn out. And see what was left.

# CHAPTER 22

ABE WAS FUCKING GLAD HE hadn't started driving, or he'd have plowed into something right then. "*Sarah.*"

"You heard what I said." Tone firm, she stared straight through the windshield, but her breathing gave her away, shallow and a little too fast.

His eyes dipped to her breasts, those magnificent breasts he'd always loved. They seemed to swell in front of his eyes. "Are your breasts already more sensitive?" he asked before he could stop himself.

"A little." Her response was husky. "It's just the start."

Cock rigid, Abe nonetheless wanted to quiz her about her sudden invitation. *Don't be an idiot.* It was a ringing slap from the part of him that knew the physical stuff between them had never been just sex… no matter what Sarah might believe.

After driving to her place, he parked inside her garage beside her little red car.

He'd have hauled her into a kiss the instant they walked into the house, but he wasn't in charge today; this was Sarah's show. She greeted an excited Flossie and made sure the dog was happy to play outside before she led him to the

196

bedroom, kicked off her heels, then placed her purse neatly on the vanity.

Sarah always had a purse with her, and it always had some cash in it along with a credit card and her phone. He remembered how they'd once gone to a party to celebrate a close friend's birthday, and in the rush to leave, she'd forgotten her purse at home. She'd remembered halfway to their destination, asked him to go back; he'd tried but it had proved impossible in the traffic.

That was the day he'd realized how badly Sarah needed the security blanket of her purse. She'd been near tears by the time they arrived at the party, had only seemed to breathe again after he gave her his wallet and phone, told her to look after them both. That was one time he hadn't been an asshole to her. He'd kept her tucked close to his side all night, taken her home as soon as he could without it being an insult to their hosts.

And he'd started to understand that Sarah didn't just need a little cash at hand—usually all it was was a fifty. She needed a phone too. Where Sarah went, so did her phone and enough cash to get her home. The purses were vehicles for those two things, but they also just made her happy, as beautiful musical instruments made him.

"You still hoarding purses?" Having kicked off his own shoes and socks, he sprawled on the bed with his legs stretched out, body braced on his elbows.

A sheepish look from the only woman who'd ever gotten to the heart of him. "I can't help myself," she admitted as she removed the pearl necklace he recognized from their wedding.

She'd been a magnificent bride, statuesque and with an innate sense of presence he didn't think she'd ever realized about herself. He remembered how she'd glowed—and he remembered what they'd done to each other in bed that night, her body arching under his caressing hand and her arms holding him possessively close.

"Yeah?" His voice was rough. "How many in your collection now?"

That was another thing he hadn't been an asshole about: he'd bought her as many purses as she wanted, had often come home from tour with three or four that he'd picked up along the way. It would've been better had he taken her with him so she could choose her own favorites, but that was done. Abe wouldn't excuse his behavior or forgive himself for it, but he intended to do better now.

Sarah looked so guilty right then that he chuckled, his chest going all tight. "I bet if I hunt around this house, I'll find a dedicated purse room."

"No comment." A sudden, dazzling smile that caught him right in the solar plexus. "Don't tease me. You were such an enabler."

He grinned past the emotions crashing through him… and Sarah reached back to undo her zipper. "Let me." He wanted to adore her, seduce her, addict her.

She hesitated for a taut second before dropping her hands.

He rose to go stand at her back, then kissed the bare skin of her exposed nape, her hair up in a sleek knot.

Sarah shivered. Her skin was warm and toned and flawless under his lips, her curves just made for his big hands. Quickly unzipping and pushing off her dress because he loved Sarah naked, he let her step out of the dress, then unhooked the black lace of her bra.

It joined the dress on the floor.

Out of patience, he cupped the heavy weight of her breasts from behind, rubbing his thumbs over the swollen nipples that had always been sensitive. When she cried out, he petted her breasts, whispered, "I'll be careful." It was a sensual promise. "Treat you so well, Sarah." A kiss to her throat, her body melting back into his.

His cock pulsed.

Shuddering, he moved his hands from her breasts and down her body. Splaying the fingers of one hand over her abdomen, he slid his other one into the lace and satin of her panties. One arm rising to hook around the back of his neck, Sarah rasped his name. It was as if she'd clasped his cock in those long, capable fingers of hers, squeezed.

"I've got you," he said, kissing his way up her throat as he stroked his fingers through her lush folds.

She was liquid with need for him.

He felt like a fucking god.

Tugging on the plump bud of her clit, he wasn't prepared for her to pull away his hand and spin around to face him. He'd opened his mouth to ask if he'd touched her too roughly when she went to work on his shirt buttons.

*Oh.*

More than willing to be stripped by Sarah, he stood in place and let her undo his shirt, push it off. She pressed kisses across his chest, his shoulders. He loved that she was tall enough to do that, that they fit together like they were two halves of a whole.

Moving one hand to her ass, he cupped a cheek, stroked.

Her breasts rising and falling in a rapid, harsh rhythm, she dropped her hands to his belt buckle. He was wearing his favorite old belt—it was simple black leather but had a slightly tricky clasp… which gave Sarah no trouble at all. And he remembered this was his wife in his arms.

*Ex*-wife, the civilized part of his brain reminded him for the umpteenth time.

Fuck that, Abe muttered silently. Sarah was his and he intended to put his ring back on her finger. He had no intention of repeating his stupidity in letting her go. Not this time. Gripping her chin as she was undoing the button on his jeans, he dropped his head and kissed her long and slow and deep, his other hand thrusting into her hair to unravel it.

He licked his tongue over hers, drank her in.

Sarah moaned in the back of her throat but pulled away. "I want you naked."

He smiled even as his cock jumped. "So you do know how to talk dirty." Fisting his hand in her hair as she ducked her head, her skin no doubt hot with a blush but her fingers busy, he tensed his abdomen in an effort not to bring things to a premature end.

It was hard. Not only was she touching him, she was nearly naked. The position of her arms pushed together her breasts, creating a deliciously deep cleavage that put all kinds of sinful ideas in his head. "You're killing me, sweetheart."

"You're the one with your fingers brushing my…"

"Brushing your what?" Abe teased her with those fingers, caressing her through the gusset of her panties. "Did you mean to say your pussy?"

Shivering—and proving she was still delightfully susceptible to a bit of dirty talk from him—Sarah pushed down his jeans and underwear at the same time. She closed her fingers around his cock before he could step out of the clothes.

"Jesus, Sarah, I—" He lost his mind and his words as Sarah went down on her knees in front of him.

Flicking her eyes up to meet his gaze, she took his cock into her mouth.

Abe's grunt of pleasure had her lashes lowering as she sank into her self-imposed task. He realized he was tugging too hard on her hair, tried to get himself to relax, but *oh, sweet fuck*— The sight of his wife with her lips stretched around his cock, the feel of her tongue pressing up against his length, the heated wet, her nails digging into the backs of his thighs as she gripped him with open possessiveness.

Abe barely managed to give Sarah a warning that he was about to come.

She pulled away her mouth but then gave him that sultry smile of hers he only ever saw in bed, and cupped her breasts in sensual invitation. Abe lost it. Gripping his cock as his balls drew up impossibly tight, he came all over his wife's full breasts.

Legs shaky afterward, he somehow untangled himself from his clothes, then tugged Sarah to her feet. "That was hot." He kissed her, one hand gripping the back of her head as he thrust his tongue into her mouth.

Her throaty moan was all the encouragement he needed.

Shoving down her panties to partway down her thighs, he touched her between her legs, felt how swollen she was, how wet. Her body clamped down on the single finger he slid inside her. Brain hazing, he withdrew the finger and said, "Hold that thought."

First he stripped off her panties, then he tugged her into the bathroom.

Using a wet facecloth to wipe her breasts clean after lifting her up onto the counter, he kissed her again and again. She didn't resist, hooking one of her legs around his hip, her arms locked around his neck. He'd come blindingly hard just before, but he'd been wanting Sarah forever. He knew he'd be ready again soon. He decided to spend the time driving his wife crazy.

Petting her thigh, he flicked out his tongue to tease one nipple, then the other before getting serious and sucking one to luscious wetness. At the same time, he ran one finger along the seam of her sex, putting just enough pressure on her clit to make her tremble.

"*Abe.*"

He released her nipple after one last flick of his tongue and inserted a finger inside her slick sheath. "What do you need, sweetheart?"

A clenching of her inner muscles, her lips shaping a single word. "You."

Groaning, he managed to wedge in another finger. "You can take a third, can't you, Sarah?" His fingers were thick, but his cock was thicker.

Bracing her hands behind her on the counter, Sarah arched into his fingers in a silent answer. He pressed the pad of his thumb against her clit as he began to push a third finger inside. The pressure was exactly what Sarah needed. Screaming, she held on to his wrist with one hand as her body spasmed around him, those hidden feminine muscles promising his cock so much pleasure that it came back to life in a rock-hard surge.

Pulling out his fingers—and inciting a cry of pure feminine

outrage that made him grin—Abe spread her thighs wide and, pulling her forward, thrust deep inside her in a single motion while she was still in the throes of orgasm. Her nails dug into his shoulders as her head fell back, his name falling from her lips over and over.

"You feel too damn good," he groaned. "But don't worry. I've got plenty of stamina thanks to your sexy mouth."

"Oh God, *Abe.*"

He rode her through the last shudders of her first orgasm, then got to work on heating her up for a second. And a third. She was boneless when he finally came inside her, when he marked her in the most intimate way possible.

Holding her cuddled up against him, their bodies yet one, he hoped she knew he was loving her.

SARAH LAY IN BED AFTERWARD, her mind hazy and her breath still short.

Abe had always done this to her, turned her into a mass of trembling flesh that was all nerves and sensation and need. But he'd satisfied her too. As he had tonight. Even when everything else had gone wrong between them, the sex had been phenomenal.

During their marriage, she used to call it "making love"—at least in her own head. Her stupid mushy heart had liked the sound of it… but she had to be honest now. They weren't making love now, hadn't been making love then. No… she had been.

Because she'd loved Abe in a way he had never loved her.

*Careful, Sarah. Don't you fall again. Don't you let yourself be broken when you've barely put yourself back together.*

"Only until the baby comes," she said on a driving wave of fear and primal protectiveness.

Abe leaned up on his elbow to look down at her, all gleaming brown skin and taut muscle. "What?" He ran his free hand over her abdomen and hip.

She shivered, held on to her thoughts through sheer strength of will. "This," she whispered, looking away from him because facing a sexually sated Abe and having rational thoughts were mutually exclusive events for her. "Us."

His hand went motionless on her skin. "I thought you said I could have a role in our kid's life if I proved myself and my sobriety?"

She turned onto her side so she was facing him—and he was scowling now, so she could hold an actual conversation instead of being led around by her hormones. "Of course you're going to be a father to our child," she said at once. "I want that more than anything." Memories crashed into her without warning. "You *have* to stay clean though, Abe. I can't handle all that again—and our child shouldn't have to."

His jaw muscles tensed, as did his shoulders, but he didn't get angry. "Yeah," he said, "I get that. I won't fuck up our kid's head by getting shitfaced."

"That's what I meant about us too." She took a deep breath, and his scent, it was like a drug through her system. "It'll confuse our child if he or she finds us in bed together, or if they figure out we're having sex."

Raising his hand, Abe brushed her hair off her face, a passionate intensity to his gaze that held her captive. "Only if we aren't together in reality by then."

Her heart slammed against her rib cage, hope spiraling upward in a golden burst. It was tough, so damn tough not to jump into the arms of that hope. "We self-destructed, Abe," she whispered. "No matter how hard I tried, I couldn't get through to you about—"

"I had to be ready first." Abe's voice was rough, brutally honest. "You couldn't help a man who didn't want to be helped."

"It wasn't just that." Then she said it, said the most hurtful thing. "You didn't love me."

Abe's face closed off. She'd seen that a hundred times before, should've become used to it. But it still hurt just as badly as the first time he'd shut her out. "There you go," she said through a throat gone raw. "Leaving me behind while we're naked in the same bed. I never felt as lonely as when you did that."

# Chapter 23

SARAH'S SOFT WORDS HIT ABE hard, drawing blood. He knew that hadn't been her intent. Sarah had always had a heart of pure mush. "I'm sorry," he began, because it was time to stop being a coward, to man up and admit his terror.

"It's all right, Abe." A sad smile, her fingers brushing his lips. "You can't force love. I don't expect it, wasn't trying to guilt you into a false confession."

No, he would not let this bullshit stand. "That man you knew during most of our marriage?" he said, tugging away her hand and pressing it against his heart. "He wasn't Abe. Or he was a fucked-up version of me." The music had survived his addiction, but the drugs had damaged everything else. "But I was stone-cold sober the night I met you and I'm stone-cold sober now—and no woman, *no woman*, does to me what you do. I fucking *love* you. Always have, always will."

Sarah's throat moved as she swallowed, the thickness of her lashes coming down over the dark of her eyes for a long, still moment. "The physical connection isn't enough," she said, and he knew she didn't believe him.

His world threatened to shatter.

But then he realized: words were easy. It was the doing that was hard.

He'd have to *do*. He'd have to love her until she had no choice but to trust in his love.

Cupping the side of her face, he slit open his veins. "I'm a coward, Sarah. So scared of losing you like I lost Tessie, so *terrified* of having my heart torn out of my chest that I tried to push you away, deny my love." Abe felt as if he was fighting for his life. "But you're it for me, Sarah. The only woman I will ever love."

He and Noah, they'd had a conversation about love not long ago where he'd told Noah something his mom had asked him before his and Sarah's wedding: *Was Sarah a woman he'd have run off with if given the chance?* When Noah repeated Abe's mother's question, Abe had hesitated, said he wasn't sure.

What a load of fucking horseshit.

All it would take was the slightest encouragement and he'd have her in front of a justice of the peace so fast she wouldn't even have time to get a wedding dress.

But Sarah didn't speak. Her hand lay unmoving on him, her expression still, but there was nothing to say she believed his declaration. Abe didn't panic; he'd known this wouldn't be easy. He'd hurt her brutally in his self-protective terror, savaged that soft heart. He had to earn back her trust, earn the right to fight for her love.

"Give me till the baby comes," he bargained. "If you don't think we'll make it at that point, I'll agree to whatever you want. We'll be friends, co-parent, nothing more."

Sarah's fingers curled against his chest. "I don't know if I can," she said at last, the words falling like rocks on his hopes.

"I was *so* alone, Abe. I waited for you to call me after that night, to come for me. You never did. You left me all alone."

He heard the tears she was trying not to shed. They eviscerated him. "I've got no excuse for that." Sarah had no family in the city, no one to whom she could've turned. "I didn't do it on purpose, that much I can say."

Dark eyes met his, stark knowledge in their depths. "Did you take drugs after I left that night?"

"I took a bunch before we ever spoke."

Her pupils dilated. "What? You weren't sober when we fought?"

Abe could've taken advantage of that fact to play Sarah's soft heart, but he wasn't that guy, wouldn't ever use her. "Doesn't excuse what I did," he said flatly. "And yes, I took more after you left, a shitload of them. And I kept doing it for weeks, chasing it down with the hardest liquor I could find."

"The others—"

"—were all out of town."

She lifted a hand to her mouth, horror a bleak shadow across her beauty. "You were alone that entire time? You could've—"

"Killed myself?" Abe nodded. "Yeah, I know." Another ugly truth he'd had to accept, stop hiding from. "Noah's the one who eventually found me. I was messed up and fucked up." No way to pretty that up. "He called the others, waited until I passed out at a club, then they hauled me into rehab."

"I'm glad." Relief sent a tremor through her. "But the fact you didn't think to call me once you came out of the drug haze... it proves my point."

"No, it doesn't." Muscles bunching, Abe sat up with his elbows braced on his knees, the sheet pooling around his waist.

He rubbed his face with his hands, felt the harsh stubble already forming on his skin though he'd shaved before picking up Sarah. Then he admitted the worst of it. "I was angry at you," he said, one hand gripping the wrist of the other. "Out of it or sober, I woke up thinking about you, *only* you, every single day, and I was *so* goddamn angry with you."

He heard the rustle of sheets as Sarah sat up beside him. "Because I touched the piano?"

"Because you made me *feel.*" He squeezed his wrist hard enough to cut off the blood flow. "Before you, I could self-medicate with drugs, numb myself to the extent that nothing mattered and I could forget that I'd buried my baby sister when she was only eight. A baby sister who looked to me as her hero—but I could do nothing when the cancer began to eat at her. *Nothing.*" His demons howled, dark and twisted inside him, and suddenly all he wanted was the numb nothingness of drugs, the false ecstasy that shut out the agony of brutal reality.

Shoving off the sheets, he got out of bed and pulled on his boxer briefs. Then he dropped to the floor and began to do push-ups, making sure to keep his form viciously straight. If Sarah thought him mad, she didn't say so, remaining silent as he fought the clawing darkness that wanted to haul him back into the abyss.

Abe wasn't about to go. Never again.

He spoke on an upward push. "But no matter how many drugs I took," he said, "as soon as you walked into a room or even if I suddenly thought of you—and I thought of you a hell of a lot, especially when we were apart—my heart would wake up, start to beat your name, and part of me hated you for it. For having the power to call me back, to keep me from drowning in numbness." He went down, his nose almost to the carpet, pushed up again, repeated the movement, waited for Sarah to speak.

"I didn't know you felt anything for me." Her voice shook. "Even before you said what you did that night, deep inside I thought I was just a convenient sex partner. Forgotten as soon as I was out of your sight."

"Never that." He did three more push-ups before he had the emotional control to continue speaking. "I wanted you from the instant you told that silly knock-knock joke at the party where we met. You laughed so hard at your own joke and there was such joy in you... I wanted that for myself. I wanted you to look at me with that open delight."

SARAH STARED AT ABE'S MUSCLED body as he continued his punishingly strict movements, not a single part of his body out of alignment. "I didn't tell you the joke," she whispered, the events from that night unspooling in her mind like a film reel in full color.

She'd crashed the Beverly Hills party with a girlfriend she'd met at the minimum wage job she'd been working at the time, her earnings barely enough to cover her tiny room in a terrible part of town. Graffitied hallways redolent with the smell of alcohol and other noxious substances, gunfights in the street, screaming matches between couples and family members that came right through the paper-thin walls, that had been her reality.

It had still been safer than her childhood home.

However, determined to better herself and not scared of working hard, she'd kept putting on her cheap but neat "interview suit" and applying for jobs that paid a little more. That day she'd had one rejection too many—and the interviewer had leered so hard at her she'd had to go home and shower before her shift at work. The asshole had all but licked his lips as he spoke to her chest.

So when her work colleague said she had a contact who could get them into a fancy party, Sarah had said, "What the hell. At least they might have some nice finger food to eat—I can save a few bucks on groceries."

Sarah had dolled up in a little black dress, figuring most people wouldn't be able to tell at a glance that it was a knockoff of a knockoff—and black dresses fit in everywhere in LA. That much she'd learned in her time in the city.

Her colleague had been as good as her word; she'd gotten them into the party courtesy of a friend who was on the catering staff. But the other woman had disappeared with an older man not long into the party, leaving Sarah alone and feeling out of place and not sure how she'd get back home since her friend was the one with the car and they were outside the public transport area she knew well.

She'd decided to wait, see if the other girl came back.

Feeling stupid hiding in a corner, she'd made herself approach a group of people who didn't look too snotty, told them the silliest knock-knock joke. And when one of the women had laughed, she'd laughed too, so happy and relieved that she wasn't being rejected.

Abe hadn't been in that group.

"I know," Abe said, his muscles rigid as he held himself in position using only one arm, his other one folded over his back. "I was standing behind you at the time."

Sarah frowned; she hadn't met Abe until almost fifteen minutes later. They'd run into one another at the bar when she'd gone to get a glass of water after the group with which she'd interacted had all separated to see other people. Men had come on to her once they realized she'd been separated from the herd, invitations in their eyes, but Sarah had never been into meaningless sexual encounters. She'd always been looking for *her* man. For home.

Then Abe had asked her if he could buy her a drink sometime, and boom. "Did we meet by chance?" she asked, her heart thundering.

Abe did two more push-ups before angling his head to shoot her a heartbreaker grin. "Of course not. I stalked you."

That racing heart of hers, it turned all gooey inside her. Never, not *once* during their relationship, had Abe given any indication that he'd chosen her, wanted *her*. Part of her had always believed that it was pure luck she had the right to call this gorgeous rock star her husband, that she'd just had the right timing.

To know that he'd deliberately sought her out at a party filled with beautiful, sophisticated women... It changed the dynamic of their entire past.

Sarah tried to think past the rushing in her ears, the heat in her cheeks. "Why did you do that if you didn't want to feel?" It made no sense.

"Because I couldn't stay away from you, couldn't stop watching you from the instant I first caught sight of you." Abe finally stopped the push-ups and sat down on the carpet, his hands braced behind him and his body right there for her to ogle, the tiger tattoo prowling up the side of his rib cage making her want to trace the lines of it with a fingertip. "The idea of anyone else laying a finger on you infuriated me."

She just stared at him, her entire understanding of their past in pieces. "You never said anything."

"I married you." His eyes held hers, refusing to let her look away. "And I held on to you even when I knew I was screwing you up, messing with your head." He clenched his jaw, his abdominal muscles an iron-hard wall. "By the time I got clean, got over being angry with you, and came to haul you home, you were with that fucker Vance."

She heard the whip of anger, felt her own fury bristle to life. "I was in a bad place, Abe. My husband had abandoned me after all but calling me a gold-digging slut."

Abe flinched but Sarah carried on, so angry at him. That anger had been growing inside her since the day she first realized he wasn't coming for her. "I never intended to get into a relationship with Jeremy." Hadn't wanted to be in a relationship with anyone but Abe. "He just happened to come by the night I saw pictures of you painting the town red with half-naked groupies. You had your goddamn hand on a woman's ass, her tits almost falling into your face! What was I supposed to think?"

"Fuck." Abe didn't talk again until he'd completed ten more push-ups. "I don't remember most of that night." Another push-up. "I only saw the photos after rehab, after I had the poison out of my system."

Sarah's anger turned into the crushing pain of knowing she could've lost him forever during that binge. Then, because Abe had stripped away his own shields, she did the same with part of hers. "All my life, I figured my body was the only thing of value I had. I don't mean that in a mercenary way." She tried to find the right words. "I thought my body made people like me, so that's how I tried to form relationships."

Sometimes she wanted to go back to the naive, needy, romantic girl she'd been and just hug her, tell her she had far more to offer the world—and that the boys who took advantage of her desperate hunger to be loved weren't worth her emotions or her heartbreak.

"Even you only seemed to really like me during sex." She swallowed. "So when Jeremy came on to me while I was numb from seeing those tabloid shots, imagining you with those groupies in our bed, I thought, what did it matter? Even if you'd rejected the only thing I had to offer, at least he wanted it." She hugged her knees, unable to add the rest: that she'd already been vulnerable because of her screaming aloneness. The tabloid images had been the last straw.

Loneliness was her greatest fear.

She'd never told Abe why, never told anyone. Today she found herself wondering if she should... but keeping secrets tended to harden them to stone inside a person. Her chest ached with breathlessness, the pain an old one. She'd hidden her origins for so long, telling people as little as possible.

"One thing we have in common," she said. "I don't remember most of that night either." She'd gone away inside her head, woken to find a naked Jeremy asleep beside her.

Abe's jaw worked, his hand fisting on the carpet. "I got clean before coming to get you," he ground out. "And I shot up the day I realized you were with Vance."

She was the one who flinched this time.

"No, Sarah, I'm not blaming you." Abe rubbed his hands over his head. "Cocaine is my demon. Alcohol was my crutch. All I'm saying is that you meant enough to me to break me."

The declaration threatened to break *her*.

"Let me show you," Abe said in that voice that held nothing back, that stripped him bare. "Give me a chance to be the man you deserve."

Sarah was so scared. Not just for herself but for her baby. She didn't want to be a single mom, but she'd far rather be that than be with a man who didn't value her. Her mother had done that, allowed her "boyfriends" to beat her up, use her up, until one day one had gone too far. Sarah had repeated that pattern with Jeremy and with Abe.

Abe had never been violent, not physically, but the emotional wounds he'd inflicted still bled. Never again would she put herself in that position. She didn't want the nightmare that had scarred her to mark a third generation.

She looked at the tattooed and pierced rock star who'd once been her husband. In many ways, the man he'd become since their divorce was a stranger to her, one who'd taken her on a midnight dessert date and who looked at her with eyes filled with what she wanted to believe was love. What if it wasn't just a fleeting fantasy? What if Abe *had* changed? What if he did truly love her? What if he could be a wonderful father?

It was the last that swayed her most. Sarah wouldn't protect her heart at the cost of stealing her child's chance to have a father full time.

"All right." She trembled within, terror and hope colliding to create myriad fractures. "But if things aren't working by the time the baby is born…"

"Then we act like adults and make an agreement to look after our kid the best way we can while not being together."

Sarah nodded.

Rising from the floor, Abe walked to the bed, looked down at her. "You want me to go home today?"

Sarah thought of all the lonely nights she'd spent aching for Abe, of all the lonely nights that might yet be in her future. "No." She got up out of bed, found her robe. "Stay."

Touching her fingers to his jaw, she smiled through the fear and the hope that was a flight of butterflies in her stomach. "You can go tire out Flossie while I put together some dinner. I'm starving."

Abe smiled, kissed her fingertips. And it felt good, felt right.

# CHAPTER 24

SARAH WOKE THE NEXT MORNING facing away from Abe, her body curved into the muscled warmth of his. He had one arm under her head, had thrown the other over her waist. It was a heavy weight, but one that made her feel safe, protected. His other arm though, it had to be numb. Still, she didn't move, not wanting to ruin this moment.

Sunlight arced through a gap in the curtains, fine dust motes sparkling in the air. It was early enough that she could hear the birds tweeting loudly as they went about their business, no car sounds to break the peace. And she was all wrapped up in Abe.

Her eyes threatened to sting.

This had been one of her favorite fantasies during her marriage to Abe: just lying in bed with him on a Sunday morning, lazy and warm and with nowhere in particular to be. It had rarely happened though.

*No more living in the past. Live in today.* It was an order to herself. This would never work if she allowed herself to be held hostage to their painful history.

"Mmm." A rumbling sound from Abe before he cuddled her even closer, pushing his thigh up between her legs.

Naked as they both were, she could feel his morning arousal hot and demanding against her back, but he wasn't pushing for sex. He was just... holding her. And the tears, they came ever closer to the surface. She swallowed them in mute desperation.

Abe settled again.

Sarah barely breathed until it became clear he was still asleep. Relaxing, she allowed herself to wallow in this moment when a romantic fantasy had finally come true. Her lips curved a little shakily. Finally that teenage girl who'd haunted the romance novels section of the library and who'd believed in true love was having her faith justified.

At least for this moment.

That moment lasted for over half an hour. Abe apparently woke up in stages when he was sober and in no hurry to be anywhere else. He nuzzled and cuddled her, never releasing her from his grip. When she said a smiling, "Good morning," all she got was another rumble from his chest.

It was over five minutes later—according to her cute little bedside clock with its old-fashioned bells atop a round face—that he pressed a kiss to the curve of her neck and said, "Morning, beautiful."

That teenage girl, she just melted. Sarah the adult attempted to stay firm, but it was near impossible with Abe sounding so lazy and drowsy. Maybe—a sudden stab of worry—he didn't even know who it was he was snuggling.

"Sarah." He rubbed his bristly chin against her shoulder at the same time that he ran his hand down the curve of her waist and over her hip. "God, you're sexy in the morning."

She laughed because a smooth operator, Abe wasn't. "And you're clearly in the mood for something." His erection felt like hot stone against her back.

He nibbled on her shoulder at the same time that he cupped her between the legs. That quickly, her laughter turned into a moan. He knew her far too well; he used his fingers to play lazily with her clit until she moved restlessly and parted her thighs in a silent invitation. Taking it, he lifted her thigh higher and entered her from behind in a slow, deep slide that made a throaty moan emerge from her mouth.

Pushing home, Abe gripped her hip and nuzzled at her as he moved in tiny increments, less thrusting than rocking.

A thousand emotions twisted around and inside her, building and building. Somehow this lazy morning intimacy felt far more powerful than the wild passion of the previous day. Maybe because he was holding her, maybe because…

Sarah didn't have the words or the thoughts for it. She just knew she'd shatter if he didn't… do *something*.

"What do you want?" It was an erotic question in her ear, but even as he spoke, he was touching her again, using one big finger to stroke her clit exactly the way she liked. Then he began kissing her throat.

Pleasure broke through her in small, pulsing explosions. Like little fireworks going off inside her. When Abe rolled her over onto her front without breaking their intimate connection, she went, let him cover her, his hands sliding under her body to cup her breasts while he moved lazily in and out of her.

He was still so hard, and in this new position, his cock hit places inside her that tore new moans from her already pleasure-drunk body. When he said, "One more time, sweetheart," she tried to shake her head, but it felt too heavy, her veins filled with sweet sugar syrup rather than blood.

Abe moved one hand from her breast down to play teasingly at her navel, going an inch lower with every brush until she was holding her breath in anticipation of a more intimate touch. Then he did it, and with his hand so tightly pressed under her body, the pressure on the blood-flushed button of her clit sent an erotic shock through her entire body.

"Again," he murmured at her whimper, kissing her throat at the same time that he pressed down *almost* too hard on her clit. But Abe knew her body, knew how to stay on the right side of the line.

Bucking up in shocked pleasure, she clamped down hard on him with her inner muscles at the same time. He groaned, shoved deep, pulled out and thrust back in, in a rough pounding that had her clawing at the sheets as her body spasmed again and again. Then he was pulsing inside her, hot and wet.

He collapsed on her afterward, his breath that of a runner who'd just sprinted to the end of his endurance. His muscles quivered against her—and oh, she loved that she'd done that to him—but he still managed to brace himself on one arm only seconds later so that he wasn't crushing her.

"Fuck," he gasped. "I hate being a big bastard at times like this."

Sarah's own breathing wasn't exactly steady when she said, "I can take a little more." Yes, he was a big, muscled weight, but she liked feeling him all over her.

Taking her at her word, Abe lowered himself until she felt deliciously crushed, surrounded by his scent, enveloped in the wild heat of him. He brushed her hair off her face, kissed her cheek. The sweet, unexpected caress made her toes curl. "Morning."

She smiled in a way she knew was silly and happy. "Good morning."

Stroking his hand down her side, Abe cupped her breast with lazy possessiveness. "What do you have planned for today?" Another sweet kiss.

"Nothing major." She couldn't stop smiling. "I thought maybe I'd read or bake." Normal, ordinary things that she cherished. "And Flossie and I usually go for a more fun walk on Sundays."

"Can I eat your baking?" Abe nuzzled her.

She turned her head to smile up at him. "Yes, but I might put you to work as my assistant."

"Bring it on."


ABE SAT CLEAN AND SHOWERED in Sarah's kitchen. Since he had no fresh clothes at her place, he was just wearing a towel, while she'd pulled on a large T-shirt and panties as well as fluffy socks. "The tile floor on this side of the kitchen is too cold," she said to him when he teased her about the pink socks.

"I like them—very cheerleader." He waggled his eyebrows. "Did I ever tell you about my cheerleader fantasy?"

Rolling her eyes and laughing, Sarah passed him the last of the ham from the fridge, the rest of their breakfast supplies already on the table. "I need to go grocery shopping."

Abe didn't grocery shop. It wasn't that he thought he was too good for it—he just didn't think about it. He had a housekeeper who came in once a week and who made sure the house was clean and he had food in the pantry. If he ran out of something midweek, he grabbed it from a local convenience store. But if Sarah wanted to go grocery shopping, he was in. "We can go after breakfast."

Sarah halted in the process of pulling out slices of bread from the toaster. "Since when do you grocery shop?"

He grabbed the coffee carafe, topped off his mug. Sarah was sticking to one cup a day for the duration of her pregnancy, going with decaffeinated drinks the rest of the time. Today that meant some fruity herbal tea.

"I used to go with my mom when I came home from boarding school," he told her.

"You must've missed your folks when you were away at school." Sarah's voice was careful.

It took Abe a second to figure out why: he'd always shut her down when she'd asked about his family during their marriage. Back then everything had reminded him of Tessie, and he hadn't been able to handle it. But that Abe was in the past. This one could think of his baby sister without breaking... and he'd promised not to hurt Sarah.

It was a promise he'd damn well keep.

"Yeah," he said, the grin that spread over his face unexpected and real both. "I was a bit of a mama's boy, to be honest."

Sarah's face lit up. "You?" she said as they sat down to eat. "I don't believe it."

"Seriously, I was." Abe grabbed a slice of toast, reached for the butter. "I mean, I didn't run to her if someone talked shit to me or anything like that, but I used to enjoy doing stuff with Mom."

Grinning again, he shook his head. "I'd complain if she asked me to go to the mall or the grocery store with her and pretend I was bored out of my skull while she shopped, but secretly I liked hanging out with her."

Sarah's smile was huge. "Did you ever let on?"

"Naw. But I think Mom knew. Somehow she always had to do a ton of stuff when I was home from boarding school."

"What about your dad?"

Abe took a deep breath. Losing his father so soon after Tessie had been a hammer blow neither he nor his mother had expected, and sometimes Abe still forgot his dad was gone and would go to give him a call to ask his advice. "I loved him," he said, his voice gritty. "He was older than my mom, a little more set in his ways, with some old-fashioned views, but he was always so proud of me."

Abe swallowed the emotion choking him up. "He wanted me to be my own man, whoever that man was." He shook his head. "I was so scared of telling him I wanted to pursue a career in rock music instead of going to college, but all he said to me was that a man had to be able to support himself and his family, and if I could do that with music, that was all that mattered."

Shifting to sit beside him, Sarah ran a gentle hand up and down his back. "I'm sorry I never got to meet him."

"He would've liked you." Abe could almost see his father's smile at that instant, quiet but deep. "This business you've created with your own hard work—it's something he would've appreciated."

"You had good parents."

Sarah's wistful tone made Abe realize he knew next to nothing about her childhood. She'd told him her parents were dead, but the only other thing he knew was that her mom had been Puerto Rican, her father African-American—though, he remembered, her dad's grandmother had been Japanese.

And that was it, that was all he knew about her early history.

"Your folks?" he asked gently after she'd eaten a spoonful of muesli. "Not so good?"

Her face closed up. "No, they were fine," she said, so quickly she almost tripped over the words.

Abe wasn't about to let it go, not this time. If they were to make it, both of them had to be honest and open with each other. "Sarah." He closed his hand over her nape. "Talk to me."

Huge, dark eyes met his. Ducking her head, she didn't say anything else. He was frustrated but knew he couldn't force her—and she didn't need any extra stress right now. So he let her eat her muesli while he demolished the toast and ham and cheese. Not the most traditional breakfast, but Abe wasn't fussy.

Hell, he'd been known to eat cold pizza for breakfast after a bender.

"You want some?" he asked when there was only one piece of toast left on the plate.

Sarah shook her head. "No, you have it. This muesli really fills me up."

Abe had given up all hope of getting an answer to his earlier question when she said, "My mom was seventeen when she had me." A voice so quiet it was almost soundless. "My father was her high school boyfriend."

Abe rose, topped off his coffee, poured Sarah some more tea from her little pot.

"Predictably," she said after taking a sip, "they didn't last long. The two of them crashed and burned eight months after I was born." Her eyes turned faraway, her focus distant.

"My father wasn't a deadbeat though. He got an apprentice position at an auto shop, helped my mom with money for food and rent after her parents kicked her out. He even took shifts with me so she could go out with her friends." She took a deep breath. "Then he died in a car accident when I was three, and that was it."

It sounded so final, as if with her father had gone all hope. "I'm sorry, sweetheart." He put his arm around her shoulders. "It must've been tough, not having your dad there as you grew up."

"I sometimes wonder what my life would've been like if he hadn't been in that crash. Everything I know about him says he was the more stable of my parents."

Another pause to take a sip of tea, another shaky breath. "After my father died, my paternal grandmother helped babysit me, but she was too infirm to take me full time. She passed away when I was about nine." Her fingers squeezed at her mug, her throat moving as she swallowed convulsively. "I loved her. She was so kind to me. I think she was the only person other than my dad who really loved me."

Abe frowned. "What about your mom? Given that they kicked out their own kid, I'm guessing your maternal grandparents won't win any 'Parent of the Year' awards."

Lips pursed tight, Sarah nodded. "They were religious—and not the kind of religious anchored in compassion and helping the less fortunate. No, they were the kind of religious that makes a person cold and unforgiving. According to them, my mother had brought shame on the family by having a child out of wedlock and they didn't want anything to do with her. I've never met them."

Abe felt his hand fist under the table, his jaw a brutal line. "Yeah well, you probably didn't miss out on much." He cuddled her closer.

She came, putting her mug on the table and placing one of her hands on his thigh. "They called me the 'spawn of shame.' My mom let it slip once when she was drunk."

Abe wanted to strangle the older couple. "So, your mom drank?"

"Just the odd weekend bender. Her drug of choice was men, and they were the only thing about which she cared. I basically raised myself after my grandma passed away." She blinked really fast, as if fighting off tears. "My mother blamed me for all her lost dreams and opportunities."

Abe felt his jaw lock at the pain inherent in that last statement, knew he shouldn't interrupt, but he couldn't stop himself. "You had no choice in being born. And being a young single mom doesn't mean the end of everything."

"I know," Sarah said softly. "I didn't for a long time, but then I met my best friend, Lola. She was a teenage mom too, and though her folks didn't kick her out, they were dirt-poor and working all the hours of the day themselves, couldn't really offer her much help. She raised her son with sheer grit and determination, and he *adores* her."

"I think I'll like Lola."

A trembling smile. "I know you will—but she's probably going to want to deck you."

Sucking in a breath, Abe winced. "I can take it." Lola had been there for Sarah when she needed a friend—Abe would give the woman any leeway she wanted. "So, your mom never settled into a stable life."

Sarah shook her head. "We had a rotating front door—one man after another, all of whom were going to be 'different,' going to be 'the best.' All of whom were knights in shining armor and so what if they didn't like her 'brat.' It wasn't like she liked the brat either. Just a whiny mouth to feed, no good for anything, useless."

Fury roared through Abe's veins. He wished he could go back, change the past, but he couldn't. All he could do was hold Sarah, love her.

Shadows across her face, even darker and more vicious. "She always chose violent men. My father was her single good decision." Her hand rose to her cheek, to the spot where Jeremy Vance had hit her.

Shoving away from the kitchen chair, Abe stalked to the window, pressing his hands against the counter as he fought the rage vibrating under his skin. "Did that asswipe hit you? While you were together?" He'd never forget how Sarah had looked that night, so shocked and lost and shattered.

But it wasn't until this instant that he understood just how much Vance had hurt her soul. His blow would've awakened nightmare memories of her childhood. Abe didn't have to read very hard between the lines to know that her mother and her mother's boyfriends must've hit Sarah.

"No." Sarah's response was immediate and firm. "That was the first time—and I wouldn't have stood for it even if you and the others hadn't been there to support me. I was *never* going to be that woman, the one with fist-sized bruises under her shirts and heavy makeup to hide the black eyes."

Abe's gut filled with ice. Suddenly he knew where this was going. "One of them went too far?"

# CHAPTER 25

"HE BROKE HER NECK." TEARS clogged her voice on the starkly brutal answer, but she kept speaking. "Then he set fire to our trailer. I crawled to her room, tried to drag her out... until I realized... until I realized..."

Striding back to her, Abe tugged her up into his arms. He went to speak but she wasn't finished. "The police caught him. He's serving life in prison." A shuddering sob. "She wasn't a good mom, but she was still my mom and he killed her."

"Fuck, you were a strong kid." He knew she must've testified to send that murderous bastard to prison.

"I got put into foster care after that." She wiped her face on her T-shirt. "It was a bad place. More violence along with a son with wandering hands and a way of looking at me like I was meat."

Abe gritted his teeth together, his muscles rigid.

Sarah continued to talk. "After the prick cornered me one night, grinding his crotch into me and telling me I was going to get it and I better not say a word or his parents would kick me out for being a slut, I packed up what little I had and left."

"How old were you?"

"Fifteen."

He crushed her close, his heart thudding. Fifteen-year-olds didn't last long on the street without attracting the attention of certain predators. Especially fifteen-year-old girls as beautiful and as well-developed as Sarah must've already been. His muscles bunched, his rage returning on a black roar at the idea of her being hurt that way.

"You okay to keep talking?" Abe would never force her back into hell.

"You might as well know the rest," she said, her head turned to one side on his chest and her arms down by her sides instead of around him. "I didn't have any real money. Just a few dollars given to me by a cop who felt sorry for me."

A short pause, her breathing jagged. The next words she spoke were haunted. "After hours walking down the highway alone in the dark"—echoes of fear in her voice—"I hitched a ride out of town with a trucker. And I gave him what he wanted because he told me we'd be together forever, that he'd take care of me, make sure I never had to be alone in the dark again. I'd watched men make promises to my mom and break them over and over, should've known not to believe him, but I was so alone and so scared."

Abe was so far beyond anger now that there was no word to describe it. What the fuck kind of asshole took advantage of a grieving fifteen-year-old? "If you ever see him, point him out and I'll break his nose, and you can kick him in the nuts."

A wet laugh and Sarah's arms slipped around him at last, as if she finally trusted that he wouldn't let go, wouldn't reject her. "He left me in Los Angeles two months later. Just drove out while I was using a restroom." Nails digging into his skin.

"I had such dreams of the big city, of the lights and the pretty people, but I found those things don't exist for girls with no one."

His gaze blood red, Abe kissed her temple, braced to hear the worst.

"I was *so* lonely. Easy prey for the smooth-talking predators." Another rasping breath. "But I'd learned from my experience with the trucker, and then for the first time in my life, I had a stroke of luck. I was squatting in an abandoned building with a bunch of other kids and getting ready to run to avoid a drug dealer I already knew wanted to pimp me out, when the police raided it."

Abe kissed her temple again, so fucking scared and angry for the girl she'd been. "That doesn't sound like good luck."

"The cops didn't want to deal with us kids—they were after the narcotics den in the basement. So they handed us over to a local charity organization. Most of the others ran off first chance they got, but I stayed." She shrugged. "I hadn't been on the streets long enough to make friends or have other loyalties, and at least with the charity, I had a place to sleep where I didn't have to worry about being assaulted."

Abe could feel himself trembling within. "Sarah, sweetheart, why didn't you ever tell me any of this?" She'd said her parents were dead and that she'd been on her own for a while, never once mentioning that she'd been on her own from the time she was *fifteen*. "Why, baby?"

Sarah pulled away, her movements jerky as she walked to the sink and began to rinse the dishes, put them into the dishwasher. Abe resisted the temptation to demand more from her, resisted the temptation to be the raging bull he so often was.

Instead, he helped clear away the detritus of their meal, then grabbed the magnetic notepad she had on her fridge.

It was one of those novelty items with Shopping List in fancy font on the top. Below, Sarah had jotted down a few items in her distinctive handwriting with its wide loops and generous curves. "Milk," Abe said, noting it down. "Eggs. Ham, since I ate all of it. Bacon too." *Please, Sarah, talk to me. I won't let you down this time.* "Doughnuts. Cake. Chocolate-covered pretzels."

"*Abe.*" Sarah finally spoke, shooting him a scowl at the same time. "Just put vegetables. I'll pick from whatever they have at the Farmers Market."

Wanting to hold her again, he forced himself to stay in place. "What else?"

"I'm nearly out of flour." Dishes all stacked in the dishwasher, Sarah started to open and shut cupboards, calling out items for him to add to the list as she went. "I just wanted to fit in," she said in the middle of checking the cupboard in which she kept her canned goods. "You had such a lovely mother, a great extended family, incredibly strong roots and the kind of friendships that are forever. I didn't want you to think I was a throwaway person."

Abe crushed the grocery list, his fist clenching without his conscious volition. "You were *never* that."

"I made myself that," Sarah insisted. "I was twenty-one when I met you, and yet I'd made no real friends, not even with the charity workers who helped me take the GED." Her hand tightened on the edge of the cupboard door. "The loneliness was horrible, but I guess I'd been burned so badly that I thought it was safer to keep my distance from people in general." She looked at him after an eternity. "Until you."

And he'd kicked her so goddamn hard in the heart that he'd thrust her into the arms of a manipulative fuckhole who turned out to be an abuser. Right goddamn back into the nightmare she'd tried to escape. "I was only ever interested in your background because it was yours. It didn't matter where you came from or who your parents were."

"You don't understand." Sarah shook her head, her curls wild. "You've always had this solid foundation behind you. Always had the Bellamy name, always had people you could rely on. It's different when you come from nothing and have no one."

"You have me." Abe moved to cup her face. "Whatever happens, however this ends, you have me. *Always.*" Never again would Sarah feel alone and abandoned. "You hear me, Sarah? I'm here for you and our baby. Today, tomorrow, always."


ABE'S PASSIONATE WORDS CONTINUED TO ring in Sarah's skull as she walked with him through the permanent pathways of the Farmer's Market at 3rd and Fairfax, his hand clasped firmly around hers. It made her afraid that he knew so much about her, had glimpsed the scars that marked her… but then hiding her needs hadn't saved them the last time around. If Abe had known that loneliness was her terror, if he'd understood how her childhood had marked her, would he have left her behind all those times?

"These oranges look good." Abe bagged up a bunch. "Vitamin C is good for you."

"I'm starting to think you're going to be a pain in the butt the entire pregnancy." Sarah mock-scowled, even as bubbles of delight popped through the heavy darkness of this morning's conversation and the attendant memories.

Abe touched his hand to her lower back after paying for the oranges and taking the bag, then nodded ahead. "Those look like avocados. I heard something about healthy fats."

Shoulders shaking, Sarah walked over to the stall and bought several avocados that weren't too ripe. No one bothered them the entire time they were at the market, and they left it loaded down with fresh goods as well as a huge caramel-covered apple that was Sarah's delicious nemesis.

"I have one every six months," she told Abe as she ate a slice after they got into his SUV. "Otherwise, I'd be here every week, stuffing my face."

"Well, I guess it was once fruit," he said dubiously.

Ignoring him to munch obnoxiously on her treat, she had sticky fingers when he pulled up at the grocery store where they planned to quickly pick up a few other items. "Do you have a bottle of water?" She wiggled the fingers of her right hand at him.

His eyes turned dark, intense.

Gripping her wrist with a gentle but firm hand, Abe tugged her fingers to his mouth and sucked in a finger, swirling his tongue around it to clean off the caramel.

Sarah whimpered.

"There," he murmured after he'd patiently and calmly cleaned off each and every one of her fingers, his eyes locked with her own the entire time. "Done."

Putting a trembling hand on the door, she went to push it open. She needed fresh air, needed to find her senses again. Abe was somehow out of the SUV and around to her side before she knew it. He put his hands on her waist, lifted her down… and she caught the flash of a camera going off.

Flinching, she instinctively angled away her face, while Abe turned toward the man who'd taken the shot. She felt his body bunch, and that was enough to spring her into action. Placing a hand on his chest, she said, "Abe. No drama. I can't handle it."

"Bastards," he muttered but wrenched his attention off the photographer. "We're just going to the freaking grocery store."

Sarah took a deep breath. "At least I look good."

"You always look good." Abe tucked her hair behind her ear. "Why do you straighten your hair? It's so pretty curly."

Sarah had never thought of her hair as pretty. It turned into a tangle if left to do what it would. One of the charity workers had given Sarah her first set of straighteners, an old pair that the woman's teenage daughter had decided to replace. It had been a revelation to see that her hair could be corralled, could be sleek and shiny.

"I don't want to look messy," she admitted.

"Sarah, your messy is blow-off-the-roof sexy." A deep rumble of sound, his chest vibrating against her touch.

Things melted inside her. "I won't straighten it after I wash it tomorrow," she promised him. "But I refuse to go out in public with crazy hair."

Abe snorted, as if the idea of her with crazy hair was simply impossible—and the man had *seen* the crazy hair any number of times. "Let's go get these groceries. Ignore the vulture."

Locking the SUV, Abe took her hand in his and they walked through the parking lot to the store. The photographer—who really did look like a vulture with his pasty white face and black handlebar mustache—suddenly popped up from behind his camera to give Sarah an oddly delighted smile. "Finally!" He fist-pumped the air. "I get to have a payday. Basil, this is your lucky day!"

Astonished, Sarah paused, making Abe halt. "What?"

"A rock 'n' roll reunion," Basil said in his unexpectedly refined English accent, snapping away. "No one's broken this story yet. I get to have an exclusive." He gave her an ingratiating look. "How about a kiss, love?" He held up his camera. "I mean, it'd make the story."

Sarah was about to shake her head when Abe spun her into his arms and, bending her over, laid one on her. A hot, possessive one. She gripped at him in surprise even as her brain short-circuited, was still breathless when he let her up.

"Now scram," he told Basil. "Go get your exclusive."

The photographer, his eyes near delirious, was already pulling out his phone. "I'm scramming and I'm going to be rich! *Rich!*"

Sarah didn't find her voice again until they were nearly at the entrance to the grocery store. "What was that?" Abe didn't play to the media, didn't have the patience for it.

"What the hell—the man already had photos. Why not make things clear?" A searing glance that set her aflame just when the air-conditioning inside the store had begun to cool her overheated cheeks. "I want the world to know you're mine."

# CHAPTER 26

SARAH SAT IN HER GARDEN a couple of hours after lunch, Abe's words still echoing through her head. He'd gone home to change into fresh clothes but promised to be back by four thirty so they could take Flossie for a walk along a dog-friendly beach.

Right now Sarah's dog was dozing beside her garden chair, protected from the sun by a wisteria-covered wooden awning she'd put up herself after buying the necessary items at the hardware store. It had been hard and she'd made several time-consuming mistakes, but now, each time she glimpsed it, it reminded her that she was strong, that even alone she could survive and thrive.

That didn't mean she didn't still fear loneliness. She always would, the scar too old and too deeply set into her psyche—but she was no longer held hostage to her need. Her friendship with the woman who sat opposite her, a pitcher of fresh lemonade on the small wooden table between them, had been the first step in Sarah's journey to build a social life outside of the man with whom she was in a relationship.

She'd finally confessed to Lola about her renewed relationship with Abe four days ago, but had said nothing about the pregnancy. She *couldn't*, the fear of speaking too soon and losing her baby keeping her mute. As if the two were connected. It wasn't rational, but Sarah wasn't rational on that point.

Taking a deep, quiet breath, she returned to her earlier thoughts. "If I'd been the woman I am now during our marriage," she said to Lola, "I think it would've had a different outcome."

Lola's face, small and gamine under a cap of exuberant fire-engine-red hair, soured. "That ex of yours making you question yourself?"

Sarah shook her head, because this wasn't about Abe. "No, it's just that I was so passive back then, so afraid of rocking the boat and losing my only anchor that I never called him on his behavior." Yes, she'd gotten upset about his drugs, but not about how he'd left her behind to go on tour.

"If he ever again started to treat me the way he did back then," she said slowly, "I'd not only call him on it, I'd probably throw a few things at his gorgeous head, then kick his ass. Hard."

Lola laughed that big, honest laugh of hers, her blue eyes crinkling at the corners and her pale white skin flushed from exposure to the sunshine. Sarah's friend wasn't a natural redhead, but she burned like one if she wasn't careful.

"The rock star know you're not a wide-eyed ingénue anymore?" Lola asked after the laughter faded off into a smile, her gaze dead serious.

"I was never that." Sarah thought of the book about the entrepreneur Abe had sent her, about how he'd asked after her business more than once. "He knows—and he seems more than okay with it." She drank some lemonade. "I don't know if I'm just imagining it... but I could swear he's proud of what I've achieved."

"He damn well should be," Lola muttered. "You've made it in a town full of broken dreams and lost hopes." Taking a sip of lemonade, too, Lola tilted up her chin in a questioning move. "I'm getting the feeling things are more serious than they were even a couple of days ago."

Sarah told her best friend about the incident in the grocery store parking lot. "He was never so openly possessive of me before."

Lola had been around the block. Twice. Both times with men who appeared wonderful on the surface but turned out to be rotten underneath. The then twenty-year-old father of her son had turned out to be a wanted bank robber who'd disappeared into the ether after discovering she was pregnant; the husband she'd married at twenty-five and divorced at twenty-eight, a serial cheater.

Lola's view of men was slightly jaundiced as a result. When Sarah pointed out that Lola's son was an amazing young male with a solid core of honor, Lola would respond with, "My kiddo is a rare unicorn and he'll make some woman very happy one day. The rest of us have to deal with the toads."

So Sarah wasn't surprised when Lola raised a perfectly manicured eyebrow and said, "Easy for a man to be possessive and supportive when he wants a woman in bed. You should see what he's like if he's not getting any."

Used to her friend's acerbic ways and well aware Lola had a sweet and generous heart under her spiky battle armor, Sarah grinned. "That would be cutting off my nose to spite my face," she said in a solemn tone. "I *love* being in bed with Abe."

Lola rolled those eyes that could be as changeable as the clouds. "What am I going to do with you?" She poured them both a second glass of the crisp, cold lemonade. "Seriously though, while I admit your ex is panty-melting hot—"

Sarah almost choked on her lemonade. "Hey!"

"As I was saying," Lola continued, her eyes dancing, "the man is delicious, but do you really believe he's changed? Drug addicts aren't the most reliable people."

"I know." Sarah had lived the nightmare, watched helplessly as the man she loved gave his life over to a destructive, seductive poison. "It feels different this time. *Abe* feels different."

She paused, tried to find the right words, petting Flossie when the dog raised her head. "Before," she said, Flossie's fur soft under her palm, "he'd go into rehab when the others in the band forced him, but that was it. This time around he's seeing a counselor trained in addiction." He'd mentioned it in passing at the grocery store, after the counselor gave him a call to confirm a meeting later that week.

"He found the counselor himself, is committed to making every session." That was the most crucial thing—Abe had taken cold, hard responsibility for his demons. "If he's on the road, he says they do the session via a phone call."

Lola gave a small nod. "Okay, yeah, that's a big deal coming from a rock star used to making his own rules."

The other woman sat back, her hair glowing in the sunlight that managed to pierce the wisteria canopy. "Look, I trust you to know your ex better than I ever will," she said, "but as your friend, I'm duty bound to remind you that the bastard broke your heart the first time around, broke it so badly you left your-self wide open to a bastard like Jeremy." Lola curled her lip.

"I have to take responsibility for my own choices, Lola." It was the only way she'd grow, the only way she'd keep becoming stronger.

"No, you don't," Lola said with a scowl. "Because that would mean so do I—and I'd rather blame my exes for everything, from global warming to the bad dye job I had at thirty-two."

Laughing, Sarah put down her half-empty glass of lemonade. "And, like I said, I've changed as much, if not more, than Abe."

Lola's gaze was piercing. "Yes," she said at last. "You're much stronger these days. Even after the hurt of losing Aaron, you didn't bow to Jeremy and hand him the kind of control over your life and business that he wanted."

A stab of grief inside Sarah's heart, but she was learning to bear it now. *Had* to learn, because wallowing in sadness couldn't be good for her pregnancy. Breathing through the grief, she kissed Aaron in her mind, then imagined another baby in her arms less than eight months into the future.

A healthy, breathing baby with Abe's heartbreaker smile and his dark, dark eyes.

Her heart melted, sorrow buried under hopeful joy... but she wasn't a foolish girl this time. She was a woman. And she intended to demand everything from the rock star who was her lover.


ABE RETURNED IN TIME TO meet Sarah's friend, Lola. Pre-dictably, the redhead gave him the stink eye and, when Sarah was distracted by Flossie, promised to beat him bloody if he hurt Sarah again. Since Lola was five-foot-nothing with no hard edges except those in her eyes, the threat held zero weight—it was the fiercely protective love in her gaze that mattered most.

"I cherish her," he said quietly.

Lips pursing, Lola said, "Hmm," and he knew he'd have to earn her trust.

Fair enough.

After Lola left to do some shopping for her son's upcoming birthday, Abe and Sarah headed off to the beach with Flossie. The dog raced off ahead but always returned after fifty meters or so, at which point she'd dart into the waves for a couple of seconds before shaking off the water and racing out and along the sand.

Holding a shawl loosely around her upper body, Sarah laughed at Flossie's antics as strands of hair that had escaped the knot at the back of her head kissed her cheeks. "You'd think she was a puppy instead of a very respectable middle-aged dog."

Abe, however, wasn't thinking about Flossie except to keep an eye on the dog so she didn't inadvertently scare any of the children on the beach—not that they seemed the least terrified of her tail-wagging friendliness. "We need to tell my mom," he said. "About the peanut."

"The peanut?" Sarah's eyes almost swallowed her face. "Oh."

Abe's gaze landed on where she'd spread her hand over her belly. His lips kicked up, his heart doing that crazy thing it did every time he thought about holding his kid. "Someone's going to get a photograph of you doing that and then it's all over, and Mom's going to be pissed we didn't tell her first."

FLUSHING, SARAH DROPPED HER HAND while scanning the beach for any signs of a photographer lurking in the distance. Nothing. *Phew.* Because Abe was right. Diane *would not* be pleased to find out about the existence of her future grandchild from the tabloids—and Sarah was already the ex-wife who'd walked out on her son.

"Call her," she said. "Right now."

"She's in town tomorrow night."

"What?" Coming to a standstill on the sand, she glared at Abe. "Don't try to tell me that's a coincidence, Abe Bellamy."

"I swear to God it is." He held up his hands, palms out. "She's on some cruise deal with her best friend, and they stop in LA tomorrow. I'm supposed to have dinner with her—we set it up weeks ago."

Sarah was nowhere near ready to face Abe's mother, but she knew it was inevitable; at least if they did it tomorrow, they'd be ahead of the media. Perhaps that would make Diane a little more kindly disposed toward Sarah. Not that Sarah's ex-mother-in-law hadn't always been lovely and kind—but that was before a bitter and messy divorce fueled by anger on Sarah's part, the same on Abe's.

No mother was going to look on such an ex-wife with a kind eye.

Sarah inhaled deeply of the salt-laced air, exhaled as slowly. Then did it again.

"Okay," she said on the second exhale, "let's do it—but please warn her that I'm coming along to dinner. I don't want her feeling sandbagged." That Sarah was pregnant with Abe's baby would be a big enough shock as it was.

Abe ran a hand down her back, the piercing in his eyebrow glinting in the sunlight. "It won't be so bad. My mom's not the type to interfere in her son's life."

"No," Sarah admitted. "But she adores you, Abe."

"I think she likes you a lot more than you realize."

Sarah wanted to believe that *so* much, but she wasn't hopeful. "Go on, call her." Get the first shock over with.

Frowning a little at her no doubt wary expression, Abe pulled out his phone.

Sarah walked ahead a little so he could talk to Diane in privacy, Flossie bounding along the very edge of the water a couple of feet in front of her. After jumping back with a yelp at being splashed by a rogue wave, Sarah's drenched and bedraggled dog padded back to Sarah with a highly offended look on her face.

"Don't you dare shake yourself off near me," Sarah ordered.

Since Flossie didn't exactly look convinced by the laughing warning, her body held in position for a hard shake, Sarah bent down to pick up a piece of driftwood, threw it as hard as she could. "Go! Get the stick!"

Flossie took off like a rocket just as Abe's hand landed on her lower back, the warmth and strength of his big body a silent caress and his voice a familiar rumble as he asked, "When did you get Flossie?"

"Not long after our divorce was final." Sarah wanted to cuddle into him... but part of her remained skittish, afraid of giving him even more pieces of herself.

Then Abe wrapped his arm around her and tugged her close. Her heart ached.

Sarah was glad when Flossie returned with the stick in her mouth and Abe broke contact to wrestle it from her, throw it again. It felt too good to have him treat her as precious, as beloved. She couldn't bear it.

Yet when he cuddled her again, she couldn't say no, couldn't pull away. Because much as her feelings scared her, Abe was her greatest weakness, the only man who'd ever seared her to the soul.

"You get her from the pound?" Abe held her close as they walked, just another couple taking a lazy Sunday walk with their playful pet.

Eyes stinging, Sarah swallowed. "I found her on the side of the road," she said, thankful her voice sounded normal. "She'd been hit by a car." Sarah could still feel how Flossie's broken body had trembled under her touch, her poor dog so scared and hurt.

"I took her to the vet, stayed with her until she was sedated." She hadn't even thought of just dropping Flossie off and leaving her there alone. "Then, since she wasn't wearing a collar and had no microchip, I went back to the residential street where I'd found her, knocked on doors—but nobody knew where she'd come from. I even made up flyers and distributed them in the area."

Like Sarah, Flossie had been lost and alone in this huge city. And like Sarah, she'd had so much love to give, her eyes lighting up every time Sarah went to visit her at the vet's. "When no one claimed her…"

Throat thick with the memories, Sarah reached down to pet a huffing Flossie just returned from her latest stick retrieval. "I took her home, and it was like she'd always been mine." Another petting rub before Flossie abandoned the stick in favor of playing in the water again. "She was my strength after

I lost Aaron, always there, nudging me out of my sadness and forcing me to get up, take her for walks, interact."

"What about Vance? Where the hell was he?"

"He hadn't really bonded with the baby," Sarah said, thinking back to how quickly Jeremy had shrugged off the loss. "It was hard for him to understand my grief."

"Jesus Christ, Sarah, I can't believe you're defending that asswipe." Abe's voice was harsh.

Sarah understood his response, hadn't actually been defending Jeremy: she'd just been stating a fact about the other man, one that had exposed a lack in him she'd been unable to truly comprehend. However, like most people, Jeremy had more than one aspect to his nature, wasn't just a one-dimensional villain.

"He was kind to me after I left you." She'd been so fragile, so fractured, her love for Abe a thousand pieces of shattered glass inside her, cutting and making her bleed with every breath. "Whatever his motives, he supported me at a time I needed it most."

Maybe he'd done it because, deep down, he'd seen her as vulnerable, a woman who'd be easy to control, but that didn't alter the fact that it was Jeremy who'd made sure she ate, Jeremy whom she'd called when she needed a friend. "He helped me at a time when I had no one else."

# Chapter 27

SARAH COULD'VE STABBED ABE WITH a hunting knife and it would've hurt less. "You still in touch with him?"

"No." His wife's glance was that of a furious valkyrie. "I can remember who Jeremy once was to me without forgetting who he became."

Muscles locked, Abe forced himself to confront another heartrending truth. "You came into your own with him," he said. "You became a businesswoman, became confident and so fucking strong." While with him… Hell, he'd sucked up all her energy—she'd spent it on trying to keep him alive. It had left her with nothing for herself.

"No," Sarah said at once. "It wasn't Jeremy who encouraged me to become independent, go into business. *I* made that decision—I never again wanted to be in that position, lost and alone and reliant on a man's money."

Spinning around to face him, she pointed a finger at his chest. "Sometimes I'd feel guilty that I was building my new life using your money as the foundation, but then I'd remember all the shit you put me through." Her eyes sparked fire. "I *earned* that settlement after all the times I had to get rid of your drug stash, all the times I had to call the paramedics, all the horrific nights I spent alone wondering if I'd get a call from Noah or Fox or David to tell me that you'd been found dead with a needle stuck in your arm."

She was trembling, fury raging through her. "From the instant I got up each day to the instant I finally slept, I worried about you. And you kept on piling on the shit. The least you could do was help me get on my feet afterward!"

God, she was so strong and angry and beautiful. And Abe wasn't about to argue with her. "I never cared about the money," he said with a shrug. "Fighting you in court was never about the settlement." He'd been so furiously hurt that she'd left him that he'd become a Grade A asshole.

"I know." Sarah's anger was still dark fire in her eyes, but she slid her arm around his waist, ran her hand over his back. "You were always ridiculously generous with me." An unexpected laugh. "Remember when you gave me a credit card the first time?"

Abe rubbed one hand over his head, decided to just admit the truth. "Um, no?" He shrugged. "I just told the accountants to set up accounts for you, then passed on the cards."

"Of course you did." She rolled her eyes, but a little smile tugged at her lips. "When I got the first card, I was so happy that you cared enough to make sure I had a little spending money—then I realized my card had a six-figure limit and almost had a heart attack right there in the handbag store."

Abe grinned. "Because, of course, the first thing you thought to buy was another handbag."

"Oh, shut up." Shoulders shaking, she elbowed him. "I only figured it out because when I went to pay, the shop assistant's eyes bugged out. She said she'd never seen a black card in real life. I had no idea what that meant, so I did an online search." A shake of her head. "Forget about the cheerful pink, fifty-dollar handbag I wanted, I could've bought the entire *store* with that card!"

Chuckling at her still-scandalized response, Abe kissed her temple. "I'll get you one for your next birthday."

Her laughter undid the knots around his heart, gave him hope that the past didn't have to define their future.

AT FOUR THE NEXT DAY, Abe picked up his mom from the cruise ship terminal in San Pedro. He hadn't told Sarah that he was actually seeing his mom well before dinner, but that was only so he could make sure his mom didn't inadvertently hurt Sarah. He knew she'd never do it on purpose—Diane Bellamy just wasn't that kind of a mean-hearted person.

And his love for his mom was why he'd told her he was bringing a guest without identifying that guest as Sarah—that wasn't a bombshell he'd wanted to drop on her over the phone. Now she bustled around his kitchen making tea. He'd have tried making it for her except that, according to his mom, he could make the finest tea taste like dishwater.

Hey, at least he'd dropped by a bakery and bought her favorite cake.

"How are Fox and Molly?" she asked. "I was so sad to miss their wedding."

"They understood." His mom had been getting over a stomach bug at the time, hadn't been well enough to attend. "They loved the gift you sent."

NALINI SINGH

A beaming smile. "Oh, good. I donated to the charity like they asked, but I always like to give newlyweds a little something beautiful, too."

Taking a seat at the counter, he watched her small form move about with vibrant energy as she told him about the cruise and her best friend and the games they played onboard. "This particular ship is full of people my age," she said. "You'd be bored out of your skull, but I like the time out from the stresses of work. And sometimes I get to dance." A faraway smile. "No one dances like your daddy though."

Mind filling with the last time he'd seen his parents dance—at a cousin's wedding about two months before Gregory Bellamy's death—Abe smiled. "You two were pretty smooth together."

His mother winked. "You get your rhythm from Gregory, but you get your style from me. He once rocked the most hideous orange-and-paisley bell-bottoms—not that he ever admitted it, not until I found photographic evidence in an old yearbook."

Delighted at the thought that his quietly stylish father had once succumbed to the lure of orange bell-bottoms, Abe accepted the cup of tea his mom handed him, grabbed the cake plate, and took it all out to the wooden outdoor table by the pool. His mom followed and the two of them sat in simple quiet for a while, the sun sparkling on the blue water, before Abe took a breath, laid one arm on the table, and opened his mouth to speak.

But the woman who'd given birth to him beat Abe to it.

"You look good." A gentle hand touching his cheek. "Better than I've seen you look since before we lost Tessie. I feel like I have my boy back." Her voice broke.

"Shit, Mom, don't cry."

"Abraham Joshua Bellamy"—his mom sniffed—"don't you use that language around me, or I'll wash your mouth out with soap."

Groaning, Abe got up and went to kneel by her chair. "Why are you crying then?" He reached up to wipe away her tears. "Stop it."

She continued to cry while patting at his shoulders with hands that had eased a hundred childhood injuries. Tiny and full of energy, his mom had always been a powerhouse career woman, but she'd never let that get in the way of being his mom. Unlike Noah, who also came from wealth, Abe had never had a nanny, never felt as if he didn't have enough time with his mom.

Abe didn't know how she'd done it.

"Here." Digging in the handbag she'd brought out because her phone was in it and she'd wanted to show him some photos from the cruise, he pulled out a lacey handkerchief he'd known would be in there, thrust it at her. "If you don't stop crying, I won't give you any cake."

Rising when she continued to cry, he pressed a kiss to her forehead. "*Mom*."

Her smile was sunshine through her tears. "My beautiful Abe, so big and gentle." It took a couple more minutes, but she finally dabbed away the remnants of her tears.

Abe refreshed her tea, then pushed a slice of cake toward her before taking his seat. He hated it when his mom cried—it reminded him too much of her shattered state after Tessie's death. Abe, his mom, his dad, they'd all broken. Tessie had been the baby, meant to outlive them all—it had been impossible to believe she was gone, impossible to accept it.

"You're sober," his mom said after a sip of her tea, and it wasn't a question.

"As a judge." It was an ironic comment given how many judges there'd been in the extended Bellamy family line. "I promise you I won't ever again fall back down that rabbit hole," he said, his gaze locked to the paler brown of her own. "You don't have to worry about me anymore."

"I believe you." Sunshine dawning on his mom's face, a sudden piercing lightness to her. "There's a resolve in you I've never seen before." She drank more of her tea, expression turning thoughtful. "You know, the last time I saw that look in your eyes, you were about to marry Sarah."

Abe almost dropped his tea. "What?"

"In the vestibule before we went in, I asked you if she was a woman you'd run away with." Twin lines between her eyebrows, she leaned back in her chair and shook her head. "I never should've asked that, never should've interfered."

Abe's abdomen grew tight at the reminder of the time he'd wasted, the love he'd neglected until it had curled up and perhaps died forever. It fucking hurt to think that, to even consider that Sarah would never again look at him as she had then. "I didn't take it that way. To be honest, I was barely listening." His mind had been on the tall, beautiful, fascinating woman he was about to marry.

His mother smiled at his confession. "You never answered me that day," she said after eating a little cake. "All I got from you was that you had no time to chat, that you had to be waiting at the groom's spot or Sarah might change her mind."

A pause, Diane Bellamy's eyes looking into the past rather than at Abe. "Yet all the time before that, you'd been so cavalier about your wedding, about Sarah. Until I thought she was an opportunistic groupie taking advantage of the grief that held you prisoner."

His mother's voice softened as it always did when she spoke of Tessie, but the echo of her own grief was overlaid with endless love. "I was so sure… and then I saw her walk into the hotel ballroom." Diane Bellamy shook her head. "She didn't look around at the expensive decor or check out the famous guests. She looked only for you, and the smile that lit up her face when she saw you waiting for her, I'll never forget it."

His mom sniffed again, her voice breaking a little as she said, "And I knew that girl loved my boy. So *much*."

Abe thought of the pearl necklace Sarah still cherished; he'd seen how carefully she stored it in its box, how she always kept it separate from her other jewelry. His mother hadn't given her the gift before the wedding but *after*—when she'd taken it off her own neck to put it around Sarah's.

Abe had never realized the significance of that until this instant, and it gave him hope his mother would accept what he was about to tell her. "I'm seeing Sarah again," he said, knowing there really was no way to build up to it.

Putting down her teacup with a rattle, his mom stared at him before taking a deep breath. "I can't say I'm surprised. What you and Sarah had, it was special." A frown, her next words not what he would've expected. "You hurt that girl, Abe. I love you, will always love you, but I saw her light dim day by day in the time she was with you."

Abe flinched. "I'm not that guy anymore." A self-protective asshole pushing away the best thing in his life out of fear that she'd die on him too, leave him in the most final way. "She's pregnant. The baby's mine. Ours."

Diane Bellamy had reached for her teacup again, was just picking it up when he spoke. The cup dropped to the gritty stone below their feet with a crash, shattered. Ignoring it, his mother asked, "How far?"

"Not far. But Sarah keeps doing that thing with her hand"—he demonstrated the protective action that caught him in the heart each and every fucking time—"so some paparazzo's going to catch it soon. I wanted you to know before that." And he'd wanted to tell her before he picked up Sarah for dinner, so that if her reaction was negative, he could shield Sarah from it.

Drawing herself up, his mother frowned at him. "I want to see her." It was a demand. "She never came to me after you two blew up because I kept my distance in an effort to give you both your privacy. I didn't want to be an interfering mother-in-law."

Grabbing his mostly untouched tea, she drank it down, then put the teacup back in its saucer. "This time around," she said, her tone brooking no argument, "I want her to know she can count on me. Even if it's my son she's angry at."

Getting up, Abe lifted his mom off her feet, squeezed her into a bear hug.

"*Abraham,*" she said. "Put me down at once!"

Abe held her for a minute longer. "Thank you," he said afterward, his voice hoarse. "Sarah needs a mom on her side." And his mom was the best advocate anyone could ever have.

# CHAPTER 28

SARAH WAS STILL SITTING AROUND in sweatpants and a T-shirt even though Abe was supposed to pick her up in less than an hour. She'd woken early to take care of work matters so she'd have plenty of time to prepare, yet here she was. At least she'd showered and brushed her hair. She hadn't done anything else however, and now she was rapidly running out of time to dry and straighten it. But her guts were twisted into a panic.

Abe's mom was going to hate her for coming back into his life.

She swallowed, put a trembling hand to her forehead, dropped it a second later. "You can deal with this, Sarah."

Only she wasn't sure she could: it wasn't just about Abe and their baby, it was about how much Sarah respected Diane Bellamy. To be rejected by her…

*Buzz.*

Sarah jerked at the sound of the gate buzzer and, jumping to her feet, ran to the window that overlooked the front of the house. Abe's black SUV stood at the gate. Groaning, she found her keys and used the remote to open the gate for him before padding downstairs and opening the door to step out onto the stoop. Flossie zipped out in joyous, tail-wagging welcome.

"You're early!" she called out to him as he opened his door. "I'm not ready."

He threw her a gorgeous grin, gave Flossie a quick pat. "You look perfect." Then he ran around to open the *passenger* door.

Sarah froze.

This was *not* how she'd planned to meet Abe's mom for the first time since the divorce, with her hair barely brushed and wearing an old white tee over gray sweatpants that had a hole in one knee. She never wore them except when doing things like cleaning the garage or weeding.

The only reason she'd pulled them on today was so she wouldn't be naked while she stared at her wardrobe and tried not to throw up in panic. And now the woman she desperately wanted to impress was walking toward her. Diane Bellamy was as elegantly dressed as always, her black hair in a neat bob and her face made up with exquisite perfection, her flawless skin a sunkissed brown.

"My dear Sarah." The older woman drew her into an embrace scented with White Diamonds before Sarah could snap out of her frozen state. "It's so good to see you."

The words, the tone, they got through the ice. Trembling, she slid her own arms hesitantly around the petite form of Abe's mom; she couldn't speak, entirely too choked up. Abe's eyes met hers over his mom's shoulder, and in them was an intensity of emotion that stripped her raw.

Pulling back from the embrace when Diane Bellamy released her with a kiss on her cheek, Sarah made a gesture to welcome the other woman inside. She was bewildered by the warmth of Diane's greeting, only found her words after swallowing hard twice. "I'm so sorry. I'm not dressed for g—"

Her former mother-in-law took her hand with a deep smile, squeezed. "I know what it's like when guests barge in unexpectedly. Let's go in so you can dress. Abe can take your adorable dog for a walk."

"I guess I have my orders," Abe said with a wry smile before whistling for Flossie. "Time for a walk, Floss."

Sarah's pet, ecstatic about an outing, ran off to get her leash, then joined Abe. That quickly, Sarah was alone with Mrs. Bellamy. "You like tea," she said, remembering her manners. "Come in, let me make you a cup."

She managed to do that without dropping anything or making a mess, and once Diane Bellamy had her cup in hand, the older woman urged her to head on up to dress. "I hate feeling unprepared myself," she confided. "Abe's father could never understand why I had to put on makeup to go to the corner store, but it just made me feel more confident."

Climbing the stairs beside the other woman, Sarah felt a fragile hope. "Especially with people taking photos," she said softly. "At least if I'm dressed nicely they have to work much harder to take ones that are unflattering."

"I worry about you and Abe living in the spotlight," Diane said with a frown. "You do what you need to do to handle it." The tenured law professor took a seat on the small vanity stool Sarah had in her room, then nodded at the wide-open wardrobe. "You always look stunning in color."

Taking the hint and happy to have some direction on a day when she felt as if the ground had fallen out from under her feet, Sarah pulled out several dresses in bold colors. "This one's my favorite," she said, holding up a dress that was pure sunset. Not orange or red or yellow but a stunning color that was a blend of all three.

Despite the vivid shade, the dress itself was light and summery with a high neckline. The dress hugged her body to the hips before opening out just slightly into a bias cut skirt. "I don't really look good in A-line dresses that have a flowy skirt, but this gives me that feeling while suiting my body."

*Stop babbling, Sarah,* ordered the small part of her brain that wasn't completely thrown by having her ex-mother-in-law sitting in her bedroom.

"It's a wonderful choice." A twinkle in her eye, Diane added, "And my dear, if I had a figure like yours, I wouldn't care about full-skirted dresses. I'd be buying up as many slinky, body-hugging things as I could!"

Sarah was surprised into a snorting laugh.

Horrified, she clapped her hand over her mouth, but instead of frowning at the unladylike sound, Diane threw back her head and laughed until Sarah was cracking up again.

Ducking into her large attached bathroom after she'd finally caught her breath, the right bra for the dress in hand, she left the door partially open so she could talk to Diane while she dressed. The distance made it easier to say, "Abe told you?" She had to know if her former mother-in-law had all the facts.

"About the baby?" Pure joy in those words. "I'm so happy for you both. And for myself. I'm already planning how I'll spoil my first grandbaby."

Knees a bit shaky, Sarah leaned against the wall to catch her breath. She wanted to say so many things, admit her fears, but the words wouldn't come. So she finished putting on the dress before walking out into the bedroom.

"You're lovely." Getting up with that sweet comment, Diane put her cup on a bedside table, then took a seat on the bed so Sarah could sit at the vanity to do her makeup.

Sarah's hands threatened to shake as she picked up her compact.

"Losing a child is difficult."

The quiet words had Sarah forgetting all about the makeup. Dropping the compact, she turned to face the other woman's eyes, eyes that held an old, deep sadness. "Yes." It came out raw, torn out of her.

Abe's mother just held out her arms.

Sarah went into them in a jerk of emotion, let herself be held in a soft maternal embrace by a woman who understood the loss of her baby as even Abe couldn't. She and Diane didn't speak, just held each other.

LATER, AFTER SARAH HAD WASHED off her face and hidden the ravages of tears with makeup, she glanced at her hair and sighed. If she tried to fully dry and straighten it now, they'd miss their dinner reservation. So she got out the curly-hair goop she kept on hand for emergencies and worked it into her wildly kinky hair so that at least it wouldn't go fuzzy.

That done, she picked up her treasured pearl necklace from the special velvet-lined box where she always kept it... and saw Diane dab away another tear of her own.

It made her smile, hope a bright flame in her heart now.

Necklace on, she found her shoes, her purse. "Thank you,"

she said as the two of them prepared to go downstairs, Abe and Flossie having returned ten minutes earlier.

Diane turned to tuck Sarah's hair behind her ear, cup her cheek, her next words intense with emotion. "I'm here for you, Sarah. Anytime you want to talk about the baby, ask my advice, anything at all. Even if it's Abe you're angry with, don't feel you can't come to me and talk." Dark shadows in her eyes. "And call me Mom, okay? I so terribly miss having a daughter."

Sarah nodded jerkily, swallowed back the surge of emotion inside her, and—after a quick hug—they both headed down the stairs. The big man who waited at the foot of those stairs looked at Sarah in a way that tangled her up until she could hardly breathe.

Flushing, she stopped so that they were eye-to-eye. "What?"

He ran his fingers through her curls. "You." A quiet murmur, his touch a possessive promise. "I'm not letting you go ever again."

Sarah sucked in a breath, the flame of hope white-hot.

# PART FOUR

# CHAPTER 29

SAFELY PAST THE TWELVE-WEEK MARK in her pregnancy with no signs of complications, not even any morning sickness, the baby still safe inside her, Sarah couldn't imagine being happier. Her and Abe's relationship made her heart hurt in the best way, Diane had become a cherished maternal figure in her life, she had a beautiful circle of friends, and her business was growing in exactly the way she wanted.

She felt like she was walking on air.

Then Abe asked her if they could tell his bandmates about the baby. Because, somewhat shockingly, she and Abe had managed to fly under the radar with the media—at least on that point. Handlebar-mustachioed Basil *had* gotten a payday with his reunion story, but sadly for him, it hadn't been a big one because of a political sex scandal that had broken the same day.

That scandal had very quickly buried the news of Abe and Sarah's reunion, and they'd done nothing to reignite that interest. Sarah had known they couldn't keep the news of the pregnancy quiet forever, but she still wasn't ready for Abe's request—though, of course, he was right: it was time.

Especially since she'd already told Lola—the other woman knew Sarah well enough to have picked up the delicate changes in her face and body. A week earlier, she'd asked point-blank if Sarah was "cooking up a tiny human-shaped bun in a certain oven." It had made Sarah laugh, admit to it.

"Yes," she said to Abe now. "I want Molly, Kit, and Thea to know too."

A day after that conversation, however, she fidgeted in the passenger seat of Abe's SUV.

Abe closed his hand over her thigh, bared because she wore shorts paired with a floaty top. "Hey, you good?"

"No," she admitted, folding her arms and slumping into the seat. "I should've let you announce the pregnancy without me."

"*Sarah.*" Abe ran his thumb over her skin. "It'll be easy—we can tell everyone at once at this 'pool-warming' of Noah and Kit's."

Sarah nodded. "I know." The other couple was excited about their new pool, had invited everyone over for an inaugural swim. "Are you sure they won't mind me being there?"

"Sweetheart, quite aside from the fact you're friends with the women, the guys all know we're together, even if we haven't done a couple thing with them yet—they've just been giving us space by not prying."

Abe ran his knuckles over her cheek. "Only reason you didn't get a separate invite is because they expect us to turn up together. I think they figure we must be ready to admit our relationship by now." A grin. "I mean, they only have so much patience—except for Thea the whole lot of them have been pretending not to have seen that photograph of our kiss for months."

That made sense. Of course it made sense. Especially since Kit had chatted to Sarah about the pool just the other day, her words holding an expectation that Sarah would be there this weekend to see it. "I'm crazy," she announced.

"You're just nervous." Pulling the SUV to a stop on the side of the quiet Pacific Palisades road, Abe turned to face her, closing his hand over her nape. "So am I." He grinned. "Shit, I'm going to be a dad."

Sarah released a breath she hadn't been aware of holding. All she had to remember was that they were in this together, a unit. She wasn't alone. "Should we plan how to tell them?"

"We'll figure it out as we go." Moving without warning, he kissed her with a scorching heat that made her moan in the back of her throat as her legs pressed together. Abe put his free hand on her thigh in response, sliding it high enough that she had to nudge him off before things went past the point of no return. "You are not making me naked on a public road, Abe Bellamy."

A wicked smile, then one more kiss that melted her bones before Abe settled back into the driver's seat. They didn't speak again until he stopped at the gate to Noah and Kit's large property, but he kept his hand on her thigh anytime he didn't need it to drive. It felt great. Wonderful. The stubbornly romantic girl in her loved it.

"Kit gave me a remote for the gate," Abe told her. "It's in the glove compartment."

Locating it, Sarah pushed the button to open the gate. She made sure to close it behind them afterward, conscious Kit had once had a dangerous stalker. Even though that stalker was now locked up in a psychiatric facility, Kit was a well-known actress and Noah a rock star. Fans who wouldn't normally intrude might forget themselves if given such a wide-open opportunity.

"What in the name of all that is holy is *that?*"

Glancing forward at Abe's exclamation, Sarah felt her eyes widen. A hot pink Ferrari sat next to the crouching red beast of Fox's Lamborghini. When Abe came around to open her door—she'd kind of gotten used to that, liked him to do it— she let him help her out, then went over to examine the car while he let Flossie out from the back.

Her pet barked excitedly at this new place before running over to lean her warm body against Sarah's leg while she peered inside the astonishing car that was causing Abe to mutter epithets under his breath.

"I think I see diamantés," she told him, nose pressed to the glass of the window. "And wow, there might be pink fur on the foot pedals."

"Oh, for fuck's sake."

Rising to her full height, she turned toward Abe. Giggles threatened. "You look like you're about to cry."

"I am. Who the hell would do that to a beauty of a machine?" Shuddering, he threw an arm around her shoulders, drawing her snug against his muscled heat. "Come on, I can't look anymore. Look at Flossie—she can't believe it either."

She laughed softly as he led her toward the sounds of splashing and conversation, was still smiling when he opened the gate to the pool area and said, "Who the hell brought the pink horror?"

They walked into laughter and play and friendship.

Flossie was in heaven, racing around the pool and barking hello at everyone.

In the chaos, Sarah heard several shouted, "Hellos" including "Hey, Sarah!" and suddenly she felt silly for being nervous. These were all their friends.

"Your pool is amazing," she said to Kit when Noah and Kit surfaced after a dive.

Pushing her hair off her face as she treaded water by the side of the pool, Kit met Sarah's eyes with the sparkling amber of her own. "Did you see the waterfalls?" She was positively bubbling. "Noah got those for me."

"I had to basically steal a builder," Schoolboy Choir's guitarist said from beside Kit, the golden skin of his shoulders beaded with water. "He was working for Beau Flavell at the time—I spun Beau a line about true love and winning my girl and he fell for the romantic bullshit." Though Noah's words were offhand, the way he looked at Kit was anything but.

It was clear the bad boy of rock and roll was permanently off the market.

"Ignore him, Sarah," Kit said. "He secretly wanted the waterfalls too." Laughing when Noah threatened to push her under the water, she said, "Come join us. The water's glorious."

Sarah hesitated. She wasn't really showing yet, but...

Sliding his arms around her from behind, Abe said, "Listen up! We have an announcement!"

Everyone waded closer. As if sensing this was important, Flossie padded back to stand beside Sarah. Her heart began to pound with all those eyes on her, her breath coming faster... until Thea's voice cut through the air. "Is this like a reality-show pause? Dum, dum, dra-*ma*."

Laughter filled the air, their friends yelling at them to hurry it up.

"I'm pregnant," Sarah blurted out before Abe could say anything.

Surprise on more than one face, but it wasn't the bad kind of surprise. It was the suspiciously gleeful kind. Whistles and congratulations filled the air the next second, the two of them bombarded with handshakes and wet hugs that had her beaming as Abe's grin threatened to crack his face.

It was about five minutes later that Sarah finally had a chance to go behind the privacy screens of the newly built pool cabana and change into her deep green tankini with its fun white-on-green polka-dotted bottoms. The tankini style was her number one swimsuit of choice—she just felt prettier in it, and she liked being able to swap the tops and bottoms around to make fun combinations.

Abe whistled from where he'd already changed into his boxer-brief-style swimming trunks. "Sexy doesn't do you justice," he said, so much appreciation in the eyes that shaped her body that she might've lost her breath there for a second or two. "You still have that red bikini?" Abe asked. "The one that was all teeny tiny triangles and string?"

Sarah blushed; she'd bought that scandalous bikini for their honeymoon but hadn't had the nerve to wear it on the white sand beaches of the tiny Fijian island where they'd spent a week. Instead, she'd only ever worn it beside their pool at home when it was just her and Abe. "No." She paused. "I didn't take it when I left. What did you do with my clothes?"

Scowling, Abe said, "First, I went in your wardrobe and sniffed your clothes like a pathetic fool."

Sarah almost melted where she stood at this further evidence that he'd missed her, really missed her. "Then you threw them in the pool?" she guessed, remembering his fury during their divorce.

"Something like that." A shamefaced shrug. "I was an asshole."

"Don't feel bad." She patted his cheek. "If I'd had access to your clothing, I'd probably have taken scissors to it. Especially your favorite suits that you got on Savile Row."

Horror on his face. "You have a mean streak."

Winking, she sauntered out, well aware he was watching her ass. It made her grin deepen. Once outside the cabana, she dropped her hat on a lounger, then slipped into the crystalline blue waters of the pool to swim lazily out and join Molly.

The glee hadn't quite faded from the other woman's features.

"How long have you known?" Sarah asked. "About how serious Abe and I had become?"

"Well"—Molly smiled that wide open smile of hers—"I kind of figured out he had it bad when he kept messaging to ask how you were after Zenith."

Sarah had seen one of those messages, hadn't quite known how to handle Abe's obvious concern when she'd convinced herself he didn't care about her. "That was a while ago."

"Yes, but then he started missing dinners with the rest of us and being unavailable when he usually wouldn't be..." An affectionate shoulder nudge. "It wasn't hard to connect the dots. Especially after David flat-out asked him."

"Oh." Sarah looked over to find Schoolboy Choir's drummer sitting on the edge of the pool with Abe, both their legs in the water. David was having a beer while Abe was sticking to a nonalcoholic version Noah had stocked for him. The two appeared to be chilling, talking about nothing in particular. "Abe said he'd spoken to David, but I wasn't sure how seriously anyone was taking it."

"Are you kidding?" Molly shook her head. "After seeing you two at Zenith, we all knew it was dead serious." The other woman danced in the water. "I'm so happy for you both. An adorable little Abra baby! I'm going to buy tons of tiny New Zealand branded infant clothes. So many that your baby's going to grow up thinking he or she is a Kiwi!"

The other woman's joy was infectious.

Wait. "*Abra?*"

"Like abracadabra. Abe and Sarah equals Abra, get it?" Molly collapsed into laughter at Sarah's no-doubt-dumbfounded expression, giggling when Sarah splashed her. "I didn't come up with it, I swear. The fans on the message boards did." She wiped her face. "You two have a small but devoted fan base that's been hanging on, waiting for a reunion. Right now they might be the happiest people on the Internet."

"Abra?" Sarah's shoulders began to shake. "Abe's going to love that."

That set the tone for the day. She had the best time at the party. She was still more comfortable with the women, but when Noah sat down in the lounger next to hers a while later and started up a conversation, it felt normal, everyday. Just a woman speaking with one of her man's closest friends.

"You and Kit look really happy together," she dared say five minutes into their conversation.

"I'm fucking crazy about her." Noah's eyes followed his lover as she dived into the water to retrieve a colored ring from the bottom of the pool, she and David currently tied for most retrievals. "Head over heels."

The blond male frowned without warning. "Give me a sec."

Disappearing into the house, he returned not long afterward with an acoustic guitar and a notepad with a pen snugged to its side. "Can you write this down for me?"

"Sure." Sarah put aside her pineapple juice, then listened as Noah began to play while quietly working out lyrics.

Abe wandered over a couple of minutes later, having just come from the pool. Grabbing a towel to wipe off his face, he took a seat on the end of Sarah's lounger and listened in.

She had trouble concentrating with him all but naked so close to her, droplets of water dripping over his body. Telling herself she could pounce on him later, she managed to get her hormones under some kind of control and continued to take notes for Noah.

"You need a different chorus," Abe said at one point.

Noah made a suggestion, Abe refined it, and the two of them kept going.

At some point, Abe took her foot and began to massage it absently while he and Noah worked on the song. Sarah had never felt as included in the group, in Abe's musical family. Fox and Molly's wedding had been a special event, but this was everyday life—and Sarah was very much a part of it.

Close to tears, she was glad Abe was focused on the music. It left her free to watch him and to enjoy this moment when she was truly Abe's lover.

# Chapter 30

Late the next night, as Sarah lay sated and lazy in Abe's arms, he said, "How about we make this permanent?"

"What?"

"Move in together."

Memories smashed into her of the last time they'd lived together, of how she'd watched helplessly as Abe tumbled deeper and deeper into the abyss. "No," she said on a crash of emotion, fear gripping her heart in a vise.

"Sarah, we're spending every night together anyway."

"So? Is it getting inconvenient to bring over a change of clothes?" She knew he'd forgotten today.

"That's not it and you know it." Abe leaned over her, glowered. "I hate not having you with me, not seeing your stuff all over the bathroom counter or your books on the nightstand."

Sarah's jaw set. "Too bad." She poked at his chest. "I'm not ready to take that risk yet."

Abe blew out a breath. His jaw worked. When he finally spoke, it was to say, "I'm pissed off." He got out of bed, began to dress. "I need to go work it off."

Blinking at the blunt statement, Sarah sat up in bed, pushing back her hair from her face. "What are you going to do?"

"Go hit the gym."

"At this hour?"

"I have a twenty-four-hour membership." Bending down, he curved his hand around her nape and smacked a hard kiss to her lips. "Since I only have workout gear in the car, I'll have to go to my place to shower and change afterward, but I'll be back later if you still want me to spend the night."

Sarah nodded. "I'll wait up."

She wanted to call him back when he walked out, but part of her remained wary of Abe's commitment to sobriety. She needed to know he could deal with it if they fought, that he wouldn't turn to alcohol and drugs.

So she let him go.

And she hoped he'd come back to her the same wonderful man with whom she was falling ever more desperately in love.

ABE HIT THE WEIGHTS AT the gym, his demons tearing at him with every fucking rep. "You bastards aren't going to win," he said and lifted.

The goddamn bloodthirsty creatures wouldn't shut up. That was when he remembered what David had said to him a few days after the near miss alcohol-poisoning incident. *Don't be a proud shithead. Reach out when you need a friend.*

Deciding tonight qualified, Abe made the call. And though it was late, the drummer didn't hesitate. He just asked where Abe was, then joined him. They all used this gym, so Abe didn't have to let David in—the other man had his own pass key.

Having arrived in workout gear, David came straight to the weight room and began to warm up. "I think we're the only two in here" were his opening words.

"Good. I hate the posing grunters," Abe said with a scowl. "Why can't they just do their workout without sounding like a bunch of baboons on steroids?"

David grinned. "I like that—I'm going to use it." The drummer got to work.

He couldn't lift as much as Abe, but he could lift far more than he should've been able to given his weight and height. David was in hella good shape.

"Did I pull you away from Thea?" Abe asked after over ten minutes of companionable quiet.

"She was working in her home office." David didn't pause in his steady reps using some serious free weights. "I left her with a kiss and a promise that we wouldn't do anything to get our faces in the papers." A grin. "I do not want to piss her off, so let's not get into a fight."

"Damn it!" Abe muttered. "I called you over here specifically to beat your ass."

Giving him the finger, David said, "You get that e-mail from the label?"

"Yeah."

The two of them talked about the label, about music, about David's upcoming wedding. The one thing they didn't talk about was Abe's sobriety. They didn't need to. Having his friend here was enough.

Afterward, as they grabbed ice-cold bottles of water from the fridge in the little break area that featured a juice bar during the day, Abe leaned up against the nearest wall and said, "Sarah won't let me move in."

David swigged half his bottle before replying. "Can't blame her, man." He flipped a chair around, took a seat with his arms braced on the back. "You must've been hell to live with."

Abe thought again of the day he'd thrown Sarah's books in the pool, then the furniture. And that had been one of the tamer incidents. "Yeah." He pressed the cold bottle to his forehead. "I just want to be there for her... and I want the chance to show her I'm not the man I once was."

David ran his fingers through his sweat-damp hair. "I get it." After wiping his face on a towel, he rubbed at his jaw, eyebrows drawn together over the golden brown of his eyes. "I guess you have to court her."

"What?" Abe scowled at the man who'd been his friend since they were thirteen. "I can't write memos." No one but David and Thea knew what David had written in those magic memos, but they'd certainly worked. Which was why Abe was listening to advice that included the word "court"—because David was about to marry his girl, while Abe couldn't even get his to trust him enough to give him a key.

"Abe, you were married to Sarah." David raised an eyebrow. "If anyone knows what she likes and needs, it should be you."

Abe thought of the books he'd sent her; he'd seen them neatly placed on her bookshelf. All except one, which was on a side table with a bookmark in it. He'd done okay there. She'd also enjoyed their dessert date. "Like we're still dating?" The idea felt false to him. He and Sarah were far beyond anything superficial.

"Not dating—more like showing her that you pay attention to what's important to her." David finished off his water. "That doesn't end after you're in a relationship. It's always." A shit-eating smile. "I'm not admitting anything, but it's possible I may still write Thea memos."

Abe pointed at David, eyes narrowed. "You're a disgrace to rock stars everywhere."

"Do I look like I give a flying fuck?" Grinning, David put his drink bottle in the recycle bin, caught Abe's when Abe lobbed it over, and did the same. "You going to shower here?"

"Nah. I had workout clothes in the car but nothing else. I'm going to head home to change." Then he'd drive back over to Sarah's.

"I'll shower at home too." As they walked out, David said, "Look, man, I know this is none of my business, but seems to me that Sarah never got the romantic stuff women like. You two hooked up, got married, and that was it."

"Yeah, I know. I'm going to fix that." He'd made up his mind to give Sarah what she needed this time around. "Thanks for tonight." He held out his fist.

David bumped it and they went their separate ways.

HE WAS HALF EXPECTING SARAH'S home to be dark when he finally drove up, but the windows upstairs glowed with light and the gate opened seconds after he pushed the buzzer. The garage door began to lift up almost at the same time. He'd just finished parking beside her zippy red car when the internal access door opened, Sarah haloed by the light on the other side.

She was dressed in pajama shorts and a T-shirt, her hair loose and wild around her head. She looked all sleepy and soft.

Jogging up, he shut the door after nudging her inside and cupped her cheek. "You were asleep." He nuzzled her.

Yawning, she kind of cuddled into him, her hands folded up against his chest. "I nodded off while I was reading."

Abe loved holding her, wanted to do it all night. "Come on, let's get to bed."

She led him upstairs, crawling into bed and watching him with sleepy eyes as he stripped and dropped his clothes on top of his duffel.

"You want me to wear pj's?" It was the first time that had come up—they were usually naked when they tumbled into bed.

A slow smile. "Do you even own pj's?"

"No," he admitted. "But I brought a pair of sweats."

"I like you barefoot and bare to the skin."

Grinning at the cheeky response, he got into bed with her, then reached over to turn off the bedside lamp; it plunged the room into darkness but for a little diffuse light that came in through the curtains.

That was enough for him to see Sarah's face when he stretched out his arm so she could pillow her head on his shoulder. Turning to brush her hair off her sleepy-eyed face, his heart this huge, tight thing in his chest, he said, "Good night, sweetheart."

Sarah's lips curved. "Good night, gorgeous."

He pressed a soft kiss to her lips as her eyes closed, brushed his hand over her abdomen in an unspoken good night to their baby, then he held her close and they slept.

ABE WOKE UP WITH THAT heaviness in his limbs that came from a long, deep sleep where he hadn't been chased by endless dark dreams. Stretching out, he reached for Sarah. She was gone, her space in the bed cool. "Sarah?" It came out a gritty rumble as he lay on his front, still not quite fully awake.

"Good morning, sleepyhead." Walking out from the bathroom dressed only in a thigh-length robe tied at the waist, Sarah leaned over to kiss the back of his shoulder. Her hair was dry but damp at the ends and around the edges, her scent of some feminine soap that made him want to tug her freshly showered body into bed and make her dirty all over again.

"You were sleeping so deeply I didn't want to wake you," she said with a smile.

Happy now that he knew she was all right and not suffering from morning sickness or something, he reached for her. "Come back to bed."

Avoiding his hand with a chuckle, she walked over to the vanity. "I'm starving."

Turning his head, he saw her pull her hair into a neat knot on top of her head, then stick a bobby pin through it to hold the curly mass in place. He loved watching her do stuff like that. Normal stuff. Everyday stuff a wife would do in front of her husband. He wanted to wake up to such sights every damn day for the rest of his life.

"Want to go out for breakfast?"

"You're as slow as a snail in the morning." Affectionate words, laughter in her expression when her eyes met his in the mirror. "I'll have pancakes and bacon ready by the time you make it down." Blowing him a kiss, she headed out. "Don't be late or I'll eat it all."

Forcing himself to move, Abe yawned again, stretched, then walked into the shower. His muscles ached slightly from last night's lifting session, but nothing unusual. Just the good soreness that came from a session where he'd pushed himself until things were no longer easy. The hot spray felt good on his body, the water pressure just right.

Making quick work of it because he wanted to be with Sarah, he cleaned up, then dug out his toothbrush and brushed. He didn't want to give her any reason to hesitate to kiss him—a man had to cover his bases when he was trying to win back his wife. He thought about shaving, but right now he was still in stubble territory and Sarah didn't mind stubble.

Once dry, he emptied the duffel of a pair of fresh jeans and a shirt in dark gray with short, folded-back sleeves that made his arms look amazing.

Sarah liked his arms.

This was all about Sarah.

Dressed, he padded downstairs, following the sound of pumping music to the kitchen... to find Sarah dancing in front of the stove, her hands above her head and her body curving and swaying with the beat. The robe was thin, caressed her body like a lover. He leaned against the doorjamb and waited until she'd flipped out the pancakes currently on the griddle before walking over and tugging her into his arms.

"Dance with me."

She switched off the stove with a deep smile, and then the two of them danced barefoot in the kitchen. Abe spun her out, caught her and a kiss at the same time before moving with her in time to the beat, one of his hands low on her back, the other on her hip. Sarah had perfect timing. He'd always loved dancing with her. It felt like they were one body as they moved past the stove and around the island.

Her long legs brushed against his every so often, her hands locked around his neck, her hips and ass moving with a feminine fluidity that made him want to beg for mercy. And her face, it glowed with happiness.

"Enough," she said after three songs, her breath coming in pants and a delighted heat on her skin. "The pancakes will get cold." Rising on her toes, she pressed her lips to his. "Let's eat."

It turned out she'd already made the bacon as well. He went to the fridge, pulled out a carton of the fresh blueberries they'd bought together, put a small bowl by her plate—after washing them. Who knew what chemicals were on the fruit?

"I know." Sarah laughed. "Vitamins and shit."

The word "shit" sounded so incongruous coming from Sarah's lips. "Exactly." Popping a few blueberries into his mouth, Abe took his seat.

Then they had an ordinary, everyday breakfast together, neither one of them having anything major planned that day. Sarah was all caught up on her business paperwork, and since she was now successful enough not to have to cover absences herself, she could afford to take time off when she needed it. The only thing that might require her attention was if she got a call from a current or prospective client—she dealt with all those herself.

Abe, too, was free, he and the guys having decided to take a break with their songwriting sessions for the new record.

Midway through breakfast, Sarah admitted she was craving a hot chocolate, so Abe got up and made her one. He'd seen the good-quality dark chocolate she had in her pantry, and he was able to jury-rig a double boiler to melt it just right. He even knew how to use the handheld frother she had in her cutlery drawer.

Her eyes, which had widened when he reached for the block of chocolate rather than the mix she'd tried to point him toward, turned as huge as saucers when he put his creation in front of her, the delicately frothed top dusted with chocolate.

Taking a little sip, she sighed that dreamy little sigh he usually only ever heard in bed. His cock jumped. Ordering the damn excited thing to settle down, Abe retook his seat and enjoyed his wife's bone-deep pleasure.

Another sip, her eyes closing for two long seconds before she lifted her lashes again. "When did you become a barista?" Her voice was husky, her pupils dilated. "This is the best hot chocolate I've ever had."

"It's my one and only specialty." A wave of memories as bittersweet as dark chocolate. "Tessie loved hot chocolate, so I learned to make them. Otherwise, she'd have me going out at the crack of dawn to buy a 'real hot chocolate with foofs.'" He indicated the frothed milk to explain the last.

Sarah's expression went soft, her dark eyes liquid. "You did that for her?"

"Yeah. She was my baby sister, you know?" So small and always so excited to spend time with him. "I was her hero." It came out harsh. "She looked at me that way right to the end, even when I couldn't keep her safe, even when the pain was agonizing." Eyes hot, he stared at the table. "Some damn hero."

# CHAPTER 31

"YOU WERE THERE FOR HER." Putting down her drink, Sarah reached across the table to tangle her fingers with his. "Her big brother loved her and she knew." Voice thick, she said, "*That's* what matters."

Abe thought of the games he'd played with Tessie while she lay in a hospital bed, her tiny body ravaged by disease, and wished Sarah could've seen her sparkly smile, the way she had of laughing so infectiously. "She was a character," he said, wanting... *needing* Sarah to see Tessie as he'd seen her.

"One time, when she was five, I made her a hot chocolate but forgot to froth the milk." An unexpected smile curved over his lips, his sister's infectious laughter a faraway echo in his mind. "She gave this big sigh and said, 'Abam'—that's what she called me, after hearing Mom say Abraham one day. Anyway, Tessie does a dramatic sigh and says, 'Abam, this is atrocious.'"

Startled laughter from Sarah, the sound wrapping him in countless fragile chains he had no desire to escape. "How did she even know the word?"

"I have an aunt who uses it." Abe found himself grinning. "That summer, it was Tessie's favorite word. Everything was atrocious—the hard thing was not encouraging her to use it. She just sounded so damn cute being all prim and proper. Like a disappointed little schoolteacher."

He found his phone, scrolled to the folder he kept on it of his favorite photos of his baby sister. Bringing up a particular image, he turned the phone toward Sarah. "Mom would do her hair up in these pigtails and she liked to wear pretty dresses and little socks with patent leather Mary Janes." Exactly as she was dressed in the photograph he'd snapped in their family backyard. "That summer she told me my dirty sneakers were atrocious."

Sarah had taken his phone, was going through the images with gentle care. "There are lots of pictures of her all dirty and in playclothes."

"Oh yeah, pretty dresses or not, she could roughhouse with the best of them." Abe rubbed a fisted hand over his heart. "One rainy day right before she got sick, I was chasing her around the yard and we both slipped on a patch of mud, right onto our faces. I was worried she was hurt… but Tessie laughed and laughed and laughed."

His voice broke.


SARAH HAD NEVER SEEN ABE cry. *Never.*

Today he ducked his head, his shoulders rigid; she knew he was fisting his free hand hard. Her own eyes gritty, she put down the phone and, sliding her fingers from his, got up and moved around to tug his head gently against her stomach. "It's okay," she whispered, one hand stroking the back of his head. "You're allowed to cry for her."

His arms locked around her, and though he didn't cry, he held on so tight that she'd probably have bruises tomorrow. Sarah didn't mind. Not when this was the first time in their entire relationship that Abe had allowed himself to be vulnerable with her.

His body trembled.

Swallowing her own response to his pain, she just held him, this big, strong man who knew how to love so deeply that the loss of his little sister had almost destroyed him. He'd love their baby the same way, she suddenly realized, the understanding perfect and clear and bright. She never had to worry about her child feeling unloved or unwanted like she had.

Abe Bellamy knew how to love the innocent.

ABE WASN'T USED TO ALLOWING anyone to see his weaknesses, but as they sat down to finish breakfast ten minutes later, he realized that having Sarah hold him hadn't felt like weakness. It had felt right. She was his wife; of course she'd hold him if he needed it.

*Ex*-wife.

Shut the fuck up, he told the annoying voice in his head that insisted on piping up whenever he thought of Sarah as his wife. That stupid, needling voice that insisted on reminding him of his idiocy needed to be thumped. Wishing the voice was corporeal so he really could thump it, he helped Sarah clean up after breakfast, was about to ask her what she wanted to do today when he got a call from Thea.

"Jeez, Thea," he said as Sarah motioned that she was going upstairs, "I just saw you the other day. You gotta control your violent passion for me, or David will get jealous."

"Ha-ha." Dry as dust, her tone made him laugh. "Now that the comedy portion of the morning is out of the way," she continued, "I called to tell you that you and Sarah have been well and truly outed. Be careful of possible paparazzi at the gate."

Abe clenched his jaw, had to force himself to relax it so he could speak. "Do they know Sarah's pregnant?" He kept his voice low; the last thing Sarah needed right now was to worry about an intrusive media storm.

"No, that's still under the radar," Thea reassured him. "But a photographer got a very clear photo of you two kissing on her doorstep, and *G&V* decided to publish it front and center. You know how things get when they decide to push a particular story."

Yeah, Abe knew; the damn blog was gossip central for the entire entertainment industry. "Why now?" He'd figured people had gotten their kicks already, would leave him and Sarah in peace. "I kissed her in broad daylight for the photo shot by that weasel, Basil."

"Social media's been buzzing quietly but consistently with the Abra hashtag for weeks. I think *G&V*'s clicked onto the fact you two have a deeply devoted following—that equals more visits to their site, more ad revenue, the usual." Thea's tone was pragmatic. "From the number of comments already on the article, I don't think this'll be the last time they feature you."

Abe shrugged, his muscles no longer knotted up now that the first slap of anger had passed. "We'll continue to be boring and straitlaced and they'll find juicier targets soon enough." A "clean-cut" singer or model would get caught snorting coke, or a glamour couple would break up, or some celebrity kid would throw a tantrum.

Abe had lived in the glare of fame long enough to know it was a fickle beast.

"I'm not sure it's going to work this time, Abe," Thea warned. "Especially after they twig to the pregnancy. For now I'll see what I can do to head them off, buy you both a little more time and privacy."

Hanging up after thanking the publicist, Abe was about to go up and share Thea's intel with Sarah when he caught sight of a card propped up on the bookshelf. He'd noticed it that day he'd helped Sarah clean, had smiled because it was the one he'd sent her, but now the image on the front had a sick feeling churning in his gut.

It was a fairground.

Memories, harsh and unforgiving, punched through the misty veil created by the shit he'd been putting into his body during that time, of a night when a bright-eyed Sarah had asked him to accompany her to a fair. He'd said a flat no. One of Tessie's final outings after the doctors let her come home because there was nothing more they could do had been to a local fair—he'd carried her fragile body all wrapped up in blankets, stood beside her with his arm around her on the merry-go-round so she wouldn't fall off her horse.

She'd died two days later.

And Abe couldn't even smell kettle corn or cotton candy without wanting to break the world into a million little pieces.

Only he'd never explained that to Sarah. He'd just turned her down, tried not to see the tears she was trying to fight back, then fucked off somewhere else.

The sick feeling grew stronger. "Suck it up, Abe," he muttered. "And do better this time around."

Making a few quick calls on the heels of that order, he went up to the bedroom. "So Thea had some news," he began, then wolf-whistled.

He'd caught Sarah just as she finished hooking up her bra, her back to him and her fingers quick and clever. Her panties were the same dark blue lace as her bra, the color lush against the rich brown hue of her skin. That bra cupped her spectacular breasts as if it had been painted on, while the lace of the panties drew his attention to her equally spectacular ass.

Throwing him a startled look over her shoulder, Sarah smiled, looking a little shy and pleased at the same time. "What's happened?"

Abe didn't want to go there just yet, didn't want to steal her smile. "I'm sorry, I've lost my mind after seeing you." Walking over to grip her hip from behind, he tugged her back against him. "How about we just stay in bed?" Kissing her throat, he slid one hand around to play his fingers over her navel.

Her belly was still only curved the gentlest amount, nothing anyone who didn't know her intimately would notice.

Moaning and laughing at the same time, his wife spun around to face him, her hands on his chest. "I want to go out."

He sighed and stroked the sleek line of her back. "What do you want to do?"

"Flossie needs to be taken for a walk first of all."

Flossie looked up from where she was sitting comfortably on the bed Sarah must've made. Her tail began wagging like a metronome at the word "walk." Abe patted Sarah on the butt. "You spoil that dog."

"I know, but she's so wonderful." She kissed his jaw. "Beach walk again? I liked that."

Abe had zero willpower where Sarah was concerned. "Yeah, why not—but we might meet a few more vultures today." He told her what Thea had shared. "You still want to do the beach deal?"

Sarah thought about it, but only for a second. "Yes. How much scandal can they wring out of a couple taking their dog for a walk?" Narrowed eyes. "I'm stronger now, not so easy to bully."

"You're fucking amazing, that's what you are."

First, however, they went to visit Aaron after Abe gave a couple of paps in cars the slip. No one was going to make a quick buck with Sarah's grief. She didn't cry today, just spoke to her lost baby with purest love as she made sure his resting place was neat and tidy and his toys were where they should be.

Flossie sat beside her on one side, Abe on the other.

Pressing her lips to the stone that marked Aaron's grave an hour later, Sarah said, "I'll see you again soon, Baby Boots."

"Later, kid." Abe touched his hand to the stone before the three of them rose and walked to the SUV, a sense of peace in the air.

Heading to the beach, they hung out there for two hours, were more than ready for lunch when it rolled around. First, they made sure Flossie was hydrated and fed, then let her out into the fenced backyard. Exhausted from playing in the waves, she went to the spacious outdoor doghouse that was her official abode—not that Abe had ever seen Sarah's beloved pet spend a night there—and snuggling in, started to snore.

Meanwhile, Sarah threw together a salad and he grilled some chicken and they ate. After they'd sat for a while, relaxing, Abe took a deep breath, said, "There's a fair in town. You want to go?"

Sarah's body went motionless. And it felt as if time stopped.

"Okay," she said softly after an endless instant.

"I have to tell you something first." He swallowed, blew out a breath. "I have to tell you why I don't like fairs."

And he did, hiding nothing. None of the anger that had lived in him for so long. None of the violence of which he was afraid he was capable. None of the pain of that day when his baby sister had ridden the merry-go-round until she couldn't stay awake any longer.

Sarah cried, but she said, "We have to go. You have to remember the joy she felt that day, hold that in your heart instead of the fury that lives there now."

Abe wasn't sure he could do that, wasn't sure he wouldn't rage at the world the instant he set foot in the fair, but he would walk into hell itself for Sarah. "Let's go."

# PART
# FIVE

# CHAPTER 32

TWO MONTHS AFTER THEIR DATE at the fair, a date that had begun in teeth-clenched control for Abe and ended with him kissing her in the shadow of a Ferris wheel while she held on to a fluffy toy cat he'd won for her, Sarah no longer worried about the media or any other outside pressure when it came to their relationship.

If they messed up the beautiful, precious thing growing ever stronger between them, it would be on her and Abe, no one else.

Today she was about to step out on Abe's arm and into the full glare of the spotlight. The media intrusion hadn't been too bad over the past weeks. All thanks to a genius move on Thea's part right when interest in Sarah and Abe's relationship had been growing at dangerous speed—she'd told them to stop avoiding the media, to go to certain specific and stultifyingly nonglamorous locations where they were sure to be photographed, and to make no effort to deny the relationship.

Turned out cooperation and easy access to photos of them as a couple soon lowered their monetary value to nil as far as the vast majority of paparazzi were concerned. Why hang out all night at the gate waiting for a photo opportunity when ten other photographers also had shots of them? Thea had effectively flooded the market with so much sheer ordinariness that no one cared.

"As Schoolboy Choir's publicist," Thea had said the last time she'd come over for a coffee, "that might have been the worst possible thing I could've done, but as your friend, I take a bow."

Sarah had sent the other woman a huge bunch of flowers after the media interest died down to near zero. So much so that no one had clicked to her pregnancy. Part of it had to do with how careful they were anytime she needed to see Dr. Snyder or had to go for a scan, but mostly it was due to her height and body shape—she was carrying the baby in a way that meant her bump remained small.

Meanwhile, the peanut was developing right on schedule.

She'd worried the dress she'd chosen for tonight's red-carpet event would give it away, but Kit had been right: the Grecian-inspired gown, the color a frothy and luscious green, cascaded over her body in a joyous fall of color without accentuating her belly. If the crueler elements in the media decided to call her fat for not choosing a formfitting gown, that was fine with her—so long as they left her in privacy. Because while Sarah had toughened up enough to deal with the attention, that didn't mean she *wanted* it.

However, she didn't feel fat. She felt glorious. Her breasts looked fantastic in the dress—the heavy globes well supported by the halter neck, and her arms were beautifully toned as a result of her pregnancy-appropriate exercise routine. She patted her belly, promised her baby she'd keep her body strong, healthy.

Abe's arm slipped around her from behind. "You're worrying about the baby."

"A little." That fear lived in her always, wouldn't totally fade until she held their baby safe in her arms. "But mostly I'm excited for tonight." Turning around, she took in his black-on-black suit, the shirt open at the collar just enough to make him James Bond sexy. "You are so ridiculously hot," she said, running her hands down his chest. "Stop it."

Grinning, he dipped his head to take a slow, smoky burn of a kiss. "Sweetheart, you annihilate me in the hotness stakes." His eyes went to her hair, her curls wild around her head. "I fucking love everything about you."

Sarah still wasn't sure about the wild mass on her head, but she couldn't deny Abe this. Not today, not when he and the band were about to perform for millions around the world. "I'm so happy for you. Your performance will bring down the house." Schoolboy Choir wasn't up for any awards since they hadn't released an album within the year encompassed by the awards, but they were to give one of the banner performances of the night.

"And next year," she said, "watch out world." Every piece she'd heard from the album they were currently putting together was phenomenal. "You'll win everything there is to win."

Dark eyes held her captive. "I've already won."

Sarah's defenses were so low by now that they were barely holding. Yet something held her back from the final commitment, kept her from accepting the silent offer Abe made each time he touched her, each time he kissed her.

Maybe it was just a matter of time: twenty-one weeks, give or take, wasn't that long in the scheme of things. Five months and a bit. Not that long when you considered how long Abe had ridden a self-destructive cycle of self-abuse.

Ducking her head, she fiddled with her dress so it fell just so. "Is the limo here?"

"Yes."

What she didn't realize until she opened the door and they walked out was that it was a stretch limo. She gave an excited little jump. "Are we all going together?"

Noah pushed open the back door and stepped out before Abe could answer. "Looking gorgeous, Sarah." The guitarist held out a hand.

Taking it, she let him help her inside. Molly patted the seat beside her, and Sarah slid in. Noah and Abe followed within seconds, and then the interior filled with music and chatter and offers of champagne or juice.

The men all wore black suits without ties, though Fox and David had gone for crisp white shirts rather than the black chosen by Noah and Abe. Kit's dress was a sparkly gold sheath, while Thea wore slinky red, Molly a lush midnight blue. All ankle-length, in line with their agreement to glam it up tonight.

She took a photograph with the women, then went to send it to Lola; her closest friend had met Thea, Molly, and Kit several times by now, was beginning to build bonds of her own with them.

"Oh, that's a great shot," Molly said over her shoulder. "Can you copy in Charlie as well?"

Sarah smiled at the thought of the petite blonde who'd recently sent the peanut a tiny All Blacks rugby jersey. "Not a problem."

Lola was in Houston for her dad's birthday party, but she'd told Sarah she'd be watching the events, starting with the red-carpet coverage. Charlotte was also planning to do the same in New Zealand. Both women replied within moments.

Lola: *Knock 'em dead, you goddesses.*

Charlie: *Eep! I'm making the popcorn now. Can't wait to see everyone on screen! Good luck to the guys from both of us!*

"We look freaking amazing!" Kit declared right then, to loud cheers. "And I hope that asshole reporter who implied I had a nose job ends up with the worst case of itchy hay fever to ever torment a nose."

Sarah grinned and joined in the clapping for Kit's curse.

The ensuing moments were joyous noise, words shouted across the limo and spoken over others' heads, but it wasn't harsh. No, it was the sound of happiness, of a group of friends and lovers heading out for what promised to be a great night. Sarah found herself chatting alone with Thea at one stage, when the publicist swapped seats with Molly so she could sit next to Sarah.

Sarah had always been intimidated by Thea, wasn't quite over it even now they were so much closer. Not only was the other woman sleekly beautiful, she had a cutting intelligence and fierce confidence. It was rumored she ate paparazzi for breakfast, then crunched their bones for a midmorning snack.

Sarah could well believe it.

But as with Lola, Thea had an incredibly kind heart under her battle armor and was ferocious in protecting her own.

"Hi." Sarah held up her flute of sparkling water.

Thea clinked it with her champagne flute. "No taste for grape juice? I made sure the limo was stocked with your favorite kind."

"I'm scared I'll spill it, and then there goes this dress." Sarah petted the fabric. "I'd probably burst out crying."

"Remind me to tell you about the time I all but poured coffee on myself fifteen minutes before a meeting while wearing a white sheath dress," Thea said dryly. "I had to send my poor intern on a clothing run to the nearest boutique that knew my size and style. The girl was so terrified she'd make the wrong choice that she talked the boutique owner into giving her ten dresses for me to choose from."

"I can't imagine you spilling coffee on yourself," Sarah admitted. "It's like asking me to believe that you're a mere mortal."

Thea burst out laughing, the gorgeous golden hue of her skin flushed with delight. "Excellent," she said afterward. "That means my campaign to convince people I'm a shark who sleeps with one eye open continues to be a success."

Sarah grinned. "I'm glad you're on my side."

"Always."

Sarah thought of the portfolio Thea had built on Jeremy, digging up things Sarah hadn't even known existed and that could get Jeremy blacklisted within his industry. "It's insurance," Thea had told her. "I want you to have all this so that if he ever threatens you, you can quietly slip one of these pieces of information into your response—and make sure he knows the proof is held elsewhere and will be released if he doesn't back off."

"Thank you." Sarah's words came from the heart. "For everything you've done for me."

Thea nudged her gently with her shoulder. "It's what friends do."

Sarah didn't point out that they hadn't been friends back when the violence happened. Thea, she'd learned, had trouble with overt acknowledgement of her kindness. "How're the wedding plans coming along?" she asked instead, grateful she had so many wonderful women in her life.

Thea's gaze softened, her eyes going to David before she glanced back at Sarah. "I can't wait to be married to him," she said. "I want to put a damn ring on his finger so the entire world knows he's mine."

Sarah smiled. "I'm pretty sure that isn't in question. He's crazy about you, and he doesn't care who knows." Just like Abe made no effort to hide his love for Sarah.

It made her breathless each time he took her hand, or put his on her lower back, or laughingly stole a kiss on the beach. He'd figured out pretty quick that while Sarah was shy about public displays of affection, she liked what he did to her.

In front of her, Thea's expression was open, unshielded, exposing a very private side to this strong, powerful woman. "David's my North Star," she said quietly.

Sarah's eyes stung at the simple, passionate declaration.

Taking a shaky breath, Thea sipped from her champagne before continuing. "My parents and David's parents are as thick as thieves, and they're lining everything up for a big wedding." Her face glowed. "I don't care as long as I get to marry my man."

Sarah could already almost see Thea's tall and svelte body in an elegant wedding dress, her hand on her father's arm as they walked down the aisle. "Have you chosen your gown yet?"

Thea had just parted her lips to answer when the limo came to a halt. Putting down her champagne flute, she said, "We're here," then snapped her fingers. "Foxy, you exit first. Everyone's gaga to see you at your first formal event post-wedding."

"Do you ever take the night off?" Fox asked, picking up Molly's hand to press a kiss to the back of it.

David was the one who answered. "Yes. I have to use rope and hide all her gadgets, *and* unplug the Wi-Fi modem so she can't use my gadgets, but yes."

Pointing a finger at the drummer while everyone else grinned, Thea said, "You are in trouble."

"I love being in trouble with you."

The sound of the crowd outside poured into the car as the limo driver opened the back passenger-side door. Sarah felt a sudden clutch of nerves in her stomach as she watched Fox step out, then extend a hand to help Molly out. The other woman's movements were sexily graceful. Meanwhile, Sarah was suddenly feeling less Amazonian goddess and more fat pregnant lady.

"Can we go last?" she whispered to Abe when he shifted down the seats to face her on the other side. "So everyone's occupied with the others in case I fall flat on my face?"

"You're too elegant to fall," Abe said. "And even if there was a risk, I'd never let it happen."

Nerves continued to do the samba in her gut.

Lines forming on his forehead, Abe turned to Thea while Noah and Kit were making their exit. "You two go ahead. Sarah and I will be the rear guard."

Thea patted Sarah on the hand. "You'll *own* this. I happen to know for a fact that an entire busload of Abra fans camped out for an entire day so they'd have primo seats to watch the red-carpet arrivals, and you two are their number one couple to see."

"You're making that up," Sarah said huskily.

Thea crossed her heart. "No lies. Your people are out there."

Oddly, that did make her feel a touch better. It was nice to know there were people waiting beyond who had nothing but happiness in their hearts for Abe and Sarah.

"As for the paps," Thea continued, "remember, they want your photograph, not the other way around." A steely tone "You don't need the publicity to succeed—so in your head, you can tell them to go screw themselves. But don't forget to smile while you're doing that—under no circumstances do I want to see anything but a kickass woman with confidence blazing off her. Got it?"

Nodding, Sarah stared wide-eyed at Abe as David got out, Thea following.

"Yes," Abe said, "she's a little scary, but that's why we love her."

"I heard that," Thea said as she exited, her hand in David's.

Abe reached over to lift Sarah's hand to his lips, the kiss tender. "I've got you, Sarah. Trust me."

# CHAPTER 33

SARAH NODDED JERKILY AND FORCED herself to shift to the other side of the limo after he got out so that she'd be ready when he extended his hand to her. Then he did, and she was moving. One leg, two, lift her body out without hitting her head or tangling her heels in the dress, and wow, she was standing on two feet with Abe's hand locked to hers and she hadn't tripped or fallen or embarrassed herself.

That was when it hit her, the roar of shouts and the storm of lightning flashes from the media camped on either side of the red carpet. Sarah wanted to crawl back into the limo, but then Abe squeezed her hand and Thea's words reverberated in her head. She didn't need this publicity—these people couldn't hurt her with what they chose to write about her or any unflattering pictures they chose to print.

Tonight it was about supporting and celebrating the man she loved.

That was what was important.

Looking up at him with open pride, she said, "I love you in black. Did the four of you decide together to wear suits?" She'd looked up footage from previous awards events out of curiosity, knew that while David was known for his designer suits and Abe for his slick sense of style, Noah and Fox often turned up in jeans and band T-shirts.

Today, however, all four men were wearing flawlessly cut suits, and they looked incredibly hot together as a group. They'd be changing for the performance but would get back into the suits for the rest of the night.

"Yep." Abe kept his hand possessively around hers. "My idea." He held her gaze. "I told them we should do it because it was Fox's first big public thing with Molly after they got hitched. But it was really because this is my first time out with you at a formal deal now that you're not totally pissed at me anymore."

Sarah's stomach flipped. The intensity of his expression… Breathless, she whispered, "You're a wonderful man."

Abe's smile was that heartbreaker one against which her remaining defenses stood no chance. He broke their handclasp, but only so he could place his fingers on her lower back, warm and heavy, and they moved on down the red carpet behind Thea and David. Sarah wasn't actually expecting too much attention from the media—she'd never attracted it, wasn't glamorous enough or famous in her own right.

Molly, she knew, would love to be in her position, but unfortunately the incident with the recording of her and Fox had put her on the media radar. No matter how hard Molly tried to stay out of the spotlight, the other woman attracted a level of attention Sarah simply didn't. Thank God.

"Why are they yelling at us?" she muttered under her breath half a minute later.

Abe moved his hand in a circular gesture on her back. "They want photos," he murmured, then leaned in close and kissed her cheek.

"*Abe.*" That kiss had sent the yelling into overdrive. "Why did you do that?"

"So they know you're special." Sliding his hand around to her hip, he tugged her closer against him. "Stay with me."

Sarah knew he couldn't protect her against the vicious people who lived to tear others down, the ones who'd no doubt call her "fat" and "big boned" when they weren't snidely predicting the end of her and Abe's rekindled relationship, but she was a woman now. Not a naive girl who thought her only value lay in what others thought of her body. "Let's do this."

"First, look to the right and past the media phalanx."

Sarah followed his gaze, saw the raised audience bleachers that had been put up for those lucky enough—and determined enough—to get what had to be a very limited number of seats. Those seats provided a bird's-eye view of the red-carpet arrivals area.

*ABRA* ♥ *Forever!*

She began to laugh. "That sign is *huge!*" Lifting her hand, she waved at the group that held the sparkling, glittering sign.

They went insane with excitement, waving back as they jumped up and down. Then, as if they'd planned it, they organized themselves for a selfie with Abe and Sarah in the background.

When Abe grinned and leaned in to kiss her again, she was pretty sure one woman fainted dead away.

Abe's lips brushed her ear. "Your boobs look phenomenal in that dress."

She burst out laughing again, feeling as if she was made of pure delight. "Hey, my face is up here."

Grin wide, Abe led her closer to the paparazzi. And the cameras went wild.

THE BAND'S PERFORMANCE WENT OFF with a rockin' boom.

According to Thea, Schoolboy Choir was being talked about all over the world as the highlight performance of the entire event—and there had been a number of very good performances from other artists.

Pumped, everyone was ready to celebrate, and they headed out as a group to one of the big after-parties held in a glitzy bar. Sarah wanted desperately to celebrate with Abe's bandmates and the women, but she hadn't been feeling the greatest toward the end of the show, was now close to throwing up. She knew she had to go home before it got any worse, but she didn't want to ruin the night for Abe.

"Hey." It was a rumbling murmur against her ear, Abe's body a big, warm wall that blocked out the noise of voices raised to be heard over the thumping music. "What's the matter?"

"I think morning sickness has finally decided to hit—at night." She hadn't felt anywhere near this nauseous during her last pregnancy. Panic gnawed at her, twisting and churning in her gut and adding to the nausea. She'd call Dr. Snyder tomorrow, make sure nothing—

"I'll have the driver bring the car around."

"What?" She rubbed at her forehead, her face suddenly unbearably hot. "Abe, no. You should enjoy the night."

Abe locked his arm around her, the fingers of his free hand already working his phone to send a message. "I'm not that guy anymore, Sarah." Pressing a kiss to her temple, he began to move, heading for the exit and always making sure his body took any unintended bumps from the crowd.

Sarah looked up at one point to see David glance across from the other side of the room. Abe must've made some kind of silent sign because the drummer gave a slight nod. A minute later and she and Abe were out of the hot, crowded club and into the clear night air. Sarah sucked it in and immediately felt better, but it was all relative: her queasiness didn't subside.

"I don't know what to do," she admitted as they waited for the limo to pull up, her voice wobbling. "I never really had morning sickness with Aaron. Do you think everything is okay?"

"I'm sure everything is fine," Abe said with a confidence that boosted her own. "And I read up on stuff online. Lots of women say saltine crackers help. I got you a box, put it in the pantry."

Sarah blinked, staying snug against Abe's body. "When?"

"A couple of weeks ago." He cuddled her impossibly tighter when a photographer got too close, the camera flash going off like a strobe light. It made her stomach roil even more, bile rising to her throat.

*No. She was not going to throw up here and end up on the front page of a tabloid.*

Hiding her face in Abe's chest while trying to make it appear as if she was just tired and snuggling in, she drew in his scent. He wrapped his arm around her shoulders, and though she could feel his muscles trembling with brutal tension, he didn't strike out at the photographer physically or even vocally. Instead, he kept his attention on her, telling her he could see the limo turning into the street, that it'd be at the curb in front of them in seconds.

Then it was and he was opening the door, getting her inside.

Sarah didn't speak once she was safely inside the limo, just squeezed her eyes shut and breathed. She managed—barely—to hold it together until she was home. At which point she ran to the nearest toilet and threw up.

She was aware of Abe holding back her hair, of him using a wet cloth to wipe her mouth after she was done, but then the nausea rose again. By the time she was finally finished, she felt like she'd been hanging over the toilet for hours. "I want to shower and get into the most comfortable pj's I have."

Abe helped her to her feet, then up to the bedroom after a short detour to the kitchen to get some water down her. When he lifted his hands to undo her dress, she let him, but shook her head after the dress fell to the floor. "Alone, okay?"

"I'm leaving the door open." Abe's expression was dark. "So I can hear if you fall over."

"I'm not feeling weak. In fact, I'm starving." Her stomach rumbled on cue. "I want toast with peanut butter and jelly."

"I can do that." Abe kissed her forehead, then patted her ass in a distinctly possessive way. "Shower."

Feeling far less icky after that pat, which said her lover wasn't put off by what had happened, she took off her underwear and smiled down at her belly before stepping into a nice hot shower. When she finally got out and dried off, it was to discover Abe had dug up her yellow microfleece pajamas with the moon and stars on them.

Feeling hugged even though he wasn't physically present in the room, she pulled on the pj's, ran a comb through her hair, and was done. Especially since the scent of toast was hot and delicious in the air. Ravenous, she ran downstairs and into the kitchen and snatched the toast right out of Abe's hand as he finished putting grape jelly on the peanut butter. Groaning at the first bite, she managed to wriggle onto a counter stool and waved at Abe to keep slathering the other slice with peanut butter.

He grinned and got on it. That was when she noticed he'd taken off his suit jacket and rolled up the sleeves of his shirt. She had a seriously hot rock star in her kitchen, making her peanut butter and jelly toast, and even though she'd just thrown up in front of him, he was giving her looks that said he liked what he saw.

A lot.

Sarah's toes curled. As she finished the first piece of toast and reached for the next—after sipping from the glass of milk Abe had poured for her—she decided she was going to let him show her exactly how much he liked the view. Given the night thus far, her body and her hormones were clearly out of whack, but she didn't care with arousal hot and damp between her thighs.

Second piece of toast finished, she drank the rest of the milk.

"More?" Abe asked, having munched on a piece himself while she demolished hers.

"You."

ABE HAD BEEN DRINKING A glass of water, almost dropped the glass at Sarah's statement. Putting it down with extreme care, he gripped the counter. "You were just—"

"I'm fine now." His wife began to unbutton her pajama top, her teeth sinking into the lush fullness of her lower lip.

308

Abe couldn't take his eyes off the smooth richness of her skin as it was revealed inch by inch. Then she shrugged off the pajama top, exposing the full mounds of her breasts, her nipples deliciously tight, and he had to squeeze his eyes shut.

Jaw clenched, he said, "Sweetheart, you're killing me."

"I am so aroused right now, Abe. Please fuck me."

That was it. Sarah never said things like "fuck."

Going around the counter at light speed, he scooped her up in his arms and resolutely avoided her kiss while carrying her to the bedroom. If she kissed him, it was game over and he was damn well going to get her to a comfortable bed before he lost it. He dropped her gently on that bed short seconds later, came down over her.

Stroking his hands up her rib cage, he molded her breasts with his hands, sucked on her nipples. He was a little rough. Sarah moaned and twisted under him, her hands gripping at his shoulders. Brain hazed, Abe moved down her hot fucking body, pulling off her pj bottoms as he went. Spreading her thighs, he would've licked her, worshipped her, but she said, "Abe, please, *please*. Now."

He gave up trying to get off his shirt. Undoing his belt, he managed to shove down his pants and underwear enough to release his cock, and then he was pushing up Sarah's thighs and sinking into her.

Despite his own blazing arousal, he found the willpower to go slow, loath to hurt her, but she arched her back and pressed the heels of her feet into the backs of his thighs, urging him to go deeper, harder. "*Sarah!*" Releasing her thighs, he pressed his hands on either side of her head and bent down to kiss her.

Wet, deep, all tongue, it was sex with their mouths.

Wrapping her legs tightly around his hips when he came up for air, Sarah rocked up.

He groaned, pulled out, thrust back. And then his brain exploded and there was only the molten pleasure of satisfying the demanding woman in his arms. He felt like a god when Sarah screamed and clamped down tight on his cock as her body spasmed in orgasm, her throat arched and her breasts pressed up hard against him as her nails dug into his biceps through his shirt.

AFTERWARD, FLOPPING OVER ONTO HIS back so he wouldn't crush her, he threw out an arm across her. Taking the invitation, she snuggled her head on his shoulder.

"Why are you still dressed?" She began to unbutton his shirt.

Wrecked, he lay there and let her. "Are you going to have this much energy the entire pregnancy?" he asked when he could finally speak. By which time Sarah had successfully unbuttoned his shirt and was stroking his chest while dropping kisses wherever she could reach.

A wicked smile from the hellaciously sexy vixen in bed with him. "Can't keep up?"

"I'll make the effort." He ran his hand up the slope of her back... and Sarah's face changed without warning.

Jumping out of bed, she ran to the attached bathroom.

Abe heard her retching, got by her side ASAP. He hated watching her suffer, but there was literally nothing he could do but keep her hair off her face and hold her when it was over.

# CHAPTER 34

T HE NEXT FOUR WEEKS WERE hell for Sarah. She spent most of them throwing up her guts. There were a few more instances of scalding arousal that Abe turned into bone-shattering pleasure, but mostly she felt miserable.

Only two things made it bearable: Dr. Snyder's assurance that the peanut was fine... and Abe.

A small, wary part of her half expected him to give up as the morning sickness continued without pause, but he stuck. He got her food when she needed it, held her though she looked like death warmed over, touched her with tenderness and love, was there no matter what. She was his number one priority.

Even Lola was moved to grudgingly admit that maybe Abe *was* different this time around.

One week, two, three, and Abe stayed. Not only that, he never made her feel anything but wanted and loved. Even after she woke him up six nights in a row by racing out of bed. He was always there. Until Sarah no longer expected him not to be. Until she relied on him to cuddle her after and make her feel better.

It wasn't until the end of week four that her body decided it had made her miserable enough. She woke up feeling fresh and happy and starving and snuggly warm. Abe was like a furnace—Sarah had used to sleep under a comforter. With him spooning her as he usually did in bed, she didn't even really need a sheet.

Stretching out against him, she gently stroked her bump. It was a far more defined curve than she could've imagined a month earlier, as if the baby had decided to change position and plonk down in front of her belly.

*Hang on, Peanut,* she said silently. *Just a few more months.*

A bigger hand joined hers, Abe's breath warm on the back of her neck as he said, "Baby, we're still in bed." It was a drowsy rumble.

She smiled, that smile cutting deep into her cheeks. "We are."

"It's light out. I don't remember waking up in between."

"You didn't." Laughing, she turned to face him. "I didn't throw up once, and I feel *so* good. Let's go eat."

"We've been here before," he said darkly.

"This is different." She pressed her lips to his. "I'm starving. I want pancakes with syrup and berries and all that good stuff. I know a place."

Abe cuddled her close. "Gimme one more minute."

She kissed his chest, waited. "Okay, minute's over. Wake up."

He called her a torturer but rose, stumbled into the shower after she'd already jumped in and out. He did dress quickly afterward though, and they were ready to go fifteen minutes after waking up.

She'd worn loose clothing to hide the bump, but the one good thing about morning sickness was that she and Abe had gone out so little over the past month that the media had lost interest and wandered off to juicier pastures. As a result, the drive to the breakfast place went by with absolutely no paparazzi intrusion. Once there, Abe let her order for them both. She made sure to add bacon and eggs and toast to his order of pancakes, then after a thought, asked for fruit salad as well.

Abe was a big guy and he burned energy. Especially given how much he exercised—with her so sick over the past weeks, he'd stopped going to the gym. Instead, he'd taken to working out in her backyard so he'd be close if she needed him—and wow, he was incredible to watch when he got all hot and sweaty.

Fox, Noah, and David had come over to hang and work out with him, but though every member of the band made nice eye candy that she was perfectly happy to admire, Abe was the only one whose body made her mouth water.

She had to feed that muscle.

For herself, she got a giant heap of pancakes with berries and syrup.

Their waitress, an older bleached blonde named Betty, beamed as she brought over the food. The hair might've been an incongruous shade for her age, but her bones were the kind that meant she'd be beautiful until she died. "You two were so cute together at the awards." Plates on the table, she patted Sarah on the shoulder with the familiarity of old acquaintance, though this was the first time they'd ever met.

Sarah smiled at the genuine warmth in the other woman's tone. "Thank you."

"I saved the clippings for our walls just in case you two ever came in."

Those walls bore all kinds of memorabilia and articles about the celebrities who'd eaten at the diner.

"Really?" Sarah hadn't given a thought to the media coverage of the awards. She'd been too busy trying to keep down her food. "Can I see them?"

Abe, who'd already started to eat, scowled. "Forget that shit, Sarah."

"I want to see." She glared at him. "I looked really good that night and so did you."

"Yes, you did!" Betty hurried off to get the clippings.

Digging into the pancakes in the interim, Sarah moaned. "These are so good."

Abe stared at her mouth. "Stop making those sounds or you won't get to finish the stack."

Shivering, Sarah licked her tongue playfully over her lips.

Betty returned with the clippings before the smoldering rock star across the table could pay her back for her teasing. "I'll leave you to look at them in peace," she said with another friendly pat on the shoulder. "Just holler if you need anything."

Sarah had really only wanted to see the pictures, but Betty had brought the articles too, and wow, the media had actually portrayed her in a positive light—not simply as an accessory, not as a throwaway groupie. No, she'd been listed as Abe's ex-wife and "a rising business mogul."

She giggled. "Mogul. Ha! Someone likes hyperbole."

"Hey, you'll be a mogul before you're done," Abe responded. "I'll be your boy toy forever."

Laughing and blowing him a kiss, she continued to look through the clippings. "I told you—we looked amazing." She held up a photo of that moment when he'd made her laugh by commenting on her breasts. The photographer had caught them in the instant before they faced the cameras. Instead, they were looking at one another, their smiles deep and their eyes full of light.

"I want this photo," she said to Abe. "Do you think Thea could get me a copy?"

"She can probably twist someone's arm." Abe took the clipping from her. "Yeah, this is a good one." His eyes went from the photo to her. "You're so damn beautiful, Sarah."

Her heart kicked. This man, he— "Oof."

Abe's eyes lit up. "Peanut's kicking again?"

"Your peanut has taken up break dancing I think." Their baby's movements had become increasingly more vigorous over the past month. Sarah loved it, loved knowing their child was happy and healthy and growing inside her.

And as always when the baby moved, Abe came around to place his hand on her belly, see if he could catch a kick. When he did...

No fear of the past could compete with the raw joy in her heart. "Not that long to go now."

"I can't wait."

THEA CALLED THEM TWO HOURS after they returned home. "A sweet photo of you two is doing the social media rounds as of an hour ago," was her opening statement. "It's of Abe kneeling by your chair, Sarah, his hand on the bump."

"Tabloids?"

"No, original tracks back to a personal account. Looks like a fan caught you two being adorable together and snuck a pic to squee over. It went viral pretty quick."

Sarah's phone buzzed right then, Thea having called on Abe's. When she swiped the message, she saw that Thea had forwarded her the photo. One look at it and her heart, it melted right into the soles of her feet. "It must've been that young couple sitting by the door that took it."

"Angle's right," Abe said, his eyes on her, his face unsmiling. "You okay with this?"

"I knew it was coming—the bump's hard to disguise these days." Sarah stroked his arm. "Do you think this'll escalate, Thea?"

"I don't think so." The publicist sounded like she was moving as she talked. "Give the photographers a few more chances to take shots, then you should be home free until the birth except for the odd paparazzo hoping to get a scoop of some kind. At which point it'll become an arms race to see who can get the first shot of mini-Abra."

Scowling, Abe said, "No one's taking photos of the peanut."
Sarah nodded firmly.

"Leave it to me," Thea said, tone steely. "Shark, remember?"

Fully trusting Thea to take care of that situation when it arose, Sarah turned to Abe after they ended the call. "Are you mad?"

"About the photo?" He shook his head. "You're right. It was going to get out, and this way at least it was a fan excited about the news rather than someone out to make a buck."

And she realized he really didn't care that the photo had exposed his heart to the world. Because while his hand had been on the bump, he'd been looking into Sarah's eyes in that shot. No one could miss the tenderness in his expression, the potent love that underlay it.

*Marry me again.*

Sarah parted her lips, closed them before speaking the words that wanted to escape, fear having taken a clawed grip around her heart. Too happy, she was too happy. And it had only been just over six months. Half a year.

It could still all go horribly wrong.

Her baby could die.

Abe could fall back into addiction.

Life could shatter.

# CHAPTER 35

TWO WEEKS AFTER THE SUDDEN stab of panic that had terrified her and nothing had gone wrong—though Sarah couldn't quite forget the fear, the scars life had left on her psyche far too deep. She kept reminding herself that their baby was perfectly healthy with a strong heartbeat, while Abe and Sarah, they were an interwoven unit. He pretended to snore when she went to do her business paperwork, but more often than not, he'd play his keyboard to keep her company.

That keyboard now had a permanent spot in her house, but they also went over to the music room at his place several times a week so he could play the piano or jam with the guys. Sarah usually spent the time catching up on her own work, and if Lola or one of the other women was free, they'd meet for lunch out by the pool.

Abe hadn't brought up where they'd live after the baby was born and neither had Sarah. She adored the home she'd created, but quite aside from being much bigger, his place was far more secure. If she did move in there, Sarah thought, she'd be bringing her furniture and artwork.

No more blending into the woodwork like she had last time around.

"You look like a warrior about to go into battle," Abe said as she began to climb the ladder of the private jet that was to be their ride to Bali.

Sarah glanced over her shoulder. "I was telling myself I'm a business mogul now and I need to act like it."

Abe bowed from the waist. "Boy toy at your service."

Her fear pushed away by a deep wave of love, she smiled and continued into the plane. Noah and Kit had entered just before them, and the four of them chatted as they grabbed their seats and settled in.

They were the only ones on this flight.

Fox and Molly had left a week earlier, as Thea wanted her sister to spend time with her family. David, of course, had gone with Thea.

"I'm so glad the morning sickness subsided in time for this and that Dr. Snyder cleared the trip," she said to Abe after they were underway. "I would've been so bummed to miss David and Thea's wedding."

"Yeah, me too." Abe's response was absentminded, his attention on the magazine he was reading. "Bastard would've held it over me forever too."

Sarah just stared. The two of them had missed Charlotte and Gabriel's wedding because she'd been shaky with her pregnancy not past the first trimester, but this was another matter altogether. David had been Abe's best friend since they were *thirteen*. But it was clear that Abe was serious. He'd have missed his best friend's wedding had she still been feeling like crap. He'd put her first. Again.

This man would never again leave her behind while he went on tour.

Swallowing rapidly, she turned to face the window, the plane pillowed on fluffy white clouds. It felt like she had wings of her own, lifted aloft by the emotions inside her. The fear wasn't dead, would remain until she held their happy, healthy baby in her arms, but the hope that had been dented by that fear? It was back, and it was glorious.

BALI WAS AN EXPLOSION OF greenery, huge flowers, lavish scents, and heavy humidity. Living in Los Angeles meant Sarah was more than ready for the heat. It was the humidity that took some getting used to, but the baby seemed to like it well enough after a day settling in.

"You're just like your brother, you know that?" she whispered to the peanut a couple of days after their arrival as she stood on the balcony of the lovely little hotel Thea had arranged for the closest friends and family. "He kicked like a champion too."

The baby's response was another kick.

She smiled and returned to the suite to pull back her hair in preparation for visiting Thea's family. It was just too hot to leave it down. "Up, lazybones," she said to the gorgeous man who was sprawled in their bed, the white sheet just barely covering his butt. "What time did you get in last night?" She'd woken when he arrived, but only long enough to exchange a kiss.

There'd been no alcohol on his breath, no sign he was anything but dead sober.

"Ass crack of hell," Abe muttered and pulled his pillow over his head. "I hate being the goddamn sober driver."

Unable to resist her lover even when he was grumpy with lack of sleep, Sarah sat on the bed and pressed a row of kisses down his back. Where before she'd have been sad and angry and terribly lonely if he'd spent nearly an entire night away from her, last night she'd had a delicious dinner with the women, then curled up to watch a movie.

She'd been about fifteen minutes into it when Abe sent the first message: *David, Noah, and Fox just had these evil drinks. Now they're telling the worst jokes I've ever heard and laughing their heads off.*

It had made her laugh, write back: *Make sure you get David back in one piece or Thea will murder you.* Thankfully the wedding wasn't today, or all four men would've been in the doghouse for how late they'd gotten back.

"So the bachelor party was a success?" she asked, continuing to stroke his warm, muscled body just because she could. It was on her second downward stroke that she brushed something at the top left of his butt.

Frowning, she nudged down the sheet to reveal a gauze adhesive pad. "*Abe.*"

"It's a freaking daisy," he muttered, his head still under the pillow. "Noah decided we should all have daisies tattooed on our asses."

Sarah fought valiantly against her laughter. "You were supposed to be the sober influence."

"We were all in such a good mood. I didn't want to be the party pooper." He finally pulled away the pillow. "How bad is it?"

Peeling away the bandage, Sarah pressed a kiss close to the edge of the reddened skin. "You clearly had a tattooist who liked you. It's teeny, maybe half an inch. But it's definitely a daisy." She patted the bandage gently back in place. "Did you all get it in the same place?"

"I'm pretty sure David's is actually on his butt cheek. At least it's not yellow," he muttered. "Fucker wouldn't shut up about wanting it to be yellow-as-the-sun, and Noah was egging him on, telling him orange would be a better choice. Whatever the hell was in those drinks, it turned all three of them into lunatics."

Sarah gave up trying not to laugh. Snorting with it, she was still giggling hard when her phone buzzed with an incoming message. It was from Thea: *Abe had ONE job. ONE job!*

Crying because she was laughing so hard, she showed Abe the message. He groaned and said, "Tell her I saved it from being in Technicolor," and hid his head under the pillow again. But he couldn't hide forever since they were due at Thea's family home for lunch.

When they arrived, it was to find three very hungover men nursing black coffees strong enough to strip paint. They groaned at seeing Abe.

"Don't tell us," Fox begged. "I don't even want to know how I ended up with a goddamn daisy on my ass."

Abe's grin was evil. "You actually wanted a bunny rabbit."

Fox banged his head on the table. "Never again. Never, ever again."

Leaving the men to commiserate over their misspent night, Sarah went to find Thea and the other women. It turned out the bride-to-be had spent the morning laughing too. "My poor

David. He looked so befuddled when I pointed out his new ink." Eyes dancing, she shook her head. "Thank God Abe sent David's younger brothers home early though."

Thea's mother came bustling in right then, with Thea's sisters in her wake.

Sarah adored Thea's family. They just enfolded everyone in love until it was impossible to do anything but smile. After seeing Sarah's belly the first day, Thea's mom plied her with food anytime she was in the vicinity, to give her a "fat, happy baby." She also buried her in childrearing advice. It was wonderful. Especially since Abe's mom and David's were also present, having flown in a few days earlier to relax. All three of them treated Sarah with maternal affection, but it was with Diane that she had the strongest bond; she knew she could ask Abe's mom anything.

By the time the wedding rolled around the next day, Sarah felt as if she'd been talking and laughing nonstop for twenty-four hours and counting. If Molly and Fox's rock-and-roll backyard wedding had been them, Thea and David's traditional and family-oriented fusion wedding was just as perfect for the drummer and the publicist.

The small wedding pavilion had been raised slightly and set up on lush green lawn beside a lake, fine gold curtains tied to the four sturdy poles that held up the white-painted structure, and the carpet a haunting blue. Guests sat in chairs that allowed a direct view of the pavilion, the decorations along the aisle and around the pavilion simple white splashed with color from hundreds of fresh flowers.

Their scents filled the air.

David stood waiting outside the pavilion, his suit a sharp black with a pristine white shirt and a tie of deep gold. His groomsmen—Fox, Abe, and Noah, plus David's two handsome younger brothers—were wearing identical suits except their shirts and ties were black.

Sarah ran her eye over Abe. She'd fixed his jacket for him a little earlier, before she came to take her seat between Kit and Diane. *Beautiful man.*

"We got lucky, didn't we, Sarah?"

Sarah turned at Kit's comment to see that the actress's distinctive amber eyes were on a certain blond guitarist who stood beside Fox. "Yes," she said, just as lyrical music began to play.

She saw David's entire face light up as he turned to watch for Thea, and then they were all rising to their feet and angling their heads toward the arbor through which Thea would descend. Sunshine poured down onto it from the other side.

Framed within the light was a breathtaking bride on her proud father's arm.

Sarah sucked in a breath.

She'd seen Thea during the morning pamper session for the ladies, but this...

Tall and slender, Thea looked like she'd stepped from the pages of a fashion magazine but for the deeply unsophisticated delight on her face. Her "dress" was actually a sari of rich gold silk shot with metallic threads of vibrant cerise, the neatly fitted blouse she wore beneath it the same cerise. Embroidered bands of gold circled the cap sleeves of the top.

The part of the sari that fell over her shoulder had been lifted up and draped stunningly over her intricately dressed hair, held in place by fine gold jewelry that ended with a teardrop of filigreed gold at the top of her forehead. The way she wore the sari was more traditional than Sarah would've expected of the stylish and urbane publicist if she hadn't known that Thea had taken her grandparents' views into account.

Sarah had asked Thea if she minded, but the publicist had smiled and shaken her head. "For me, a wedding is about family. I could never hurt my grandparents by not respecting their wishes." Another beaming smile. "As well as all my sisters and my best friend, I took both my grandmas with me to choose the wedding sari—both of them! My mom too." She'd shaken her head. "Let's just say those three women have *opinions*."

"Someone with more opinions than you?"

A wink. "Maybe not." Thea had run her fingers over the sari, her expression poignant. "I love this outfit. It stands for me and for the people who made me who I am today. I could want nothing more."

Molly, and Thea's best friend, Imani, walked behind Thea with a number of other family members, including Thea's two younger sisters—who were smiling hard enough to crack their faces. Everyone wore vibrant color, with Thea having gifted Molly and Imani with saris of deep cerise and indigo blue to wear to the wedding since they were part of the bridal party.

Her aunts had taken charge of putting the two women in the traditional garment.

In her hands, Thea carried a garland of lush pink and white blooms that matched the one David had in his hands when Sarah glanced back to the men.

Thea's mom had provided the flowers for those garlands. She was also the one who'd tucked lush white blooms behind Kit, Molly, Imani, and Sarah's ears. And it was Thea's paternal grandmother who'd lent the bride her earrings of polished seashells. Given her income, Thea could've dripped with gemstones, but she wore those old, beloved earrings with pride.

Sarah's eyes stung as she watched the other woman pass. Thea's own eyes were only for David; she seemed wholly unaware of the gasps in the audience, of the photos being taken. As at Molly's wedding, Sarah couldn't help but remember her own wedding day. Unlike Thea's elegant sari, her dress had been big and poofy and sparkly, the kind of Cinderella dress of which she'd always dreamed and that she'd thought was the height of fashion at twenty-one.

She bit back a smile as she sat down with everyone else; her marriage might've imploded, but Sarah had never regretted that dress.

Thea reached David.

Exchanging garlands, they linked hands and stepped into the wedding pavilion.

The ceremony was simple and heartrendingly beautiful, a blend of the traditional and the new, of David's cultural mores as well as Thea's. No one could miss the love David wore on his sleeve—and Thea, this tough, strong woman, she wore her own love for the drummer as openly.

Sarah dabbed away a tear, emotion thick in her throat. And smiled at seeing the way Thea's sisters giggled as David leaned in to kiss his new wife.

"Wouldn't it be cute if once they were grown, Thea's sisters ended up with David's brothers?" she whispered to Kit, the romantic in her loving the idea.

"I heard the two girls talking this morning," Kit murmured. "They were giggling and saying how David's brothers were 'super cute.'" A sparkling smile. "So you never know."

A heartbeat later, they all rose to congratulate the happy couple, clapping and crowding around to take photos. Sarah stayed back, careful of the peanut, but Abe found her and got her through the crowd so she could offer her delighted congratulations.

Thea returned her heartfelt hug with gentle arms. Her joy in being married to David was incandescent, the way the two kept touching their fingers to each other's a silent statement of togetherness. In between, David exchanged back-slapping hugs with his family members and bandmates, his grin so deep that it might well carve permanent grooves in his cheeks.

Sarah sniffed again.

Sighing, Abe handed her a pristine handkerchief. "I bought it for the waterworks."

She elbowed him. "Shuddup."

He pressed a kiss to her curls. "Softie."

Sarah melted.

She'd felt a bittersweet joy at Molly and Fox's wedding, happy for the other couple but sad that she and Abe had broken. This time she could almost imagine walking down the aisle all over again with the only man who had ever owned her heart.

It scared her in a beautiful way.

# Chapter 36

AFTER THE HAPPY ROMANCE OF Bali—and the relatively low-key response when news of the pregnancy first broke—it was a shock to return home to endless paparazzi cameras and judgmental articles that implied Sarah had "lured" Abe back, then "trapped" him. Sarah knew she shouldn't read those articles, but she wasn't superhuman. Sometimes she couldn't help herself.

"Do you feel trapped?" she asked Abe sharply one morning while they were still in bed.

Yawning, he opened one eye. "What?"

"By the fact I'm pregnant." Sarah glared at him.

He groaned and reached over to close a hand over her thigh under the sheet. That thigh was naked because she somehow always ended up naked around Abe. She'd pulled the sheet up over her breasts and tucked it under her arms, but beneath it she was as bare as the day she'd been born.

"Abe, stop stroking my thigh and answer the question."

"I am answering it." He scowled at her. "Why the fuck would I feel trapped when I get to wake up to you every morning?"

Sarah's lower lip quivered.

"Aw, shit." Rising up into a seated position against the headboard, he ran a hand over her hair before tugging her gently toward his chest. "I'm sorry. I didn't mean to growl at you."

Sarah snuggled up to his chest, not even sure why she was crying. His answer had been wonderful, romantic. "I'm so pregnant!" she wailed.

"Definitely." Abe sounded like he was smiling.

She thumped a fist against his chest. "Stop laughing."

Chuckling openly now, he wrapped both arms around her. "I can't help it. You're finally doing the hormonal pregnant-woman thing." Pushing one hand into her hair, he tugged up her head and kissed away her tears before coaxing her into a slow, deep kiss. "Good morning, beautiful."

Feeling all wrung out and yet oddly happy, Sarah smiled. "Good morning, gorgeous." She petted his pecs, sighed over just how pretty he was.

"Um, thanks?"

She frowned. "What?"

"I don't know if I like being described as pretty. Noah's pretty. I'm ruggedly handsome."

Sarah hadn't realized she'd said the words aloud, but now she smiled and pressed a kiss to the closest part of his chest. "Pretty Abe."

"If you weren't pregnant..." His threat lost all force when he kissed her, the tenderness of the touch making her eyes tear up all over again.

"Sweetheart." Expression darkening, Abe shook his head. "For the record and so you don't ever have to think about it again: I don't feel trapped. Far from it. Fuck, Sarah, *I* want to trap you. Forever. I want my ring back on your finger and I want to wear yours and I want the world to know you're mine."

Shock froze her tears, turned her breathless. "Did you just…"

"Ask you to marry me again?" Abe nodded. "I was planning to wait until you were more sure of me, but I don't ever want you to worry about why I'm here. I'm here because I *want* to be here."

Rubbing at her eyes, Sarah sat back on her haunches.

Abe's eyes went immediately to her nude breasts.

She blushed and picked up the edge of the sheet to shield herself, not because she didn't love the way Abe looked at her but because she wanted to talk… Yet she didn't know what to say. That was when she realized that the fear that had hit her before Bali was still there, a wary shadow she couldn't quite shake, a shadow formed of a lifetime of pain and neglect and loss.

Deep inside, where she tried not to look, she was *so* afraid this was all a mirage that would disappear if she reached out and tried to claim even more happiness for herself and their baby.

And last time around, the best part of their relationship had been before marriage. What if history repeated itself? What if they simply weren't built to be husband and wife?

*I want my ring back on your finger and I want to wear yours and I want the world to know you're mine.*

The memory of his words stopped her heart all over again.

Dark eyes held her own.

Mute, she dropped the sheet and leaned toward Abe. He took her invitation, loved her with tender hands and a raw need that made her feel so wanted it almost hurt.

SEVEN WEEKS LATER AND SARAH still hadn't given Abe an answer, the words locked inside her throat by that quiet, insidious fear she couldn't shake off. But other than that visceral fear that held her back from saying yes, being eight months pregnant was glorious. The peanut no longer had enough room inside her to keep on playing football. These days it was all sharp pokes with a tiny elbow or foot and what felt like impatient twisting as the baby tried to get comfortable.

Which could get uncomfortable for her, but Sarah loved the sign that their little rock baby was alive and thriving. Sometimes when she petted the part of Peanut's body that was jabbing at her, she got a response. Last time, it was Abe who'd done it—and it had felt as if the baby was playing with him—pulling back, then pushing out again.

Abe's expression had been priceless, fascinated and astonished both.

"You sure you want to do this?" her lover murmured now in the back of the limo that was ferrying them to an early evening party. It was to celebrate the birthday of a record executive who'd helped Schoolboy Choir sign their first deal.

"We'll go for a little while." She closed her hand over his thigh, the fabric of his black pants slightly rough. "I feel like seeing our friends, and I know Marty's important to you all."

Abe's knuckles brushing her cheek. "Not as important as you."

She'd become almost used to those words. Never would she take them for granted, but she believed them now, knew Abe meant what he said. "I'll tell you when I'm ready to go home," she promised. "Mostly I plan to find a comfortable spot and chat with Molly and the other women." Sarah knew they wouldn't leave her alone; they never did at such events.

It was wonderfully strange to find herself circled so protectively by Abe's tribe… that was now also part of her tribe. "I also have a bone to pick with Noah about the ice cream he brought over last week." Sarah hadn't been able to stop eating the stuff. "He's responsible for at least five extra pounds."

Abe nuzzled her. "I don't see any extra pounds." One big hand shaping her hip. "How about you get naked and show me where they are?"

Giggling like a teenager and feeling far too carefree for a woman who was currently eight months pregnant, she bit playfully at his ear. "Limo's stopped."

The driver opened the back passenger-side door half a minute later.

Murmuring, "We'll pick this up at home," Abe exited, then helped her out.

Her dress flowed around her. Sarah had tried on more formfitting formal gowns that showed off her bump, but as with the gown she'd worn to the awards ceremony, she loved the softer lines of this strapless dress. It hugged her breasts with some spectacular tailoring that involved crisscrossing pieces of fabric, then flowed down in heavy lines that suited the deep midnight blue of the material.

Molly had found the gown for her in a store that sold vintage gowns from Hollywood's golden era. She'd gifted it to Sarah for her birthday, sweetly happy that Sarah loved it so much. The best thing was that it'd be easy to tailor it to suit her post-pregnancy body too.

As for jewelry, having swept her hair into an updo that exposed her neck and shoulders, Sarah had chosen to wear statement earrings of heavy silver.

That, however, wasn't what she was actually wearing. Because Abe had surprised her with another set of statement earrings tonight—and these were created of diamonds. Not just transparent diamonds of perfect clarity but also vibrant pink diamonds that were a glorious accent to her gown. The earrings sparkled and caught the light and were no doubt ridiculously expensive, but what Sarah loved most about them was that Abe had admitted to spending hours in two different jewelry stores in an effort to find exactly the right pair for her dress.

Even had they clashed terribly, she'd have worn them.

Curling her hand around his biceps, she admired his own form. He'd chosen to pair a fitted black shirt with his black pants. The shirt hugged his pecs and arms and made her want to jump his bones. She wasn't the only one, she saw when they joined the party. Several women made eyes at him.

Abe rubbed her lower back. "It's not too crowded at least."

Ignoring the women trying to flirt with him when it was obvious Abe wasn't interested, Sarah glanced around. "Is that Kit over there?"

Abe followed her line of sight. "Yeah. Noah's with her."


ABE BEGAN TO WEAVE HIS way through the large room, careful to keep Sarah always in the protective curve of his arm. For the most part, people didn't get in his way—there were some advantages to being a big guy with tattoos and a visible piercing.

"Abe, Sarah."

Abe stopped and exchanged handshakes with Marty, after which the tall, thin man leaned toward Sarah and accepted her kiss on the cheek. "Happy birthday," she said and lifted the little bag she was holding.

"Oh, you shouldn't have," Marty said, though his tanned-to-honey-brown skin flushed in pleasure. "I asked for donations to the scholarship fund I help administer."

"We did that," Sarah reassured the other man. "But everyone should get presents on their birthday, even if it's just a small thing."

Unhidden delight in his eyes, Marty took the bag. "Can I look?"

"Of course," Sarah said, her hand not on her belly but curved below it, as if she was supporting it.

Digging inside the gift bag, Marty came up with a small but rather battered jewelry box of deep red. He looked curious rather than dismayed. Abe was curious too. Having no idea what the hell to get a man who was filthy rich and whom Abe knew only from the music world as opposed to a personal friendship, he'd left it up to Sarah.

As he watched, Marty flipped open the box and gasped. Loud enough to capture the attention of several people nearby, who peered over to see what had him so excited. "My dear," he whispered, "where did you find these?" He turned the box so people could see what lay within: cuff links that appeared to be hand painted with a miniature scene that reminded Abe of the traditional Chinese paintings he'd seen in a museum one time.

"My secret," Sarah said with a smile. "A little bird told me you collect vintage cuff links—the seller told me these are meant to be part of a rare set."

"They are!" Marty pressed a hand to his heart, his ring finger bearing a dramatic ring set with a square sapphire. "The artist only ever painted a hundred overall. And they're in the original box too!" In raptures at this point, the other man closed the box and hid it away in the bag before enclosing Sarah in a hug. "Thank you." It was heartfelt.

Sarah hugged him back, said, "You're welcome. I'm so glad we got it right."

Eyes shining after they broke apart, Marty leaned in to whisper, "I'm going to disappear from my own party for a few minutes to put these beauties with the rest of my collection." Leaving them with a conspiratorial smile, he snuck out through a side door.

Kit and Noah, who'd drifted closer, immediately asked what was up. Kit shook her head when Sarah told her. "How did you know about his collection?"

"He mentioned it in an interview once." Sarah shifted a little on her feet as she often did to find a comfortable position now that the pregnancy was so advanced.

When Abe rubbed at her lower back, she threw him a smile that made his heart twist itself into a thousand knots. God, he was so gone for her. Head over heels, like that song Noah had written for the new album.

"You're showing me up," Kit teased with a mock-scowl. "Did you see Marty hired Florentina Chastain to do a full dessert bar? Her people just brought out peach tartlets with a dark chocolate garnish."

"Oooh." Sarah lit up.

Curving his hand over her hip, Abe said, "You want me to grab you a plate of dessert stuff?"

"No. I'll waddle over with Kit—half the fun is in the choosing."

Tall and statuesque, Sarah was far too graceful to waddle. Abe watched her as she and Kit wandered over into another room where Abe could just glimpse the edge of the dessert bar. "We fucking lucked out with our women, man."

"Hell yeah." Noah raised his champagne glass, his eyes on Kit until she disappeared inside the other room. "You and Sarah, you look good together."

"I know," Abe said smugly.

"Modest too." Noah's dry tone was belied by his grin. "How's Sarah doing with the media stalking?"

Scowling, Abe folded his arms across his chest. "Better than I am. She's got this Zen thing going on—so long as the baby's okay, she just ignores the vultures." As Thea had predicted, the media interest was relentless at this point, every damn pap and his dog aiming to get the first images of Abe and Sarah's child. "Thea told me the tabloids have put a fucking bounty on pictures of the peanut. Some international magazine is offering a million right off the bat for an exclusive."

"Assholes." Noah's lip curled. "You know we'll all play interference, get you and Sarah out of the hospital without anyone getting a photo."

"I know." His friends had stood by him through the worst times of his life; they'd never abandon him or Sarah now. "I mean, I'm going to be a proud dad who boasts about his kid till people are sick of it, but if and when a photo goes online, I want it to be our choice."

"I get you." Noah nodded at the open balcony doors. "You want to step out for fresh air? Looks like Kit and Sarah found some friends."

Abe looked up, saw Kit and Sarah had moved back into view. "I recognize Imani," he said, identifying Thea's friend and work-mate. "The blonde must be a friend of hers." Since it was clear Sarah was having fun, he followed Noah out to the balcony.

"You're gritting your teeth," Noah pointed out once they were outside, Marty's pool glowing like a blue jewel just beyond.

"I'm having trouble letting her out of my sight," Abe admit-ted. "I get this fucking knot in my gut worrying about her."

Just like Fox and David, Noah had been at Tessie's funeral. He understood the fear that gnawed at Abe, that had him jerk-ing awake deep in the night just so he could make sure Sarah was still breathing. But the guitarist didn't point out that Sarah was healthy and strong, that she and the baby would both be fine.

What he said was, "You weren't like this the last time around."

Throwing back the ice water he'd picked up off the tray of a passing waiter, Abe said, "Last time around, I was so fucking scared of loving her the way I wanted to love her that I did eve-rything in my power to fight it." His hand clenched around the glass. "And I lost her."

This time around, Abe had no shields, no protective walls. His heart was wide-open.

But he was terrified Sarah's no longer was.

# CHAPTER 37

ENJOYING HER CHAT WITH IMANI, Kit, and Imani's screen-writer friend, Sarah stayed in the dessert room until her bladder began to protest. That didn't take long, of course, not with how pregnant she was. Excusing herself, she hunted out a restroom.

The door had a sign on it saying Powder Room, and she thought that a cute whimsy on Marty's part until she stepped inside and saw the size of the space. It really was a powder room, with seating and mirrors in this section, huge vases of flowers sitting in two corners. The actual restrooms—two of them—were beyond another door.

When she returned to the section with the mirrors, she found it was no longer empty. A lone woman stood in front of the central mirror on the right, touching up her makeup. She had skin the same shade of rich brown as Sarah's, but that was where the similarity ended.

Where Sarah was tall, this woman was five two at most. Where Sarah was rocking a baby belly and full breasts made even fuller by the pregnancy, this woman had a flat stomach and perky breasts. And where Sarah wore a flowing gown, the other woman's sparkling silver dress came to just past her butt and could've been painted on.

Sarah didn't feel bad at the contrast. They were both beautiful, she thought, just in different ways. And one day in the future, Sarah intended to find herself a sparkly painted-on dress too. Just to shake things up. Because there was still a rock groupie inside her—even if she was only interested in one particular rock star.

Smiling, she paused to check her own makeup in the mirror. She had her lipstick in her clutch, decided to touch it up. "Stunning dress," she said to the other woman.

"Same." The falseness of the single word was so obvious that Sarah had to stifle a laugh.

Some women just couldn't get over instinctive bitchiness.

"You're with Abe, right?"

Surprised the other woman had spoken again, Sarah said, "Uh-huh," and began to apply her lipstick.

"I heard he was clean."

Not liking the poison already dripping from the woman's voice, Sarah didn't dignify the intrusive question with an answer. She finished off her touch-up and, capping her lipstick, dropped it into her glitzy mirrored clutch. That clutch was probably a little too loud, but Sarah didn't care. She liked how it glittered. What she loved most of all was that Abe had bought it for her a month earlier, for no reason except that he'd passed a store with the clutch in the window and thought she'd like it.

A "just because" present.

It made the romantic girl inside her sigh and melt.

Smiling deep within, she went to leave... and the petite bitch blocked her path.

"You really think he's into you?" the woman said, her words a sneer. "Fat and pregnant isn't a turn-on, you know."

Far from being hurt, Sarah was furious. "What the *hell* is your problem?" she snapped.

Jerking back, the other woman clenched her jaw. "He would've married me if you hadn't trapped him the first time around," she hissed. "No wonder he was driven to drugs."

"I'd worry about your own drug use," Sarah said, no longer feeling like being polite. "A collapsed nose isn't particularly attractive. You should talk to your surgeon about that."

Leaving the other woman spluttering... and surreptitiously touching her surgically perfect knife blade of a nose, Sarah pushed out the door and made her way to the balcony. Her cheeks felt hot, as did her body.

"Sarah." Abe's voice from behind her the instant after she stepped outside. "I was looking for you."

Breathing in, then out, Sarah was expecting his hand on her hip. Abe had a way of touching her when they were out, branding his claim on her. She liked it. "I just met the nastiest woman," she said to him. "Petite, black, about five two, tight curls in a bouncy cut, razored cheekbones."

When Abe looked blank, Sarah wanted to smile in smug satisfaction. Yes, she wasn't feeling the least bit polite or nice right now. "She said you would've married her if I hadn't come into the picture."

Abe snorted. "Then she's high. I wasn't ready to marry anyone—then boom, I got hit by the Sarah-hammer and that was it." Scowling, he looked over her head as if searching for the bitchy woman. "She upset you?"

Sarah had no hesitation in answering. "Nope. I was furious, not upset." She was just touching his chest in a calming gesture when she spotted warm brown eyes and a wide smile heading in her direction. "Molly!"

"Hey." The other woman drew her into a hug. "I was hoping you'd still be here. We got held up by a breakdown that caused gridlock."

Fox was already bumping fists with Abe, and pretty soon, Noah and Kit were there, with Thea and David arriving soon afterward. The entire Schoolboy Choir family.

Her family.

Then Lola arrived, Abe having finagled an invitation for Sarah's best friend and her current plus one, and things turned even more wonderful.

Despite what she'd said to Abe in the limo, Sarah had such a good time that she stayed for far longer than she'd expected. She even danced with Marty, who snuck her away to admire his cuff link collection.

"My husband thinks I'm mad," he confided to her. "But he still gets me a pair every time he travels. Usually they're ridiculous, the most chintzy, touristy things—but I adore them."

Only when her body began to protest did she ask Abe to get them home.

That night, as she lay in bed with him spooning her, she smiled. She'd taken that powder room bitch down a peg and not allowed her to do the same. It had felt good. And frivolous as that incident was in the grand scheme of things, it had reached the fear inside her, as if it was the final piece of a complex puzzle.

Maybe because it had shown her, once and for all, that she wasn't a hostage to fate, that she had the ability to fight for her happiness. "Abe?"

"Hmm?" Yawning against her, he ran his hand over her belly and up to cup her breast.

Her smile deepened. *Fat and pregnant, my ass.* She was hot and pregnant, as demonstrated by the rock star in bed with her, one who couldn't keep his hands off her. "The first time around, with us, I wasn't confident."

"You were young." A pause. "So was I."

Yes, she thought, he was right. They'd both been so young then, struggling to find their place in the world. She could forgive that young couple, forgive the wounds they'd inflicted. Lifting Abe's hand, she pressed a kiss to his palm. "Be honest with me," she whispered in the darkness, confronting a large part of the fear head-on.

"Always. What is it?"

"The drugs—have you felt the need to go back on them?"

Abe blew out a breath. "I'm an addict, Sarah. I always will be." Another deep breath, another exhale. "That's the only way sobriety works—if I admit that, if I accept it." He pressed a kiss to her shoulder. "That demon whispers to me from time to time. You know it; you've seen me working out at all kinds of random hours. But no matter what, I've never, not once, felt tempted to give in. You know why?"

"Tell me." The words came out husky.

"Because I know the second I touch drugs, I lose you and I lose the right to be a parent to our child. You wouldn't even have to throw me out. I *do not* want an active drug user raising our child—so the second I do drugs or take a drink, I give up the woman I love and I give up our child. That's not going to happen."

It wasn't a pretty speech. It was hard and rough and raw, but it was exactly what Sarah needed to hear. Tears rolling down her face, she struggled to turn, laughed midway. "Help me, dammit."

Abe kissed her instead. Her shoulder, her neck, every part of her he could reach. When she finally managed to get onto her back, he leaned over her to turn on the bedside lamp. "No tears," he said in a gruff tone as the light washed across her face, but the kisses he dropped on her cheeks were tender, his hand as tender where he cradled her face.

Half smiling, half crying, she stroked his jaw. Her heart ached. "I loved you before," she whispered, then shook her head when the light in his eyes began to dim. "I thought then that I could never love you more... but I do."

Fighting the fear that clawed at her, trying to hold her back, she said, "The man you are now, he's the man I dreamed of all my life."

Shuddering, Abe buried his face in her neck.

He didn't speak for several long minutes, his breath jagged.

"Abe?" She put her hand on the back of his head... and she realized he was trying not to cry. This big, strong man was struggling not to cry because she'd told him she loved him. She'd never been that important to anyone.

Her own tears began to fall again.

He kissed her when he raised his head, his thumb stroking over her cheek. And he kissed her and he kissed her. She felt her bones liquefying under his touch, and when he lowered his hand to between her thighs, she shuddered and held on to him as he played her body like a fine instrument. Pleasure rose in a heavy wave.

She surrendered, gave in.

TWO DAYS LATER, SARAH SCOWLED at Abe when he said, "Let's go out."

"I'm in my pj's and I want to stay that way." It was only six p.m., but Sarah had decided eight months of pregnancy gave a woman a certain latitude—especially after she'd spent an hour on the phone with a particularly demanding client.

Pressing his hands on the sofa on either side of her, Abe smiled that heartbreaker smile. "Please."

She gave a huge sigh, though butterflies danced in her stomach—damn but the man was sexy. "You'll owe me big-time."

"Done."

Getting up and dressing in a pretty jersey dress in a vibrant shade of orange that Diane had insisted on buying her the last time they went shopping together, she called down to where Abe waited in the downstairs hallway, Flossie by his side. "Shall I put on proper makeup?" She'd brushed on enough to feel ready, but it was just the lightest touch.

"No, but take some."

*Huh?* She went to open her mouth, then thought to hell with it and put some makeup in a little carry bag. As she zipped it up, she paused. Was Abe planning to take her somewhere? Bubbles of excitement skittered under her skin. Maybe—she bit her lower lip—he'd ask her to marry him again.

She knew she was the one who should ask since she was the one who'd effectively turned him down by never giving him an answer, but the romantic girl in her clung to the dream of being asked by the man she loved. "Should I take some clothes?"

"No, I already packed for you."

Her mouth fell open. "Did you pack purses to match the clothes?"

"Who the hell do you think you're talking to?"

Laughing at his insulted tone, she padded down the stairs with the makeup kit and her current everyday purse. "Here, put this with the other stuff." She handed the makeup bag to him. "Are you going to tell me where we're going?"

"Nope."

Sarah decided to go with it. "One last adventure before the peanut arrives?"

"Something like that." Abe helped her into the passenger seat of the SUV, then went around and tucked her makeup kit into the luggage he had in back.

Flossie was already in the backseat. When Sarah asked if Flossie was going with them, Abe told her their pet would be jumping off at her favorite doggie hotel. "Don't stay up too late," Sarah told Flossie as Abe locked up the house.

It was as they were pulling out of the gate that she frowned. "Hey, where are all the photographers and reporters?" They'd been on her like white on rice for months, would hardly disappear when she was only weeks away from giving birth.

Abe's grin was smug. "We have good friends."

"What did you get them to do?" Sarah pushed at his arm when he just chuckled. "It must be one heck of a photo opportunity if they drew away the entire crowd."

"Oh, it is." Abe smirked. "You can read all about it in the tabloids tomorrow."

Amused by his smugness, Sarah decided she could wait and settled in for the ride after they dropped off Flossie. Of course, she had to keep making him stop so she could visit the restroom, and they'd only been gone maybe two hours when he pulled into what appeared to be a little family-style hotel.

"Here?" Wildly curious, she took it in. The hotel was pretty and old-fashioned with its wooden frame and climbing roses, and even as they stopped, a well-dressed couple stepped out as if to welcome them.

Opening her door, Abe got her safely on the ground. He grabbed their bags with the help of the male half of the couple she'd seen—who turned out to be the owners—while the woman walked with Sarah. "We've put you in a downstairs room," the other woman said with a smile. "I know when I was pregnant, climbing stairs got old fast."

"Tell me about it." Sarah patted her abdomen to reassure the peanut of her love; difficulty with stairs or not, Sarah adored her and Abe's baby.

"Here we are." Opening the door to what proved to be a lovely suite decorated in rich blue and white with creamy yellow accents provided by roses placed in a glass bowl, the other woman walked in. "We prepared a little tray of snacks." She gestured to where that tray sat on a coffee table with curved wooden legs. "Just light things—crackers and fruit and chocolate. Our kitchen is full-service twenty-four hours, so just pick up the phone when you're ready for dinner."

The other woman opened the folding doors at the back of the living area. "This leads into our private garden. Many of our guests enjoy sitting here for breakfast or after dinner."

Sarah could see why—the bougainvillea was colorful even in the soft lighting created by the old-fashioned lamps, and she could see palms as well as a thick carpet of velvety green grass. "It's beautiful."

A deep smile from her blond host, the woman's glossy bob shining in the light. "Anything you need, anything at all, let us know."

The hotelier couple departed soon afterward, leaving Abe and Sarah alone in the living area. She explored, with Abe following lazily. The bedroom was spacious, the four-poster bed huge and covered with an ivory-colored spread. There was also a window seat tucked below a curved window, books on honey-colored shelves. In the bathroom, she found lovely little toiletries.

"This is wonderful, Abe," she said, trying not to be disappointed that he didn't appear to be setting things up for a proposal.

*Take charge of your own happiness.*

Nodding inwardly at the piercing thought, she decided she'd ask him as soon as they returned home. She'd get candles, roses, make it romantic, surprise him. "How did you find this place?" she asked, smiling at the thought of proposing to her rock star.

"I know people." He held out a hand. "Come on, let's sit in the garden for a bit before we eat. We have places to go tomorrow."

She frowned, her proposal-planning derailed midthought. "We're not staying here?"

"Nope."

He refused to tell her anything else no matter how creative she got with her persuasive tactics. And Sarah could get plenty creative with a naked Abe Bellamy.

# Chapter 38

THE TWO OF THEM HAD a long, lazy breakfast the next morning after long, lazy showers. It was eleven by the time they set out. Sarah was in a comfortable dress suitable for travel that Abe had packed, but she definitely didn't have to worry about it being a hard journey. Abe stopped all the time. Sometimes so they could admire a view, other times so she could use a restroom, still other times so they could exchange kisses.

It didn't take her long to realize they were heading for Vegas. "We going gambling?"

"I thought you'd enjoy a shopping trip. You can buy lots of purses—the SUV has plenty of room."

Sarah began to laugh. "You're taking me on a prebirth purse-shopping extravaganza?" God, but she adored this man.

"Babymoon, right? That's a thing."

"Yes, but I never expected you to know that." She was tickled he'd thought of it. "Let's do this."

Thanks to their meandering path and constant stops, they didn't arrive in Vegas until around five that afternoon. Not tired in the least thanks to all the breaks she'd had to stretch her legs and to just relax, Sarah looked around curiously as they checked into a newly built hotel that screamed luxury.

She'd been in Vegas before, but never with Abe. However, the memory of being left behind while he went on tour, it no longer hurt. They'd been two different people then. This was who they were now... and Sarah's Abe, he was devoted. She couldn't wait to ask him to be her husband.

"It's not as much fun before dark," she whispered in the elevator.

"Yeah, Vegas is a night town." He tipped up her chin, dropped a kiss on her lips. "We'll paint it red tonight."

"Did you pack the right clothes?" Vegas—and especially this hotel with its hushed air of old money—was *not* jersey dress territory, not even for an überpregnant woman.

Abe grinned. "Maybe."

Narrowing her eyes, she said, "What are you up to?"

"Nothing." His laughing eyes belied his reply.

"Hmm."

Kicking off her shoes the instant they were in their suite, Sarah stretched. Then, while Abe tipped the bellman who'd brought up their luggage, she padded over to the floor-to-ceiling window and looked out at the uninterrupted view of the Strip. It'd be spectacular at night.

"Will you dance with me in front of the window tonight?" she asked Abe, feeling silly and romantic.

"Anything you want."

Something in his voice made her turn around.

Her hands flew to her mouth, her eyes stinging. Because her rock star lover was down on bended knee, an open ring box in the hand he held out.

"Marry me again, Sarah?" he said, his throat moving as he swallowed. "I promise to do it right this time, to love and cherish you like you deserve, to be the best man I can be." His hand trembled. "I will always be there for the peanut and any other children we have. I'll be a good dad. And I'll love you forever."

Unable to speak, Sarah just nodded, the movement jagged.

A smile breaking out over his face, Abe reached for her hand, tugging it away from her mouth to slide the ring onto her finger. It wasn't her old ring, the one she'd posted back to him because it hurt too much to look at it. That one had been big and sparkly and pretty, but without much of either one of them in it.

This was big and sparkly too, but the platinum band was carved with musical notes. "What?" She just pointed with her other hand, her voice too wet and shaky to make much sense.

Rising to his feet, Abe wove his fingers through hers. "It's from this." He began to sing, the bluesy tone of his voice a caress and the words he sang so raw and passionate and stark with love that she began to sob.

"It's called 'Sarah,'" he said afterward, leaning forward to kiss away her tears.

That only made her cry harder.

Enfolding her in his arms, he just held her. "I love you."

"I love you too," she managed to say, sniffing against him. "Sing it again," she ordered when she could finally speak.

He did, without letting go of her. This time he kept his voice soft so she wasn't overwhelmed, but the words, they were as powerful.

Abe was smiling by the end, the smile of a man who adored the woman in his arms. "I'm going to need a whole suitcase of handkerchiefs around you."

She pushed at his chest without force. "Shuddup." It came out wet. "I'm so happy," she whispered a little later. "This is the best day." The romantic teenage girl she carried in her heart, she was a complete, happy mess right now.

"It's not over yet." Abe wiped away her tears after tugging her into the bathroom so that he could dampen a facecloth and dab off the mascara that had run down her cheeks. "I thought you said this stuff was waterproof."

"They're liars."

"What do you say to getting hitched tonight?"

Sarah's mouth fell open. "Tonight?" It came out a squeak.

"We're in Vegas." Abe's grin was pure sin. "I'm sure we could find a wedding chapel."

Heart thumping, Sarah felt her own grin break out. "Let's do it." Why not? She wanted to be his wife again. So much.

Reality intruded a heartbeat later. "Wait, Mom—"

"Will understand, trust me." He thrust a hand into her hair, his kiss so hot she nearly combusted then and there. "But we have time to send a driver to kidnap her and get her on the private jet I have waiting in Chicago." Another grin. "I hoped you'd say yes."

Sarah wanted to bounce up and down. "Lola? The guys? Molly, Kit, and Thea?" Eloping was wonderful, but she wanted their family with them.

"I told them I was going to ask you," Abe said, looking a little unsure. "I needed their help to get you out of LA without a media tail."

Sarah felt teary-eyed again. "They all helped?" The love inherent in that act overwhelmed her.

"You don't mind?"

"Of course not."

Smile returning, Abe said, "I'll message the guys now, tell them to haul ass to Vegas. You call Lola—she can hitch a ride with David and Thea." He glanced at his watch. "Let's aim for a midnight wedding."

"Okay." It came out breathy.

It only took them ten minutes to get the word out.

That was when it hit Sarah. "What am I going to wear?" It was too hot and she was too pregnant to traipse around rush-shopping, but her heart gave a regretful twinge at the idea of marrying the love of her life in a dress designed more for comfort than style.

Sarah shook off the regret. She was about to marry Abe. Nothing else mattered. "Let me see what you pa—"

"Hush." Taking her by the shoulders before she got to the suitcases, Abe nudged her into an elegantly upholstered armchair. "I told you I've got this figured out."

He made a quick call.

Someone knocked on the door less than five minutes later. Going over to open it, Abe invited in people pushing two racks of the most stunning clothing. A couple more followed with a table on which were piled clutches, purses, fascinators, and other accessories.

A curvy older woman oversaw it all.

"Oh my God." Sarah's hands rose to her mouth again. "I get to choose from all this?"

"Sweetheart, you can have every single thing if you want."

Blinking back the tears, Sarah jumped up—or as close as she could come to a jump—and threw her arms around Abe. "Thank you," she whispered.

For giving her romance. For caring enough to set all this up.

*He'd written her a song.*

She almost started crying again at the memory of how he'd sung to her.

"Always, Sarah," Abe murmured against her ear. "*Always.*"

He told most of the staff to leave in the next couple of minutes, but the two who remained behind—the curvy woman and a male with the solid look of a boxer—were kind and knowledgeable, and they'd brought clothing suitable for a woman who was Sarah's height and pregnant.

Having found her center again in his arms, Sarah said, "Shoo," to Abe. "I don't want you to see my dress before the wedding."

"I'll be downstairs. Call if you need me."

She knew he'd answer.

The man she was about to marry kept his promises.


ABE'S MOTHER THREATENED TO CLIP him around the ear when she arrived in Vegas, but she was laughing as she did so, her delight open. "That man just turned up at my bridge game." She poked him in the stomach. "If you hadn't called ahead and if I didn't know him as your driver, I'd have slammed the door in his face."

"That's why I sent someone you knew." Abe lifted her off her feet with his hug. "I got you a room so you can rest a little."

"Forget that. I'm ready." His mother adjusted her jaunty yellow hat. It went with her stylish skirt suit. "Where's Sarah?"

Abe gave her the suite number, watched her go up to join Sarah, Lola, and the other women. Around him, his friends were in the charcoal-gray suits they'd worn to Fox's wedding, while Abe wore a slightly darker suit Sarah had chosen for him the last time they'd gone shopping. Dark gray shirt inside but no tie, because she liked him without a tie.

Not wanting Sarah to guess what he was up to, he hadn't brought the suit with him. David had picked it up, brought it over. Abe had changed in the room he'd booked for the drummer and Thea, and now he, Fox, David, and Noah stood at the bar just off the check-in area. "Thanks for coming," he said to his friends.

"Don't make us hurt you," Noah said without heat, then slapped Abe on the back. "This is awesome. No fucking reporters, just family and friends."

Abe looked at Fox. "You and Molly have trouble shaking them off?" The other couple, Noah, and David were the ones who'd distracted the media so Abe and Sarah could make their getaway, with Thea playing informant and feeding certain pieces of information to the right sources.

Kit and Lola had been backup.

Now, Fox groaned. "Christ, it was like trying to shake off an army of rabid rats." Running a hand through the chocolate-dark strands of his hair, he said, "I finally had to park my SUV in a mall parking lot and duck inside with Molly, come out a side exit and get into Kit's car. Lola managed to pick up Noah and David in an underground parking garage—the media doesn't know her car, so it was easy for her to drive out."

"They totally bought it." Noah's eyes gleamed. "Oooh, news hot off the press, the members of Schoolboy Choir at one another's throats over some unknown woman—total public meltdown. David even threw a punch at Fox after we shouted down the restaurant."

Abe glanced at David. "Thea?"

"She says it's great publicity, especially since it'll be obvious by tomorrow that we were fucking with everyone. Of course, if Sarah had said no, you'd be in the shit."

"Worth the risk." Abe couldn't imagine his life without the woman who was about to become his wife again. "Sarah's worth every risk."

David's phone buzzed. "Thea," he said, after reading the message. "Their limo is here."

"Then we'd better start walking." Abe had chosen a chapel not far from the hotel, one with the requisite Elvis impersonator.

If he and Sarah were getting married in Vegas, they were getting married Vegas style.

Walking out with his best friends into the light and color of Sin City, Abe wanted to whoop with joy. Somehow managing to keep it together, he took several deep breaths. *Soon*, he told himself. Soon Sarah would be his again. All official and public and permanent. Very permanent. No way was Abe messing this up a second time around.

They arrived at the chapel to find it more tasteful than could be expected.

Ten seconds later, a white-jumpsuit-clad Elvis hustled them to the head of the aisle and took up his position with an "A-ha-hah" and a hip swivel.

"Right," Abe said, settling his suit jacket when it didn't need to be settled. "Shit, why am I so nervous? I already married Sarah once."

David was the one who answered. "It's because this time around you know exactly what's on the line, how precious it is."

Yeah, he did.

The sound system came on, filling the chapel not with the wedding march but with the song Abe had written for Sarah. He'd recorded it alone two days earlier, given the CD to Elvis's assistant. Around him, he felt his friends go still as they recognized his voice.

Then he saw Sarah enter on his mother's arm, Lola, Kit, Thea, and Molly following. Everything else receded. His Sarah had chosen a strapless gown in a rich emerald green that made her skin glow. The fabric gathered together in a kind of a knot between her breasts before waterfalling to the ground. It was stark and simple and stunning.

She'd left her hair in wild curls about her head, tucking only a vivid red rose behind her ear. Her sole pieces of jewelry were the ring he'd put on her finger and a delicate diamond necklace Abe remembered his father giving his mother on their twentieth wedding anniversary.

The bouquet in her hand was a profusion of color.

She looked like his every dream come to life.

"There you are," he said when she reached him, immediately taking her hands into his after she passed her bouquet back to Lola. His beaming mother waved him down, kissed his cheek, then did the same to Sarah before stepping back to let Elvis begin the ceremony.

Mostly all Abe remembered was the unhidden love in Sarah's eyes and the joy flooding his veins. When Elvis declared them husband and wife, he couldn't hold it in. He gave a roof-shaking whoop and then kissed a laughing Sarah until everyone hollered and Elvis offered to rent them a room.

Grinning, he clasped Sarah's hand in his and they walked out as a group... straight into the flash of a camera.

Basil froze, his eyes huge in his pasty face. "Shit," he whispered. "I think I just got the exclusive of a lifetime."

Abe looked at Sarah, lifted an eyebrow.

She laughed and, turning to the photographer, said, "It's your lucky day, Basil." She tilted up her head, Abe bent, and they kissed while their friends showered them in flower petals the women must've brought in with them.

Vegas sparkled and shone around them, bystanders gathered to applaud, but all Abe cared about was the woman in his arms. The woman who was now his wife.

# CHAPTER 39

B ASIL, FOR ALL HIS FAULTS, proved to be an amazing wedding photographer. He even sent a whole set of the images to Thea—after he'd gotten his exclusive splashed all over not the tabloids but *the* glossiest magazine in the business. "I always wanted to be a wedding photographer," he'd written in the accompanying note. "With the money from this exclusive, I can follow my dream. Thank you."

Going through the photos the week after the wedding, Abe reveled in the joy he saw on Sarah's face in every shot. The same joy suffused his.

According to Thea, the social media outlets had gone crazy.

Abe ignored the noise of the world, he and Sarah cozily ensconced in a spacious villa an hour from Los Angeles that he'd rented so they could have a small honeymoon, free from media intrusion, before they went home to prepare for the baby's arrival. That'd happen in about two to three weeks, depending on if the peanut decided on a little extra womb time.

David had dropped off Flossie too, the villa owners happy to welcome a canine guest. Abe had known Sarah would miss her pet if they were apart too long, and Flossie had settled right in, was currently curled up at Abe's side on the sofa, as interested in the photos as he was.

"Abra is now set in stone," Thea had said when she came by with the photos a couple of hours earlier. "My favorite headline so far is: Abracadabra, Rock Reunion!"

"Kill it," Abe had ordered. "Kill it dead now."

"Too late."

Abe didn't really mind the sobriquet. What the hell. He was with Sarah. What did he care?

"Abe." Sarah's voice was shaky.

He turned his head to look over the back of the sofa, got up at his first glimpse of her face. "What's wrong?" She'd gone to the restroom after a quick look at the photos, had been excited to come back and look through them more slowly, but now her skin was pale, her hand on her abdomen.

"I think I just had a contraction." She swallowed, her fingers trembling. "It's too early."

"Only by a couple of weeks," he reassured her even as his own heart thumped. "You okay for me to drive you or should I call an ambulance?" *Stay calm, Abe. Stay calm.* "We're not that far from the hospital you wanted to use if I put pedal to the metal."

"You drive." She winced, but it passed quickly. "I don't think the baby's in a rush." Her voice held, but he heard the tremors beneath. "We should have plenty of time."

Taking his cue from Sarah, Abe drove fast but not recklessly. No way in hell was he getting into a wreck; no way was he hurting Sarah or the baby. At first it all proceeded slowly with Sarah's contractions quite far apart. He was beginning to calm down, thinking they'd have plenty of time to get her settled in at the hospital—hell, the doc might even send her home until the labor was more advanced. He'd read that some women were in labor for twenty-four hours or more.

All hell broke loose about twenty minutes—at normal speed—from the hospital, Sarah's contractions suddenly coming far too close together for his peace of mind.

"Another one?" he asked when she gasped, his hands white-knuckled on the steering wheel.

Sarah breathed in and out in short bursts. "Y-yes."

"We're almost there, sweetheart."

Sarah kept breathing jaggedly.

"Hey, yell at me, swear." Abe didn't dare take his eyes off the road. "I'm the one who put you in this position, right?"

"I-I... help—" The rest of her words were a scream.

*Oh, Christ.* "Should I stop?"

"Hospital. Doctors."

Right, of course she'd want the hospital and the doctors. Abe increased his speed... and yeah, there was a cop behind him right that instant. "Fuck." Pulling over, he rolled down the window and waited until the older man swaggered to the window, ready to tell him this was a goddamn emergency.

"License and regis—"

"I'm having a fucking baby!" Sarah screamed before Abe could speak. "Unless you want to deliver it, get me to a hospital. *Now!*"

The cop's mouth fell open before he jerked out of his shock. "Follow me," he said to Abe, then ran back to his squad car and pulled out, full sirens and lights going.

Abe fell in behind the police vehicle, grinned. "Hey, the peanut's going to have one hell of a birth story."

Sarah laughed, sounded surprised into it. "Don't tell our baby I swore," she said, her breath a throaty gasp. "I was lady-like. Got it?"

"Got it." He focused on staying on the cop's tail, following his path exactly as the vehicle cut a swath through LA traffic.

Screaming into the emergency department of the nearest hospital, Abe jumped out and got to Sarah's side as medical personnel poured out. Sarah swiveled in the seat, legs hanging out... then gripped his hand, sheer terror on her face. "Abe, my water just broke. I think the baby's coming."

Abe didn't even think about it. He just scooped her up and ran into the hospital, the nurses following. No fucking way was he allowing the news choppers overhead to get images of his wife and child in such a vulnerable moment. It was to the medical personnel's credit that they raced past him to show him into a room.

He laid Sarah down on the bed.

She wouldn't release his hand, and the pain ripping through her made her incapable of speaking. Abe was the one who explained that the baby was early by about two weeks. He also quietly mentioned the stillbirth to a nurse, made it clear Sarah and their baby were *not* to be separated unless it was a medical necessity.

Time passed at the speed of light. Later, he'd find out it *had* been fast. Twenty-five minutes from the time he laid Sarah down on the bed. But in the moment, it just felt like controlled chaos to him—Sarah's contractions coming closer and closer together, sweat dampening her hair, then the medical staff telling her to push, *push!*

And then, while his heart was pounding like that of a race-horse, his only focus Sarah's exhausted face, a lusty cry broke the air.

"I want to see," Sarah sobbed. "Please let me see."

"Here you go." The nurse to whom Abe had spoken placed their strong, healthy baby boy on Sarah's chest. "We'll have to take him for tests, see if he needs a little extra help, but his lungs definitely seem fine."

Smiling, sobbing, Sarah kissed their baby's head as Abe dared put a gentle hand on that tiny body. "He's so small," he whispered, shaken to the core.

She sniffled. "Only compared to you." Light filled her eyes. "He's all right, Abe. Our baby's all right."


THEODORE "THEO" GREGORY BELLAMY WAS very much all right. Healthy and strong and, right now, sleeping in his daddy's arms.

"I have a kid," Abe said, not for the first time.

David touched a finger to the tiny hand fisted against Abe's T-shirt. "You have a kid. Shit."

"Don't swear." Sarah scowled from the hospital bed where she sat dressed in the pj's Lola had bought for her on the way to the hospital.

Abe's mom was on her way from Chicago, so excited to meet her grandson that she was a bubble of pure joy.

"Right, sorry." David held out his arms. "Can I hold the little guy?"

Abe put their son in David's careful hands.

"Look at that face," Fox murmured, peering over David's shoulder. "You two made a mini Abra."

Punching the lead singer lightly on the arm, Abe couldn't stop smiling. "Did you see his hands? He's going to play the keys, I can tell."

"I dunno," said a new voice. "I think those are a guitarist's fingers."

Walking in, Noah drew Abe into a back-slapping hug while Kit went over to join Thea, Sarah, Molly, and Lola. "Congratulations, man."

"Sarah did all the work," Abe said, sending her a smile that was probably a little goofy.

Her responding smile was exactly as goofy and it melted his heart. He went over and wrapped an arm around her shoulders, dropped a kiss on her hair. "A wedding and a baby in less than two weeks. I think we should slow down now."

Sarah laughed softly and held out her arms for Theo. "Look at him. Pure sweetness."

"Yeah. I already love being a dad."


THREE WEEKS LATER, DRESSED ONLY in white boxer briefs, Abe walked back and forth on the gritty stone paving beside the pool, Flossie pacing beside him and the night air balmy and quiet apart from the screaming and furious tiny person cradled against his bare shoulder.

They'd moved into his larger place post-birth because it had better security and a lot more private space where the media couldn't pry—but Sarah had brought her place with her in all the décor. Including endless bookshelves in the music room, which had been transformed into their family room.

Abe loved it.

The day before, he'd mounted a sweet photo of Aaron beside his favorite picture of Tessie, and they'd all smiled at seeing those two beloved faces on the wall while Theo slept in his mother's arms.

Right then, however, sleep was the last thing on Theo's mind.

Abe stroked Theo's little body, the fabric of their baby's blue one-piece soft under his hand. "Come on, kid," Abe said without halting his rocking, patting walk. "You're well fed, warm, and dry." He patted Theo's diaper butt, a butt he'd personally cleaned up and reclad after waking to the baby's first cry. "Why don't you let your parents and your grandma catch some shut-eye?"

Theo just wailed louder.

"Good lungs is an understatement," Abe said, continuing to walk, Flossie loyally following his lead. "Lead-singer material right there."

He turned to kiss an angrily scrunched-up face, his hand careful to support Theo's head. "It's fine. I don't need sleep." Love, huge and endless, filled his heart. "All those nights of partying are finally coming in handy." Blinking gritty eyes as his son cried even louder, he kept walking.

It took thirty minutes for Theo to wear himself out and finally fall asleep.

Yawning, Abe carried him upstairs and would've gone into the nursery except a sleepy Sarah whispered his name. She'd risen up on her arm, her hair a gorgeous tumble around her shoulders. "How long was he awake?" She rubbed her face.

"Forty minutes or so." Abe sat down beside her with Theo in his arms. "How long do you think he'll stay down?"

"AN HOUR IF WE'RE LUCKY," Sarah said, leaning over to kiss their baby's soft cheek. "I'll take the next wake-up call." She was utterly exhausted, sleep-deprived... and madly in love with both the big man seated on her bed and the tiny child he held in his muscular arms. Abe was just as sleep-deprived and as exhausted as her, but he'd proven endlessly patient.

Where others might've crumbled under the stress of a newborn, Abe was thriving. He soaked up the advice Diane gave them both about how to care for a baby, his joy in being a father open—he was already "teaching" Theo the piano by holding their baby in his arms as he played.

Theo always listened intently—and every so often, Sarah would wake in the night to the music of Abe playing the piano. It seemed to settle their little rock baby better than anything else. "Music didn't work today?"

"The peanut's a harsh critic." Fisting his hand in her hair, her husband tugged her into him for a kiss that was slow and lazy and lush. "How about it?" he murmured. "Got enough energy to make a different kind of music?"

Sarah's toes curled. "Let me put him down." She took that precious, warm weight, overwhelmed by love. "I feel like snuggling him a little." Carrying Theo across the carpet and into the adjoining room, she put him in his crib after a long cuddle. "Dream happy dreams, sweet baby."

She tiptoed out and slipped into bed beside Abe... to find him fast asleep on his front, his breathing deep and steady.

Laughing softly, she pressed a kiss to his shoulder. He stirred long enough to say, "I love you, Sarah."

"I love you too," she whispered, tracing his lips with her finger.

He pretended to bite at it, though his eyes were already closing again.

"My Abe," she whispered, stroking his bristly jaw before settling down against him to sleep... just as a whimper came through the baby monitor.

Abe started awake. "I'll—"

"Shh. I'll go." Slipping out of bed, she scooped up Theo, who was all wet eyes and trembling mouth. "Mommy's here," she said, snuggling him close.

He didn't cry this time, apparently just needing a little cuddle.

When she walked into the bedroom, Theo in her arms, she found that Abe had turned onto his side and was facing the nursery. Though his eyes were heavy, he'd managed to open them. "I'm a lucky man."

Sarah's heart just burst, her own eyes stinging.

Going to sit in bed beside his sprawled form, she rocked their baby as she watched her husband sleep. No doubts. No fear. This, her and Abe, their family, they were forever and always.

# EPILOGUE

FOUR MONTHS LATER AND THEO watched wide-eyed and smiling from Abe's arms as Noah promised to love and cherish Kit until the earth stopped turning and the stars stopped shining. The peanut was an honorary groomsman, complete with his own tiny suit that matched those worn by Fox, Abe, and David.

Looking at his happy little face, you'd never know this was the same baby who'd screamed down the house six weeks running.

These days, Theo had his mother's Zen going on.

Sarah stood on the other side of the bride, her smile misty as she watched Kit speak the same promise in return. It was as well Abe had already given her a handkerchief. Yep, there she went, wiping away a tear.

"...husband and wife!"

Abe grinned as Noah went in for the kiss. He'd expected laughing passion or maybe a raw lip-lock, but his hands cradling Kit's face, the guitarist kissed his new wife with a tenderness that had every single woman in the room sighing and all but melting into the floor.

Abe shook his head. "He really doesn't give a flying you-know-what about his bad-boy image does he?" he said to David.

David shot him a laughing look, his golden-brown eyes shining with happiness for a friend who'd found his way out of the darkness that had haunted him for so long. "Says the man holding a baby and avoiding the *F* word."

Abe grinned as Noah and Kit turned to walk back up the aisle, the guests showering them in flower petals that fell softly over the fine lace of Kit's long veil and train as beams of sunlight gilded the entire scene. That light came from endless rows of delicate glass windows, the venue the ballroom of a venerated country home.

Sarah had told him Kit had been firmly against the big wedding her parents wanted to throw her and Noah until her mother dragged her to this place. "It's so elegant and lovely, it's no wonder she buckled," Sarah had said. "Especially after Thea found her that incredible gown. It *needs* a dramatic venue."

Of all the Schoolboy Choir weddings, Noah and Kit's was undeniably the biggest, with a large number of glitzy guests. But Abe knew the grandeur was mostly for Kit's mom and dad—they weren't exactly perfect parents, but they loved their kid in their own way and Kit loved them back.

Noah and Kit had held a much more intimate wedding breakfast earlier today, with only their closest friends and family, including Noah's sister, Emily. And of course Abe and the others had taken Noah for a bachelor party—where they'd had their daisy tattoos transformed into an obscure symbol David had found on the Internet.

He'd told them it meant friendship. He'd been drunk at the time.

The women had gone dancing, come back tipsy and happy.

"Did you save me a dance?" he asked his wife as she joined him to follow the bride and groom down the aisle.

"I saved you every dance." It was a husky whisper just as Theo tried to dive-bomb into her arms.

Sarah laughed, which made their son laugh.

It was the most beautiful music in Abe's life.

# AUTHOR'S NOTE

I HOPE YOU ENJOYED *ROCK WEDDING*! Before you go, I have two pieces of news!

First up, if you'd like to get a glimpse of David and Thea's wedding from their point of view, or if you're wondering about that astonishing pink Ferrari from the pool party, then head on over to my website (www.nalinisingh.com) and sign up for my newsletter. Both short stories (*Sunshine* and *With this memo...*) are included in the Welcome newsletter. If you have any trouble accessing it, drop me an e-mail: nalinisinghwrites@gmail.com.

I'm also working on other short stories set in the Rock Kiss world that I hope to share through the newsletter over the coming months.

Secondly, while *Rock Wedding* is the final book in the Rock Kiss series, it's not the last time you'll see the Rock Kiss gang. You'll notice we didn't get to attend Gabriel and Charlotte's wedding in this book—that doesn't seem fair to me! Which is why we'll be checking back in with them in my next contemporary romance, coming in 2017. The story will feature one of Gabriel's hunky rugby-playing brothers.

NALINI SINGH

And, last but definitely not least, if you missed the earlier books in the Rock Kiss series, they are: *Rock Addiction* (Molly & Fox), *Rock Courtship* (David & Thea), *Rock Hard* (Gabriel & Charlotte), and *Rock Redemption* (Noah & Kit).

Thank you for reading, and here's to plenty more story adventures together!

~ xo Nalini

# Acknowledgments

THANK YOU TO EACH AND every one of you for taking a chance on this new series from me. I hope you've enjoyed this rockin' ride! I had a ton of fun writing each book and I'm looking forward to doing further contemporary romances. (I mean, how can I leave those rugby hunks hanging, right?!)

To all the bloggers and reviewers who've supported this series, thank you. You're awesome.

A special shout out to Rahaf and Leena for your wonderful feedback on the draft, and to Nephele and the TKA team for all your work. Jenn - thanks for shooting the amazing cover image! And Frauke - I love what you did to turn the image into a cover.

And last but not least, a great big thanks to all the sexy, bad boy rock stars who inspired this series!

# ABOUT THE AUTHOR

NEW YORK TIMES AND USA TODAY bestselling author of the Psy-Changeling, Guild Hunter, and Rock Kiss series Nalini Singh usually writes about hot shapeshifters and dangerous angels. This time around, she decided to write about a gorgeous, talented keyboard player and the woman he's never forgotten. If you're seeing a theme here, you're not wrong.

Nalini lives and works in beautiful New Zealand, and is passionate about writing. If you'd like to explore the Rock Kiss series further, or if you'd like to try out her other books, you can find lots of excerpts on her website: www.nalinisingh.com. *Slave to Sensation* is the first book in the Psy-Changeling series, while *Angels' Blood* is the first book in the Guild Hunter series. The website also features special behind-the-scenes material from all her series.